THEY BROUGHT A
NATION'S COMING OF AGE . . .

FRANCIS MARION "FOX" GAIRDEN—Hot-headed and ambitious, his search for love and honor takes him from South Carolina to the mills of the North, from the fetters of a British man-of-war to the frozen peaks of the Appalachians.

HUGH VARDRY—A powerful, philandering Connecticut mill owner, his brutality lies hidden—until one desperate moment.

ANNE VARDRY—Hugh's widow craves love from the man who fought her husband. But will their tempestuous passion be tainted by Hugh's blood?

ADELLE DURANT—Defying her parents, Paul and Lily, the dark-eyed, headstrong beauty flees Philadelphia to the salons of Charleston—and into the arms of her cousin Fox, whom she vows she will not share with another.

Praise for Coleen Johnston's
THE GUARDIANS:

"A page-turner that is explosive and action-packed. Outstanding!"

—*Rendezvous*

The Gairden Legacy
by Coleen L. Johnston
from St. Martin's Paperbacks

The Inheritors

Coleen L. Johnston

SMP

ST. MARTIN'S PAPERBACKS

THE INHERITORS

Copyright © 1994 by Coleen L. Johnston.

ISBN: 0-312-95284-8

Printed in the United States of America

St. Martin's Paperbacks edition/August 1994

10 9 8 7 6 5 4 3 2 1

For Joyce Flaherty,
pioneer

And as the sun breaks through the
darkest clouds,
So honour peereth in the
meanest habit.

—William Shakespeare
The Taming of the Shrew
Act IV, Scene 3

THE GAIRDEN LEGACY:
1706–1766

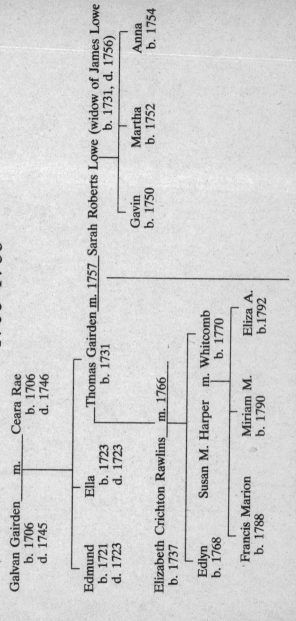

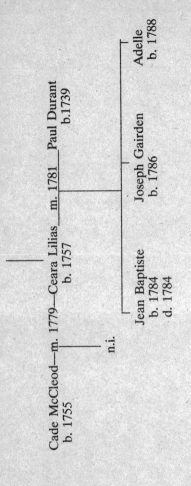

Cade McCleod—m. 1779—Ceara Lilias—m. 1781—Paul Durant
b. 1755   b. 1757   b. 1739

n.i.

Jean Baptiste   Joseph Gairden   Adelle
b. 1784   b. 1786   b. 1788
d. 1784

❊ Part One ❊

1808

1

Fox Gairden swung the club easily, left arm fully extended, right arm powering the thin wooden shaft back down to meet an imaginary ball, snapping the grass as it passed.

"Ready then, Fox?" Jurian Hudson called.

Francis Marion Gairden nodded, used to the familiar nickname. He had been named after one of his father's heroes from the War of Independence, General Francis Marion, and nicknamed for him, too—Fox, short for Swamp Fox. The General had been a short, stocky man with a limp. His namesake was tall, lean and quick. Like the General, though, he had a single-mindedness that annoyed some and inspired others.

Jurian had only been able to coax him out to try this new game called golf today by promising to attend the Independence Day speeches at the Exchange later in the day. Just now Jurian was impatient. "Simply do as I do," he commanded. "There's nothing to golf but hitting a ball. Even a scholar like you can do it." Jurian laughed, took a swing at the small brown ball and watched as it arced off to the left side of Harleston's Green, where he had set up a makeshift course. In Columbia, where Fox was a student at South Carolina College, the game had not yet gained attention. Fox could think of a dozen young men who would be eager to learn it, though, and he pictured them playing it on the college common. But he did not include himself in the picture. He had taken to spending his free time at Colonel Thomas Taylor's cotton mill, much more fascinated by the machines than by his studies. Hardly suitable for a gentleman, Jurian Hudson had been quick to point out when Fox told him about it. "We *grow* cotton, Fox," he had added, "we don't *need* to do anything else." But Grandfather Gairden had said the future was in the spinning of cotton. Fox planned to be part of it.

Taylor's mill was now closed down temporarily because of financial problems, college was out of session and Fox had come home for a visit. Home to hear his father tell him, "I don't care if you are at the top of your class, Son. Forget Taylor and his mill. And don't listen to your grandfather. He'd have us all buried in worthless weaving manufactories if he could. I broke free of it. You will, too. Your education will put you on an even footing with any planter's son." Home to his mother's gentle persistence in pushing him toward a romance with her best friend's daughter, a lovely but plain girl of fifteen who looked at him with longing eyes but never spoke. Even a Fourth of July golf match with aimless Jurian Hudson took on a sweet promise compared with the alternatives. Besides, Hudson had a sister.

Fox stepped up to the tee, placed his feet apart the way Jurian had instructed, looked at the brown leather ball and swung his club like the wand that it was, sending the ball sailing high over the head of his partner and into the gravel at the far end of the green.

"You've played before, Mr. Gairden," a voice behind him stated.

"Good day, Miss Hudson," Fox said, forgetting the ball and Jurian down the green as he took in the sight of Sally Hudson in a short-bodiced gown of lemon muslin, neatly embroidered around the deep neckline. She wore a matching shawl draped over her bare shoulders and looked out at him from beneath a gypsy hat that tied at the side of her chin. Her maid attended, slowly moving a fan decorated with scenes of Greece back and forth against the humid air. "Do you play?" he asked.

"When no one is watching." She tilted her head as she untied her hat ribbons and took off the broad-brimmed straw creation. Her hair was cropped short and curled around her face like one of the Grecian sylphs on the fan, and her eyes were of the same dark, coffeelike shade. She handed the maid her hat and opened a parasol, twirling it just a little as she rested it on her shoulder. "I haven't the strength to hit it very far."

"Your brother tells me that to hit it straight is just as important. Isn't that right, Jurian?" he called out to his friend, who had collected the balls and was returning to the tee to join them.

"Quite right. Good morning, Sally. What brings you out in the heat of the day?"

"Curiosity. I had to see what golf is. And, of course, I *had* to see Fox, too. Welcome back to Charleston, Fox."

"Thank you. It's good to be home. Might I beg you for a waltz at the Izards' ball tomorrow evening, Miss Hudson? Provided you approve, Jurian."

"I'm certain I must approve lest you beat me at this game I'm 'teaching' you." Jurian was gracious, but Fox could tell he was anxious to get on with their game. "You might even take lunch with us on the city green today, unless your family has other plans. We do have enough for guests, don't we, Missie?" he asked of the maid.

"Cook always pack plenty, Mist' Hudson," she said, never ceasing to move the fan so that a cooling current might fall across the dimpled cheek of her young mistress.

"It would be my pl—," Fox started at the same time Jurian said, "We'll meet you on the city green, Sally." Jurian turned away without waiting for a reply and took another practice swing.

"Can't I watch and walk back with you?" she asked, ceasing the twirl of her parasol while she looked from Fox to Jurian and back with a pouty smile.

"Of course. We should be much distressed were you to leave, Miss Hudson," Fox said before her brother could answer. "And perhaps you'll join us in chasing these odd little balls around the green." Taking a certain amount of perverse delight in watching his friend sputter inwardly at the prospect of entertaining his sister when he wanted to do nothing but practice at golf, Fox added with an innocent smile, "No sport should ever come before a lady."

"Very well then, Sally. Do come join us—don't just stand there teasing from behind your parasol."

"But I don't want to soil my gown. I'll watch from here."

Jurian blew out a deep breath of exasperation, but Fox nodded his most polite dancing-class bow. "Of course, Miss Hudson. As you wish. Jurian, your turn." Fox took momentary leave of the lady and resumed activity with his friend. He'd missed the intriguing ways of Charleston ladies this past year at Columbia, he thought as he glanced back at Sally Hudson. There hadn't been much time for socializing. Fox filled his lungs with the rich Charleston air and smiled. Coming home had been a good idea, after all.

Once again Jurian took a masterful swing at the ball and then drove it far to the right, while Fox took an easy swing and sent the ball straight to the other end of the green. "I shall retrieve this time," he said, conscious of Sally Hudson's eyes on him as he jogged down the length of grass, barely pausing to scoop up one ball before he continued over to pick up the other one, then returning not even winded. He had worked hard in the mill this past year, lifting, carrying, running up and down stairs, and his body was taut and trim from it. Sally's appreciative glances told him she noticed.

By the time the golfers, Sally and her maid joined the Hudsons at midday, the city green was crowded with colorful canopies. Beneath them stood long tables of cold meats, breads and cakes. Servants attended with fans and cool drinks. Young people moved from one shady canopy to the next, taking a sip of cold tea here and a sweetmeat there. Sally Hudson, though, stationed herself in the center of the Hudsons' large, striped canvas pavilion and waited for others to come to her. She leaned forward, using her folded parasol as a balance, and flirted with young man after young man. Fox managed to give her what he thought was a rather gallant smile of his own when he caught her eye. She looked away. Fox smiled. She played flirtation by her own rules. He *was* going to enjoy himself at the Izards' ball tomorrow night. Even dancing with the longing-eyed fifteen-year-old might not be so bad.

Fox took a last glance Sally's way and caught her looking back before he pulled her brother away from the charms of a Miss Elwood Jurian had only just met.

"We'll see these lasses later, Jurian, and many more with them," Fox whispered in his ear. "Come along, now. Let them miss you a little, talk about you. They'll be all the more eager for your company later."

Jurian kissed the young lady's hand and excused himself, then fell into step beside Fox for the walk to the Exchange, where a large group of men and a few elderly women waited in the street for the patriotic program to begin. Already the firing of cannons at the Battery could be heard and soon a parade of dignitaries would make its way down Broad Street. "Ah," Jurian said, catching sight of someone across the way, "I'll catch up with you later. I need to speak to Edwin Myer."

Fox nodded as his friend hurried off, then drew back his shoulders and settled in to wait for the program to begin. This October would mark the twenty-seventh anniversary of Cornwallis's surrender at Yorktown, and today's program was a celebration of that victory. Charleston's three surviving Sons of Liberty were to be honored. Fox waited patiently through the whole program to hear the last of them, his grandfather, Thomas Gairden. Fox smiled as he watched the old man walk, straight and proud, to the speaker's stand where there was no shelter from the sun overhead. Perspiration streamed from beneath the battered tricorn hat sprouting a white cockade Grandfather wore, but his eyes were bright, his lips always formed into a little half smile. While many in the crowd looked wilted and tired, Grandfather looked eager, if not especially fresh. Cheers rose in a great swell as one of Charleston's few surviving war heroes looked out over the crowd.

"Today we celebrate an' remember all that was bought with blood twenty-seven and -eight years back —not just by General Marion's men or General Sumter's men, but by of all those who fought for the rights of men. In the twenty-seven years that have passed since the British left Charles Town, as we called it then, we've found that telling what those rights are is not so simple as we'd thought twould be. The business of building a government that can endure throughout our lives and the lives of our children and their children is a hard business, but one every veteran, and every citizen, must attend to—for we hope that never again will we be forced to shed blood in the search for justice.

"I remember the spirit of those of us exiled in St. Augustine. I remember what it was like to leave, to lose my home, and I remember our final victory. But I do not glory in the memory of war. I glory in the result: a nation where men can air their differences, then settle them, not with might but with reason.

"Still I say this day that while the Revolution is behind us, the troubles with England remain. While underpriced British goods flood our markets and while British men-of-war impress sailors from our own ships, we cannot think ourselves completely free from the troubles we fought for with such zeal.

"Let us celebrate this day, and give thanks to God for our many blessings, but let us remember these wise words from an Irish friend of freedom who said, 'The price of liberty is eternal vigilance.' May our vigil into eternity be blessed. Thank you."

Fox clapped louder than the rest of the crowd, smiled more broadly, and caught a wink from Grandfather Gairden, who never missed a chance to twit the British. No matter that he was now seventy-seven years old and a wizened figure of the man he had been in the Revolution, the Scots-Irish sense of right and justice in him burned bright as ever. He would be fair, but he would give as good as he got. He embarrassed Fox's father sometimes, popping in as he did at his law office with a bit of news about the way France and England were edging the United States toward a war, warning against the British factors in the city and the way they were controlling the business that should be rightfully in the hands of Americans like his son. But, of course, he had their best interests at heart. He always had. And he had reasons, too, for his feelings.

Grandfather had returned from the war to find his manufactory burned, his house gutted, and the new nation in a deep depression that made getting back into business all but impossible—unless one drew upon the ready credit of the British, a road he was not willing to travel. He had fought a long fight to regain an economic position in the city, but he had never lost the political position he had won before and during the war years. His place in the city and in the state was secure. He had been one of those reluctant rebels who had tried all of the nonviolent channels he could to resolve the difficulties with England, but finding them hopeless had given himself wholly to the move for liberty. It had cost him dearly, but he had never regretted it.

As a small group of musicians began to play the stirring songs of the Revolution, Fox watched a circle of men crowd around Grandfather Gairden. Some of them, those who hadn't met him before, studied him for clues to the man behind the words. They might even unravel a few of his mysteries, Fox mused as Grandfather chatted easily with the group, but never all of them. He had been with Grandfather every day of his life up until he left for college, had heard many of the same stories over and over, and he still wondered if he would ever know all of Thomas Duncan Gairden. Always something new appeared. A new idea. A new bit of his past. A new bit of his freely offered advice. He was of a different age, and part of Fox wanted to hang on to what his grandfather was while part of him wanted to be very different from the man who so often now lived in the past.

A red-white-and-blue bunting hung across the front of the platform where Grandfather had been speaking, and now, standing in front of it, he made a striking silhouette. A patriot larger than life before the colors he had fought so hard to defend. One young man's face flushed as Grandfather took the man's hand between both of his and spoke some words Fox couldn't hear. Words a young man could cling to, even if he was the son of a wealthy planter who didn't have to worry much about eternity or vigilance, no doubt.

"I don't suppose they'll be singing 'La Marseillaise' this year the way they did a few years back."

Fox turned to find Carlin McPherson just behind him, looking toward Grandfather as he spoke. Fox laughed, glancing back over his shoulder at the older man. "I don't suppose. Now that Monsieur Bonaparte seems more a threat than a friend, that tune has lost its favor."

McPherson worked a small acreage with three slaves, but his passion was politics. He would have been in the legislature except that he had not the property to commend him to such a position. Fox noticed the rough cloth of his shirt, darkened around the neck from infrequent washing, and thought that life was not easy for the small planters. Once McPherson had been a good-looking man, before long days in the sun had aged him. Even now, despite the leathery look of his face, he wore his hat at a jaunty tilt and he folded his arms across his chest with the confidence of a man who wasn't afraid to say what was on his mind.

"We might all be singin' it again if we get into a war we can't win. Still we need to put England in her place. I'm afraid the revolution he was talkin' of isn't over yet," McPherson said with a nod toward Thomas Gairden.

"Grandfather doesn't favor war," Fox said. "That's why he hopes Madison will follow Jefferson as president. No doubt you've heard him speak of it." Fox lifted his eyebrows as he made the remark. Few in Charleston for any length of time had missed hearing

Grandfather Gairden's political views or reading them in his letters to the editor of the *City Gazette*.

"Ever'body says they're against war, Francis, but most aren't when it comes right down to it. Your grandfather's no different." At this last, McPherson raised an eyebrow and nodded a firm, knowing nod.

Just as the musicians began to play "Liberty's Reign," Fox heard a voice raised over the music and shifted his eyes to the speaker. A man with a sunburned face and wavy blond hair had pushed in close to Grandfather and was almost shouting. "You favor Mr. Jefferson's plans because they benefit *you*, while they kill commerce in the North. Shipping is the lifeblood of this country, and if it cannot go on, if goods cannot be bought and sold, there will be no more United States of America, but only frail domiciles once again, ripe for the plucking of England or France. Republican principles be damned! I say Jefferson's mind is highly addled on the matter, and we can only hope to elect a successor with more a head for reason."

"Mr. Jefferson, with his 'addled' mind, is helpin' see to the establishment of commerce within our own nation, something I've been trying to do for fifty years." Grandfather stopped a moment, appraising the tall stranger. "I don't believe we've met."

"Hugh Vardry. Down from Connecticut." He nodded to Thomas Gairden, but made no move to shake his hand. "I'd wager you've done business with England yourself in the course of that time, Gairden." Vardry lowered his voice, but still there was an edge to his words. Fox made his way to the edge of the circle for a better look.

"Shipyards stand idle in the North, goods are scarce and prices are high," Vardry went on. "Folks have had about enough of Mr. Jefferson's embargo. I see the Charleston docks are piled high with cotton that can't get out, too. Is that helping commerce here? Is that why you fought the Revolution?" The blond man's face reddened angrily, and Fox tensed his fists, not waiting for Grandfather's reply.

"Surely you don't accuse my grandfather of selfishness?" Fox said, stepping forward. "He has sacrificed much in the interest of this nation. He is willing to sacrifice again, but he is *not* willing to see us in the midst of a war with England once again. British mills can't keep running very long without our cotton. And British mouths will go hungry without our rice. We have a peaceful means for bringing England around to our way of thinking, and we support Mr. Jefferson in his use of it." As he spoke, Fox made his way to stand beside his grandfather, and his dark eyes locked with Vardry's sallow ones. At nineteen, Fox was tall as his grandfather had been, with a shock of dark brown hair he combed straight back and a pair of black eyes that parted the air before them with their intensity.

Vardry drew up his chin, set his square jaw and clenched his teeth just before he started to speak, then stopped himself and started again. "You rich slave owners think you can have everything your own way by controlling Congress and electing presidents from the South! Nonimportation never worked before the Revolution, and it's not working now. The only way to have peace is to be ready for war! This country needs a president who'll listen to what the rest of us want!"

"We own no slaves, my grandson and I," Grandfather said, "but even if we did, that has nothing to do with Jefferson's plan. Nonimportation worked in South Carolina before the Revolution," Grandfather said evenly, "because the majority of us honored the agreement. The flow of British goods in this colony was all but stopped in 1769. Things were different in your part of the country."

Vardry seemed not to hear Grandfather's subtle re-
buke. His eyes were set on Fox, sizing him up the way a
hound does a scent. "England can get her cotton elsewhere. She can shut you down the same way she shut
down your indigo plantations when she ended the
bounty. One day there'll be cotton plantations standing
idle the way the indigo ones are now. Don't be
deceived . . . Mr. Gairden, is it? No economy can
survive on the basis of one crop."

"There is more to South Carolina than cotton, sir,"
Fox said, making no attempt to sound as even tem-
pered as Grandfather.

"Little more, I'm afraid. I've just spent a month traveling your state looking for a site for a cotton mill. And
there are sites aplenty, but nobody wants to invest in a
mill because everyone's too busy getting rich from cotton." Vardry's words caused a small stir among the circle of men, and inside of Fox. Surely he was mistaken.
There were plenty of men with money in South Carolina to foster such investment. There had to be. Fox
planned to start his own mill just that way.

"You'll begin to feel the pinch down here soon
enough, I'd say, Gairden," Vardry said, smiling as he
took note of the reaction his words had received.
"Soon you'll see planters who can't pay their creditors
because they can't sell their crop. Then you'll see that
they have no money to buy these domestic goods Jefferson is so fond of talking about, either, and so the
whole stupid business will not have helped you one
whit. We need trade with England and we need it
now."

The musicians stopped their playing. All eyes turned
to the debate raging beside the speakers' platform
where the red, white and blue seemed now less promi-
nent than the black of Hugh Vardry's coat and
breeches and the high color of his face. Grandfather

stood by with his lips drawn tight in that look he always wore when he knew he was right, even against all arguments to the contrary. But Fox felt his own color might be approaching the shiny red of Vardry's face, and now he, too, felt perspiration seeping beneath his hatband.

"We are not strangers to hard times, Mr. Vardry," Grandfather said. "And we don't fear 'em. But we are engaged in the work of building a nation, and we cannot do that by building up the commerce of other nations instead of our own. Washington and Adams would have us little more than subservient states of England. Jefferson and Madison see the need to assert our independence, whatever the cost—short of war. If we can learn to think in terms of the future, rather than in terms of gain, we will all profit in good time."

"You're a bit gray at the muzzle to be speaking so fondly of the future, are you not, old man?"

Fox's eyes widened. "I challenge you to defend that remark, Mr. Vardry! You are entitled to your political views, but no one is entitled to deride my grandfather."

Thomas Gairden grabbed Fox's arm, shaking his head in jerky defiance. "Nay, lad. Let the man be!"

"I'm afraid I cannot, Grandfather. And I'd be less than a proper grandson if I did."

Vardry's mouth turned down at the corners in a bitter laugh. "He's right, Gairden. His honor's at stake. And all of us from the North know there's nothing more important in the southern states than honor. In fact, I find that there's not much else in the southern states besides honor. They call North Carolina the Rip van Winkle of the United States, but I'd say South Carolina's even sleepier."

A collective gasp went up from the circle of men, and from the broader group of listeners who had begun to pay attention once the musicians had stopped.

"Name your second, Mr. Vardry," Fox said, clench-

ing his fists at his sides and feeling his grandfather's
sigh of disgust hot on his shoulder.

"I have none. I'm traveling alone. I shall defend myself alone."

Vardry looked confident, almost as if he welcomed
the dawn of the next day that would bring him face-to-
face with his young opponent, but Fox did not look
away. "I shall do the same, sir," he said.

A gossipy hush rippled over the crowd as the word
was passed at the same time the arrangements for the
duel were made. Fox took in a deep breath and
scanned the crowd for Jurian's face but did not find it.
He was aware of the eyes on him and of the way
Grandfather stomped away muttering something about
Fox's being "bad as that banty rooster Marion."
Grandfather thought dueling should be outlawed. So
did a lot of other men. Fox's classmates at South Carolina College, though, had all agreed that dueling was
necessary. As they practiced each evening with their
firearms out behind the main hall, they knew there
were things that could be settled no other way.

Tomorrow at dawn Fox would have a chance to
prove them right. And tomorrow night, he would waltz
with Sally Hudson.

The next morning, Fox watched as his father inspected
the weapons Vardry had brought to the Washington
Race Course where the duel would take place. Whitcomb Gairden had none of his own father's height but
was instead small and fine boned like his mother, Eliz-
abeth, who had died just last year. His small hands
were better suited to holding a pen than to throwing a
shuttle, or so he said when Fox asked him why he had
become a lawyer instead of a weaver. Though Fox had
heard his Grandfather lament often and loudly over his
inability to give his son a proper start in the world

thanks to the British devastation of his property during the war, Whitcomb was intelligent and quick and made his own way to a modest success. Success enough to send his own son, Fox, to the new college at Columbia. It was a fine school, one most in the state favored, and Fox had worked hard to make his parents and especially Grandfather, who was such a firm believer in the value of an education, proud of him. Would he dissolve that pride here today over a point of honor? He shrugged. If he did, and the honor was upheld, then the death was not wasted.

The heavy mist of a Charleston morning was just ascending when a chaise approached, and Fox saw his grandfather get out. Fox closed his eyes for a moment, gathering strength.

"Thought I should be here since 'tis my name you're defendin'," Thomas Gairden told his grandson. "You know I don't approve of this business, and I'll stop it if you'll let me, but if your mind's made up, then I can only pray for your safety—an' his."

"I thank you, Grandfather, but Vardry returned my letter of challenge without an apology. He means to duel, and so we must. If you try to stop it, Vardry will then tell it about that in the South we have not even honor. You'd not have that, would you?"

"Lots of people say lots of things, lad. I've said some myself I've come to think better of. An' some would see Mr. Vardry for what he is—a bully and a braggart, an' a bitter one at that. Hardly worth givin' up your life for . . ."

"I don't intend to do that, Grandfather. I'll take care of myself."

"I've seen men who limped all their lives over affairs more trifling than this. Men who've lost eyes. Hands. I'd not want that for you, lad. Something like this when you're young isn't over after the shots are fired—'tis with you all your days. Look at Aaron Burr—ruined over a duel."

"I've not the position of a Burr to lose, Grandfather. I'll be all right." Fox looked into Grandfather's eyes, dark under the sagging wrinkles of the skin above them. While the eyes stared straight at Fox, they seemed to see nothing of him.

"If you kill him, you'll never be the same. Not quite," Grandfather said, his eyes still far away.

Fox took his hand and shook it. "I won't kill him, Grandfather. I'm certain of that." Still the wrinkled face he knew so well did not respond for a moment, and there was no squeeze of his hand. Grandfather's hand felt cold. There was no impish wink this morning, no half-smile. Fox forced a smile of his own, and shook the cold hand again. "I'll make you proud, Grandfather," he said.

Grandfather nodded, but did not speak, then stepped back as Sam Rutledge, the attorney hired to serve as judge for the duel, called for the principals to take up their weapons.

"Mr. Vardry. Mr. Gairden. Choose your weapons." Fox avoided Vardry's face as he reached into the box to pick up one of the muzzle-loading pistols. Whether Vardry looked cocky or concerned, Fox didn't want to know it, didn't want to know anything that would rattle him, confuse him. He was a good shot with a pistol, short range or long. He would do what had to be done.

"One. Two. Three. . . ." Rutledge called off the paces, and the two men stepped slowly, like toy soldiers being pushed along by a small boy's erratic motion, until the final command. "Turn and fire!"

Fox whirled, pivoting on one foot, and took aim. Arm extended fully, body posed slightly forward the way he had been taught by friends at school, he now

saw Vardry's face. And Vardry's face was all he saw as
his finger pressed the trigger and the ball spun across
the morning air. The calm calculatedness of that face
collapsed in an instant. His mouth fell open, his eyes
flew open, white with pain as the missile hit. His body
jerked, balance gave way to agony, and the blond man
dropped to the earth.

Fox rushed to him, oblivious of the blood that ran
from his own thigh and onto the white breeches he
wore tucked into tall black boots. Whitcomb Gairden
and Sam Rutledge reached Vardry first, and Fox saw
Rutledge shake his head. Nothing wrong? Or . . . Fox
threw his pistol aside as he reached the trio and knelt
down.

"He's dead," Rutledge said.

"Dead?" Fox touched Vardry beneath the nose to
feel his breath. There was warmth, but no breath.
"Dead? I didn't mean to—"

"He hit you first, lad," his father said. "Threw off
your aim. You couldn't help it."

"Such are the ways of duels," Rutledge added. "It
isn't the first time. It won't be the last."

Fox could not look at Vardry's face. He knew he
should. He knew he should because he might see that
it no longer carried the contortions now emblazoned in
Fox's mind. But he could not stand to carry the death
look of the man with him either. He closed his eyes,
fighting both images back.

"Mist' Gairden! Mist' Gairden! Come quick!" At the
cry from Grandfather's driver, Jesse, both Mr.
Gairdens looked toward the chaise, then rose and ran
to help Jesse, a small, aging man himself, who struggled to lift Grandfather up from where he had fallen
forward off the chaise seat.

Again the kneeling by the body. Again the check for

breath. This time, Fox's father raised an eyelid. Nothing but white. The white of death.

"I think it would be best if I went away for a while," Fox said that afternoon, meeting alone with his father in the library of their home on Maiden Lane.

"No one in Charleston will fault you for what happened today." His father did not look at him as he spoke. "Vardry provoked you, you challenged him, he shot first, you defended yourself. A gentleman can do no more." Whitcomb Gairden, bulged with the inactivity of his job and middle age, sat smoking a heavily carved pipe, looking over his ample belly to the tips of his boots, but not at his son.

"It's not that—though I wonder what the talk will be at the Izards' ball tonight. No, it's Grandfather. I know you must blame me."

"I don't. I would never—"

"Still, I think it best to leave."

"To go back to the college, of course."

"No. Not there. The session does not resume until September. The mill is closed. I expect to go north."

"North? Whatever for?"

Fox swallowed hard, struggled for the words. "To tell Aunt Lily what happened. And to see what it is that I have killed."

Whit Gairden shifted in his seat and Fox could feel his distaste for the term he had used. Grandfather Gairden had always spoken of the sanctity of life, of the need to stop bloodshed. And the words had not been lost on his son, who had spent all of his years in a quiet law office where there was certainly no killing and very seldom even a raised voice. Fox, now that the deed was done, had a feeling for what his deed had cost his father. The only way to ease the burden was to absent himself, to take away the constant reminder of what he had done, of the failure his father must feel.

"That will be a long journey, my son," Whit Gairden said, still looking at his boots. "I wish you well."

2

Fox could tell by the tears welling up in Aunt Lily Durant's eyes that the news was unexpected. He looked around, everywhere but at her—at the cleanly furnished room with its straight-backed armchairs near the hearth and at the small writing table by the window. A patterned floor cloth, no doubt from the Durants' own looms here in Philadelphia, covered the wide planks of the floor, and the hems of heavy, bottle green draperies lay gracefully puddled on the floor. The room had a simple elegance to it that was different from the more elaborate interiors he was used to in Charleston.

Fox shifted his weight from leg to leg, adjusted the stock that felt too tight at his neck, touched his earlobe thoughtfully, awaiting Aunt Lily's response. He had told her Grandfather was dead. He had not told her how he died.

"It was sudden, then? No pain?" she asked, folding her hands in close to the waist of her blue-and-yellow-plaid gown.

"So sudden I had no proper chance to say farewell. You see, it—"

Aunt Lily's husband, Paul, a man nearer Grandfather's age than her own, nodded solemnly. "He wanted it that way. He often joked of dying by a single shot. This was almost as quick."

Fox colored. "It was the sound of a shot that brought it on, Uncle. It was the sight of my shot claiming an-

other man's life." He watched his uncle's face, but saw
that Paul Durant didn't understand. "I fought a duel.
And it was the sight of it that killed him."

Fox sensed a stiffening in the room, as if everyone,
of a sudden, were unable to take in a breath or let one
out. All movement ceased. All eyes were on him, yet
for a moment, an invisible barrier separated them, Fox
and these blood relatives he'd come to Philadelphia to
see. Then Aunt Lily broke through it and reached up
to touch his cheek.

"So the Gairden blood has not cooled, even in two
generations." She shook her head in resigned understanding.

"I was defending him," Fox said. "I was defending
him against a complete stranger whose name I had
never heard before that day. The man was the worst
kind of Federalist, shouting Grandfather down in front
of the whole of Charleston."

"You did the right thing." Adelle Durant, Fox's
cousin, spoke with a lively certainty. The starched muslin of her petticoat rustled softly as she rose and came
to stand beside him, a little shorter than he, but her
eyes meeting his with a level compassion. Fox remembered how, as children, he had told stories of ghouls
and goblins during the humid, late evenings of her one
visit to Charleston. The old ghosts of Charleston were
friendly images to him, but not to her, he'd found. She
had cried and his own mother had had to comfort her
into a restless sleep. They were only months apart in
age, and as he looked at her now he saw that she was
no longer a frightened little girl.

"Thank you, Cousin," he said, heaving a deep sigh
and swallowing back the choke in his voice. "I wish I
could share your certainty." He shook his head, unable
to explain the whole of it, and looked back toward
Aunt Lily. "I've come to face the consequences of my

actions—to atone, if I can, for the taking of another human life, to make amends."

"There is no need of that," Aunt Lily was quick to say. "We know you had only the best of intentions. Papa was at the end of his days—"

"And your grandfather was no doubt proud of you," Paul interrupted. "He did not approve of wanton killing, but he was ever the champion of the oppressed and a believer in people standing for beliefs. That is how he came finally to approve of my marriage to his daughter." Paul placed his arm around his wife's shoulders. "We believed ourselves meant for each other, which, indeed, our twenty-seven years of marriage proves we must have been. And he gave us that, gave us his blessing. He was a good man. I have missed him over these years we have been so separated by miles. I thank God that you, Lily, saw him one last time when you went to Charleston with the children." He kissed her lightly on the cheek, still holding her.

"He warned me—begged me—not to play out the duel." Fox went on with his explanation as if his aunt and uncle had not even spoken. The memories came flooding in, and now that he had started talking about them, he couldn't stop, not even for a comforting word. "But I had made the challenge. I assured him that the man would be no more than injured, so certain was I of my skill as a marksman. What he knew that I didn't was that the opponent cannot be counted upon to do as we expect. He feared I would be maimed, or even killed. He was afraid for me."

"Your grandfather understood the unpleasantnesses of life because he had known many of his own." Paul Durant paused, looking into his wife's eyes, then back again to his nephew. "I can see, Fox, that you are very much like him, and no doubt that is why he feared so much for you. Your own father has been content with his practice and his family and has not involved himself in affairs of government the way your grandfather might have hoped. In you, no doubt, he saw the flicker of his own youth."

Fox caught the look that passed between his aunt and uncle. "Was there something?" he asked.

"Your grandfather was attacked by a murderer when he was about your age," his uncle told him, "and in the fight that ensued, the murderer was killed. The experience of it never left Thomas. I know he wouldn't have wanted you to repeat it, even in a fairly fought duel."

"So that was what he meant." Fox thought back to the day of the duel and remembered Grandfather's words: "If you kill him you'll never be the same. Not quite." "But I never knew—"

"It was a family secret, though it needn't have been. Now both of you children know about it," Aunt Lily said. "I know of it only because Paul told me. Papa had confided in him years before, and it helped to explain why Papa held some of the beliefs he did. He couldn't tell you about it, either, Fox, but he did not want you to have the same kind of pain he had known himself. That's how he was."

"That *is* how he was," Paul echoed, smiling at the memory. "But this is *you*, Francis Marion Gairden. And you must get on with your life. Stay with us a while, Fox. We can put you to work in the mill—your father writes us that you already have some experience. Your cousin Joseph went west to Pittsburgh and left the weaving business, but he writes us he hopes to return. He's selling boats to people heading down the Ohio. A good business, but one that won't last long, I'm sure." Paul shook his head. "You might help us here until he returns."

"I appreciate the offer, Uncle. First, though, I'm determined to find the family of the man I . . . I'll be off to Connecticut as soon as I've rested and bought a horse."

"That is very honorable, Fox, but is it wise?" his uncle wondered. "The family will need time to accept the news of the death before they will want to hear anything you may have to say. If you go too soon, they will have nothing but anger and harsh words, *if* they will see you at all. Don't rush into something that will only bring you more pain. Stay here with us."

"I can't." Fox shook his head as if to drive away temptation. "Even though I know they've already received word of Vardry's death, I must try to explain."

Paul Durant whispered softly in his wife's ear, and she nodded. "I have to go out for a while," she told Fox, kissing him first on one cheek and then the other. "Stay and talk to Paul. I will see you at dinner."

"We shall make a chicken pie for you, Fox," Adelle said, rising to leave. "I seem to remember it was quite your favorite when we visited your house."

"What a good memory you have, Cousin." Fox nodded absently.

Closing the sliding parlor doors after her mother had gone out, Adelle was framed for a moment between them. She had her father's fine, French features set into a heart-shaped face, and a small, pouty mouth that reminded him of the way he had known her as a child. Her eyes, though, met the world directly and purposefully. Her actions appeared crisp as her muslin, and while Fox felt tired and restless, she moved about with quick, resolute steps. She nodded and lowered her eyes, then snuck a last look and smiled at him before the heavy doors closed.

"I think I may know how you feel, Fox," Paul said once they were alone. "You think if you talk to the family, if you explain, then it will all go away—you will be able to forget it and go on with your life. And perhaps you will. But more likely this thing will be with you always. You will never forget the sight of the man's face or the wound in his chest. One day you will smell air that has the same scent the air had the morning of the duel, and it will come back to you, fresh as if it were yesterday. Or you'll see a man you think is Vardry —a face in a crowd you'll look at twice, only to find it isn't him, because he is dead, after all. I know, Fox, because I still see the faces of men I killed in battle. I see their faces, the way they fell. I see them and I wonder why it was them and not me. Why was I the one to live on? Why was I spared?"

"But if you could have talked to their families, maybe it wouldn't be that way. If you could have explained—"

"I could not even explain it to myself. How could I ever have explained it to them?" Like so many veterans of the Revolution, Paul Durant had a pride in what he had fought for, but also a sadness. One of President Washington's dying wishes was for an end to all wars, and veterans like Uncle Paul echoed that sentiment wordlessly every time their thoughts turned to those blood-drenched days. Uncle Paul dressed, though, with the flair of an actor, or dancing master, in a ruffled shirt and brocaded waistcoat. Still a dashing figure, Fox thought. The kind a young woman would go against her father to win.

"But mine was a duel, an agreement. The family will understand that."

"They may understand it, and you may understand it, but understanding will never compensate for loss— for either of you. And feelings go deeper than understanding, no matter how much we may wish it otherwise. We cannot help what we feel, because most often we don't know where our feelings stem from, where their roots are."

Fox sighed and swallowed hard. Uncle Paul had voiced what so far he himself had not been able to express. It was a bad business, this killing, just as Grandfather had warned him it would be. If I had only known. Fox caught himself and chided himself for the weakness of even thinking it: I wouldn't have listened even if I had known. I was certain the duel was the right—the only—course.

"I'm going, Uncle Paul. I must. Honor demands it."

"Just as honor demanded that you fight Vardry? Where did that lead, Fox? Honor is an elusive master —one you cannot always obey."

"But I've been taught—"

"I know what you've been taught. I lived in Charleston many years myself, you know. I know its mind. But I tell you this: Its mind is not the mind of the rest of the nation. Here in the North they run over those who live for honor, because here they live for profit. I, too, have had to adjust my ways to keep up with the never-ceasing drive to be better, and faster, and richer, that is part of this new merchants' world. You will see it, too, if you stay long enough. Up here they don't hold with the pace in the South, and feelings are growing stronger against slavery as well. Even Adelle has attended some meetings at the Presbyterian church on the subject of abolition—quite a thing for a Catholic. There is a Society for the Abolition of Slavery here now. You may meet with some unkind remarks, as I did, even though you have never owned a slave. Some are rather quick to forget that until quite recently slaves were common here, too."

"Vardry, the man I . . ."—Fox slipped past the word—"said the Carolinas were like Rip van Winkle— asleep. He was jealous of the money being made in cotton, I think, and he appeared the kind of man who would be quick enough to buy up some slaves if they could make him rich." Fox caught himself. "Forgive me for speaking ill of the dead, Uncle. It's only that I still get angry sometimes when I think of the abusive manner in which he spoke."

"I can see that this duel was not something taken lightly. And from what you say of the man and knowing that his family may be very much like-minded, your errand seems all the more admirable. Whether you follow your honor code and seek the Vardry family is up to you. Only know that we do not expect it of you, and we will not think less of you if you choose not to go. You will be welcome to stay here as long as you like. Going back to Charleston may not have much appeal for a while."

"No, it doesn't. But I must go to Connecticut—no matter what kind of reception I get. At least I'll know I tried."

"Of course, Fox," Uncle Paul said, patting him softly on the shoulders. "It is important to try, always to try. Your grandfather taught me that. I can see he taught you well, too."

"He did, sir . . . and, ye gods how I shall miss him." For the first time, Fox let the tears run down his cheeks as he looked away, out the window and across the way to his uncle's Oxmoor Mill, its waterwheel circling effortlessly and spilling troughs of water into the bracing autumn air.

When he turned once again toward his uncle, his eyes still not as dry as he would have liked, Adelle stood silently in the doorway, her eyes large and dark as she took in the scene before her. He hadn't heard her open the doors, and even if he had, he probably could not have collected himself any more. Fatigue and grief had caught up with him. "Excuse me," he said, hurrying past Adelle and out the front door.

* * *

Philadelphia's streets were laid out in a perfect grid, and most of them were paved, with sidewalks raised a foot to keep passersby from being spattered with mud or run over. There were blocks and blocks of businesses and neat-looking houses, but it was a very different place from Charleston. It was a world of gray, where smoke rose from the tall chimneys of manufactories. A world without ornate wrought-iron piazzas and walled gardens. Men and young boys worked at sweeping in the streets, and women hung laundry out to dry in the cool, damp air. All of them seemed to hurry and to take little notice of anything but their tasks. Fox saw all these things today, whereas yesterday when he had run out of his uncle's house, he had seen nothing, noticed nothing. Absorbed in his own guilt he had wandered for nearly two hours before he had been able to return to the Durant house ready to converse with his aunt's family once again, and to face Adelle's warm, forgiving eyes when he felt so unworthy of forgiveness. The evening had passed quietly, but by the next morning Uncle Paul had announced that Fox must be up and about.

"Papa suggested I take you to see the new waterworks, since we're to be the first city in the United States to have water piped to our homes," Adelle said. "A few already have it, but some of the time it doesn't work. They're going to replace the wooden pipes with iron ones, if you can believe that."

"I've read something about it. It sounds quite modern."

"There's a great deal of machinery inside the building in Centre Square, but it's the building itself I like," she said as they approached the circular domed building of white marble. "Quite grand for a pump house, isn't it?"

"Classical lines," Fox replied with a nod. "No reason

not to make it beautiful, I suppose. I think it's very nice." Taking her arm in his, he felt her energy flow between them, circling in that link of arms, and Fox let it overpower the guilt that had weakened him since the duel. The feeling made him smile. "And now that we've completed one of our assigned tasks, what's next, Cousin?"

"The university. They've taken the mansion that was built for the president of the United States—the one Mr. Adams refused to live in because he thought it too grand. The university bought it at a public sale and uses it for the main college building now that the government has moved to Washington City."

"I hear most of the senators and congressmen wish they could be back here instead of in the mud and half-finished buildings of the new capital," Fox said, matching his long strides to Adelle's brisk pace.

"They have Mr. Hamilton to thank for being there, or so I hear. He wanted to control everyone's money, and in order to get it he took the war debts of all the states upon the new government in exchange for putting the capital in the South." She opened her mouth again and took in a quick breath instead of speaking. "I'm sorry, Fox. To bring up Hamilton, I mean. You probably think I—"

"Because Burr killed him in a duel, you mean? Not at all. I can't expect people not to talk of such things. Not at all. But I thought we were a nation, not a north and south," Fox ventured, changing the subject back to the capital again.

"So far we are," she conceded, "but you must agree that there are those who might wish us other than one nation." Glancing his way, she did not slow her gait to wait for his reply.

"I must agree," Fox said, "though I'm not at all ready to agree that such a division would fall along geographic lines. There are those in both the North and the South who would have us still England's puppet, and those who want no such thing."

"And you would make Republicans of them all if you could, would you not, Fox?"

"Not by dueling, if that's what you mean."

"Not at all. Of course that's not what I meant." Her pale skin flushed with color and she looked away.

"I'm sorry, Adelle," Fox said, catching her by the arm to stop her so that he could apologize. Still she looked away. He took both of her arms in his hands and tilted his head until he could look her in the eye. "I know you didn't mean that. I've forgotten how to talk with a lady, I've been so preoccupied with this Vardry business." Her arms were tense and he realized it was not so much hurt as anger that made her look away. He chanced a smile.

After a moment, she returned it. "All right," she said. "And I've forgotten that my southern cousin is not like the rest of the southerners we hear about up here."

"In the South, you know, we marry our cousins," he said, giving her arms a playful squeeze before he dropped his hands to his sides again. He could easily have held her there longer. It felt good to touch another human being, to connect with more than a handshake.

Adelle started walking again, though not as fast as before. "I know," she said, looking at him as though the thought was foremost in her mind. Now it was Fox who looked away.

"I belong to an abolitionist group, against Papa's wishes." Adelle changed the subject in a way that left the last few statements still audible in Fox's mind. "He's afraid I'll be harmed physically in a riot or some other action. I don't care if I am. I, too, would make

Republicans of people, Fox. I believe in the rights of all people, and I don't believe we should let Britain control our policies, no matter that she's at war with France. We have a right to carry on our business with France as we always have, and I think Mr. Jefferson can convince them of that by peaceful means, like the embargo. I *do* think he might free his own slaves, though, to show people his principles go deeper than just ink on paper."

"You have been listening at those meetings of yours, haven't you, Adelle?" Fox was not surprised at her knowledge of the political issues. After all, such topics had had the country on the brink of civil war all summer. But he was surprised at her passion, and somewhere inside him, a bit of defensiveness stirred. "It's not against the law yet—owning slaves, I mean. When it is, Jefferson will comply. I'm not so certain about others. Plantations need slaves—"

"Why do plantations need slaves any more than mills need slaves? Plantation owners could pay their employees just as mill owners do."

"In a way, they do. They give them food, clothing and shelter. Other employers pay only just enough for their employees to have those things, nothing more. There's very little difference from that standpoint."

"Unless you're a slave. Owned like cattle. If there is so little difference economically, why not just pay them and be done with it?"

Fox and Adelle stopped on a street corner, waiting for a coach to pass, and he paused as he sought his answer. He had almost been defending slavery, he realized, rationalizing it just the way he had the need to duel. When he spoke again, he uttered a truth he had never before felt free to state. "Because they're afraid of them," he said.

He saw her look of disbelief mixed with the knowl-

edge that what she had just heard was an intimate ad-
mission, a private comment that shocked him as much
as it did her. "That's why there's a nine fifteen curfew
and why armed patrols walk the streets of Charleston
at night," he went on. "They're not watching for
thieves or vagrants. They're making sure no Negroes
are out there. Slavery is a system of control that is destined to fail, because no one individual can ever control
another. Not completely."

"Then why not stop it? Why not get rid of the system?"

"They're more afraid of that, I suppose. Slaves have
made men rich. They don't want to see it end."

Adelle stepped down from the sidewalk and they
crossed the street taking long, hurried steps as a wagon
pulled by two lathered horses rushed toward them.
"I'm so glad you've come, Fox. Now I know the aboli-
tionists are right," she said. "If you stay here with us, I
want you to come to a meeting with me and tell them
what you've just said."

"I don't know, Adelle. I'd feel like a traitor saying
those things to anyone but you. No one would ever say
that in Charleston."

"You're not in Charleston anymore," Adelle reminded him.

"But I'll go back, and I'd still remember what I said
up here."

"You *should* go back there and say it, too, Fox. Say it
loud and strong."

"I don't think I have it in me to be a revolutionary,
Adelle. I'm not like Grandfather . . . was. And you
know Mama's family owns slaves. Her sisters live on
rice plantations with hundreds of them. They would
not likely welcome someone who spread it all over the
North that they were scared of their own slaves. Or
someone who said the whole system was wrong."

"Well, if you're not welcome there, perhaps you'll stay here. I'd like that, Fox." This time it was Adelle who stopped and touched his arm.

It was there again, that feeling he remembered from the only other time he had ever seen her, when they were no more than children playing jump rope and hide-and-seek. He had kissed her when he found her once, and she had looked surprised, then kissed him back. They had been fast friends for a month all those years ago. This time they were older. This time a kiss would have a much different meaning.

"You're very kind, Cousin. You've all made me feel welcome, even though I came as the bearer of such sad news." He took her hand and kissed it lightly. "But I cannot stay. The commitment I must honor may take me some time." He felt grief come over him just the way it had during his days under sail from Charleston, and before him he saw the leering face of Hugh Vardry. He forced it away as best he could. "For now, we'd better tour this university so that we can honestly tell your parents we've seen the appointed sights today." He squeezed her hand gently before he let it go, and watched her eyes as she chanced another look into his.

"No game of hide-and-seek before you go?" she asked.

"So you haven't forgotten, either."

"I have a very good memory," she said. "You said so yourself."

"That you do, Cousin." Fox felt people watching them as they stood somewhat too close to each other on the walk before the large square building that was now the University of Pennsylvania. Once again he took her arm, but he didn't draw her in quite as close as he would have liked as they started up the walk to the mansion. Between them stood the awareness that he had not really answered her question. For a few moments they walked in silence.

"It looks like a university more than a home, don't you think?" she asked at last. "Papa says they've had a difficult time gaining students because they have no religious affiliation. They've been forced to include an academy and a charity school in order to establish themselves." When there was no response from Fox, Adelle went on. "The small building with the dome is the medical school, guided by Dr. Rush. He saved many here during the yellow fever epidemic when I was a child. Lots of people don't like the pilasters," she went on. "They say it looks as though the upper and lower stories are reversed. I think it's lovely."

"And so do I. It reminds me of some of the Charleston buildings, with its broad stair and tall windows."

Fox kept his eyes focused on the building's graceful facade as Adelle went on analyzing the building's attributes. If he expected her to melt into tears or flit into giggles as Sally Hudson might have done when faced with having to settle for less than she wanted, Fox found that Adelle was something different from the Charleston standard of womanhood, though she had learned well from her mother what it meant to be a lady. The little girl he had known had fascinated him in a tomboyish sort of way. The older Adelle had a new fascination for him that both attracted him and yet daunted him, too. She had a strength that, just now, he wasn't certain he had. Perhaps after he had settled this business with the Vardrys he would have it again. He would once again be the Fox Gairden who liked fast horses, a good argument and a pretty girl. No matter what Grandfather had said.

"Let's walk down to the docks," Adelle suggested suddenly, before they had gone completely around the block where the university stood. "I'll show you where

Grandfather landed when he came here from Ireland. He told me all about it when we visited you in Charleston that time, and when we came home I made Mama take me down there. Cranston's Wharf, he called it, but they don't call it that anymore. He told me how he walked down Market Street and bought bread at the baker's and there's still a baker's on Market Street. I always imagine it's the same one."

Adelle's energy revived itself even as Fox felt his lag under the weight of his mission. Still the day passed far too quickly to suit him. "Did your father tell you to keep me so well occupied?" Fox asked at last.

"He did," Adelle replied, without guile.

"Let me guess—and you are to make life here so inviting that I will abandon my plans to go on to Connecticut. I will then regain my senses and return to Columbia and my studies, just as *my* father wishes."

Adelle returned the smile Fox offered. "Something like that," she admitted.

"Please don't let the whole family produce a conspiracy without telling me, Adelle," he asked. "I really haven't lost my mind—not all of it, anyway."

"Papa knows that. We all know it. We just want to make things easier for you."

"Believe me, I appreciate everyone's concern. It's just that seeing the Vardrys is something I have to do. I don't know if the man left behind children, debts, a wife. I know nothing except that they deserve to be told at least a part of what happened, the least painful part. I think I can give them that. I think I owe it to them."

"That is very honorable, Fox, and I commend you for it. I'm not certain I could face them if I were in your spot."

"I had a dream that I was on a ship, far out at sea, and I wanted to get off but the captain wouldn't let me off until I scrubbed the deck with a tiny brush. I had to do it or be eternally at sea. This trip to Connecticut gives me the same feeling the dream did. If I don't do it, I'll never rest, I'll be eternally at sea. Do you understand that, Adelle? Does it make sense?"

"It does, Fox. And we all know you're right to want to do it. We just don't want to lose you now that we've seen you again after all these years."

"And I would gladly stay were things different. But they aren't. I've done what I've done, and now I must do what I must do. I can only trust you'll understand."

"You can always trust me," she told him, squeezing his arm in hers as she emphasized the *always*.

Fox squeezed back, hearing in her words a little of the voice he'd never expected to hear again. Grandfather.

It was late afternoon when they made their way back to the Oxmoor Mill on Germantown Road in what was known as the Northern Liberties of Philadelphia. Entering by the roadside door, Fox had his first look inside his uncle's mill. Larger than Colonel Taylor's mill back in South Carolina, this mill was also different in that its specialty was flax rather than cotton. Still, the racket of the machines was the same, and the waterwheel that drove them was of the same overshot type. Fox walked behind Adelle, looking about him, at once fascinated with it all.

"This way, Fox," Adelle called to him from the bottom of a narrow wooden stairway. "Papa's office is up here."

Fox hurried to catch up, still looking behind him at the warp dressing room as he mounted the stairs, then nearly bumped into Adelle where she stopped on the landing at the sight of a stranger in her father's office. "Papa's busy," she explained in a hushed voice. "Mama's in there, too."

Adelle was clearly perplexed by the business in the mill office, but did not hesitate to turn her back on it when Fox suggested she show him around the manufactory.

"Mama grew up in Grandfather's manufactory, and she believes I should have the same experience," Adelle told him as she showed him around. "I've worked many an hour here over the past ten years. Mama got to go off to London to school for four years when she was a girl, but she does *not* believe I should have *that* experience. There, of course, we differ, for I long to see other places. Joseph does, too. He's been a terrible disappointment, leaving here and going off with dreams of the West. But I'm going, too, one day."

Just like her mother, he remembered Grandfather saying about Adelle, smiling as he said it. Aunt Lily had run away with a Loyalist just before the war broke out in 1775. She had not married Paul Durant until after her first husband died, near the close of the war. Both marriages were to men her father did not approve of—at least at first. But she had had her own reasons for what she did, and she had stood up for them. Adelle had inherited that spunk.

Flax, tow and hemp were processed and spun, twisted and then woven, she told him, getting back to the tour again. The mill produced two main products, a coarse linen fabric and an even coarser bagging, along with twine and yarns in finer weights. Fox coughed against the fiber particles that filled the air like a tan fog, and saw Adelle fan them away from her own nose as they walked through the spinning room. Vats of water stood by each jenny; a young boy sprinkled the water onto the fibers as they passed to make the long, line-spun linen threads. The tow linen, made from the shorter, less desirable fibers, was spun dry, and in that room each worker covered her face with a white scarf that was ever layered with dunes of fibers across the nose and under the eyes.

At the touch of Adelle's hand on his arm, Fox knew it was once again time to follow, and they made their way up to the mill office. This time, they found his aunt and uncle alone, both of them looking slightly dazed.

"Who was that man?" Adelle asked, slipping into a familiar seat against the wall. Fox remained standing, leaning back and folding his arms across his chest, still thinking of all he had seen downstairs.

"That man," Uncle Paul said, "has just told us that the widow Shaves has taken a husband in Europe and wishes to divest herself of some of her holdings, including this mill. Our lease includes an option to buy. At last we can do it, if we wish."

"This embargo against English goods has made it possible for us to sell more bags and yardage than ever before," Aunt Lily said. "If ever there was a good time to buy the property, it is now."

"We may need to take in another investor," Uncle Paul was quick to add, "as we did when we added more spindles and cards, but that should not be difficult."

"If only Joseph were here to help us now," Aunt Lily said. She shook her head, chiding herself, Fox could tell, for even thinking such a thing. She was a handsome woman, but had worked hard here in Philadelphia, and the years were beginning to show in a few gray hairs and a missing tooth. A half sister to Fox's father, she had the Gairden softness of heart and tenacity of spirit, making Fox want to reach out to her as she thought of her absent son.

"I don't think you should pin your hopes on Joseph." Adelle's curt statement was spoken like a true younger sibling, Fox thought, recalling similar conversations in his own family. "Just because he wrote that he would like to come home doesn't mean that he will."

"What do you think, Fox?" Uncle Paul asked. "You've some experience in a cotton mill. What would you do?"

"I would buy, and I would expand," Fox said, without any hesitation. "You're right about the market just now. It's getting bigger every day. Grandfather told me many times that the future of weaving was in the mills. People will buy the goods as long as the price can be kept down. And new machines will make the work faster, the product better." He stopped a moment, looking down at Adelle, then to his aunt and finally back to Uncle Paul.

"We could use you to stay here and help us," Uncle Paul offered.

"I would like that, but I can't promise it now, not knowing what I may find in Connecticut. I'm afraid I can't let you pin your hopes on me either, just now."

"You are Papa's spirit reincarnate, Francis Marion Gairden," Aunt Lily said with a smile.

Odd, Fox thought. I thought that of Adelle. "I take that as a very great compliment, Aunt Lily," he said. "And if I can come back, I will."

Fox thought Adelle smiled when her father shook his hand and thanked him, but once again he sensed a distance between them, just as he had back on the university steps. Fox gave Aunt Lily a hug, then took Adelle's hands in his. You want more than I can give, Adelle, he tried to tell her in his look and in the way his thumbs rubbed gently across her fingers. He caught the glance that passed between Aunt Lily and Uncle Paul. They sensed the beginnings of something between him and their daughter, yet he could not tell how they felt about it. And he did not know himself.

As quickly as it had come, Adelle's disappointment or whatever it was seemed to leave her. She brightened, transforming her pouty lips into a warm smile.

"We hope you will come back, Cousin," she said, her vitality abounding and surprising him as it did each time he realized how she shared her energy with those around her. "And in the meantime, I'll take over for Joseph if you'll let me, Papa," she said. "I'll help you."

"I knew you would, Adelle. But we'll make room for these young men when they come back to us, won't we?"

"Aye, Papa. We won't be selfish—there'll be plenty of work to go around."

Fox sighed once the moment of tension was past. Perhaps she had not been so disappointed in him as in her father's assumption that Joe must be the one to help in the mill. He chanced another look into her eyes. She was the one who should be going to Connecticut. There was nothing she couldn't do.

"You'll post a letter to us once you're there, won't you, Fox?" Adelle asked as he was leaving the next morning. She stood holding Shadow's reins, petting him gently on the nose as she watched her cousin strap his few belongings on his newly purchased gelding.

"I shall try, but I might be back here before *it* is, you know," he teased.

"Not at all. The mails run daily through New York now. It will reach us in three days." She paused, looking up from Shadow's serene face. "I know you won't be back that soon."

"As usual, you are right. I fear it may take some time."

"You have many things to prove, don't you, Fox?" Adelle laid her cheek against Shadow's nose, and Fox caught the pensive look she gave him.

"As you do," he replied, looking into her eyes. She shrugged, and Shadow nuzzled at her neck.

"I suppose," she said. "I wish you weren't going yet."

"And I wish I hadn't come at all, because then I wouldn't have to leave so soon. But the longer I stay, Adelle, the harder it will be to go. And if I don't go . . ." He let the sentence trail off, remembering the dream of the eternal voyage. He shook his head, unable to say more.

The faces of his aunt and uncle as they came down the walk to bid him farewell showed regret, apprehension and yet pride, too. There was a sadness in the farewell that was not just from parting, but from an unidentifiable sense of loss they all shared. Still, there was hope. Aunt Lily and Uncle Paul had once walked their own difficult roads. In their eyes, he saw an understanding of what might lie ahead. In Adelle's, he saw the trace of a tear.

"I'm off," he called out, reining Shadow around to the left as he fought back his own emotions. "My thanks to you." With a wave, he was gone, not to the West of his cousin Joseph, but to the East and another frontier.

The morning he rode into Connecticut Fox was thinking about his name. Carrying around the memory of
General Francis Marion had been a heavy responsibility for Fox all of his life, even if half of the boys born
each year in Charleston seemed to be named after
Marion or some other war hero. Marion was the
toughest of them. The shrewdest. Was Fox like him at
all? he wondered. Just now he wished he could hide his
head in a swamp instead of facing the Vardry family.
He could feel it already, Uncle Paul had been right: It
was too soon. The Vardrys wouldn't want to see him.
The whole trip would have been in vain. He should
have stayed in Charleston.

"Can't catch the Swamp Fox!" That had been his
battle cry when he played with his boyhood friends.
Calling it out he would sneak into the hackberry
thicket that hid his secret place behind a lattice under
the veranda—the place he'd found, and kissed, Adelle
all those years ago. None of the other boys had ever
found the hiding place. Only Adelle. He should have
known then she was more than a match for him. But he
hadn't. No, it seemed he was destined to learn everything the hard way. No doubt this visit to the Vardrys
would be more of the same.

"Relative?" the barman in Derby wanted to know
when Fox asked for directions to the Vardry home.

They were nosy, these New Englanders. Now he was
going to be nosy, too. "Does it make a difference?"

"Might." The barman, a head shorter than Fox, bent near as he spoke. Deep wrinkles fanned out from his hazel eyes, as though he had narrowed them countless times, squinting for an answer. "She don't talk to ever'one. An' they don't talk to her."

"I see." Again Fox wished for a swamp, for total submersion. "Well, I have business with the family."

"No family. Just missus. Not much on business, I'd say." The barman took Fox's empty glass and wiped the bar before him, as though he'd be the judge of when Fox was done.

"Another, please," Fox said, not wanting one.

"Hmmp," came the barman's reply. "Out on Beaver Creek. You'll find it."

"I need to post a letter," Fox said. The barman's words on Vardry were clearly used up.

"In that pouch. Goes out tomorrow." The barman kept his eyes on the keg he was tapping and kept his back to Fox.

"I'll have it ready." Fox let the whiskey roll across his tongue a half-dozen times before he swallowed it with a grimace unbefitting a Carolinian and left the tavern, steadied for his mission.

Riding to the top of the ridge above the town, Fox looked down on Derby with its colorful houses and riverfront row of shops. Water tumbled over the rapids of a small stream that emptied into the Housatonic, and Fox couldn't help but think it would be a fine place to build a mill, the damming would be so easy. Bad financial luck must have been the thing that sent Hugh Vardry sailing for the Carolinas, for it surely hadn't been lack of mill seats. Dreading his mission as he was, Fox could still see the possibilities here, many more of them than he had ever seen in South Carolina with its slow, flat rivers ambling through the coastal plain. Rivers in Connecticut were tumbling, boulder-strewn, bawdy affairs filled with power. Fox patted Shadow's shiny black mane. "Why would a man leave such a place, Shadow, and seek out mills in Carolina?" he asked, blowing out a chestful of pent-up questions in the air he pushed through clenched teeth. "Perhaps we'll never know, but by God we're going to try to find out."

Beaver Creek was a good-sized river by Carolina standards, a gurgling stretch of liquid energy that fed the Naugatuck River. Sturdy maples guarded the summits of craggy banks where lichens covered ancient rocks like spattered paint and cedars tipped, shallow-rooted, into the rocky cut of river. The road along the creek forked, and Fox followed it another couple of miles on a gentle grade until at the top he saw a small mill, its breast wheel slowly turning in a jerky rotation, missing a half dozen or more of the buckets that caught the water and caused the wheel to keep on turning.

Fox reined Shadow into the drive, then rode to the creek's edge for a closer look. Branches and weeds clogged the trash rack above the wheel, left there by spring flooding, he supposed. No sign of cleanup. The mill was quiet.

He was standing, arms folded across his chest, surveying the head race and wheel motion when he heard a door close and looked up to see a young woman pointing a long, ancient musket at him. She was plainly dressed in black homespun and heavy black shoes. Around her shoulders she wore a gray homespun shawl that was pulled down under her arms and tied at her waist in the back. Heavy clothes for August. Mourning clothes. Her hair, a dark brown color, was pulled back in the severe way that a maid or a servant might wear it, and her eyes appeared large and dark against her pale skin.

"What do you want?" she said, holding her finger tight on the trigger.

"I'm looking for—"

"What you're looking for isn't here. My husband's dead. Gone. Next time I find somebody out here I'll shoot! Now, get away."

"I'm not here about the mill. My name is Gairden, Francis Marion Gairden, and I've come from Charleston."

The barrel of the heavy gun wavered slightly, but the woman made no move to lower it. She looked too young to be Vardry's wife, but then he was the sort of man who would have liked young women. He had been rather good-looking, the kind who could attract women. This one appeared shy and frightened, just the compliant type a man like Vardry would no doubt have enjoyed. Fox felt an instant sympathy for her, and no fear of her weapon, oddly enough, but a shock at what he saw in her eyes: a bitter hatred that simmered in the pretty darkness.

"You shot him?"

"I did. I've come to offer my apologies to his widow —to you—and to all in his family. To offer my help if it's needed." Help was needed, that was clear in everything from the poor way the woman was dressed to the way the door sagged on its hinges behind her and the rust on the musket barrel. Fox felt a new surge of guilt over the deprivation he saw. "He fired first, caught me in the leg just as I was firing. My aim was ruined. Instead of his arm, I hit his head. I don't think he felt any pain." How feeble the words seemed. At once he realized that no one can truly know the pain another feels. Had there been a second of intense agony that seemed to stretch for long minutes inside Hugh Vardry's wounded head? He would never know. Not quite.

"He's gone," the woman said, holding the musket

steady, "and I don't want to hear any more. You've done what you came to do. Unless you are actually after the mill. I had an idea there might have been more to Hugh's duel than just words. There was usually money involved somewhere."

"I'm sorry, Mrs. Vardry. I didn't mean to intrude. I just wanted to—"

"I don't care what you want. I'll burn this mill down before I'll let it pass into the hands of another. It's *mine*, no matter what he promised anyone else. Now, get along. Go on."

Shooing him away with the musket barrel, she never once lowered it or loosened her grip on the trigger. Still, she was a slight woman and he could have knocked the gun aside and bested her in a single lunge had he wanted, but he didn't. He wanted to explain.

"I've come a long way, Mrs. Vardry," he said. "I won't hurt you . . . I mean no harm . . . you don't need to hold the musket on me . . . I promise. I only want to explain. I don't expect you to like me, or even to understand it all, but I thought you'd want to know . . . how it happened, I mean."

"I don't need you to tell me how it happened. I *know* how it happened. It was something like this: Hugh made the rounds of the county, dealing on land or mills or crops, which he had no funds to support, and then when he was called on it—by you, I suppose—he challenged you. And he bargained with you. If he won, he took your holdings. If you won, you were entitled to his, including this mill." She stopped here and lowered the gun, dropping the tip of the barrel into the rocky soil at her feet. "You see, it wasn't his first duel. It was only the first one he lost."

"He didn't make the challenge, Mrs. Vardry. I did. He insulted my grandfather and I called him out. I never meant to kill him, I hope you can believe that. I was only defending my grandfather's honor. Until the day of the duel my life was full of happiness and good fortune. Since that day, I have known no happiness and fear I will not until—"

"Your guilt is absolved? Is that it? I should say I forgive you and then you can go on about your life as it was before? Very well then, you are forgiven! Now get on with your life, Mr. Gairden, and leave me to mine."

Sunlight flickered across her face, shadowed by the arc of the hand she held above her eyes to shield them from the midday glare she had to look into when she looked at him. He walked toward the corner of the mill and leaned against it, out of the sun. "Your forgiveness has a bitter ring to it, Mrs. Vardry. I wonder if it is forgiveness after all, or contempt. Perhaps if I could explain—"

Now it was she who stepped out into the sunlight, and he who looked against the bright sun as she turned her back to him. He left the security of the mill's wall to close the distance between them, but she kept her direction toward the river. And he waited.

"You know, Mr. Gairden, I knew he wouldn't come back. I knew it the day he left, long before you ever shot him." She turned to him, a single tear streaming down her left cheek. "But can we give each other absolution? Never. Hugh Vardry will never die for either of us. And so you see, Mr. Gairden, your coming here was a wasted trip."

"I did not know your husband," Fox said, "but I know the honor code of Charleston. When your husband spoke wrongly of my grandfather, it was my duty to challenge him. My obligation. And I did send him the required note offering the option to deny the challenge, but he refused. He seemed to almost relish it—"

"Because he was a man who never missed a shot. He used to practice, right over there," she said, pointing to a small open area to the north where the skinned tree bark told of much target practice. "He would not have been afraid of a duel. I'm only surprised it is you who lived to tell about it and not him. You're fortunate to still have legs to walk on and arms that work."

"He wounded my leg, and that has healed. But what was killed, I think, was something in my heart which I cannot seem to heal. I admit I had hoped talking to you might help that. I'm sorry that instead I've only renewed your pain. I shall leave now, as you wish."

She still stood, back to him, looking off across the river. Fox was already starting back toward his horse when she began to speak again. "I suppose you heard his views on slavery before your duel of words came to an end."

"I believe he made a comment to my grandfather about slaves—about how the South felt itself above the rest of the nation because it had a force of slaves to do its work. Then in the next breath he said he wanted to build a mill in South Carolina, where he would no doubt have had to hire slaves as help because there are no hordes of jobless immigrants to do such work, as there are up here."

"Build a mill? With what? I wonder. The debts he ran away from here with? He had grand ideas, Hugh did. But he knew next to nothing about a mill."

"And you did?" Fox walked around to face her, yet she did not meet his eyes.

"He plucked me from my father's house in Massachusetts where I had been weaving since I was eight years old. No, I knew little enough then of mills, but I knew weaving, and he had visions of getting rich by building a spinning and weaving mill, instead of just a spinning mill as most others were doing. I was tired of my parents' house, tired of the long days that stretched between Sundays, which were the only days I was allowed to see young ladies—or young men. My father thought Hugh quite a match, although he knew nothing about him other than what Hugh told him, and like you, I was too young to know the difference."

"I'm sorry." Fox shifted his weight uncomfortably after the tale of regret was told. "We all make some unfortunate choices in our youth, I suppose . . ."

"Ah, yes, but you are a man, and bad choices are considered part of the necessary experience for a man's life. For a woman it is different. A woman must pay for hers. I am Hugh Vardry's widow, tainted with the legacy of debt and deceit he left behind, no matter what."

"But you could go away from here. Sell the mill, go back to your parents or to live with another relative, perhaps."

"As a pitied widow? You would sentence me to a life of covert looks and whispers? Of wearing black and never laughing? No, my family would not welcome me. You see, I've not written them in all the time I've been away. At first it was because I was so glad to *get* away, then it was because I'd got out of the habit, and finally it was because . . . Well, anyway, I don't want to go back. I won't go back. I'll stay here. This is my home now, this is my life, if you can call it that. And at least I'll have no one telling me what to do. I've had enough of that," she said, looking at Fox at last, "and I know better than to want it again."

"You could go west. Lots of people are. My cousin Joseph Durant from Philadelphia left for the Ohio and found work. They'll be needing weavers out there, I imagine."

"I can weave here, Mr. Gairden. I don't need to go west for it. If weaving is all I'm to do, I can save myself the lions and floods and whatever else it is I'd have to endure there. No, sir, I'm not leaving here. I'm going to do what my husband failed to do: make a profit at this mill. Seven years of my life are in it already. I have nothing to lose."

"The embargo may mean a healthier market for our own manufactures, but of course no foreign markets. The man I worked for in South Carolina had to close his mill. The South Carolina Homespun Company right in Charleston is behind in its financial obligations. We need the embargo, and I think Mr. Jefferson is right to use it, but we're all going to have to grit our teeth for a while until England finally comes around to our way of thinking."

"Well when she does, I'll be ready. Now if you'll be on your way, Mr. Gairden, I'd appreciate it."

"I won't trouble you any longer, Mrs. Vardry. As I said, though, I wish I could be of help to you. I could clean out the trash rack and fix those missing buckets on the wheel—whatever you need."

"No, Mr. Gairden, please. I'll get it done."

Fox thought he saw a softening in her eyes just then, but it was clear there was no point in protesting further. Still he knew she needed help, even though she obviously didn't want it from him. "I'm planning to take a job at Lapham's Mill upriver," he fibbed, plucking out of the blue the name of a mill he'd heard about from a man in the Derby tavern. "Thought I might see a little of the country here before I go back to Charleston. If you change your mind . . . if there's anything you need . . ."

"I won't change my mind, Mr. Gairden. I can't. My task is set before me, you've helped see to that."

"I can understand your anger, Mrs. Vardry. But if I could only help—"

"You can help by going away and leaving me alone. I've got to do this myself."

"Very well, then. But I will stay close at hand for a

few months, and I will come back. I will not let you struggle alone if things don't go as well as they should."

"This isn't Charleston, you know. There is no code of honor here you have to live by."

"I have my own, wherever I go. I'm afraid I can't get rid of it even if I want to," he said, smiling for the first time since he'd come. "The curse of the South. My apologies. Farewell."

"Farewell, Mr. Gairden. I'm sorry you came so far to find a bitter, ungrateful widow. It's only what Hugh left behind."

"I'm glad I came. It is your grief that makes you bitter. And it might help you to know that my grandfather died at the sight of my duel with your husband, and that I have my own grief and my own bitterness. Neither of us is alone. Not really. Good day."

He reached for her hand to kiss it, as he would have in parting in Charleston, then caught himself, though he noted a slight movement in her hand. She might have responded. She might have lifted the musket again. He didn't know. He only knew that for a moment her grief and his own had touched, so very different though they were, and he rode off determined to try once more. To give her time, and to give some to himself. He did not want an endless voyage, for either of them.

Dearest Uncle Paul, Aunt Lily and Cousin Adelle,

I have located Mrs. Vardry, although I cannot say I've done what I set out to do. It is obvious her husband left her with a great deal of debt, and I have offered my help to her in reestablishing her mill. Thus, I will be staying on here for some time, instead of returning to Philadelphia as soon as I had hoped.

Let me express once again my gratitude for your loving attention while I stayed in your home. I would

gladly return at once were it not for my obligations
here.

> With affection,
> Fox

Postscript to Adelle: You were right. This letter did
arrive before I did. But do not plan to win so handily
again upon my return. FMG

The barman at the Derby tavern placed the letter in
a leather pouch with the other pieces to be posted on
the coach to Bridgeport the following day. From there
it would go to New York and on to Philadelphia. "Find
it?" he asked, eyeing Fox with interest.

"Aye. Your directions were good."

"Pretty little piece, ain't she?"

"Aye," Fox said, dropping a penny into his hand and
then tipping his hat without saying more. He went back
outside and drew a drink from the well while Shadow
drank from the trough nearby. Nosy. Folks here were
so nosy. So why didn't they ask the poor woman if she
needed help? Perhaps it was just outsiders they were so
nosy about. Perhaps just outsiders from the South. People passed by him on their way to the row of shops, and
to the wharf, and to the tavern, the whole town a
stream he was swimming against. He splashed water on
his face and neck to cool away the August heat, then
mounted Shadow and followed the path along the river
he hoped would lead him to Lapham's Mill. He didn't
feel like asking for directions again.

4

An hour after having reached Lapham's Cotton Mill, just beyond the little town of Hemphill, Connecticut, Fox was standing behind a mule-spinning machine just the way he had only a few months ago back in Columbia, before his life had changed forever. Most of the skilled workers were English, trained in mills across the Atlantic. Owner John Lapham was both amazed and pleased to see an American who could start to work at once.

The singular faces of the other mule spinners here were not old faces, but they were formidable faces, faces of men who had labored since childhood in the factories of their native Lancashire, rising finally to skill levels that allowed them to come to America and put the lockstep nature of the English system behind them. Developing American factories needed them— couldn't function without them on any scale—and some of the English workers were so bold as to plan to work in places like Lapham's for a year and then return to England with enough coin in their pockets to buy a better life than the one they had so recently left behind. Others were glad to be away from the discontent of the English mills, where displaced hand spinners and hand weavers rioted and destroyed machinery in hopes of forcing owners to revert to the old processes that would restore their jobs.

In the continual hum of the spinning room the men's full attention was focused on their work, and they had little patience for lads like Fox, who had not learned the spinning process in the same rigorous way they had and who caused interruptions in the day's work with their questions and breakages. The perfect execution of their work was a passion to them; they would be bested by no man. They clung to their English ways and their English jargon and the English families some of them had brought with them. They bought no trouble that they couldn't handle themselves, and they brooked no complaints from their superiors without a fight.

"Gairden!" Josiah Trumble called out one gray, rainy September morning when Fox had been at the mill nearly a month. It was Fox's twentieth birthday, but the sound of Trumble's voice did not augur well for it to be a happy birthday. Trumble had a growl of a voice to him for such a small man, taking all of the Scottish lilt out of Gairden and making it sound more like "Gurdon." When Fox heard the shout he knew his supervisor had found a sliver of cotton slipped from its guides or a drawing roller out of adjustment or some other minute infraction of his machine that his unpracticed eye had not yet learned to see in time to prevent the machine from quitting entirely.

"Aye, Mr. Trumble," he shouted in reply, seeing the man's hairy forearm under his neatly rolled shirtsleeve point anxiously at the problem area. Trumble could run a machine of his own and still manage to watch over the rest of the room, which made him a very valuable employee, indeed. Fox watched him and tried to learn from him, even though he didn't intend to run spinning mules all of his life. He intended to own them.

That much he'd decided in his month here on the Furnace River. Mills were springing up everywhere despite the embargo, most of them started by men with no more money or experience than he had, but men who saw the possibilities. These new machines were changing textile production from tedious handwork to speedy production work, and those who could produce fabrics efficiently and economically stood not only to relieve themselves of hard physical work, but to make themselves rich in the bargain. It was like a race and he longed to be in it, even though worry of Mrs. Vardry's future still haunted him.

"So ye think ye want to own a mill, do ye?" Trumble asked him that day over dinner at the boarding house where they both had rooms. Trumble had no wife, no family here at all. "What do ye think it takes to start one? Money, I mean?"

"I think ten thousand dollars would give a man a good start. Add jennies and looms a few at a time as things begin to go."

"The debt doesn't bother ye then? Ye could just go ahead on somebody else's money and never mind if ye lost it?" Trumble chewed as he talked, his jaws working as quickly and surely as his hands did in the spinning room.

"We don't put people in debtor's prisons here, Trumble. Those who have money loan it out to those who don't. For a mill, they loan it out for a share of the profits. And why wouldn't they? Look at this place: Even small as Lapham's is, it's got to be making money. We can hardly spin the yarn fast enough for John Lapham to send upstairs to weave on his fly-shuttle looms. And now with English goods embargoed, there'll be an even better market for his cloth."

"Ye must have family money behind ye then, too, though, to be thinkin' such thoughts."

"You've got a lot of questions, Trumble," one of his countrymen, a fellow named Quigg, piped up loudly from the far end of the table. "Are ye testin' him for a spy, the way we used to do back in Lancashire? Ye think Gairden here might be stealin' Lapham's secrets to take on to his own mill?" Quigg chuckled as he spoke and the other men formed a chorus around him. Fox could see in their faces that the Lapham mill was several steps below what they had been used to in England.

"I'm testin' how he got the job in the spinnin' room, and what he's goin' to do with it once we have him trained proper." Trumble's face, though sallow, had a leathery look to it. He squinted one eye at his fellow Englishmen, pulled his lips down and wrinkled his nose. "Don't know as he should be makin' the same as the rest of you lads, or have his eye on my job, either one."

"I'm after no one's job." Fox tried to keep his tone light, matter-of-fact, though he half expected Josiah Trumble to tip the table over on him if he said a wrong word. "I've some schooling behind me, and when I get the experience to go with it, I hope to start Gairden Cotton Manufacturing, Incorporated."

"Might be that none of us will be mule spinners for a while if war comes," Quigg pointed out. "Jefferson and his embargo are apt to start one, I'd say—either right here or else with Mother England. No one wants it."

"There are those who do," Fox ventured. "Where I come from, in Charleston, people support the president. They can see long-term gain over short-term profit."

"Makes no difference to me," Trumble said. "I'm a British citizen. I won't have to fight in any American war."

"You will if it's with England," Quigg said.

"Hah, these pups here won't turn on their mother." Trumble dismissed the statement with a flick of his hand. "I suppose you're plannin' to vote for this man Madison come November, too, eh? He's from your part of the country, isn't he?" Trumble asked, turning his attention back to Fox. "It seems lads hereabouts are tiring of your southern states being able to count three-fifths of every Negro as population and keepin' all the power in the government."

"I think perhaps Mr. Madison is simply the better man for the job, regardless of geography," Fox said, ignoring the implication. "But he does not want war, unless all other measures fail."

"Like this 'O Grab Me' Act of Jefferson's. There's a fine kettle of fish. Jefferson found out that when Mother England says blockade, she doesn't mean it just on paper. Embargo, ha! All Jefferson's done is kill trade here in your fine United States."

"Many don't like it, I'll grant you, but if people would hold to it instead of smuggling and letting British goods in anyway, England would soon find herself in want." It was getting harder for Fox to defend the embargo, especially since he had come north and seen for himself the hundreds of idle ships in every harbor, but he did trust Jefferson's judgment, and Madison's.

"Your southern lads want war, don't they?" Quigg asked. "They want our British out of some lands down there, and up here they want to get their hands on Canada—isn't that right?"

"Your British army supplies the Indians with weapons, which are used against our settlers. That's the main reason people wish them gone. As for Mr. Madison, I believe he is more concerned with our rights on the seas than anything else. He says he will not allow our ships to be stopped and searched the way the *Chesapeake* was just last year, and the way others continue to be. We must certainly have rights over our own property. Even a Briton would have to agree to that." Fox lifted his eyebrows to Trumble, challenging him to reply.

"Quite right," Quigg piped up instead, while Trumble sat and scowled. "These navy lads get a bit carried away with their own power, don't they? Never worked in a mill and learned their place!" At this, all the men laughed, even Fox.

"What about the property called slaves?" Trumble wanted to know, stifling the humorous moment in the length of one short sentence.

"The slave trade ended this year, and that may be as much a hardship on your British slave *traders* as it is on our American slave *owners*. And, of course, the cotton mills of this very area make their profit by producing coarse, cheap Negro cloth, Trumble. If slaveholders are to be the subject here, then those who profit from their profits must be held accountable as well. There are those here in the North who speak of the end of the peculiar institution but labor to see it continue. Right now, Trumble, you have a job because slaveholders need cloth."

"Then they've a right to their property!" he announced, unfeeling, getting a laugh from the other men. This time Fox did not join in. You shallow son of a bitch, he thought. "What's the matter, Gairden? Didn't get the joke?" Trumble smiled a joyless, reckless smile.

"You're quite the jester, Trumble," Fox said, excusing himself before he said something he would wish he hadn't.

". . . a fine one to walk away from a fight . . . ," he heard Trumble saying to the other men, just loud enough for Fox to hear as he mounted the stairs to his bed. He stopped and looked back at the group of men —neither British nor American as far as he was concerned—who ringed the table, so quick to ridicule and so slow to act. Let it go, he told himself. In a few months you'll be gone from here. But whether the other men would let it go, he didn't know.

At dawn Fox returned to his post at the mule spinner. Two months had passed since the argument with Trumble, and there had been some tense moments since then, too, but he hadn't quit or been fired. A letter from Adelle had arrived several days ago, but the words were just as fresh in his mind as if the paper were in front of him.

Dear Fox,

I was so pleased that you asked me to write. If you can't be here, at least I can pretend that we talk through these letters. Joseph has returned home—with a wife, Margaret. He is thin, dispirited and very quiet. I don't know what happened to him in the Ohio, and he won't say, but he has begun to help Papa in the mill and seems content with it, so you needn't worry about how we are getting along. It is we who worry how you are progressing with Mrs. Vardry. It is a very honorable thing you are doing in helping her.

I continue to attend abolition meetings, now led mostly by a group of Quakers here in the city. Some of them have even helped slaves to escape. I do not mention such things to Papa and Mama, because they are in constant fear for my safety, though there is no need. We all look forward to seeing you, whenever you can come back to us.

Fondly,
Adelle

PS: Give Shadow a sweet for me.

So he was no longer needed in Philadelphia now that Joseph was back, and of course he was not wanted here —not by Trumble, at least. Adelle sounded eager for him to come back, and he smiled at the thought. He let himself admit it: he missed her. But Adelle deserved more than a man who had caused so much pain to others. Adelle would find herself a high-idealed reformer who would complement her interests and enthusiasm. She was so beautiful and her life so full. And then there was Mrs. Vardry. Just calling her "Mrs." made her sound so matronly when in fact she was far too young to be grieving alone. To be grieving at all, he added as an afterthought. The days of uncomplicated beauties like Sally Hudson seemed a lifetime ago instead of a few short months before. Grandfather had been right: His life would never be the same. And his obligation to Mrs. Vardry stood unfulfilled. His voyage was not yet ended, and no port was in sight.

From the first groan of the long belts that ran the machines, Fox could tell it was not going to be just an ordinary day. A freak early November ice jam on the river made the flow of water erratic, which made the belts slow and then speed up, which made the machines cease and then start abruptly, which made the long strands of roving break. Throughout the morning, the spinning room was a ferment of frustration as first one machine and then another had to be stopped for repairs.

"Gairden! You've a break there man! Is your head still back in bed? Get it righted or lose a day's pay!" Trumble had kept his distance since that night at the dinner table, but today he seemed to sense Fox's frustration and to feed on it.

Fox stopped the machine, trying quickly to splice the broken strands and put in enough twist with his fingers to allow the machine to begin again, but Trumble stood over him, watching him, and his hands felt as clumsy as if they were feet instead, and the twist would not hold. Impatience heating him like a match, Trumble started the machine before Fox was ready. Slivers of cotton snapped, strands flipping in every direction. Half an hour's work to repair. Fox stood up.

"I wasn't ready yet," he said, trying hard to hold his temper. "But it was your action that caused this mess."

"You'd best watch what you say, Gairden," Trumble growled. "It's your machine, and yours to fix. Now don't make a mistake on the rest of 'em like you did on the first one or you'll be goin' to the picking room. Permanently."

Gladly, Fox thought, but he did not speak again.

Trumble watched him for a few minutes, then stepped back to his own machine, apparently found it functioning smoothly, and came again to stand over Fox. Fox did not look up but kept his fingers moving quickly, thread to sliver. Again Trumble snapped at him.

"Gairden! Hurry up or I'll find someone who *can* get the job done."

The hum in the room was enough that it wasn't easy to hear what someone said if you were over a few feet away, but as Trumble barked out this last statement, Fox was aware of the smirks on the faces of the other Englishmen. They had planned this among them. It was systematic, almost machinelike.

"I'm sorry, Trumble," he said. "I'll try to do better."

"You'd twist a rope to hang yourself."

"Pure water doesn't run from a muddy fountain," Fox countered, never taking his eyes from the work. Repair after repair. At last, with Trumble's eyes burning holes in his back, the task was done.

When every thread was perfectly spliced and Fox was ready to start the machine again, he looked around him for the first time. Every eye on the room was on him, and for the first time in the long weeks he had been here, he saw approval in most of them. It had been a test, and he had passed it. No one would say anything, of course. The mule spinners were a close-mouthed lot, but as Trumble walked away, Fox could tell he was going to be left alone from now on. Perhaps it was a sign that he should stay here in Hemphill. No, he told himself. Your days here are numbered. You are going to check on the widow Vardry once again, and then you are going home. If you want your own mill, you are going to have to face Charleston. Will I be an outsider there now, too? he wondered. There was no law against dueling, but there were many who did not favor it. There would be whispers. "I don't want to be a pitied widow," Mrs. Vardry had said, and as Fox thought about going back to Charleston, he knew exactly what she meant.

5

His knock sounded small and insignificant in the expanse of cold, still November air that surrounded the Vardry mill. Fox tried again. "Mrs. Vardry?" he called out, "Mrs. Vardry, are you here?" He stepped back from the door, his eyes scanning the windows and the weathered clapboards, the ground where several shingles blown from the roof lay strewn about, the bare tree branches of the woods behind him. No sign of her. Fox shivered inside the wool coat he had bought in Hemphill when the cold weather began in October. It was warm, but not warm enough for a Connecticut winter. He stamped his feet and wriggled his toes about inside his square-toed boots to warm them, wishing for warmer socks. It was just as well that he would soon be on his way to Charleston, for he didn't think he could ever adjust to the constant cold of a northern winter. His hands jammed tightly inside his pockets, he was still looking off toward the woods when the door opened behind him.

"Mr. Gairden? I doubted I'd see you again." The widow Vardry stood in the open doorway, eyes still pools of darkness set deep against the white of her skin, except that they now appeared sunken, her cheekbones more pronounced. The months had not been kind to her.

"But I said I'd be back. I've been at Lapham's, just as I told you. I made the mistake of assuming you were not in need of my help. Judging from the look of things here, I was wrong. Has something else happened?"

"No, nothing's happened. Nothing at all. I haven't felt up to working is all. And that's none of your concern anyway. You can just be on your way like all the others. I want to be left alone."

"Like all the others?" At once he thought of the barman's comment. "A nice little piece." Were there men so base as to take advantage of widows? Well of course there were. Charleston gossip was full of tales of widows deceived.

"That's not your worry. I—"

"But it *is* my worry, don't you see? Can't you understand that I feel responsible for your welfare, seeing you here pale and thin, knowing that I killed the man who should be providing for you now?"

"I can understand. I just do not want to be cared for. By any man. Ever again."

She was shivering, her arms folded beneath her small breasts like a starving street urchin. Fox's eyes drifted down toward his own feet, which he stamped lightly again. "Could we talk inside for a moment? I don't want to bother you, but . . . . my feet are freezing. I've come all the way from Hemphill, you see. You must be cold, too." He saw her hesitation, but then she looked at the frosty ground and at his boots and stepped aside so that he could enter.

He saw at once that she did not live on the first floor, and he could feel it, too—there was no heat. Carding machines sat silently in nests of unspun fleece, and a thin coat of fiber dust covered every surface. A trail leading up the stairs suggested that was where she had come from to answer the door and probably where she lived. There was no other building, no house, on the premises, only a site that might once have been a house where now a few charred timbers lay angled in disarray. No fire department here as in Philadelphia. No Adelle in this Mrs. Vardry, either, he thought. No spirit, no energy, no hope. And for that she has me to thank, at least in part. Fox hung his head. What else was there to say? He could not undo what he had done.

"I need to get my shawl," she said, hurrying toward the stairs with a light step. Her black homespun draped behind her as she went, lapping each step as a wave does the shore, and Fox noticed that the heavy black shoes she had worn last time had been replaced by frayed black satin slippers that must once have been dancing slippers. He remembered dancing, remembered it as a long-ago pastime, remembered he had promised Sally Hudson a dance she would probably not ever want to claim once he got back to Charleston. He pulled his toes up tight inside his boots and felt the scratch of his wool socks. The coldness of the pine-plank floor speared the soles of his shoes, and he began to walk around the carding room to ward it off, but he kept an eye on the stairs to watch her come back down, anticipating, dreading, wanting, avoiding, wondering, knowing. They were all there, feelings that should and shouldn't have been.

"I don't know much about wool." He had allowed himself the luxury of seeing her glide noiselessly back down the narrow, worn factory steps, and now he had to pretend he hadn't. She had put on her shawl, a soft, downlike garment that fell halfway down her skirt in the back and lay loosely rolled around her shoulders in folds of variegated indigo blue that softened the whole look of her, eased the darkness of her eyes and the angularity of her thin face.

"What do you want to know? It's like cotton, only it comes from the sheep ready to spin—no seeds in it. Weeds, of course. Cockleburs and chaff. Dirt. Stink.

That's what our fluffy baas give us. You feel it on your hands, the oil of the wool. Works its way in. Good for the skin." She rubbed her hands together, and even in the dim light of the room's few windows, Fox could see that they were chapped and red.

"What do you do?" he asked, chancing it that she might keep on talking as she had about the wool. "All day, I mean? You haven't been working the mill, and I can see from your hands you haven't been working with oily wool. You haven't been eating, at least not enough. You—" Fox shook his head and bit back the words. You're going to die here, he wanted to say, if someone doesn't help you.

"I sleep. I eat. I walk along the river."

"Do you have friends to visit? Anyone who can help?"

"My best friend died last year, too," she said, seeming suddenly very distant. "She was all I had."

"I'm sorry," Fox said, keenly aware of her pain at the same time he was at a complete loss as to how to ease it. He changed the subject. "I'm headed back to Charleston, Mrs. Vardry. I wanted you to know. And I want to try one last time to explain my actions and those of your husband, if only you'll let me."

"I know without hearing the story that it was no fault of yours, and I'm sorry for you if you think it was, but I want to hear no more of it. The more you tell the more I will tell, until the memories will be more than I can stand. Say no more."

Fox shook his head. "I can't say I understand, Mrs. Vardry, but of course I will honor your wishes. I can't leave, though, without saying I shall never forgive myself for taking the life of another man, whatever kind of man he was. I shall forever ask myself why, and I must tell you that I see his face before me each and every day to the point that my head aches with the grief of a life wasted. I am not a killer, Mrs. Vardry. But perhaps I am not a gentleman, either. I thought I was, but now I'm not so sure I even know what a gentleman is."

"I believe you, and I believe your torment is genuine. But I cannot help you get rid of it. Go back to Charleston, back to your family. There's nothing more you can do here." She turned away from him, heading once again toward the stairs.

"How about money? Do you have enough money? Are you not eating and not starting up the mill because of money, because of the debts your husband left behind? If that's it, I could help. My family's not rich, but we could send you a little each month if that would help. I'll be going to work on my own mill when I get back. Once it gets going there'll be more money—"

At this she turned and looked him in the eye. "No. No money. I won't take your money."

Fox saw the quiver in her chin. It *was* money, and she was too proud to say it. "I'm sorry, Mrs. Vardry. I didn't mean to offend. It just seemed a final question I should ask to settle things before I go." He fidgeted with his coat buttons for a minute, his fingers stiff with cold. "I thank you for seeing me again, and I hope that you will feel free to write to me in Charleston should you find yourself questioning anything I've said, or needing help, or . . . anything. Now I realize I've taken far too much of your time and I'll be on my way. I hope to sail out of New York within the week and to be back home in Charleston within two."

From his breast pocket he took one of the small calling cards he hadn't had much use for during his time in the North. "You can write to me at this address if ever you should want to."

The widow Vardry took the card, holding the shawl to her with her elbow as she reached out with her forearm, but she didn't look at it, just clasped it tightly under her thumb and returned her arm to be folded in front of her, just as it had been since the moment Fox arrived. She was completely closed in unto herself, he thought, watching her. Her arms like a shield in front of her, her face drawn tight against the betrayal of a smile or quiver such as the one she hadn't been able to hold back, she was a lone warrior in a lonely fight.

"Thank you," was all she said as he bowed slightly and made his way to the door.

He lifted the latch, then paused in the open door. "I'm going to deposit some money for you at the bank in Derby. Not a lot, you understand, just some extra that's not needed for my trip home. You don't have to use it if you don't want to, but if you need it, it will be there. Once you get the mill running again, send it back to me. You have the address."

Closing the door before she could answer, he covered the distance to where Shadow was tied in a few long strides, jumped on his back and headed back toward Derby. He took one glance over his shoulder, half expecting to see her there with the musket, but she wasn't. And from then on, he did not look back.

After the raise of eyebrows Fox had encountered at the bank when he deposited two hundred dollars in the name of Mrs. Hugh Vardry, opening an account where there had been none, Fox had little choice but to take a room at the Derby tavern for the night. Darkness came early now, and a raw November wind pelted ice crystals at him as he led Shadow to the stable behind the tavern.

"Mr. Gairden," the barman greeted him.

"Did you read the letter, too?" Fox replied. "I don't recall ever telling you my name."

A chuckle rose low in the throat of the husky, heavy-bearded barman. "Not at all. Had to put the mail in a box for the driver—he's not usin' bags anymore. I noticed was all. An' I remembered. Not from around here, I thought to myself."

"Charleston," Fox said, slapping down a coin. "Whiskey. And supper, if you have some." He found himself smiling back at the nosy barman. Fox had taken to the same sort of one-word sentences the other man used like sword strokes. "Please," he added self-consciously.

The little tavern was quiet and quite dark, though an oil lamp burned above the bar, and another hanging lamp lit the middle of the room. By the time the barman brought out a plate of cooked cabbage, crisp-fried side pork and a loaf of molasses brown bread, the two men drinking at the bar had left, and only Fox remained.

"I'll join you if you don't mind," the barman said. "Name's McLaren. Francis McLaren. Figure you for a Scot like me."

"Scots-Irish, on my father's side. My mother's French." The side pork crunched and Fox pulled the tough center gristle back and forth between his teeth as he tried to bite off a chunk.

"Been to Vardry's again today, have you?"

"How did you know that?"

"Seen you come in from that way when I walked down to the wharf this afternoon. Figured it was that."

Fox swallowed the unchewed pork and hit the table with his fist in one motion. "Why does everyone look at me like that? You . . . the banker . . . What is it? What is so wrong about seeing this woman?"

"Well, laddie, she's got a reputation, you see. Most decent folks want nothing to do with her."

"But she seems nice enough. She's lonely, and poor, since she's lost her husband, but I can't believe—"

"Aye, well, believe what you like, but folks around here knows. And if she knows anything about Derby, she'll go back to Massachusetts where she came from. We don't want women like that around here."

"But you wouldn't see someone starve just because of gossip, would you? I don't think she's even getting enough to eat."

"Aye, then, but that money you put in the bank for her ought to help then, hadn't it?"

"How did you—?"

"Derby's a small place, laddie. You'd best learn that if you're goin' to stay around helpin' out lonely widows." McLaren raised his eyebrows, but not in the same suspicious way the banker had. McLaren had mischief in his eyes.

"I don't make a habit of helping out lonely widows, McLaren," Fox said, chewing once again. "Just this one."

"Aye, then, laddie. Can't say that I blame you— lookin' at her, I mean."

"I know. You said that before. But I won't be staying around anyway. Just tonight. In the morning I head for New York and the first ship to Charleston."

"Bumpy ride, sometimes, I hear, with the British coastin' along waitin' for easy pickin's."

"Those are just stories," Fox said, pushing a spoonful of the soft cabbage into his mouth. "The Britons have their hands full with Napoleon. They're happy enough to leave us alone, I'd say."

"But they need sailors for all those ships to fight Mr. Napoleon." McLaren raised his eyebrows once again. Point scored.

"Ah, but then they're like as not to comb the Irish coast for laddies needing a job, aren't they, McLaren? Lots of good tars just waiting for a chance there, isn't that right?"

"God, but the Irish have little say over their own lives. You're right about that. Still, I'd think of ridin' that horse you've got in the stable back to Charleston. Or take the stage. Ships aren't the only way, like they used to be."

"But they're the fastest way, and just now that's what I want. I want to get home. That's all I want. I've had some back luck and it's taken me months to realize that the only way I can ever really work my way out of it is to go back home where it all started and try to make a clean breast of it."

"So then, you *are* the one shot Vardry. I guessed as much. From Charleston an' all."

The pork seemed to swish back and forth greasily in Fox's stomach and the cabbage burned in his throat. "Your life will never be the same," he could hear Grandfather saying. Vardry's sneering face appeared before him, too, and the sneer turned to a laugh. Fox put down his spoon and drank another glass of whiskey. He nodded, trying to meet McLaren's eyes but not quite able to.

"You're young for it, 'course maybe not in Charleston. They like to duel down there, don't they? Young goes with hotheaded, though. Lucky you lived." McLaren had finished eating now, and he leaned back in his chair, tipping it back on two legs.

"Am I?" Fox said after a moment. "I don't really know anymore." He pushed back away from the table and took two dollars from his wallet. "I won't be needing the room after all. This is for supper, and the horse. Thanks."

McLaren hurried to his feet, leaving the money where Fox had tossed it. "Don't take offense. I only meant you're lucky to be—"

"I'm in a hurry, that's all. Good night."

"Aye then, good night. But if you're ever back in Derby—"

"I won't be back," Fox said. "Not ever." He closed the door behind him, and sleet slashed at his face before he could pull the brim of his hat down low enough to shield him. The last thing he wanted to do was ride through the stuff, but he would. To another tavern. Where no one knew the name Vardry.

⸎ Part Two ⸎

1811

6

Rhode Island
1811

"It was the British, not the lightning, not really," Fox told the mother of Arthur Grisham, the British emigrant who had been impressed with him onto HMS *Iago*. Over two years had passed since the December day in 1808 when they had sailed from New York harbor on the *Jolly Bacchus*, the first ship on which Fox could gain passage to Charleston. Grisham was bound for Martinique. Five hours out, their lives changed forever. When the *Iago* came alongside, Fox and Grisham had made sport of it. Grisham was a little older than he, on his way to work in his uncle's shipping office. His parents had immigrated to America several years earlier, but Grish still spoke with the round British tones of his birthplace. Gleaming with the good health of a hardworking life, he was the sort of man who stood out among men not because of his fancy clothes but because of his sheer stature. A man who was noticed. Only this time he was noticed for the wrong reasons. And Fox was noticed with him. Grish never arrived in Martinique. And now he would never arrive home again, either. Arthur Grisham was dead.

"The lightning wouldn't have touched him had he been on deck with the rest of us, Mr. and Mrs. Grisham. But Lieutenant Growley sent him up the mast to stay the rigging, even though he *knew* there was a risk. He *knew* Grish—Arthur—might be struck, but he sent him anyway."

Fox watched as Arthur Grisham's parents tried to accept what he was telling them. They had received no letter telling of their son's death, even though it had occurred nearly a year ago. Their faces, however, both long and thin, gave away nothing. "They weren't so hard on me," Fox went on, almost apologetically. "They knew, deep down, that I was an American and they had no business with me on their ship. With Grish, they had no such thoughts. To them he was English, and by the look of his strong shoulders and powerful build, they took him for one who'd been at sea. Since I seemed to be with him, they took me for the same."

"But didn't they ask for papers? I thought seamen had to carry papers?"

"They do, and of course neither Grish nor I had any papers other than our tickets. They merely accused us of failure to carry papers, cast our tickets aside and forced us to the *Iago*. It was a lieutenant who thought he recognized your son from another voyage and pegged him for an illegal seaman." Fox relived the moment for the thousandth time. Part of him had been indignant, afraid, angry as he felt the end of a British rifle poke between his shoulders. Yet part of him had been willing to drift with whatever tide might take him, with anything that would take him away from Derby, Connecticut, and the debris left behind from the life of Hugh Vardry. His determination to return to Charleston had weakened with each day he waited to board the *Jolly Bacchus*, even though the name of the ship seemed to carry with it the seed of good fortune. Resuming a normal life in Charleston was not going to be an easy assignment, given the visage of Hugh Vardry that hung over him like a shroud. In the instant that Lieutenant Growley had pointed his finger at them,

Fox had to admit he'd felt a kind of release, and he had let himself be impressed without a fight.

"He was such a good son," Grish's father said. His words reached Fox as through a fog. "So quick-witted. So kind. We wanted him to be a minister, like his Uncle Adam, who first brought us to the Presbyterian ways before we left England. Arthur would have led the righteous."

Fox blinked at this. Arthur Grisham a minister? His drinking indicated he wouldn't have been much of a success at it, and so perhaps impressment had saved him from another kind of unhappy life. Fox and Grish had shared many things. They had been as close as any two men can be.

"He looked after me like a shepherd over a lost sheep, that much I can tell you," Fox said. "He *was* my friend, I hope you understand. I tried to convince Growley to send me up the mast instead of your son, but he had already given the order."

Once again he remembered the stormy night aboard the *Iago*. They had taken in all sail and kept the frigate before the gale, but the rain was like a surging rapids above them, and the lightning, the awful lightning lit the cavernous skies and cast each face in a horrible silver glow. The men were ordered below decks, but they were slow in going—a lightning strike to the hold filled with metal and powder would blow them up, with no chance to jump overboard. It was when the halyard on the main mast broke loose that Lieutenant Growley ordered Grish to the top. Out of three hundred men, Grish was chosen because he was despised. No amount of explaining had been able to make the officers see that Grish was an American citizen. He had been born in London and to them he was still British. And they were determined to punish him. Every chance they got. Especially Growley, the lieutenant who had spotted him that first day on the *Jolly Bacchus*. Growley would never admit he was wrong. Would never admit Grish was not who he thought he was, though he should have known it once he saw that neither Grish nor Fox knew anything of sails or wind or watches.

"And he was buried at sea?" Grisham's mother asked. She was a woman of forty or more, Fox guessed, whose teeth were either black or gone altogether, who had already seen three of her children die: two from smallpox, one from an infected broken arm. She took the news of this one without a tear, but her lips puckered nervously in the long silences that fell between the difficult statements Fox had to make.

"He was." Fox lied to spare her knowing that Grish's body had been thrust off into the raging sea by the force of the bolt that hit him. No words had been spoken for Arthur Grisham, except by his friend. "They gave him that much, at least."

"It was not a dishonorable way to die," Mr. Grisham said, lifting his head with an air of humility.

"It was not," Fox promised, all of the pain of Grish's death once again raw inside him. Honor and death seemed to be inextricably linked, and why? What was there in honor that should cost a man like Grisham his life? "Your son's only fault was not being who Growley thought he was, and therefore a constant reminder of the lieutenant's fallibility. Growley was out to get rid of him. Kept us separated as much as possible. While I spent my time patching sails and standing watch, Grish spent his in whatever dangerous or hated jobs Growley could find for him. He served with diligence and great courage, and he never gave up. He never gave up."

Fox was twenty-two now but felt and looked much older as he left the Grisham home near Coventry, Rhode Island, behind him. The years on board the *Iago* had been hard years, each one like five years on land.

He had been flogged, humiliated and made to go without sleep for long days and nights. He had eaten weeviled crackers while the British tars had meat. He had boarded the *Iago* a weak, confused twenty-year-old. Like the sails he mended, he, too, had needed some repair. Somehow, during his two years of forced night watches and bug-infested food and humiliating floggings, he had actually grown strong. While Grish had died, Fox had been handed another chance at life. Before he could begin again, though, he needed to put two things behind him. One of them was already done: the Grishams now knew the fate of their son. The second task awaited him in Connecticut.

Trilliums and cowslips lifted their blooms to the sky under the semishade of the just-leafing maples above them, and the earth smelled of growth and abundant moisture as Fox rode once again toward Beaver Creek. He couldn't say he was happy, or sad, or frightened anymore, but he was determined. He would see the widow, then go straight to Philadelphia and from there to Charleston, just as he should have last time. Sailing from New York harbor instead of going back to Philadelphia as he had promised Adelle had cost him two and a half years of his life. Now he meant to make up that time, yet was going to keep his promise this time. Adelle . . . How often she had been in his thoughts during the endless hours at sea. No doubt she would be married by now. God, how the British had robbed him of time! Fox snapped the reins of the old mare he'd bought in Bristol, still angry. He was done being pushed this way and that by others. From now on, he would be the master of his own fate. His chest swelled at the thought of it. Once he settled his business with Mrs. Vardry once and for all, he would be free to get on with this newly regained life of his. Freedom smelled even sweeter than the spring air, and Fox snapped the reins again, anxious to get to the Vardry mill.

Dandelion greens ready to bloom sprung out here and there in the roadway, and Fox could see that the closer he got to the mill, the less the road had been traveled. Once he got within sight of it, he knew there had been no spinning done here in the years he had been away. She had given up after all and gone away. Perhaps the two hundred dollars had helped her get away, he thought, and felt good about it, though he could have used the money himself just now. The mare cantered easily to the hitching rail, and Fox tied her there to rest while he looked around. A red-winged blackbird's *cheree* rang out from a branch across the river, and the air was so clear the song sounded close as his fingertips. Fox took off his coat and caught it on one finger as he threw it over his shoulder. The spring air was still cool as it seeped through his shirtsleeves, but the sun that filtered through the leafing aspens sent patches of warmth as well, and Fox smiled at the pleasing combination.

"If you've come about the money, it's still in the Derby bank. I haven't touched it."

The rushing water had masked the sound of her step, and the widow Vardry had appeared beside him without warning. She still carried the old musket, but this time, at least, she wasn't pointing it at him. She still wore the same dress, too, now patched at the elbows and shorter than it had been where the frayed hem had been turned back yet again. And she was barefoot.

"Mrs. Vardry, I thought no one was here. I would have knocked, but everything looked so quiet." She seemed smaller to him, somehow, but he knew it actually was that he had grown. Several pounds heavier, more muscled and even taller, he had long ago sold the clothes he had left New York in to a British tar on the *Iago*. They no longer fit. Mrs. Vardry, on the other hand, was still the thin shadow of a woman he had met almost three years back. She was not so hollow eyed, not so guarded, but still pale, still gaunt.

"I don't have many visitors, and you can see the mill is still not running, and so it is quiet, I'm afraid. Ever quiet." The faraway look he remembered from before returned as she spoke, and it wrenched the insides of him just as it had the day he made the bank deposit in Derby.

"It's a poor time for a mill to be quiet, Mrs. Vardry. There's war coming. I saw the shipyard in Providence working 'round the clock, and they were drilling troops on the green there. The British scoff at President Madison's threats, but I doubt that's wise. No, a mill ready to spin or to weave sailcloth or tent canvas or blankets or wool for uniforms can make money. And high time. It's been hard going these past few years, I know."

"How would you know? You wear a new suit of clothes, are strong and fit. You know nothing of hard going, Mr. Gairden."

"Perhaps I only think I do. I've been aboard a British ship since a few days after I left you last, Mrs. Vardry. Impressed. I was fortunate enough to prove my citizenship and status to the Admiralty Court in London and gain my freedom, but not until almost two years had passed me by. But for the help of a Charleston lawyer friend of my father's on business in London, I might very well have been shipped out again on the *Iago* and been punished for the supposed sin of my lack of papers. I have known hardship, Mrs. Vardry. I have seen the death of a good friend on stormy seas. But I do not intend to let the experience stop me from living out the rest of my life."

"I'm sorry, Mr. Gairden." The widow walked a few steps away, turning her back to him.

"No, it is I who am sorry. I spoke with too much passion. I was too harsh. It's only that when I think of it all, an anger fills me and spills out before I can stop it." He moved his coat from over his shoulder to his left forearm, then folded his arms across his chest, thinking. "They gave me passage to Bristol, Rhode Island, so that I could take word of my friend's death to his parents, or I would be back in Charleston already. But since I was not far away, I thought I should visit you one last time and—" She started to speak and he stopped her. "No, let me finish. I thought I should visit you one last time and satisfy myself that you are well, because otherwise I can never free myself of your husband's death. His face appears to me in my waking hours and in my sleep. He is there to ridicule and to taunt me, though I meant him only the harm of an apology. I suppose, Mrs. Vardry, I've come here for your forgiveness, for a word from you that you are all right and that I should go on with my life."

"You are forgiven!" she shouted. "There, go on with your life and leave me alone!"

"I don't think that's a good idea," he said softly, touching her elbow and turning her toward him. He looked into pain-filled eyes which she tried to lower by looking away from him even as he moved to hold her in his view. "I think, forgiven or not, I am going to help you as you wouldn't let me before. I think, Mrs. Vardry, I owe it to you to help you get this mill running again and earn back some of the money your husband lost."

"But you're going back to Charleston."

"Charleston can wait a few months. My family knows I'm safe, and that's all that's important now. I'll earn my forgiveness, Mrs. Vardry, if you'll let me. I can see now it's what I came here to do, and in the back of my mind I think I've known since the day of the duel it was what I should do."

"You don't think I could do it alone?" The widow Vardry's brown eyes bore a flicker of defiance in them that heartened Fox. He clasped his hands behind his back, stretching his arms, and blew out a long breath.

"No doubt you could. It's just that I wonder if you *would.*"

"Because I've done nothing while you were away?"

"Well . . . why haven't you? What's happened, Mrs. Vardry?"

"Do you want to help me? Really help me?"

"Of course I do. You know that."

"Then promise me that the mill will make me rich, and that when I'm rich people will quit whispering about me. Promise me that I can buy their silence so that I can have some peace. You said it was quiet here, Mr. Gairden, but you were wrong. The whispering never stops. I hear it every day when I sit at my loom and weave for Colonel Humphreys, and I hear it every night when I lie in my bed in that drafty upstairs corner. Don't look away," she said, as Fox lowered his gaze and tried to pretend he didn't know what she meant, though indeed he didn't know the whole of it. "Don't pretend you haven't heard things or seen the way people look when you mention my name. Why haven't I reopened the mill? Because I can't face them. I can't bear the thought of what they know, or think they know. I walk six miles to a little country store rather than into Derby, because they don't know me there. And your two hundred dollars still sits in the bank in Derby because I wouldn't go there to take it out, though God knows I could have used it. Jonathan Hawke rode out here one day to tell me you'd left it

there, though why he really came was to try to buy the
mill off from under me for next to nothing."

"But you've kept from losing the mill . . . ," Fox
said, trying to make sense of things.

"By weaving for the Colonel. I've made enough to
pay off some of Hugh's debts, and with every payment
I've felt looks that would chill an August day. I won't
deal with them again. I can't." Her voice broke then,
but no tears came, though Fox could see they were
close.

"Then let me. I've taken colder looks than those
from one Lieutenant Growley, I'm sure, and I can take
these for you. As for promises, I can't make any except
that I will try."

"And in return?" Her lips still quivered as she made
this bargain that seemed so hard for her.

"In return, perhaps you can help me understand why
it was that your husband held the opinions he did, and
why he was so eager to duel. Perhaps if I could understand the man, I could understand the ghost as well."

"Mr. Gairden, your debt of honor is repaid. In full.
But I doubt I can ever begin to tell you how to understand Hugh. I never did myself."

"I'm sorry. I didn't mean to bring back painful memories," he said quickly. "I just thought it a way to
square our bargain."

She wrinkled her bare toes against the soft grass of
the riverside, and Fox waited for her to reply. She had
been considering the offer, he could tell, and something in him itched to have her say, yes, run my mill,
while something else said, it can't be done.

"I don't think you know what you would be getting
yourself into, Mr. Gairden," she said at last. "It
wouldn't be easy."

"I don't think I would know how to do anything that
was easy anymore, Mrs. Vardry," he told her. "The

British don't do anything the easy way." She almost smiled at that, and he felt a surge of hope.

"Then there's only one more thing," she said. "Don't ever call me Mrs. Vardry again. Call me Anne. Never again do I want to be reminded that I was his wife."

"Aye, aye, Anne," he said, saluting her with a crisp spring of his right arm. "My name is Fox, not Mr. Gairden. And not ever just Gairden, as I was at sea."

She offered her hand and he took it in a firm handshake that sealed the bargain he had not expected to make when he rode in just an hour earlier, the master of his own fate. He felt her draw her hand away and with it the little bit of herself she had shown him in eagerness of the clasp. He cleared his throat and turned to where the mare was tied. "I need to post a letter and find some different clothes if I'm to be a working man once again. I'll find a room in Derby for the night and then begin work in the morning, if that's all right."

"Whatever you wish. You will be in charge."

"For now, perhaps, but the mill is yours. Ultimately, the decisions will be yours. We both need to agree on that. I will look to you for approval all along the way."

"Very well, but I will look for your guidance."

Fox nodded. "As you wish." He tipped his hat at this last comment and walked to where the mare waited. Anne said no farewell and did not go back inside, but instead sat down in a sunny spot to look out over the river. She looked delicate as a doll on a child's picnic as she sat there, motionless, porcelain faced. He waved a good-bye that she returned, but the smile that had peeked out earlier was gone.

That evening, in a small room at the Derby Inn, Fox thought back over the days since he had landed in Bristol, his visit to the Grishams, and now this.

My dearest Cousin,

If you suffer me anger in the extreme for having been so long away without writing, let me only explain by saying that although I could not write, you were often in my thoughts. How I wished for your strong spirit some nights when the labor was oppressive aboard the *Iago*. As Papa has no doubt written you of the details, I won't repeat them. I lost a good friend aboard ship and visited his family near Bristol after I landed.

Now I have returned to Derby, in order that I might once more satisfy myself as to the condition of Mrs. Vardry. I have found her no better than when I left her, and at last she has accepted my offer of assistance. Perhaps I will finally put the ghost of Hugh Vardry to rest.

My assistance in the renovation of the Vardry mill is likely to take most of the summer, but when it is complete, it will be my great pleasure to visit Philadelphia again. I trust your father's mill is doing well, and I will be anxious to see the changes he and Joseph have made.

I know, Adelle, that you may well be married by now or, at the very least, betrothed, and I add it to my long list of regrets that I have had to be away from you for so long, and that I was unable even to let you know my whereabouts. If you can find it in your heart to understand some of what I have endured, please write. I spoke of you so often to the friend lost at sea that he came to feel he knew you. He was determined to come to Philadelphia with me and meet you, and you would have adored his brilliant mind and steady friendship. I have suffered a great loss. And I have missed you.

With affection,
Fox

He read the letter twice before he folded it and put his pen away for the night. She would be expecting more, perhaps, if she had been waiting all this time, but this was all he had to give. He put his lips to the paper. I don't know if you can understand my feelings, dear Adelle, for I don't think I can myself. Give me time. Please, give me time.

7

Hugh Vardry had acted as rashly in the construction of his mill as he had in his dueling, from what Fox could tell when he studied it the next morning. Built on a stone foundation, the mill was of post-and-beam construction, covered with ten-inch-wide boards lapped over each other, which was in and of itself not unlike the construction of many other mills. Vardry's mill, though, had been built of green lumber which, now shrunken over these few years, allowed light and the cool of the spring air inside the spinning room. He hadn't spent well on windows, either, and the few that bordered the room were ill-fitting and poorly spaced.

Five hundred seventy-six spindles sat idle in the big room, which Fox measured at thirty-two feet wide and seventy-four feet long—a small fortune in machinery that should have been kept running and producing during the years of Jefferson's embargo instead of sitting here gathering dust. Of course, Fox himself had been to blame for that, and now it was up to him to try to set it right. The economic climate with Britain was far from perfect even yet, and when war came, as he was certain it would, the market for yarns and cloth should be strong. He had a chance to make up some of what he'd taken away, but he had to admit, he was not certain where to start.

Wiping the dust from his hands on a rag he found near one of the jennies, he made his way down to the ground floor once again and looked over the condition

of the carding machines and drawing frames. Some of
the card cloth would need to be replaced, because the
fine wire teeth of its combs lay bent back in the wrong
direction, allowing small lumps of fleece to get into the
roving. The drive action of the machines appeared to
be in order, although there was evidence of wear on
several of the belts that spun off from the massive,
wooden horizontal shafts overhead, and that could be
dangerous.

On the stone-walled lower floor of the mill, the giant
gears that connected to the waterwheel outside stood
mute as the river ran on by outside. The bevel gear was
missing, Fox discovered, disabling the whole mill. No
wonder Anne Vardry had done nothing with the mill in
almost three years. She couldn't, not without considerable expense. But why hadn't she told him about the
bevel gear? Perhaps she didn't know as much about
mills as he thought she did. Perhaps she just wanted to
see him fail—but he didn't think so. Perhaps she knew
nothing of it. The whole matter had a false ring to it.
The investment here had been too great to simply walk
away from . . . and what of the other investors? Why
had they not stepped in to buy off at least the machinery, which could easily have been installed in another
mill? What kind of man had Hugh Vardry been?

A sawmill with enough tools to make wooden machine parts was set up in one end of the long room, and
piles of sawdust sat just where the sawyer had left them
years earlier. A stack of lumber, boards like the ones
covering the outside of the building, stood against one
wall, nicely vented for drying with short thin pieces laid
in perpendicular to the rest, a process the shrunken
boards upstairs had missed. Fulling vats stood at the far
end of the room, and while not a large operation, they
would be adequate to shrink and fluff up the yard
goods that could be made there, but probably could

not handle both that and commission work from local folks should they want it. Most of them had probably learned to take their fulling down to Humphreysville by now, anyway, Fox thought, grimacing at the difficult obstacles ahead of him.

He took note of how many people would be needed to run things and wrote them in a small notebook: machinists, three; fullers, four; sawyers, four. Working his way up to the main floor, he estimated another four for the carding room. All men, so far. Now the spinning room. Women and children would be sufficient here, eight of each to start.

Now he took the steps to the second floor where he knew Anne Vardry worked at her loom and lived. She had told him to meet her there when he finished looking around, but even so he climbed the narrow stairs with apprehension. The news he had to deliver to her was going to be unwelcome, and somehow he expected that the sight of her living in a corner of the drafty, unfinished mill attic under the heavy roof beams with windows even more scarce than in the spinning room was going to be unsettling to him, too.

Even before he could see her, he could hear the beat of her loom. She—or someone—had taken a number of the wide boards like the ones he'd seen in the sawmill and nailed them to a cross beam to form a crude partition. They hung at different lengths, none of them reaching quite to the floor. Against them, a row of wooden crates stood, Fox supposed, to stop the great draft that must sweep beneath the uneven edge of the flimsy divider. The crates were stamped HUMPHREYS-VILLE and were filled with the wool yarns that she had been using to earn her livelihood the past few years.

Fox could not help but take in the rest of the room as he approached. A small bed against one wall. A small iron stove connected with a long pipe to one of the great chimneys that stood at either end of the mill. A small chair and small table—everything was dwarfed by the tall attic roof and the width of the room. Her clothes hung over a length of rope that stretched between two of the upright beams. Unlike the rest of the mill, this room was clean except for the lint that necessarily gathered under the looms, of which there were four: two wide, two narrow. He had seen another half-dozen looms gathering dust in the unused portion of the second floor as he'd come up the stairs. There was room for more, or for storage, besides. But not room for a woman to stay here once the mill was working again.

"Two months," he said, coming to stand by the castle of the loom, where she was weaving a length of coarse shirting.

She stopped, looking at him now. "Two months? You'll need two months?"

"We'll have it running again in two months provided I can find the right people—and you must know something about that end of it. First we'll need a millwright to fix the wheel and reset the gears."

"Did you notice anything missing?" Anne Vardry lowered her eyes as she spoke, resting her elbows on the cloth beam in front of her.

"So you know about the bevel gear?"

"It was taken out and rolled into the river. If you look you'll see the shaft of it poking up, making the water run fast over it. Fish come and eat on the weeds that catch on it, no doubt. Cast iron. Do you think you can get another of those in two months, Mr. Gairden?"

The questions that had bothered him on the lower floor came back to him now, but he sensed it was not the time to ask them. "That may complicate things a bit," he said, trying not to sound overly concerned at this first, large stumbling block, "but it can be done. It may mean having all new gears cast," he added, "and that will mean greater expense. And more time. But there are people anxious to invest in such things, I'm certain. The money can be found."

"Not around here it can't." Her face showed no expression. No anger. No bitterness. No hope. She stared vacantly at the shuttle wound with plain white wool she held in her right hand. Her skin was barely a shade darker, Fox noticed.

"Something personal?" he asked.

"Completely."

Fox had stumbled into the territory he needed to map out, but asking for direction wasn't easy. "You know I won't be able to help you unless I understand what I'm up against? You know that, don't you?" He felt very young suddenly. Both of them were older in experience than they were in years, but the experiences were different, and talking about them was not going to be easy.

"I can't help you. Not with that." She shifted her eyes once again to the yardage in front of her and began throwing the shuttle back and forth with a speed that told of her years of practice at it. She had left her home in Massachusetts to get away from such a task, and instead she had sold herself into a lifetime of it— unless he could intervene. Did he owe her that? Was that what he had come here for? He had not even known Hugh Vardry. But he had killed him, and the thought haunted him once again as he watched the nervous way she fixed her eyes on her work, without ever looking up.

"I'll do what I can," he said after a few moments, considerably less certain just now that he could in fact do anything at all. He hurried down the stairs, stuffing his notebook inside his saddlebag once he was back to his horse. His first stop was Humphreysville.

* * *

As he rode up, Fox was surprised to see ten ranks of young men, eight to a rank, in identical military garb of short blue coats, white pantaloons and tall blue hats with white cockades, drilling on the green east of the mill. They appeared to range in age from about eight to sixteen, some of them too small for the long rifles they carried, but all of them stepping smartly along to the drums of the front rank. An elderly gentleman marched with them, and Fox stopped to watch.

"I'm looking for someone who might give me the name of a millwright," Fox said when the man gave the youthful militia unit their leave and sent them hurrying back to their quarters in one of the large mill dormitories nearby.

"Colonel David Humphreys, at your service, young man," the small, silver-haired man said.

"Colonel, I beg your pardon. I didn't expect to see so auspicious a personage as yourself marching the young lads. I—"

"I like to personally supervise the moral direction of the people who work for me, Mr. . . ."

"Gairden. Francis Marion Gairden, sir. And I'm honored to make your acquaintance."

"Named for a man I never met but heard astounding reports of, Mr. Gairden. Like Marion, I, too, fought in the war for our independence—served with Washington," he added, not afraid to advertise his connections, it seemed to Fox.

"That must have been a gratifying experience," Fox said, searching for a word to encompass the high and low points of serving with a man of such varied reputation.

"Highly. It opened the door to foreign service for me, and finally to this," he said, spreading his arms to indicate all of the mill sprawl that was Humphreysville.

"I haven't as many cities named after me as the great man, but at least I have this. I see to their every need—I house them, clothe them, feed them, school them, teach them honesty and virtue. Not bad for the poor son of a humble pastor."

"Not at all, sir. I, too, have hopes of building such a place—not so grand, perhaps, but productive all the same."

"And so you are looking for someone to build for you. Have you a site in mind?" The older man's eyes were shrewd, always seeking opportunity, and it pleased Fox, just a little, to be able to tell him that he had a mill as well.

"I've been hired to reopen the Vardry woolen mill, Beaver Creek," he said.

Humphreys nodded solemnly. "Good luck," he said, and started to walk away.

"Wait! Sir . . ." Fox hurried after the portly little man, going so far as to grasp him by the arm to stop him. "Why do you say that? Why do you act so?"

"Why not ask Mrs. Vardry? Let her tell you."

"I have. She will tell me nothing. I can't seem to find out what I'm up against. But she weaves for your mill. I thought you might be able to help me."

"There is a millwright named Buffin who might be interested," Humphreys said, his eyes gentler once again, "but before I'd hire him, I'd try asking Mrs. Vardry a few things, Gairden. You might find out you've hired on for something that can't be done."

"Or shouldn't be done?" Fox asked.

"Perhaps," Humphreys said.

"But you won't say why."

"I don't think I need to," Humphreys said. "I think you'll find that people here have long memories, son. Good day."

Once dismissed, Fox stood watching the Colonel

walk back to his carriage, back stiff and shoulders square as would befit an aide to General Washington. He had prospered here at the edge of Rimmon's Falls. He had given three hundred others a means of making a living. The boys in the militia, the man had told him, were mainly saved from the New York almshouse to come here for a new start. They, and the young girls, were schooled in the evenings and on Sundays. They were taught the value of hard work and thrift along with their other subjects, and religious education was incorporated wherever possible. Very positive, very admirable, Colonel Humphreys, Fox would have liked to have said. And why be so very tight-lipped about the Vardry mill? But Humphreys was in his carriage now and off to the large brick house he maintained in Derby.

Fox located the man Buffin at work on a mill called the Housaton Fulling Mill near Seymour, and found Buffin a far different sort from Humphreys. Samuel Buffin was the son of a millwright Nathaniel Buffin, who was the son of a Scots-Irish emigrant named Jonas Buffin, a joiner and carpenter, Fox learned in a quick first sentence. The brawny, large-framed man stood chewing a wad of tobacco and surveying the work of his crew, who were rocking-in the wheel pit of the mill. Enlarging it, he told Fox, for a bigger wheel and more power. When he found out Fox had work to propose, he motioned for his men to go on without him and showed Fox to a bench on the sunny side of the mill's stone foundation where they might sit and discuss the proposition.

"You may as well know at the beginning that the job is at the Vardry woolen mill. From what I've been able to gather, that ends the conversation with most folks around here."

"You a relative?"

Fox paused a moment. The barman in Derby had asked the same question. The South had no monopoly on its preoccupation with family, it seemed. "No. I'm hired by Mrs. Vardry to see things right again. The mill's been closed a good while, as you must know."

"Mrs. Vardry, eh? Either you're a good man or a fool. Which is it?"

"Why don't you tell me? No one else seems to want to." Fox's eyes were stubborn as Buffin's as he stared back at him.

Buffin rubbed the reddish stubble of a good three days' growth on his chin, then scratched an itch on his back and shook a bit at the tingling. "What is it you need done?"

Fox took out his notebook. "Repair overshot wheel, replace one bevel gear, replace belting as needed when system starts up again, repairs on building including replacing shrunken clapboards with some that fit, add windows—"

"I told 'em it was too dark in there, but they wouldn't listen." Buffin chewed thoughtfully on his tobacco.

"You know the mill? You've worked on it before?"

"Built it, sonny. Most of it, that is. Before they kicked me out."

"They? Who besides Vardry?"

"His partner, of course, Taylor Jacobs . . ." Buffin stopped in the middle of what he was about to say, trying to put things together in his mind. "She sold the mill?"

"You sound like that would surprise you, Mr. Buffin. But no, she didn't. She . . . hired me to get it going again."

"You must've needed a job bad, sonny." The hazel eyes that sat so predominantly above the millwright's ruddy cheeks watched him carefully.

"I'm just back from being plucked off a coasting vessel by the British navy and impressed two years on the *Iago*. This position seemed infinitely superior to what I'd come from." Fox couldn't quite keep the exasperation out of his voice.

"Whoa, there, sonny. No need. No need at all to say more, though I say you don't look like a sailor, nor walk like one. But if you've suffered bad treatment at the hands of the British, as my own grandfather once did, then we've something in common after all. And mayhap you've enough of the tar in you to sail that piece of bad business Vardry left behind into some kind of mill."

The man seemed to be warming to the topic, seemed almost ready to accept, and then he added caustically, "If not, you'll die tryin'."

"I plan to live a long time, Mr. Buffin," Fox said, more ruffled than he wanted to admit at the future the millwright implied for him. "I thank you for your time."

"Wait a minute there, sonny," the millwright said just as Fox was about to walk away. "I didn't say no. I'll be down, soon as I can, have a look."

"Monday?"

"Nay, not quite. Got two weeks' work here, at the very least. But if you're still lookin'—still on the job—talk to me then."

"I'm talking to you now. I'll have your word on two weeks from Monday or I'll look elsewhere."

"My word," Buffin said, extending his hand and nodding in appreciation of the way Fox had handled himself. "But in the meantime, watch your stern, jack tar," he added. "Watch your stern."

"I'm always watching it, Mr. Buffin. Always on watch."

Fox mounted his mare and reined her back toward

Anne Vardry's mill. He blew out a long breath. You owe an explanation, woman, he thought, more than I ever owed one to you, and by the blazes I'm going to get it before I have any more old men call me "sonny."

Instead of riding back to the mill, Fox took the road to New Haven and spent the night there drinking at the Bunch of Grapes, every cup of whiskey dulling the image of Hugh Vardry's contorted face until at last he drifted off into the kind of stupor he had not sought for a long while. The bad dream ceased to ache in him, and a stillness came over him in which he thought it possible Hugh Vardry and Arthur Grisham still lived. The groggy waking from the stupor brought a sharp jab of reality, making him want to seek the stupor again. He called for another whiskey.

Sleeping then before the fire where the owner led him, covering him with a flea-infested blanket, Fox dreamed that night not only of Grish but of the way the Vardry bevel gear must look from beneath the waters of Beaver Creek. He saw it rusty and covered in places with green vegetation that shimmered in the current. And his face was there, much larger than the rest of his body, and with little hands he was trying to dislodge it from the stony bottom, but the shaft end was caught between two boulders. He could turn the gear on the shaft, so well was it lodged there. The gear spun freely on the shaft, but the shaft would not budge until finally he, with his outsized head, let himself drift above the water and finally along with the current to the sea.

Riding back to Derby late the next evening, Fox thought of the mills he'd seen, and of the people he had talked to. If Buffin agreed, work would begin soon. By autumn Fox would have the Vardry mill running again. His debt would be repaid. And, with any luck, he

would be able to get back to Charleston and then on
up to Columbia to find a site for his own mill.

First, of course, there was the matter of finding out
what actually had happened at the Vardry mill, and
that meant talking to Anne Vardry. Sunday evening
seemed as good a time as any, and even though his
head still ached from last night's whiskey, he rode by
that way on his way back to his room in Derby.

The days were beginning to get longer now, with the
sun setting around eight o'clock but its twilight linger-
ing until almost nine. It was quiet, though doves sang
their evening song, and the mare's hooves thudded as
she loped along. All was still but for the motion of the
horse, the flight of small buntings and the dive of an
occasional purple martin. Fox himself, though, sat erect
and kept his eyes on the road, not interested in the
signs of new life around him but only concentrating on
the conversation to come. Who was Taylor Jacobs?
Whatever happened to him? And if he dared to ask it:
Why did your husband really leave?

He tied the mare to the hitching post at the north
end of the mill and started for the door, but Anne Vardry opened it before he could knock. The thud of Bessie's hooves had announced him.

"You'll be happy to know I've found a millwright for
you," Fox said in greeting. "Name of Buffin. Perhaps
you know him?"

The woman did not answer but stood watching him,
waiting.

"It's rude not to answer people's questions, don't
you think?" he said, smiling falsely now. "I'll try again.
I'll say: 'Perhaps you know him?' and you'll say something like, 'I did, once.' See how easy it is? I ask, you
answer. Perhaps later on you ask and I answer." He let
the smile fade from his face when he saw she was not
returning it. "I'm sorry. I thought perhaps I could draw

you out a little on the question of Mr. Buffin is all. I thought we might talk over what I've found out on my travels, but perhaps another time."

"I doubt there's any need to talk. You keep on with your work, I'll keep on with mine. We have an agreement. You offered your services. I accepted. Unless you can't keep your part of the bargain, I expect you to keep at your work. In the meantime, I will keep on with my weaving and put aside some funds to pay for what I can."

"That's one of the things I want to talk to you about," he said, unwilling to let her get away when he had so many questions that needed answering. "I've done some looking at mills around New Haven, and most of them are purely spinning mills. No weaving. Just make the yarn and sell it. Let someone else worry about the weaving. I think it might be best for you here, as well. The looms take up room that could be used to house two or three more mules—more mules, more output. More output, more profit."

"The looms will stay." Anne Vardry's chin bobbed once, just enough for Fox to see that, despite what she had said yesterday, *she* was in charge.

"But I thought you married Hugh Vardry to escape a life at the loom. I thought you'd be pleased—"

"I've just told you I'm not. The looms stay."

"I don't suppose you'd care to tell me why?"

"No, I wouldn't."

"And what if I had simply gone ahead and purchased more mules without asking you—you who told me you didn't want to talk about anything? What then? How am I supposed to know what you'll talk about and what you won't?"

"You won't. But I'll tell you."

Her face never changed, Fox thought, though he knew his was probably red. He never had been much good at controlling his temper or hiding his feelings. Either she was good at it, or she didn't have any feelings, he didn't know which. He only knew that the questions he felt he must have answers to before he could go on with the work of getting the Vardry mill running again were no more likely to be answered tonight than the simple one about the looms had been.

"Anne," he said after a few moments. "You are making my task more difficult than it should have to be."

She shrugged. "Good night, Mr. Gairden. I'll expect you in the morning."

"Not in the morning, I'm afraid. I'm off to find you some partners, and to see about the bevel gear. I trust you'll talk to these men, provided I can find some?"

"Not unless I must. I would prefer that you make the arrangements. I will sign the papers."

"Without even talking to the others? Without even knowing them?"

"For reasons of my own, I believe that would be best."

Beyond the chill of her tone, so different from the warm caress of the spring air, Fox thought he heard a sadness, a helplessness. He took a second look, but there she stood, unflinching, tight-lipped. The vow he'd made to find out from her all that had happened here fell apart like a teacup thrown against a wall.

"Good night then, Anne. Pleasant dreams." She did not even wait for him to walk to his horse before going inside and closing the door behind her. Fox swung into Bessie's saddle and rode around to the river side of the mill, gazing out onto the ever-changing surface of the stream to see where the shaft of the bevel gear might protrude. It was there all right, and . . . bobbing a bit? Perhaps it was not so wedged between the rocks as it had been in his dream. Perhaps he should take a swim in there tomorrow and look at it. Perhaps it would be possible to harness some horses to it and pull it out of there. In his dream the gear had still turned freely on its shaft. Would that now that dream might come true. Would that investors would agree to be part of such a questionable venture as this was shaping up to be. Would that he might serve out his agreement and get on with his life somewhere far from here, far from anything Hugh Vardry had ever touched.

8

"Goin' to haul that bevel gear out of ol' Beaver, are ye there, sonny?" Erastus Pratt owned a fine pair of matched Belgians that helped him make his living as a drayman over the often barely passable road from Derby to New Haven. The man was built much the same as his horses were, with a proud head and hefty arms and legs set on a beefy body.

"If the cost's not too dear," Fox replied. "I take it word of the mill is spreading?" He had been at work nearly two weeks now, and had told everyone he could about the plans for the mill, but he hadn't talked to all that many people.

"Can't hardly stop word from spreadin' here in the valley. Specially this word. Everybody knows the story of the Vardry woolen mill. Most folks want nothin' to do with it, as I suppose you've found out by now. Myself, I'm different. Don't give a whit what's done long as the bill's paid. Cost ye two dollars, sonny."

"Two dollars? That's two weeks' pay for one of my employees, Mr. Pratt. I don't know . . ."

"Then you'll have to get yourself another gear, an' that'll cost ye far more. Two dollars or go without, for sure as Jamie's in the woodshed you'll not find another to help ye."

"Two dollars . . ." Fox paused a moment, looking Pratt in the eye the whole time. "Two dollars . . . I'll give you one and a half."

"One seventy-five, then, if it'll suit ye. But that's as low as she goes."

"One seventy-five." Fox nodded and gave Pratt's hand a brisk shake.

"Got a crew to help ye, then?"

"Not unless Buffin is there with his men. The mill's not hiring yet."

"You'd better get a few men around to help with the ropes an' all. Gilly and Billy can't do it all by themselves."

"I'll find some men, but it won't be easy—not a place people want to work, though I can't seem to find out why."

"Why? I'll tell ye why. Bad business that Vardry woman is. Folks hereabouts wouldn't speak to her, much less work for her, except for ol' Humphreys down there who lets her work for him—but then he's the type who'd take in any waif and try to reform her."

Fox shook his head. Even smiled. "I've asked this question so many times, I hesitate to again, but somehow I'm going to get an answer. Just what has this woman done—or her husband, or whoever it is that everyone seems to hate so dreadfully?"

"First it was the husband and his partner, Taylor Jacobs. Between the two of 'em, they borrowed money from everybody within ten miles of here, promising healthy profits that never came. Then it was the wife, who committed adultery with Jacobs, drove off that couple who later drowned at sea, and her own husband as well, him later died somewhere in the southern states tryin' to make a new start. She stays on here like a hermit and wonders why people talk. Hmmp! Plenty to talk about, I'd say. She should've just left when Fortune Bemis wanted to buy her out, but she wouldn't. Wouldn't when William Yeardly wanted to either. Just wouldn't do, wouldn't do what was right and let folks forget. No, she stays and near taunts folks to remember. I can't figure why, no I surely can't."

"And I suppose you can't figure out why I'm helping her either, then. Is that right, Pratt?"

"Folks figure you're one who had some dealin's with Vardry in the South—you talk a little different from folks here. Maybe in business with him? Knew him?"

"I killed him," Fox said without smiling. There was no waver in his voice, no apology, just the fact, bald and unsinging. He watched Pratt's reaction change from curious to shocked. "In a duel," Fox added. "Fairly." He stopped, waited, gauged Pratt's reaction. "Now, will you be there with your horses in the morning or won't you?"

"I'll be there," Pratt replied, but Fox thought he sounded a little less certain than he had the first time he'd promised.

Buffin loaned Fox three men for the bevel gear raising. Fox and the one named Cobb took on the underwater task of rigging the ropes to the gear itself. Fox's sea training served him well for such work, and the two-inch-thick ropes were secured to the shaft and then to the gear and back again with Cobb standing by and holding a smaller rope, attached to Fox's waist, should anything go wrong. The water was nearly four feet deep, with a current strong enough to sweep away anything as light as a man, and Fox kept an arm linked around the shaft at all times. Even at that, the work took close to an hour, and by the time it was done, Fox was cold and he was exhausted. But he felt Pratt's eyes on him, and he knew it wouldn't do to let slip the impression he'd made on the man yesterday when he told him of the duel. Pratt hadn't called him sonny so far today. Fox intended to make sure he didn't start again.

He gave the go-ahead signal to Pratt, who was waiting at the top of the gorge with his team. Buffin's other two men, Daniel Spinny and Abel Clark, stood by with long wooden poles to skid the tooth-edged gear upward and to prevent it from lodging on the craggy walls of the gorge. Fox let go of the shaft, found footing in the waist-deep water and got out of the way but not out of the water. He and Cobb each took hold of long hickory poles they would use as pry bars should the gear, which was almost like a giant hook, become lodged again on the rocky bottom.

The initial pull had to come at an angle, against the current, and at first it seemed that nothing was happening. Not even a wiggle. No movement. The ropes stretched taut and Fox sensed the danger if the gear did not budge soon and ease the tension. A rope could snap, injuring or possibly even killing one of the men. He couldn't let it happen—he couldn't . . . but then the shaft moved, just enough to let it bob slightly on the water. He heard a cheer go up from Spinny and Clark and waved to them in reply, then watched the ten-foot-wide gear inch through the waters toward the low point in the gorge wall where it would be hauled to the top. Now and again he or Cobb had to use their poles, but once the mechanism was free of its long-time resting place, its snags were minor. Now let it be undamaged, Fox prayed. Let it work. He clambered up the wall and took his place at the top, where he and Cobb guided the gear off the skids and onto another set of skids, and another and another, until it was at the mill door and ready to be moved inside.

Whether Anne Vardry watched this feat of horse strength and human ingenuity, Fox did not know. She was nowhere in sight when he topped the ridge, nor when he pushed open the wide double doors at the end of the mill. Pratt seemed to be looking around for her but didn't ask anything. Neither did the others. And

Fox offered no information—just paid Pratt his dollar and seventy-five cents when the job was done and sent him on his way. Buffin's men set about the work of refitting the shaft, working as a team with few comments for Fox other than a question here and there. They spent the better part of the day on the job, but when they were ready to leave that evening, the great gear still would not turn on its shaft.

"It's goin' to need to dry out," Cobb said. "Shaft'll shrink down then I should think. No damage to the iron itself. She was lucky."

Not *you* were lucky. No, *she* was lucky. So even to these men, Anne Vardry figured into the equation, and Fox couldn't help but wonder what would happen on Monday morning when they came to work here full-time. She couldn't stay hidden like this forever. And if she wanted to, why was she opening up the mill again? She. Anne Vardry. She didn't seem the sort to deceive her husband. But, then again, perhaps he didn't seem the sort to have killed her husband, either.

Buffin's men left around eight o'clock that Saturday evening. Cobb was a farmer south of Derby, Spinny farmed to the north and Clark, who lived in Seymour and ran a pottery part of the time, went home to stay with Clark for the night. The three of them would be back, with Buffin, on Monday morning. At least he hoped they would, though Cobb and Spinny said something about planting wheat if the weather was good.

God, but the renovation of this mill was a sorry business, Fox thought. Two months, ha! Two years would be needed to get it running again if things continued as they were. And then there was the matter of the money. So far Fox 'had interested only two investors, both of them sheep farmers, both of them only willing to put in one hundred dollars. Perhaps once Buffin was at work Fox would need to sail for Charleston and find some backing there, or give up the project altogether. By next week's end, he needed to know where the money was coming from or set sail, because within a month's time he would need to begin advertising for workers. Paying the twenty-some people needed would take money, and it would be a month or more before there would be any income. Odd, he thought, how at Lapham's I thought the greatest problem of a mill was in the getting along with the know-it-all British mule spinners. Now the problem is money—and a past I cannot change. From Lapham's I was able to walk away. From this, I cannot.

Sitting on the stone floor of the basement, his back against one of the rough-sawn ten-by-ten support posts, he heard the whisper of the widow's skirt on the stair. She probably expected him to be gone, and he knew he should have stood to acknowledge her presence, but all the show was gone out of him now. It had been a long, brutally physical, tension-filled day, and not a completely successful one at that. The gear, though more or less in place, still did not work. Buffin's men, although they had spent hours on it, did not seem to know exactly what the next step should be. The gear might loosen up within a couple of weeks, or a couple of months, or never. Years at the bottom of Beaver Creek might have ruined it after all. Thank you, Mr. Vardry, Fox thought as he imagined the man having it pitched down there in a fit of temper at . . . at this quiet creature? At Anne Vardry? Just like the bevel gear, it didn't quite seem to fit.

"You broke up your husband's partnership with your love for his partner? And in his anger he savaged the mill and left you here to look at the savagery? Am I to understand that is what happened?" Fox never moved, never turned his head toward the woman as he spoke. Exhaustion and the kind of defeat he had come to know only too well soaked his body like water in a sodden sponge, making him heavy and limp.

She didn't answer at first. She waited on the last step, leaning against the wall as if she, too, were exhausted. In his peripheral vision, Fox thought she seemed to be nodding slightly, but he couldn't be certain. She wasn't smiling, or looking pleased at the handiwork she saw in front of her, that much he could tell even without seeing her. There was a feeling that had come into the cool basement with her of anguish, of deceit, of business unfinished.

"I didn't, you know. I had no love for Taylor Jacobs outside of the bonds of friendship that should develop between partners in any kind of worthwhile endeavor. But I see the voices have been whispering once again. I thought they had all silenced, but I should have known that once anything of me touched the outside world, the voices would begin again, too. They don't forget, do they? They never forget. And yet they do not even know what it is they remember. Not truly. They only think they do."

"How can they know differently if you do not tell them? How can I make them understand when I do not? I think the time has come, Anne, for you to either tell me the truth or for me to leave, for even though I made you a promise, I cannot keep it under these conditions of mistrust." Fox let his head drop back against the post, his eyes focusing on the heavy beam above him, gray with cobwebs. Dust fell into his eyes and he blinked frantically, then let his head fall forward once again.

She sat down then on the bottom step where she had been standing and began to speak so softly he had to strain to hear her. "It was Hugh," she said. "Hugh who had the affair, Hugh who caused it all to happen. . . ."

Fox turned his head in her direction, but she wasn't

looking at him. Her eyes were on the bevel gear, and she kept them there, as if she were talking to herself instead of to him. And maybe she was.

"It had all started long before I came here to Beaver Creek. Hugh had quit his farm, determined to build this mill. Taylor became his partner and put in some of the money and much of his time, but he kept his farm, waiting to see how it was going to be, waiting to see how much could actually be made in such a place. At first it went well. They did only fulling, but took in work from miles around. Then they started carding as well. When Colonel Humphreys opened his mill there was competition, but still enough work for everyone. Then Humphreys added spinning jennies. So Hugh decided he must, too. They plunged deeper into debt to buy the first machine, planning to have the Henley foundry copy it and make more. But they had troubles with it, and that's when Hugh came to North Uxbridge. He was on his way to Boston to look at a new machine being made there, and he happened to find me instead. How often I've wished that Henley had been a little more enterprising. . . ."

Fox watched her as she told the story in a soft, wistful tone that seemed to fit the silent dusk now filtering in through the open doors. She had sat on these steps before, he could tell, when her only company had been an empty gear pit, but he doubted she had ever told her story before, even to herself.

"When we returned to Beaver Creek without the new machine," she went on, "Taylor and Hugh had words. Ugly words. Taylor felt Hugh had taken time away from the mill for nothing. Hugh felt Taylor would have been angry if he'd brought back an expensive machine; the shipping from Boston alone would have been more than the purchase of another machine such as they already had. I heard it all, every word. It was the first day we were back. I was a young bride, still not quite believing I was two hundred miles from home. We lived in a small house across the road—there's nothing there now, no trace of it but the foundation stones. Nothing left after Taylor was done. At first I thought us fortunate that the mill had not gone too, in the fire, I mean. But now I don't know. Perhaps it would have been better . . ."

"Jacobs burned your house? I don't understand."

"You mean, if he was in love with me, why would he do it? Well, of course, he wasn't. It was quite the other way around. It was Hugh and Beatrice Jacobs who were infatuated with each other. Both of them had lived here all their lives. They had been sweethearts before Taylor and Beatrice married. For some reason, they resumed the relationship after Hugh and I married. And I think Taylor suspected it for quite a long time, though I never did. It wasn't until Mr. Jefferson put the embargo on, though, and Taylor had no income from his farm, and debts were owed on the mill that he began to be nervous, to look for things to be wrong. Then he happened in on Hugh and his wife one Thursday afternoon.

"I remember it so well because it was in February. General Washington's birthday, in fact, and we were going to a party at Beatrice's that evening. She had given Taylor instructions to spend the day in the woods, cutting logs for the sawmill, so that she could cook and clean without interruption. But Taylor cut his hand rather badly and had to come home to bandage it properly. The house was clean. A pot of stew simmered on the hearth. And Hugh and Beatrice were . . . there.

"Taylor was ever thoughtful and cautious. He ordered Hugh from the house, never to see Beatrice again, but acted otherwise calm. Hugh, of course, came home and told me nothing except that Beatrice was indisposed and we would not be going there for the evening. I set up a small celebration for us at home, using the drawing of Mr. Washington I'd taken from an old copy of the *Courier* as decoration. I remember it was printed on the occasion of his death, and I had placed it among my most precious mementoes to bring with me to my new home. I set it on a platter I stood upon the mantel. I found some bits of red-white-and-blue yarn to festoon the mantel corners and drew a special store of New England rum from the cellar for a tribute. We spent a quiet evening, but I found no cause for alarm in it, thinking Hugh tired from his day of helping Taylor in the woods.

"In the morning, Hugh rode off—to Derby, he said —to see about more help for the mill. Taylor couldn't work, he said, because he'd cut his hand. Still he hadn't been gone long when Taylor came, hand bandaged, driving the team of work horses he normally would take with him to the woods to skid the logs. He drove them right up to those big doors, just as the men did today, and I could hear some noises I couldn't identify, but I didn't concern myself. I had left Massachusetts to put such things behind me. Here on Beaver Creek I was determined never to set foot in the mill. I took my own horse, Ginger, and set off in the direction of Beatrice's. I thought to help her if she was not feeling well, to comfort her. Instead, I found her gone. A large trunk sat packed by the door. I sensed something wrong, but thought Taylor would have spoken of it before he started work should it have been my concern, so I left again, the way I had come. I knew no one else to visit. People here were slow to offer friendship—or perhaps I was slow to seek it. But I did not hurry back, stopping instead at the little store in Derby to buy some smoked cod. I looked about for Hugh but did not see him, and I went home.

"I could see the smoke once I got within a mile of here. And I knew it was the mill. Too many mills had burned for me not to have thought that. And I feared for Hugh, that he might be in it. Or that if he wasn't, it might bring on a rage in him that he would take out on me. He did that sometimes. But I could not turn around. I had no place to go. So on I rode.

"Of course, it wasn't the mill. It was my house. It was my few precious mementoes of home. Ginger shied from the smoke, whinnying and stamping her feet, and all I could do was hang on—I wasn't much of a horse-woman then, as I'd never ridden at home. Through the smoke, though, I saw Taylor and three of the men who worked at the mill with his team over near the gorge, but I couldn't see what they were doing. There were deep tracks in the snow, with an odd mark to them—as though something had been dragged, I remember that. I remember it because I rode across it trying to get to the house, wanting to save it, or at least something of it. But there was nothing to save. Nothing to do. But watch.

"I came in here to wait. Taylor and the men must be hauling water up from the stream, I remember thinking. I would wait here for them, and then help them soak the mill so that if the wind changed . . . But they never came. I don't know how long I stood here, dazed, I suppose. But when I went out again, they were all gone. I feared an accident. Went to the edge of the gorge. And saw the bevel gear sticking partly out of the water, for the river was low just then. And then I began to see a connection in Hugh's silence and Taylor's. And in Beatrice's absence.

"I waited for Hugh to come back. I imagined all manner of scene, but always, always there was the scene of Hugh and Beatrice, almost as if I'd known it all along—because I had, but hadn't wanted to. When by afternoon he had not returned, nor had Taylor, I rode once again to the Jacobs's house. Now cold, with reddened cheeks and stiff fingers, I guided Ginger through a snowstorm that blew in on the gray skies. This time, again, no one was home. But this time the trunk was gone, too.

"It took me some time to puzzle out what must have happened, but finally I did. Hugh had ridden out early, waiting to speak to Beatrice after Taylor left. Taylor had already told Beatrice to be ready to leave when he came back home, and so she had packed her trunk. She, meanwhile, had gone off with Hugh for a time— to where I still don't know—to lay their plans without the risk of Taylor returning again unexpectedly. That was when I came the first time. Taylor was at the same time here, taking his revenge. I have learned since that Taylor and Beatrice later made for New Haven, driving the same team and wagon Taylor had brought here for his destruction of the mill. Hugh followed them, intent on learning their destination and following them.

"Taylor and Beatrice sailed the next day on the *Hero* for New York. Taylor had a brother there, I think. Probably another calm fellow, who knows? Hugh was forced to stay behind, the weather being galelike by this time, too cold to ride, even. And he must have watched the sea and wondered, I don't know. But he never saw her again. She and Taylor were lost at sea along with the *Hero* and its crew."

It was a long tale, and Anne sighed at the end of it, spent with the weight of memories so long borne alone. But to Fox it was not the end—it in no way explained why the whole of the countryside should despise her. She had done nothing wrong. Fox started to speak, opened his mouth, but was unsure of how to phrase the question, or even if he should. Could she stand any more? Before he could decide, she answered for him.

"You're wondering now why I remain. Why I am the guilty party." She laughed a bitter laugh. "I have Hugh to thank for that. You should be able to imagine why better than most, I think. Hugh, you see, came back here after the *Hero* was lost. Thought to resume life with me and repair the mill, for now he was the sole owner. He was also the sole debtor, and a cloud hung over the operation. The men who had helped Taylor cripple the mill had done their share of talking, and they knew there was trouble between Hugh and Taylor. Somehow, from what Taylor had said in his agitated state of mind, they assumed that it was Taylor and I who had been caught in adultery—that it was Hugh who was the wronged party. Hugh, seeing an opportunity, did not correct them. In fact, he added to the story that he had caught us together and threatened to kill Taylor if he ever set foot on the place again. Taylor had retaliated by trying to burn him out, and by assuring that the mill would be inoperable by disposing of the bevel gear. Hugh played the wronged husband until he had the whole valley sorry for him, even though he owed many of them money and was trying to borrow more. Mr. Jefferson with his embargo had seen to it that no one had any extra money, and so Hugh couldn't make it work. It was then that he hit on the idea of going south, where, the story went, cotton planters had lots of money to invest. He would go there and either borrow enough to get this mill running again or to get one started there, having this machinery shipped down later."

"And he left you here . . . alone."

"He left me here to bear the wrath of every indignant matron and lecherous man who cared to bother with me. He left me here to find out the truth about things in bits and pieces—mostly in pieces of insults hurled at me when I went to the store, or anywhere that people gathered during that first week or so. After that, I quit going out at all, unless it was absolutely necessary. Only I had the truth, but my truth counted for nothing. Hugh and Beatrice had grown up here—I was an outsider. I was easy prey for every exaggeration and bit of filth anyone cared to tack onto the already lurid account making the rounds at the tavern or the other mills."

"And I took away any chance you would ever have had of Hugh's coming back and telling the truth." Fox's head throbbed and his body ached. There was near darkness in the cool basement now, the only light coming from the double doors which had opened onto so much activity so long in the past.

"Hugh was never coming back. I knew that when he left. He wanted nothing more here, nothing of me. . . . I don't know what was wrong with me . . . I'll never know that. . . ." She began to sob, she who had been so dispassionate throughout the whole recounting of the affair. Fox rose and went to her, dropping down on his haunches to put himself at eye level with her.

"There, there. It wasn't you. It wasn't anything about you. You mustn't think that, you can't." He should have touched her, put an arm around her or comforted her with something other than words, but something stopped him, and he let the inches stand between them.

"I didn't know him, you know," Fox said at last. "I had very little cause to challenge him as I did, except that he belittled my grandfather in a way that could not be ignored. But I saw in him a mixture of anger and contempt that made him seem to relish my challenge, almost as if he had known it would come." Fox leaned to his right and slipped to the floor, remembering. "He was like so many of the other Federalists I've met since I've been up here—quick to judge, certain of his point of view, disgusted with Republican ideas to the point of sneering at anyone who might favor them. I heard later —after our duel—that it was not the first he'd fought in South Carolina. Someone said he probably expected to kill me—you said he was a good shot. I don't know. And I don't truly know what happened that morning at the race course, except that my loss of balance when his shot hit my leg cost him his life."

"It was for the best, whatever it was, though I may be damned for saying so. But it freed me, in a way I never could have freed myself—"

"Not of the gossip, though. Not of untruths."

"No, not of them. Not yet, at least. But in my months of seclusion here I have had time to think, and I have finally decided that since my life goes on I should make what I can of it. I should have done it sooner, of course. But I didn't. No, this mill became my prison. I left it only when I had to—and never to go to Derby. I would walk to Woodbridge, or even to Hamden, to get supplies. No one knew me there. Your coming back was like a sign to me that it was time. I had been thinking it anyway, but you helped me decide it."

"Thank you for telling me all this. I know it wasn't easy. I know the memories must be painful."

"Sometimes they are almost humorous, if you can imagine that. I was so young. I was so naive. I made it so easy for Hugh, who was looking for someone quiet and well-behaved to fill up the space that Beatrice left behind when she married Taylor instead of him. He had a forceful, persuasive way about him I found attractive. I wanted to leave home. Marriage was the only way."

"So that is why you've not returned to Massachusetts?"

"There would be little more than servitude for me there, just as there always was. My father knew nothing but work." She turned away from him again, so that her profile was silhouetted against the open doors.

"But you are going to have a great deal of work here, too, Anne. This mill is not going to run itself just because I get the gears working again."

"I know that, but it will be different from working for my father. Or Hugh."

"You've had some poor experiences with men, haven't you? I'll . . . try not to be another one of them."

"You're already far different from the rest, Fox Gairden, or you would never have come back this time. So good luck to you, now that you know all you're up against."

She held out her hand to shake his, which was a clumsy undertaking when they were both sitting down, but they managed it, and she almost smiled at him.

Rising with an amazing amount of energy, considering the emotional story she had just told, she walked to the far corner of the mill. Fox couldn't see her. It was too dark. But he watched after her, sensing her nearness.

"I'm thankful for all you've done." She seemed to be facing away from him, her words little more than a whisper.

Fox got up and stretched, shaking off the tenderness he heard in her voice. "We're far from finished, you know. The bevel gear may never spin again. We're going to have to give it some time, according to Buffin's men."

"I can't let you do all this as a debt of honor, Fox. I've been thinking about it. Once the mill is running again, I want you to own a quarter of it."

"A partner? Are you certain—in light of what you've just told me, I mean?"

"There would have been no trouble between the partners had it not been for Beatrice. I would expect none between us."

Fox could hear the tone of defeat that had come back into her voice again. She tried to mask it with her dispassionate explanation of the first partnership, but he could hear it all the same. Beatrice had been her only friend here. Fox ached for her through the darkness, but could reach out to her only with words. "You are most generous, but I didn't come here for profit. I came out of duty. Let me get the mill running once again, and then we'll see. I don't want any bad luck to fall on us now that we've made a start. If I fail, there's no partnership to untangle. I think it best that way. My father's a lawyer, you know," he said, trying to lighten the conversation. "He's taught me to avoid legal problems rather than create them."

"All right. We shall see."

Still she did not face him, nor did she come out of the shadows. An uneasy silence fell between them. Fox walked to the bevel gear and ran his hand down the wet, swollen wood of the shaft. Like a ship's mast, it was a power source, but it would take more than wind to make this one sail. And when it did, he hoped she would not be blown off from it the way Arthur Grisham had been blown from the *Iago*. "I want to make this work, Mrs. Vardry. I do."

"And I want to be called Anne, if you recall."

Even in the darkness, he could hear the change in her tone, almost confident now. Perhaps she could give orders and run a mill—if she could stay in the dark. "Anne," he said, "say that again, tomorrow. Say it to Buffin. Say it to his men. Say it to everyone you meet. Let them know you. Don't hide yourself any longer."

"I can't. Yet. You tell them."

"I'll tell them Anne Vardry has been wronged and they'd be wise to help right it."

"They won't believe you."

"We shall see . . . ," he said, echoing their earlier words. "For now, I think it's time I go. Morning comes early."

"Safe journey," she said, and once again he heard the rustle of her petticoats as she slipped through the darkness and up the stairs.

The freshness of the evening air met him at the doorway and washed him with the scent of lilac and newly turned earth from the ruts where the bevel gear had gouged down deep. She had come a long way since that first day when she'd aimed the musket at him. Partner, though? It was the last thing he had expected when he had set off in search of Hugh Vardry's family three years back, and he wasn't too sure he wanted it now. Still, she would need help. He had given himself two months to make up his mind. Two months for her, too. But he doubted he would stay. He doubted it would come to that.

9

"We're gettin' 'er to look like something, eh, Gairden?" Samuel Buffin spoke through a mouthful of nails as he pounded in the last of the new clapboards. Six weeks had passed since the bevel gear was replaced, and the mill machinery hummed as the crew tinkered with adjustments that would send an even supply of power from the tall waterwheel to the gears and onward out through a system of shafts and belts. Three new mules were being installed on the second floor, where, so far, Anne Vardry was still living. Work was progressing on a small boarding house where she would eventually move and where future mill employees would be living as well. For the time being, though, she was still holed up with her looms, ever so quiet, seldom seen.

"Aye, it's coming along, Buffin. I only wish it was a cotton mill, sometimes. There's a king's ransom to be made in the sailcloth business just now, I expect. The way it sounds, war's not far off, and you can wager that every available ship will be called into service, private or no, and new ones built as well. Lots of canvas needed for such a venture, any way you cut it. But, I see that won't be it for the Beaver Creek Woolen Mill. Cassimeres, woolens and doeskins—that's what we'll be making. I hope."

Buffin spit the nails from his mouth and dropped them in the leather pouch that hung at his side. "So you think Mr. Madison will go for war after all this

time, do you? Think he's sick of bein' humiliated by the
Britons for so long? I doubt it, myself. I think he'd
rather let 'em walk all over us than stand up to 'em.
This negotiation business—if England feels like nego-
tiatin', she does. If she don't, she don't. Has always
been that way, I don't see what would change it now."

"She's never lacked for spleen—like in this *Little Belt*
business. When it and a half-dozen other British cruis-
ers have taken up station just off our coast, stopping
and searching every ship that passes, impressing at will,
the Mistress of the Seas simply says she didn't fire on
our *president* first. She's playing us for the fool. I think
Madison's right to ask for satisfaction not just for the
Little Belt affair, but for the *Chesapeake*, too."

"Aye, England ought to be held to account for some
of her actions, the way she holds us to account. An'
mayhap war would bring better times to us. 'Tis a poor
time to be a farmer, I'll tell ye, goods worth almost
nothing."

"I know. I worry for Mrs. Vardry here, and her debt,
but at least she'll have a go at rising above it. With the
farmers I'm not so certain."

"The widow Vardry doesn't deserve such a piece of
luck if you ask me, but then I guess you didn't."

"I didn't ask, but I'll tell you something instead.
Anne Vardry wasn't the guilty party who drove the
Jacobses away and her husband with them. There was
guilt to spread around, most of it to Mr. Vardry, the
way it looks to me. I'd ask you to have an ear for a
woman who's seen some bad times, guilty only of the
poor judgment of a young woman wanting to get away
from home. You've been fair with me, Buffin—be fair
to her, too."

Fox could see Buffin's surprise at the request. "So
you believed everything she told ye, swallowed it like a
spoonful of sugar?"

"I did. But unlike folks around here, I had reason to. I saw the husband after he left here, saw how he conducted himself and what he was like."

"And you didn't mind killin' him? Is that what you're sayin'?"

"I minded. And I still mind. But everything she said fit with the impression I had of the man."

Buffin stroked the stubble on his chin. "Hmmm." He nodded as if there might be something to the idea. "But it was Taylor Jacobs who tossed the bevel gear into the gorge down there—the men who helped him told the story themselves. Jacobs was gettin' back at Vardry for breaking up Jacobs and Vardry's wife, an' for threatening to run Jacobs out of the business and out of Derby."

"It *was* Jacobs who hobbled the mill. Mrs. Vardry told me that, too. But the reason was just the opposite: Jacobs was getting back at Vardry because he'd found Vardry compromising his own wife, Mrs. Jacobs." Fox watched interest pique on Buffin's face and smiled. "You see, don't you, how skillfully a story can be twisted to serve those who wish it? Vardry stayed on and faced not the scorn Jacobs intended for him, but sympathy instead. Jacobs, in wanting to get his wife away from her lover, opened himself to whatever Vardry wished to say about him once he was gone. Vardry, in my experience, delighted in trying to talk his way out of things, which served him well here—and not so well in Charleston."

"Well, I'll be a bloated croaker. Like you say, Vardry was a schemer. Lots of folks here had no love for him, so it was pretty easy to believe the stories about his wife, too. But I still don't see why she didn't speak up, tell folks what really happened."

"I don't think she could. At first she was too heartbroken to say anything back, and later she was too bitter. And who would have believed her? She had no friends, hadn't been born here like her husband had. She had very little money and was in fear of the wrath of her husband's debtors at every turn. She did not care to return to her family in Massachusetts. What could she do?"

"Naught but what she did, I suppose, though it seems it took her long enough to get around to it. Pity you didn't come along a bit sooner, Gairden."

"I came up here soon after the duel, but no one would talk about her, and when I came out here she wouldn't talk about it. But I don't know if I'd have been ready to help her then anyway. Not like this. No, it took impressment aboard the *Iago* and the loss of a very good friend to give me the strength to come back here. And so I expect I owe the Admiralty something after all."

"Hah! I'm sure you feel deeply in their debt!" Buffin clapped his hands at the thought, laughing. "So deeply you'd fire the first shot in either a sea or land war should you get the chance."

"I've joined the militia," Fox admitted, "as you've probably heard. Derby Rifles, actually."

"Plannin' to stay on here, then, are ye, once ye get the mill runnin' again?"

"I don't know yet. I wasn't originally, but now—"

"Now mayhap there's somethin' more to hold ye here?"

"I don't know," Fox said, evading the inference that there might be a woman involved. "I'll have to wait until later in the summer to decide, I think. Too much work for now to even think about leaving—or anything else," he added with a knowing wink. "I've hired two men so far, but we're a long way from having enough people to run the mill. And now that we've come this far, I don't want to just walk away and let it fall apart again."

"You should get a share of it for yourself, you know, or your time'll have been for naught. Don't settle for a wage—take shares or nothin'."

"You give advice you don't take yourself there, Buffin. You work for a wage."

"I've worked for shares, too, though, lad, and that's where I can make enough to keep me goin' until folks like you with little money but good intentions can pay me for my labors."

"I'm not certain it would be right—"

"Don't let a sad story or a pretty face fool ye, lad. Look out for yourself a bit, as well. Time is passin', time when you should be makin' a life for yourself, takin' a wife, raisin' some younguns to work in a mill of your own someday. Any debt you owe here's already repaid, I'd say. Shares. Demand 'em."

Fox could not imagine demanding anything from Anne Vardry, not now that he knew her story. And her, too. "I'll think about it," he told Buffin as the older man returned to adjusting the belt to the mule on the mill's main floor.

"You do that, lad. You do that. Pretend it's old Napoleon you're dealin' with, or worse yet, King George. Stand up for your rights."

"I think maybe I have to help Mrs. Vardry stand up for her rights first, and then see about my own."

"They do teach you a respect for the ladies in that Charleston of yours, don't they, Gairden? If she'd been widowed down there, she wouldn't have been in such a pickle, would she, now?"

"I don't know. I've never thought of it quite like that, I suppose. But maybe not. Although if her husband lost his honor, hers, as a widow, would be diminished as well. And Charleston is rife with gossip, just like here. No one can escape from that, anywhere."

"Well, if she ever gets rich enough, she can buy her way out of it here—though that's not likely, I don't imagine."

"No, not likely, but perhaps at least rich enough to get away somewhere and start over. If I were her, that's what I'd do, I think."

"Would you go West?" Buffin asked.

"West—I don't know. Best way to get there's on a flatboat—overland trails are killers, from what I hear. She'd need money and a man to help her either way. I'd say she'd be best off in a place like Philadelphia." Fox thought for an instant of Adelle. He hadn't heard from her since he had been in Connecticut. No doubt her life was greatly changed since the time he had last seen her, as his own was. Still he wondered, what if? What if he had gone back there after the first time he talked to Anne Vardry? What if he had worked those months in Uncle Paul's mill instead of Lapham's? Would he still have ended up on the *Iago*? Should he have given in to that urge to take Adelle in his arms? Would Anne Vardry have managed on her own if he hadn't come back?

"I'm itchin' to go west, myself," Buffin went on while Fox's mind was still on Philadelphia, "but the wife's against it. 'Fraid of Indians, I suppose."

"I think a nice mill somewhere in South Carolina's what I want," Fox said, finding no answers for himself. "I haven't seen my home in almost three years, and I'm ready to go back."

"Aye, home calls to most folks. Odd that Mrs. Vardry here doesn't feel it. But then, some families aren't all that welcomin', either."

"Hardly. But mine is—"

"And there are lots of lovely ladies in Charleston, by

all accounts. Prettiest women in the United States, one gent told me. I should think you *would* want to go back there then."

"For a married man, you seem to have ladies on your mind a good deal, Buffin," Fox joked.

"Just because there's no fire doesn't mean there's no coal in the stove," the millwright replied, jabbing Fox none too gently in the ribs.

"Oh ho, so there're more tales to tell of Mr. Buffin yet. Well, now, I'll be anxious to hear more before you're done here. And I'll be watching any young ladies I might have my eye on to see that you're not after them as well."

Both men returned to their work smiling, but it was Fox who whistled the afternoon away. Anne Vardry had one more person on her side than she had had at daybreak.

Buffin and his men were camped a short way up the mill pond in an old Continental army tent salvaged from the local militia storehouse, where it had been since the end of Washington's presidency. The army had been disbanded then, on the theory that a strong military was a threat to the fledgling government, and perhaps it might have been. Since the beginning of the embargo in 1807, though, there had been talk of war, either civil or against England or France. Looking at the tent, Fox couldn't help but wonder if the old canvas might be called into service again, and soon. This week's *New Haven Times* told of Madison's sending a detachment of regular army troops to support Governor William H. Harrison in Indiana. There was fear that the Indians, led by a man named Tecumseh, might attack at any time, urged on by the British, no doubt. The safety of the American settlers in the new territory had to be secured.

Fox shook his head. He had often heard his grandfather tell about the Cherokee War in South Carolina, about his mixed feelings at the destruction of Cherokee villages inhabited since long before South Carolina existed even as a proprietorship, and yet of his certainty that safety needed to be assured for the people who had chosen this new land as their home. All of his life, Grandfather had been a reluctant warrior, first in the Cherokee War, then in the Revolution. But when need had arisen, he had served and served well. Will I be called to do the same? Fox wondered. Somehow the idea of fighting the Indians left him with the same mixed feelings he had heard Grandfather tell of. Still, if needed, he would have to go. And he could never turn his back on what was being done on the high seas, on what had been done to Grish.

Fox had given up his room in Derby and brought a tent of his own to pitch out here by the millpond next to Buffin's. The men shared breakfasts of bacon and eggs and coffee each morning, cold bacon sandwiches at noon, and then a stew or meat each night which was prepared by Anne Vardry, who came to camp and stoked the fire, then started the slow-cooking meal and left again before any of the men came back.

Since the night she had told Fox her story, Anne had remained an unseen presence at the mill, and if he had thought a door of understanding had opened between them that evening, he had been wrong. If anything, she was more elusive, more skittish, more mysterious now than she had been before. When he went to her room —or hiding place, as he had come to think of it—she answered his questions about construction or equipment, but no more. Her answers were not sharp, but neither were they especially cooperative. And he knew Buffin's men made jokes about her—probably about him, too, for serving as her voice. There was always a

distance between him and the other men, no matter
how much he tried to close it. Even with Buffin, Fox
wasn't completely certain of where he stood. Now that
the men were camped here, it would not be seemly for
him to go to the mill to speak to her in the evening,
and yet he needed to talk to her at some time when the
conversation might go unnoticed.

His opportunity came just a few days later on an un-
seasonably cool July afternoon when Buffin and his
crew were at work on the head race gates that con-
trolled the flow of water into the mill. Fox was replacing a section of card cloth on the carding machine
when, glancing out the window, he saw Anne on her
way to the camp with a basket of food.

"Let me help you, Anne," he said, rushing to catch
up to her. "That looks heavy."

"I had some early cabbage, a few carrots. I'll start a
soup for the men."

"We'll enjoy that." Fox looked at her, chanced a
smile. She almost returned one, then seemed to think
better of it. She had disposed of the black dress she
had previously worn nearly every day and replaced it
with one in bold blue-and-cream stripes that gave her a
look of youth and style Fox couldn't help but notice.
She still kept a shawl with her at all times, almost like a
shield, despite the summer's heat, and she wore a high-
brimmed bonnet whenever she was outside. Her pale,
delicate skin was unchanged, though, and her eyes as
brown as any could be.

"You're not making it any easier for me, you know,"
he said, after they had walked a short distance in silence. She tilted her head in question. "With the men, I
mean. How can I convince them that you are so very
different from what your husband led them to think
when you insist on hiding in your rooms, slipping about
out here only when there's no chance of meeting with

another human being? How can you expect that when I leave you will run this mill alone if you will not even so much as take a step toward meeting the people who work for you and who will continue to work for you?"

"I don't wish to interfere, that is all. These men cannot serve two masters."

"Ha! We are all working for you, as I recall. Therefore there is only one mistress, and it is you—"

"And I recall that much of the money spent so far has come from your own pocket, Mr. Gairden, for you have asked very little of me."

"But that does not make me master here. It is only what I owed you. A penance. It is you who must learn to speak with people once again, to let them know you. Not all men are so harsh as your husband was, Anne. I fear for you once you are left on your own."

"But surely you are not leaving yet?"

"Buffin and his men will be finished in another week. I've purchased your first run of wool and have begun the hiring. There's another advertisement in the *Times* this week, and no doubt we'll soon have our complement of workers—all of them new people, people who know nothing of you. People you can face without shame. Beyond that, by autumn, you will need to take over. Things should be running smoothly."

"And you?"

"I'll return to South Carolina. Thanks to you, I've the experience now to start my own mill, though I must say I wish I could take Buffin with me. He's a fine millwright. I doubt if I'll find another around—"

"I'd rather you didn't leave so soon. Give me time to get to know things a bit better. I don't know much about a mill, after all. I'd have to learn."

"But once we have the spinners and the carders and everyone knowing the tasks, your job will be to buy and sell. You'll learn that in no time. You won't need me.

And anyway, if I'm to get a mill started on my own, I'll need a year or more to build it, and then still need to get it running as I have this one. If I'm to catch these good times for mills, I need to get to it, and soon, before all the mill seats are spoken for."

"I see." Anne dropped her eyes, taking the basket from his hand as they came to the makeshift plank table at the camp. She began to chop the cabbage in a wooden bowl, and Fox left without a word to go to the edge of the millpond for a pail of water he could see she would need next. Coming back, he watched her work for a few moments, wondering what she would say next, but she kept on chopping, almost as if he weren't there.

"I'll stay on as long as I'm needed, Anne," he said at last. "You know that. It is what I agreed to. I'll honor that."

At his words, she stopped her chopping and looked up at him, directly into his eyes, in a way she had always before avoided. "Thank you," she said, smiling but yet quivering at the corners of her mouth.

"But you must try to help me," Fox urged. "You must try to come out more, to take part more, or I will never be able to help you learn all you need to know."

"I shall try." Once again she dropped her eyes to the cabbage, scooping it up into her palms and dropping it into the large iron pot that made a daily trip to the fire pit to cook the supper. Her hands were small and blue tinged from working with some indigo yarns. They worked quickly and with purpose, just the way he had seen them work at the loom. They could work just as purposefully with the accounts and business matters of the mill, he knew. But to do that she would have to come out of her rooms.

"Join us out here for supper," Fox asked. "Please. The men would be honored." He caught her look of disbelief. "Truly, they would. I know they would. Come. Please."

"Me, dining with seven men? That would give the townsfolk something to talk about, now wouldn't it? I'm afraid I can't."

"Take the chance, Anne. Take the chance that instead of gossiping about you they might come to know you."

"I can't." Her eyes never left the vegetables and the ham bone she was placing in the pot.

"You're going to have to," Fox said, losing patience. "If you don't, I leave tomorrow. *You* have to meet these people, talk to them. I can see now that the only way you'll do it is if you're forced. My job is not here any longer—it is to go away and to make you do what I know you can do."

Fox was just about to turn and walk off when Anne Vardry ceased her consuming concentration with the vegetables. "Please don't," she said, touching his arm. "Don't go."

Fox took a deep breath and looked into her eyes. "You know what must happen to make me stay." He said nothing else, but walked away, wondering what her decision would be.

The men did not gather for supper until almost half past eight o'clock that evening, when the work on the gates was at a point where it could be left without harm until the next morning. The pungent smell of green cabbage and salty ham filled the evening air, and they lined up to dip out their portions of it and the fresh bread that was set out for them just the way they did every night. Fox fell to the back of the line, looking back over his shoulder toward the mill, hoping for a sight of Anne but finding none. She had called his bluff. He would be leaving in the morning.

It was quiet around the table, the men tired after the fourteen-hour day they had put in. "Tomorrow'll be another just like this one," Buffin said, breaking off another piece of bread. "But that should about do it. Double planking on that gate should've been done the first time, but Vardry—"

Buffin stopped in midsentence and one by one the other men looked up at him, then off in the direction he was looking. Coming toward them was Anne Vardry, carrying a basket. No one spoke, and for a moment no one moved, but then Fox stood up, then Buffin, then the rest, one by one.

"Good evening, Anne," Fox said, nodding to her. "I'd like you to meet Mr. Samuel Buffin, and his crew. . . ." Fox introduced them in turn and felt their discomfort almost as keenly as he felt Anne Vardry's from a few feet away. She nodded but didn't speak as he indicated each man and told a little about him, and the men nodded back.

"Won't you join us for a glass of cider, Mrs. Vardry?" Buffin surprised Fox by asking. Fox saw her start to back away, shrinking from the request like a morning glory closing for the night. "Made it myself, keep it cooled in spring. Folks say it's good."

Silence. Not a man echoed a compliment or extended a hand. It was left to Fox to speak again. "Finer than any I ever drank in South Carolina, sir." He made a mock bow to the millwright, then looked again to Anne Vardry. "Anne? Won't you?" She began to shrink away again and Fox thought to reach for her hand to pull her back. The memory of the way she had touched his arm just a few short hours ago came to him. He wanted to touch her. Very much. But only his eyes willed her to come forward.

"I brought a maple pudding. A bit lopsided from perching in my little stove, I'm afraid, but I hope you'll like the sweet of it." She thrust the basket forward toward Fox, and he could see the round of pudding nestled in the bottom among some linens.

"We don't go by looks, do we men?" he said, searching their faces as he spoke, feeling joyous and successful that she had come, that she had done what he'd asked. By the time he looked back, she had already turned and started for the mill without a word of farewell. He drew in a deep breath and blew it out again, exasperated.

"Her looks ain't bad," Cobb said in a low tone. Eyebrows raised around the table at the idea.

"That's why we don't go by looks." Spinny elbowed Fox and winked. "The proof of the puddin's in the eatin'!" There was a chuckle around the table that Fox could not bring himself to join.

Buffin, too, was silent at first. "She's a widow, not a puddin', Spinny, so get your mind back on your supper," he said after a moment.

"Aye, guess that'll be the last we see of her for another six weeks, eh lads?"

Nods of agreement went around the table as the mound of maple pudding was passed.

"She's a mite younger than I expected," Cobb observed, making soft sucking sounds as he tongued the pudding and savored its delight. "Makes a fair puddin', too, I'd say."

"An' no wonder she had her eye out for another man. Vardry was a bit long in the tooth for her, I'd wager."

"Odd she never found herself another man after Vardry died. . . . If one wasn't even enough for her before he passed on, I mean."

"I'd be willin' to volunteer," Abel Clark put in. "She has a lovely swing to her skirts, I say."

"You have a wife an' more children than you can

feed already. Leave your breeches be. There's younger men who can see to widows' needs." John Whitson, a new man on the crew, pointed proudly to himself, and laughter rang out around the table.

"I think that perhaps one man was more than enough, gentlemen." Fox tried to hold his temper, but his chest seemed to pound with the beating of his heart. "The story about her and Jacobs was a lie. It was her husband and Beatrice Jacobs who caused the trouble, only Vardry twisted the story around a bit to make himself look the wronged party."

The look on the faces was much the same look Fox had gotten from Buffin when he told him the story. Clearly these men were just as skeptical. "An' I suppose she told ye this, and ye believed her?"

Fox looked to Buffin, and Buffin looked back with an expression that said he knew what Fox was going to say next. Fox smiled. "Not quite. Vardry told me himself," he lied, watching Buffin's face to gauge the effect. The older man held back a smile, but Fox could tell he did not disapprove.

Once again silence reigned. "You knew him?" one man asked.

"We were acquaintances."

"He challenged Fox here to a duel," Buffin chimed in, changing the story once again. "Only he wasn't quite as fast on the trigger as he was at the mouth, isn't that right, Fox?"

"He was fast—just not very accurate," Fox said quietly. He felt the other men's eyes upon him. "His shot threw me off, and my shot went through his head instead of over it."

The next silence was an uncomfortable one, and Fox wondered what the men would make of this information. It would not be digested as easily as the maple pudding, that much was certain.

"They say there's only been five duels in Connecticut since the Revolution, an' four of them was out-of-staters. Couple of 'em was New Yorkers didn't want to get fined for duelin' inside their own state so they came here to do it."

"I'd like to see one once," Spinny added.

"Better to see one than to be in one." Fox got up from his place on the long bench and took his bowl and cup to wash them in the bucket of dishwater on the stump near the fire.

"Glad you made it through, anyway, Fox," Buffin said. "The more I see of little Mrs. Vardry, the more I think what you say is true. She's no evil woman—just a shy little doe lost in this big woods."

The other men were not so quick to make a judgment and turned their talk to bathing in the millpond before bed. Soon they had shed their clothes and jumped in, splashing and dunking each other, some of them swimming with strong strokes, others just picking their way along the rocky bottom and laving themselves in the deepening twilight.

Fox watched. He remembered the view from the second floor of the mill, and he wondered if Anne Vardry stood there now, watching the display. He wondered if it was shyness, as Buffin had said, or bitterness or fear that held her tongue. He walked toward the mill to make certain the tools were all inside, for the sky was almost starless. The cool day might bring a stormy night. A wet night in the Continental army tent, and in his own. He wondered what the other men were saying about Anne Vardry now. And about him. And he found that it mattered to him what they thought, more than he would have expected when he started this job three months back.

Standing near the wheel pit, Fox looked up at the

faint light that flickered in the back corner of the second floor. You've been impressed here like a sailor, woman, he thought, by the legacy of one Hugh Vardry. And it's time you were released.

10

July 21, 1811

My dear Francis,

How thankful we are to think of you alive and prospering in Connecticut. Your letter made clear to us some of what you endured during your time at sea, although I am certain it in no way depicts the whole of it. Of course we share your outrage at the British dalliance with our sentiments. The continuation of trade restrictions and the humiliation of impressment and search and seizure are as odious to us as to your friends in the North, and fervor for war heightens here each day. While you may still see it differently, I thank God that your grandfather did not have to live to see this sorry state of affairs.

Your interest in returning to Charleston was, of course, the news dearest to our hearts, and we shall do all we can to prepare for your return. I have spoken this day to two men of my acquaintance in the Camden district with regard to purchase of mill seats and have made appointments to speak with several people formerly associated with the South Carolina Homespun Company for advice that you might find helpful. I am most interested in your proposed venture and have interested two others in investing, so that you may have adequate capital at your disposal. We should be able to start work on your mill yet this autumn if you wish, or wait until spring if you are detained in Connecticut longer than you expect. But, please, do try to come home to us as soon as you can free yourself of your obligations there. You are missed more than I can say.

You will find that things have changed here since you left. Your sister Miriam was married last month to Robert Stockbook and has moved to his plantation near Beaufort. How we do wish your letter had reached us sooner, that we might have postponed the joyous event until your return. Miriam, of course, sends her regrets, but she is happily situated at Tradewinds now, far from all she grew up knowing. We do not expect to see her for some time. Eliza has a young man, too, but then, Eliza has always attracted young men. No marriage is expected at the present time.

Aunt Lily writes that Joseph has bought half ownership in the mill. They plan to begin making sailcloth, along with their other cottons. Adelle finds her work as a teacher to the mill children most rewarding, her mother says.

Business manages to go on here, although it is overly susceptible to the direction of the wind from the Crown. Still, shipping on coasting vessels and privateers makes for a goodly amount of legal work, and I am ever behind. The excitement of your proposed venture consumes me, and I hope I am right when I say your future will be more profitable than my own. There are better times ahead, for both of us, I pray.

We hold you ever in our thoughts and prayers and await word of your return.

Your loving father,
Whitcomb
Gairden

Fox read the letter over and then over again. If much had happened to him during his years away from home, much had happened to the rest of his family as well. Somehow he had held them stopped in time—Miriam still a young girl, Eliza barely old enough to stay up for a ball, Papa a respected lawyer. Times had been difficult in Charleston, Fox could tell from Papa's tone, and people there were counting on war to bring them out of it just as people here were. But then, they hadn't seen the British navy. They didn't know how the men-of-war could be lined up bow to stern and make a string halfway across the Atlantic when the United States couldn't make a string across New York harbor. But war was on everyone's mind. His own, too.

Fox reread the first paragraph, about his own mill. He had already begun making drawings and taking measurements. Whatever he could transfer directly from this mill to the one he would build for himself would save time and money. Of course, his mill would spin cotton, not wool, but the principle was the same. He made a mental note to spend a day or two at the Ludding Cotton Mill near Meriden. He'd happened to talk with the agent for that enterprise in New Haven one day not more than a month back, and the fellow had invited him to come for a visit, saying his mill was a much more advanced one than some of the others nearer to Derby. At first the idea had seemed out of the question to Fox, but now that his own mill was closer to becoming a reality, Fox felt himself reaching out for any kind of information that would help him, even if it meant a good day's ride or more.

It was already the middle of September. Papa's letter had taken a long time in reaching him. Still, if he could leave New Haven by mid-October, he could be back in Charleston within a week or two to get things ready for an early winter ground breaking. That would mean the mill wouldn't be ready to open for nearly another year beyond that, but if there was sufficient capital to carry the plans through those months, things should still go smoothly. Perhaps the need for sailcloth would be even greater by then than it was now. Either sailcloth or Union Jacks, Fox thought without smiling.

The Beaver Creek Woolen Mill had been running for almost a month now, but not without its share of difficulties. Buffin and his men had broken camp and gone off to their next job, a new mill seat upstream on the Housatonic, when the newly repaired gate began to give way, upsetting the flow necessary for the steady running of the wheel and gears and belts, and therefore of the actual production machines. Fox and the new agent, a small Ulsterman named Allen McNitt, did their best to make the repairs, but Fox could see that a whole new gate was what was called for, and he had to make the ride to the town of New Milford to retrieve Buffin, who sputtered, "Couldn't be," until he saw the gate for himself and said, "I'll be damned," instead.

"We *need* to be dammed," Fox replied.

"That's an old joke," Buffin said, knocking him roughly against the shoulder, "but at least you're still laughin', an' that's good."

Once the gates were repaired, though, the mill ran smoothly. Fox had hired people from as far away as Ireland, and from as close as New Haven, but there was no one from Derby. No one who knew anything about the Vardrys had applied, and Fox knew that Anne Vardry's troubles were not completely behind her yet. Still, with the coming of three families to work at the mill, she now at least had the company of some women, though they were older than she. For the time being they were all cramped into the single boarding house that Buffin's men had put up before they left, but soon three more small houses would be complete, these built by James and Stewart Karr, the same two men who ran the sawmill and repair shop in the mill. The mill site was beginning to look like a little town—Vardryville, she could call it if she wanted to someday. But then, she wouldn't want to.

Now it was Fox who slept in a tiny corner of the mill's second floor. Anne Vardry had moved into the boarding house, partly against her wishes, and Fox had given up his tent as the nights became cooler, and moved his cot to her old corner. He would be leaving soon. He did not want to take up a room in the boarding house when so many were already crowded in there. But he did eat with the rest of them. And each day, he saw Anne become more a part of the group.

"Will you be attending services today with the Goodings, Anne?" he asked one Sunday morning as the other boarders began to hurry out and just the two of them were left in the dining room with its unfinished floors and walls. The building was little more than a shell, one that the Karr brothers were going to have to try to finish before winter set in.

"Will you?" she surprised him by asking.

"Yes, of course. We'd be happy for your company." He tried to guess what her answer would be from looking at her face, but he couldn't tell. She was looking at the bowl in front of her and not at him. But he kept looking at her, unwilling to give up, waiting for her answer.

"I don't . . . I don't think so." She looked up then, but barely met his eyes.

"You know it *is* a meetinghouse, not a courthouse. You'll be left alone. I'll see to that."

"You see to everything, Fox. I don't really know how to thank you." Now she did look at him, anxious, tentative.

"Your going out and meeting people once again will

be thanks enough for me. In a few weeks, after I've gone, you'll forget there ever was a first time back to church, or out with others."

"In a few weeks? That soon? I hadn't thought it would be so soon." Once again her eyes were downcast, and Fox felt all he'd gained a few minutes ago being dashed once again.

"I've had a letter from my father—I think I told you I'd written him soon after I arrived here. In any case, my father has already started making inquiries about a mill seat for me. He wants me to start as soon as I get back." Still she did not look up. He reached across the table and lifted her chin with his fingertips. "And so, you see, I must go. I've stayed here overlong as it is. The sooner I go, the better you will do."

"Do you miss someone there?" she asked, looking him in the eye at long last.

"No," he answered truthfully. "No one special. It's not that." Now he looked away. "We'd best get ourselves ready for the walk to the meetinghouse. Services start at ten o'clock. You'll be ready?"

"I . . ." Once again she hesitated. Fox thought he could hear a refusal being formed on her lips, but then she seemed to brighten. "I will only require a few minutes."

"Very well then!" Fox tried not to show the amount of enthusiasm he felt at this response. Too much might scare her off. She was, as Buffin had remarked, much like a frightened doe. But she had no cause to be frightened of him. She could trust him . . . unless, of course, she was remembering the act that had brought him here in the first place. Some of the glow at her acceptance faded, but not all of it. "I shall be back for you shortly," he said, and when he closed the door behind him, he smiled.

* * *

Fox always thought of Derby as a long place when he looked at it from the hilltop that gave him a view of the whole valley. The Housatonic was navigable all the way up to Derby, and many vessels were tied up at the Derby wharves, as well as across the river toward Huntington, beyond which several ranges of irregular hills gave the horizon a layered look that dissolved into gray sky somewhere in what was called "the West." A string of houses and shops clutching at the river's shore, Derby stretched for almost a mile and a half. Near the middle of it stood the Presbyterian meetinghouse, an old frame building badly in need of repairs. There was talk of tearing it down. The Episcopal church nearby, meanwhile, was a neat, modern building. The town had been incorporated in 1675 when only twelve families lived there and its Indian name had been Paugasset. Now there looked to be almost a hundred houses along the narrow street.

Fox thought of Camden, where his own mill would one day soon harness the water of the Wateree River to run its spinning machines. It would be an advantage to have the water power the Housatonic had, rather than the slower pace of the Carolina streams. And it would be an advantage to have vessels come to port to trade, rather than to have to ship goods to port. And it would be good to have so many new people coming in from Europe each month, as happened here, all looking for work, to fill the new manufactory. But then, it was also good to have the mill close to the cotton fields —and Fox hoped desperately that that one factor would make up for all the others that seemed to favor this site in Connecticut over his own in South Carolina.

He felt Anne Vardry's eyes on him as they paused to rest on the hilltop on the way back from the meetinghouse in the valley. Abe and Tillie Gooding had gone on ahead, partly trying to keep up with their three children who ran instead of walked, and partly, Fox knew, trying to be mindful of their place as separate from that of the mill owner, and even of the agent. No matter how close the quarters in which they lived, or how frail the thread of ownership that kept Anne Vardry ahead of her creditors, she was still the owner.

Anne was winded from the climb and took in a series of deep breaths as she looked out across the valley and then at Fox. He might have taken her arm, but he, too, had a sense of his place, and did not.

"You look like you're looking at it for the last time," she said, once again letting her eyes sweep the panorama of river and ridges spread out before them. "Are you?"

"I don't suppose. I expect there will be trips to the wharf, or the store. I'll see it again. But I wonder if I'll ever see it again just like this, with the sun gleaming on the bright colors of the houses and the deep greens of the leaves. In another week or two, those leaves will be all golds and reds, and very beautiful, but nonetheless a harbinger of the winter to come."

"And you wish, instead, for the gentler days of a Carolina winter. I can hear it in your voice. The winters here are not so harsh . . . you'd see that if you stayed. I'll pay you, or give you that one-quarter I offered before—whatever it will take to make you stay. If you'll please just stay."

"You can't afford to pay me yet, and even if you could, I couldn't take it. It's not what I came for. I came to help you—no, that's not quite right. I came to help myself. And I think what happened is that you helped me more than I helped you. I feel, at last, that I can go on with my life, Anne."

"And what if I cannot go on with mine?" Her eyes shifted as she spoke, so that she looked at him only from the corner of her eye.

"But you can! You're the owner of a fine mill, one of the few women who enjoys such a position, I might add. And you're getting out again, making your place in the town . . ." He took her hand and she did not withdraw it.

After a moment she met his eyes with a frankness he hadn't seen before. "Because I went to meeting once? That's hardly worthy of being called 'making a place.'"

"But it is. It's the start, and I've always known all you needed was the start."

"Let's sit a moment, Fox, and enjoy the beauty of the day a bit longer before we go on." She motioned to a boulder in the meadow near the road and started toward it, surprising Fox with the easy way in which she spoke and moved. He followed and took a place beside her. The rock had soaked up sun the whole while they had been at meeting and now was warm even through Fox's breeches. He smiled at the pleasure of it, and she did, too, as she placed her hands on it, though none of the heat could have gone through the skirts and petticoats she was wearing. The sun fell warm on their faces, and they sat quietly for a short while, lazied by this last whisper of summer's breath.

"I had promised myself never to do this again," she said.

"To do what?" Fox looked up but found her gaze fixed on the river.

"To let myself feel beauty. To feel at all, really. I promised myself I would never open myself to the world again. I told myself that no one could be trusted except myself. And then you came." She turned to meet Fox's eyes, and in hers he could see what he had always known must be there. Not reaching out to touch it required concentration. He clasped his hands around one knee as he pulled his foot up on top of the boulder.

"I didn't do anything you wouldn't have done by yourself sooner or later. You were grieving. You were alone. But one day it would have come to an end. I just came along before that happened." Fox smiled. "I've wondered sometimes what would have happened if I'd stayed three years ago, when I first came. Would things have been different? Would I still have ended up at sea, impressed by the British, losing my friend Grish? Would I have been able to face some of the challenges I have now?"

"It was meant to be this way. For both of us." She shifted on the rock just then, and he felt the touch of her elbow in the same way he had felt the touch of her hand that day at Buffin's camp. Unintentional but powerful. He moved over, out of her space, aware of her in a way he could not afford to be. He was leaving. He was putting this part of his life behind him so that he might get on with the next part. She was doing the same. And they could not do it together.

"Perhaps," he said. "Perhaps it was. We'll never know otherwise, I suppose. You might think of coming to Charleston sometime, for a visit I mean, once the mill is making some money for you. You'd like the gentler winters. . . ." He let the sentence drift off. She wouldn't come to Charleston. Hugh Vardry's face appeared before him to remind him that she wouldn't.

Fox stood up, stretching in the sunshine of midafternoon. They had eaten their fill at the lawn dinner after services, and now he could have easily lain down on the warm grass and napped away an hour but for the odd feeling inside him of wanting to stay here with Anne Vardry, and at the same time of wanting to get as far away from here as he could go. "The others will be wondering if we're lost," he said as he swallowed back a yawn. "Shall we go?" He offered his arm to her as she rose, and she slipped hers into it, leaning on him as she picked her way through the drying weeds of the meadow but then dropping it once they reached the road again.

"In the morning," he said, "I'd like you in the spinning room with me first thing. We'll go over the machines, make certain you know their weak points so you can be looking for problems before they occur. Same thing with the carding room, fulling room, picking. Looms, I think, you already know a great deal more about than I do, and that's good, because starting this week I'm going to tell the workers that they answer to McNitt, and he answers to you."

"No! Absolutely not. I cannot. I'm not ready. I'll—"

"I'll be right there with you while you get the feel of it, don't worry. That's why it's good to do it this week. Gives you plenty of time. Gives the workers a chance to know what you expect, as well. No point in their working to please me, when pleasing you may be something completely different. Starting tomorrow, I'll be truly your agent, carrying out your orders."

"No, you can't. I'm not ready," she pleaded again. "Please . . ."

"You're ready, Anne. Just as ready as you were to go to the meetinghouse today. Just as ready as you were to get the mill running again in the first place. You just don't think you're ready. That's why I'll stay on a few days, until you know you're ready. Don't worry. I won't abandon you."

It sounded like another pledge, Fox thought as soon as he heard himself utter the words. And why was he making such a pledge when he had such definite plans to leave? In ten days he would take the packet to New York, a coach to Philadelphia as he had promised in his letter to Adelle, and then sail to Charleston. He would be there by October first, well ahead of the rough seas that could come later in the month. But he had to admit it, there was the tug of her wants to be considered, and it was not such a gentle tug as he'd once thought it would be.

"You'll stay until I know I'm ready?"

"I suppose I'll have to," he said, trying to tease her out of what he could see was a rapidly rising wave of apprehension again, "because if I were to leave when *I* knew you were ready, I'd have to leave today, and I'm not packed yet. So we'll wait a few days. You'll be ready. I promise it."

The road was dry beneath their feet, and here and there pockets of sand showed the tracks of those who had gone before them. The little mill village was quiet as they approached, the children busy with their Bible readings, and their parents engaged in teaching them.

"I don't think I can go in there just now," she said, looking toward the boarding house. "I'd like to walk some more. Beside the river, I think. Would you join me?"

"Of course. The miller has given me no tasks for today, it being the Sabbath, and so I'm free to do as I please. I might take a fishing pole, though, unless you object, and stay to fish for a while."

"No objection. I would welcome a meal of fresh fish tonight if you are successful." Her look wagered she didn't think he would be.

Fox thrust out his chin and accepted the challenge with a chuckle. Taking the pole he had fashioned from a piece of willow during the days he camped with Buffin's men, Fox caught up with Anne at the edge of the gorge, and the two fell into step on the path along the river above the millpond. Buffin's men had fished daily, rising while mist still steamed from the cool waters into the sun-heated summer mornings. Now that the mill's bell rang every morning at dawn, there was little chance for anyone to fish. Midday was a poor time to fish, he knew, but perhaps by late afternoon, as they finished their walk, he might wet his line and find a hungry bass eager to strike.

Where the path was wide enough, Fox and Anne walked side by side. In the narrow places, he went ahead, holding branches aside for her where he could. They walked in a play of shadows, interrupted now and again by the sun that poked in amongst the branches overhead, until they came up onto the top of a small bluff, perhaps twenty feet above the water's edge, where only a few low junipers hugged the rocky soil. Below them, the water fell over jagged rocks and boulders worn smooth by its timeless flow. A small tributary joined Beaver Creek just above them, cutting a giant Y in the landscape before the waters joined and tumbled into this rocky gorge. Cool air rose from the rapids with a refreshing rush that Fox felt as he leaned over to look down.

"Ummmm," Anne said, obviously feeling it, too. "Isn't it a lovely place? I like to walk up here and imagine living up here in a big, stone house that looks out over the river."

"You will one day, Anne. One day soon, if the wool business goes the way it looks as if it might. Colonel Humphreys built himself a nice big house—you can, too."

"I expect I'll lag behind Colonel Humphreys by a good bit, but I would like my own house someday. Wouldn't you?"

"I don't know. I haven't thought about it much. I've grown so accustomed to a small room, or a blanket on top of a stack of sails, or a tent and a cot. I've put my thoughts to building mills, I suppose, and not to building houses." He had to shake his head as he realized how odd that must seem to her, and yet it was quite true. He had been engrossed in hanging on to his life during his years at sea, and in her mill once back on land. But now that he thought about it, about his family's stately Charleston double house, he knew that those were fond thoughts, but not driving ones. A fine house was the mark of a man's success, but so far he had not been able to afford the luxury of such a mark. He was still busy mopping up his failures. Today, in the sun, with the tumbling waters far below him, though, he could imagine himself in a fine house—but somehow he couldn't imagine where. The house, as he pictured it, seemed to float on air, waiting for a site.

"And I left Uxbridge wanting a home, thinking Hugh would provide a fine one. Instead I found a small one waiting, and that was all right. But then it was gone and I had nothing. All the years I lived in the mill, I told myself that someday I would have a fine house on this bluff. You say you think I will."

"I do. Though I must say I'm surprised you would want to stay here, in this place, with all its memories. But, in any case, soon the house James and Stewart are working on will be ready, and you can establish yourself as separate from the workers, even if it's only by a few feet. Later, when your house up here is finished, you can use that house for your agent."

"I don't know that I want to be separate again." She didn't look at him as she spoke, but he could see that she chewed her lip nervously as she waited for his reply.

"You're just beginning to actually *live* here, Anne. For years you've just been existing—the way I was on board the *Iago*. We've both been given a new start, and it may take us a few tries to make it all work, but we've nothing to lose by trying. If you choose to do it by staying in the boarding house, then I'd say you know what's best. And I'd be happy for you."

"I don't want you to leave," Anne said, her eyes on

the ground where she rubbed the toe of her shoe into the sandy spot between two rocks.

"But you can run the mill, we've just been over that. You—"

"It's not the mill . . . I . . . I don't think I can stand it if you go." She was trying hard to hold back tears, Fox could see, but her mouth quivered at the corners and her eyes blinked again and again, each time wetter than the first.

The touch of her when he drew her into his arms hit with a thousand times the force of the touch of her elbow just a short while earlier. She was small, and as he held her to him he felt his arms could have encircled her twice around with some room still left over. He kept trying to draw her close enough to use up all that slack, close enough to stop her shaking, all the while aware of her touch, her nearness. In her was the human warmth he had not felt in the arms of a doxy in Liverpool, or anywhere else for far too long.

"There, there," he whispered, rocking slightly side to side as he held her. "Don't cry. Please don't. You won't miss me. You'll be so busy you won't even know I'm gone. And you'll have friends to be with, and you'll go to the meetinghouse on Sundays. And one day soon some rich man will come and want to buy your mill, and he'll want your hand with it. He'll build you that big house you want so much."

He felt her head thrash back and forth above the circle of his arms, and heard her mutter, "No, no, no," and he did not let her go but held her even closer. If he had, even for a moment, let himself feel what every ounce of him wanted to feel for her, he would have eased her down to the warm grass and loved her and satisfied the great craving that had seized him. And if he did, in those few moments of ecstasy, he would undo all that he had done on his journey here. This was her life he was tampering with, as well as his own. Like the rivers, they had come here from different sources, converging into this time, but they could not flow on as one. Like the rivers, their sources did not disappear but only kept renewing themselves to flow over the same jagged rocks and through the same narrow gorges. Aeons of nights and days were needed to smooth the sharp rocks into boulders, and they did not have aeons. They had a lifetime. That was all.

"I can't stay. You know that, Anne," he said. "It's only natural to fear what may lie ahead, to want someone to face it with you, but I'm not leaving you here alone. You know the work yourself, and you have McNitt to help. As the mill grows, you'll grow with it, and need no one's help. I'll do the same. I don't know yet what faces me at home, either. But I know I have to go there and try on my own."

"No you don't! You could stay here. Anything you have to prove to yourself can be proven here. Going a thousand miles away won't change anything. What can you do there that you can't do here?"

"I can find out what I am without the ghost of Hugh Vardry to drive me," Fox said, his voice no more than a whisper.

She stepped out of the circle of his arms and turned, just enough to look over her shoulder at him. She was really quite young, he thought. Her profile against the afternoon sun was a strong one. Her eyes appraised his, her nose tilted slightly upward and her lips no longer pouted but set themselves into a firm line, full and inviting. "Then I suppose I must do the same," she said, wiping away the drying tears with the back of her hand.

Fox stepped toward her again, uncertainty thick within him. Taking her by the shoulder, he turned her gently toward him once again. "You will do wonderfully well, Anne," he said. And then, knowing he shouldn't, he let his hand slide up her neck and into the richness of curl that pulled against itself where the hair was tucked up inside her bonnet. She pulled at the bonnet strings and let it drop back onto the ground. As it fell, Fox took out the pins that held her dark hair in its familiar, severe knot, letting his fingers spread it like angel wings across her shoulders. She turned her head this way and that, closing her eyes like a purring cat. Once again she stepped into his arms, this time not in pain the way she had before, but in want, and as she moved against him he lost the will that had kept him from touching her all these long weeks.

"Anne, Anne," he said, burying his face against her neck and touching his lips to her pale skin at last, and then to her lips. Her hands eagerly traced his eyebrows and cheekbones, earlobes and jawline, and she spread her fingers wide as she moved them up and down his chest, and after a while her hands urged him downward to the grass with her, where they lay in each other's arms in the afternoon sun. Her skirts slid up around her calves as they moved about in each other's arms, and at last he dared to touch that exposed softness, then let his hand slip beneath the folds to discover her sleek thighs, temptation luring him to where he had promised himself he would not go.

"I think it's time I caught some fish for our supper," he whispered, forcing out the words, "before I start what I dare not finish."

"No, Fox. Don't stop." She huddled against him, one hand slipping inside his shirt, her fingers exploring his chest in the very way he longed to explore hers.

"I must, Anne." He sat up, still beside her but his hands once again firmly clasped in front of him. "I killed your husband, Anne. And no matter how despicable he was, that memory will always stand between us. I will never be able to love you freely while that memory is with me, as it is at this moment."

"And you won't even try," she said. There was a coolness in her words, and a bit of malice, if Fox admitted the truth, but he didn't want to.

"I can't." He got up and started back down the path the way they had come, stopped and threw in his hook and worm. After a few minutes he heard her step, but she kept on going.

Tillie Gooding was already done cleaning up the boarding house kitchen when Fox returned a half hour later with the one fish he had caught.

"'Tis enough to feed ye, Mr. Gairden. Let me cook it," she offered.

Fox tried to look around for Anne without seeming to but sensed Tillie knew what he was doing. Anyway, it made no difference. Anne Vardry was not there.

"Thanks, Tillie, but I'll cook it myself. I'll make a fire outdoors since everyone's eaten here already." He went out, closing the door behind him, took a half dozen steps and then winged the bass out into the trees beyond the buildings. "No good at fishing either," he muttered, and walked back to the mill, not even hungry.

11

Two weeks later, Fox went from man to youth, just by going home to Charleston again. Inside he felt a man's failures and a man's energy, but to his family he was the Francis Marion Gairden who had gone away a confused nineteen-year-old. Until they received word of his impressment onto the *Iago*, they had thought him lost at sea, and so they had preserved him in their minds as the carefree young man they remembered. It took all of his diplomatic skills to let them know he had changed. He had been away from Charleston for three years, but he had not forgotten its subtleties.

Crossing the bar in from New Haven that first day, Fox found Charleston diminished in ways that only someone who had been away from it for a while would notice. There were ships in the harbor, but not as many as he remembered. And there was a quietness about it —little of the raucous energy he'd seen in northern and British ports. Coasting vessels came and went, trying to make their runs either within or without the limits of the ever-changing navigation laws. Cotton was loaded. Rice, too. But trade with England was still restricted, and unless some negotiations between President Madison and the Crown led to a treaty soon, there would soon be no trade at all, but war instead.

At first he told himself it was that Charleston's gentility carried over into the way business was conducted at the docks and in the taverns, but after a week or two he knew that wasn't true. Charleston was no longer the most important port on the southern coast: New Orleans had taken precedence as the purveyor of goods from the West to a steady stream of ships that would carry them up the coast and off to the rest of the world. They might stop at Charleston, but they did not *have* to stop at Charleston.

The city, though, still seemed to think of itself as the pinnacle of the cotton trade, the social center of the seaboard and the answer to all aspirations after gracious living. And, Fox had to admit, life was gay and social graces were well honed and cotton had once made planters rich. But there was a hollowness to it all that he didn't think was there just because he felt an emptiness.

He had left Derby the morning after he and Anne had spoken their last heated words on the bluff, and he had come straight to Charleston without stopping in Philadelphia because he could not face Adelle. Others would leave questions unasked, but not Adelle. She would not have to ask. She would know something had happened between him and the widow Vardry. The last time he had seen Adelle, he had thought he might fall in love with her someday—he had even teased about marrying cousins, and he had meant it. But so much had happened. And now he wasn't certain it was in him to love anymore. Perhaps that had been taken away from him just as Grandfather had, just as Grish had. Still, he often thought of Anne Vardry the way she had looked that sunny September afternoon, her profile etched against the bright blue sky. He had wanted her, and yet taking the honorable course had once again caused her pain. The sadness of having done that made him feel years older than the young man his family thought him to be.

His parents' life was unchanged. There were servants to care for the house and do the cooking. Papa went off to his office each day, but came home by midafternoon for dinner and stayed to spend the evening unless another social occasion called for his going out. The first week Fox was home he received callers nearly every day—old friends from school, friends of his family. Then his mother gave a buffet in his honor one evening, and many of these same people came again, most of them to remark on his good fortune in breaking out of the hands of the British and on coming back to Charleston. Any mention of where he had been in between was discreetly left unsaid. Unpleasantness was rigorously ignored; his duel with Hugh Vardry was never mentioned in his hearing.

Mama paraded any number of lovely young women past him, certain to make a match for her Francis with one of the good families of Charleston, and it was only with all the breeding she had instilled in him in his early years that he was able to say to her with a smile that he approved of her intentions but could not indulge himself just yet when there was so much to be done toward his new venture at Camden, and that when he could be indulged he would speak to her first.

He stayed in his father's house for two long weeks while he met with the investors his father had mentioned, and while he made his plans to go back to Columbia and renew his acquaintance with Colonel Taylor, whose mill he had worked in during his year at college. Fox tried to keep his mind occupied, to set some goals for himself and to not let himself be lulled into the slumber that was Charleston.

"No, Jurian," he told his old friend at a small dancing party the Hudsons gave in his honor one of his first evenings home. "I'm afraid I can't go out shooting with you tomorrow, no matter how many quail there are."

"But you must. Let your father take care of these money matters for you. What should you care of it?"

"I plan to own the mill, all by myself, as soon as I can pay back the investors. I want to know who they are and see that the terms are reasonable."

"But that would be work, Fox. *Work!*" Jurian spoke the word as if his mouth were full of castor oil. "I leave that to others."

"You have a fourth of your father's plantation now, don't you? Surely you have work to do?"

"I leave it to my overseer. Good man. I get out there once a year—like now, for the hunting."

"You must have great trust in him."

"No reason not to. Besides, I find the life here in the city more to my liking. Not cut out for the life of the country squire, me. Of course, you wouldn't know about the boredom of an Ashley River plantation because you've always had the life of the city. I grew up on the land."

"Of course," Fox said, picking up the not-so-subtle reminder that his father's position as a lawyer was not quite as solid socially as a planter's. Before he left Charleston, the remark would have galled him. Now, he found, he didn't really care. He took a drink of the sweet punch Jurian's mother's cook had prepared for the party and looked around the room, noting the familiar faces and how they had changed while he'd been away. "Your sister is pretty as ever," he observed, changing the subject.

"Still the little minx who had to golf with us that day, though."

"Is she? And not married yet? Too bad she got all the looks in the family, Jurian," he teased.

"Ha-ha, Fox. She's been waiting for you to come back."

"I doubt Sally's ever waited for a man in her life, Jurian. And certainly not for me."

"I wouldn't be too certain, old man." Jurian laughed, nudging Fox in the ribs. "She often asks about you."

"Only to make conversation, no doubt."

"Then what you mean is, you've not waited for her. She'll be furious, you know."

"She'll get over it. I don't do well where women are concerned, Jurian. I'm giving them up for good—Sally included. Devoting myself wholly to my new mill the way you're devoting yourself to Charleston's pleasures."

Jurian had an easy way with a joke, even on himself, and let ribbing bother him no more than low cotton prices, when the conversation came around to that. "They'll rise again, once Mr. Madison gets this shipping business straightened out with England," he said, sounding a more serious note. "And in the meantime, you'll have a good supply of the stuff for this new venture of yours. The South Carolina Homespun Company is closing its doors, though, Fox. No money in spinning cotton. Just grow it and sell it, I say. Leave the lint and the noise and expense of it to someone else."

"Homespun didn't have as good a site as the ones I saw up north, Jurian. That's part of the problem. I sometimes think I should have stayed up there—every river up there has waterfalls that can run wheels."

"But you have your eye on a mill seat, is that right?"

"I do. Or at least I did, before I left." Fox was able to mention that time without pain, but Jurian was clearly uncomfortable and unable to respond. "I'll be going up there early next month, as soon as I can, actually. Why not come along with me? You might find yourself some hunting along the way."

"Thank you, Fox, but I'll be getting Dublin Knight ready for race week. Can't really leave—"

"Fox Gairden! You've been gone too long!" Sally Hudson interrupted her brother with no more care than she had interrupted his golf game over three years earlier. "And I'm still waiting for the dance you promised me." Her gown of white silk was cut low in the front and the skirt draped elegantly from its high waist, accentuated with a silver braid. The long sleeves of gossamer net were studded with small silver brooches and edged in silver braid and a filmy lace. A short train trailed behind her, as if she were a princess, and around her head she wore a band of pearls caught in a silver clasp above her ear, her short-cropped curls hiding the jewels here and there.

"Go on, Fox. Don't stand here keeping me from the ladies all evening," Jurian said with a gentle shove.

"My pleasure," Fox replied, offering Sally his arm. The crystals hanging from beneath the lamps on the mantel reflected rainbows that dappled her bare shoulders as they circled by. She was lovely, but Fox did not for a moment believe she had spent the last three years waiting for him. He saw the eyes that followed her around the room. Among them, the most obvious belonged to Richard Celestine, the man he would be meeting with tomorrow in regard to investing in his mill. One of a long line of Celestines who had come to Charleston with other Huguenots early in the last century, Richard was mainly a cotton merchant rather than a rice and indigo merchant the way his father and grandfather had been before him. Cotton was making him richer than his ancestors had ever dreamed of being, and he certainly had money to invest if Fox could make the return look attractive enough.

Celestine had lost his wife soon after Fox left Charleston, and in Sally he no doubt saw a more than suitable replacement. He had danced with her twice already, but then, so had several others. Just now her favor fell on Fox, and she smiled up, looking into his eyes with fond interest. Fox glanced toward Celestine and nodded when their eyes met, but then he smiled down at Sally. Let the old man be a bit jealous, Fox thought, actually enjoying himself for the first time since he had come home. *He may be more willing to deal if he thinks having me off at a mill in Camden would remove a rival.*

"Thank you for the dance, Sally," he said, returning her to her mother's side and mumbling a few appropriate words about his appreciation for the party, then excusing himself to take a cigar outside. Avoiding the crush of men talking of war and politics at the front door, he slipped down the back hall and was about to go out the door when someone caught his eye. A young slave girl of about fifteen, he guessed—not so much younger than Sally herself—walked by, shoulders slumped but head held carefully erect. White cloth bandages covered her ears, wrapping around her head and down under her chin. On the left side, blood had seeped through the cloths in an ear-sized oval.

The girl kept on walking away from him, but Fox stood unable to take his eyes off from her.

"Fox? I'm coming with you." Sally was hurrying down the long hall, her slippers making a scuffing noise.

"What happened to that girl?"

"Papa caught her listening at his door during some very important business. He had her ears cut off."

"Sally, no. He couldn't have. I remember your father. He'd never have done anything like that."

"New slaves. Different from before you left, Fox. Papa said if he didn't make an example of her, the others would all be doing the same thing—and heaven only knows what else as well. We have to keep order. You do remember that, don't you, even though you've been away?"

"I'm afraid I don't remember much at all, Sally. I—"

"But then you've never had slaves, only those few free blacks. Slaves are different. Like children, Papa always says. They have to be made to mind. Ceely, there, won't disobey again. Papa said."

"I'm sure she won't."

She seemed to take his words for agreement and subtly shifted her shoulders, exposing even more breast than her otherwise generous cleavage had as they danced. She meant for him to notice—that, too, he had learned since he'd been away. "Let's not talk about her, Fox. I snuck out when Mama started talking to Mrs. Willett. I want to hear all about you." Once again she curved her shoulders forward, leaning against him conspiratorially as she led him out the door to where the night air was cool. Her gown gapped agreeably in the front, and she watched him as he let his eyes glide toward her bosom.

"Francis Marion Gairden," she said as she noiselessly closed the door behind them, "you *did* grow up while you were away." He felt her eyes appraise him, as if he were a new gown she might try on. "I am so glad you're home."

Anyone else in his position would be glad himself. The loveliest young woman he had seen since he came back was making sure she captured his attention. That long ago day on Harleston's Green he would have been only too happy to oblige her in any way she desired had she pressed against him the way she had just now, but tonight the invitation was less welcome. And then there was the matter of the slave girl. "I don't think you should be out here alone with me, Sally," he said, "old friend or no. We've both grown up while I was away."

"Are you afraid Papa will cut off your ears if he catches us?"

Fox was caught off guard by the easy way she referred to the inhumane treatment of the slave. "I suppose," he said. "I suppose that even if I've been away, I still remember Charleston gossip. I wouldn't want you to be harmed by it."

"I know how to avoid the gossips, Fox."

"But I don't, Sally."

He heard her sigh softly. "You are still a gentleman, Fox Gairden, no matter how long you've been gone."

"Jurian Hudson tells me they call you Fox. There was once another man in Charleston called Fox. Foxworth Dunne was his name. He was a pirate, I believe." Richard Celestine leaned back in his chair and flicked an invisible something from his fingertip as he spoke, his eyes never leaving Fox's face.

Fox managed to smile at Celestine's barb. "Fortunately I'm not named for him, sir, but for the Swamp Fox. He is one of my father's heroes."

"Of course, Gairden, of course. Jurian said you're looking for yet another investor for the mill you propose to build."

"I am. We plan to have four hundred spindles. The machines have already been ordered from Rhode Island. The balance will be due on them in two months' time."

"I'm not interested in machines, Gairden. I'm interested in who's to run them. I trust you'll manage your Nigras efficiently. That will make you a good manager —the kind whose enterprises men like me are eager to invest in. I could venture up to four thousand dol—"

"I do not intend to hire Negroes," Fox said, ignoring the offer.

"And whom *do* you intend to hire? There aren't enough white people in the upcountry to work a mill. The people there are growing cotton and making more money than they ever could working for you."

"I'm not so sure that's true. There are poor folks up

there, too. Squatters bumped off their land once cotton went high. Small tenants not making enough to get bigger."

"Slaves, Gairden. Labor in South Carolina is done by slaves. You've been away. Perhaps you've forgotten that. These other people will work for you until they need to get their own work done—then they'll leave you. They're too damned independent. Slaves do what they're told, when they're told."

"I've no doubt slaves could be trained to do the work. I just don't want to have to deal with overseers, and I don't want to own slaves. I don't want to have to worry about whether they want to stab me in my sleep some night." Fox lifted an eyebrow, knowing he had broached a touchy point, the unspoken topic that never left the mind of any white person of wealth. Slaves came with a price that was more than what was paid at the market. His grandfather had told him that when he was just a little boy, but it wasn't until just now that he really knew what that meant.

"Certainly you know best, Fox, what you need, but I'm not investing in something as chancy as all that. If you should reconsider, we can talk again. I shouldn't be surprised if you change your mind after you find out there aren't enough men up there to run a mill."

"It won't be a large operation, not at first," Fox said. "And women and children can do much of the work. I'll manage."

"I suppose you find the idea of hiring women appealing. Women like you, don't they?"

Fox straightened at the inference and remembered the way Celestine had watched him as he danced with Sally Hudson. "Women like men who treat them well, I think," he said, allowing an inference of his own. "In the mills I saw in Connecticut and Pennsylvania, most of the work is done by women and children. My uncle owns such a mill in Philadelphia."

"Ah, but there are immigrants coming there every day looking for work. That's not the case here."

"Not yet, but now that slaves can no longer be imported—"

"You've been away too long, Gairden," Celestine said with a laugh. "Slaves are unloaded from Africa somewhere in South Carolina every few days. Not in Charleston Harbor, of course, but in coves where they go unnoticed. There are no jobs here for immigrants— and no immigrants for mills. Think about it. You'll see I'm right."

Fox stood, seeing only that unless he was willing to run his mill with slave labor, Celestine was not going to invest there. And perhaps he was right. Perhaps he would have to change his thinking on that. But then he thought of all the mill seats in the North, and of one in particular, and he knew that he could go there and fill a mill with workers in a day's time.

He looked at Celestine's grand house, at the glossy black carriage, and remembered his elegant clothes. I will have these things someday, too, he thought, but I will not climb across the backs of slaves to get them.

❧ Part Three ❧

1812–1815

12

June 1812

"Mr. Gairden! Mr. Gairden! There's going to be war. I heard it in town." Jake Merrill didn't unhitch the team or even tie them up before he ran to the gable end of the mill where Fox was replacing shingles on the roof, and shouted the news.

"For certain? What I mean is, has it started?" Fox took a nail from between his lips and looked over the edge of the roof down to where the millwright Merrill waited, hand above his eyes to shield them from the late June sun.

"I don't know if there's been any shooting yet. Nobody knows. But they voted on it in Washington. All except the Federalists. They're pretty stirred up, from what I heard. Up in Massachusetts they're goin' hungry for a day to protest, but folks in Camden seemed relieved that Jemmy Madison finally decided to do something."

Merrill was only three or four years older than Fox, but he had been damming up creeks and building mills for over ten years, first as an apprentice to his father and then on his own after his father died. He was a short, broad-shouldered man whom Fox had never seen without his leather vest and apron. Today he wore a straw hat to keep the sun off his face, but his shirt was soaked through with sweat, and even from where Fox sat, he could smell the odor. Not that he smelled much better. They had been working long days and even by lamplight into the nights on Fox's new mill, the Valley Cotton Mill, and no one had taken much time for bathing or anything else.

"So, the Mistress of the Seas is finally going to have to back up her demands with powder," Fox said. "High time. Perhaps she'll see she can't regulate our shipping and our goods any longer. I swear, Merrill, they've never quit thinking of us as their colonies. I heard it when I was on the *Iago*. They figured we couldn't make it without them and so they might as well keep on telling us what to do."

"So will you be signin' up? To go prove 'em wrong, I mean?"

Fox hammered in one last nail, then started down the ladder. "When I'm needed. Will you?"

"So far they haven't said what militia's to be needed, but I suppose I'll go, too. I heard in town that they're thinkin' of forcin' 'em to serve—draft, they call it—and some in Congress don't hold with the idea."

"So we may not have to make any choices at all, eh, Merrill? Just do as we're told, when we're told? Why, that would be just like being in the British navy all over again."

"And you don't sound as though you'd fancy that, Gairden."

"No. It wasn't exactly the best time of my life, those months impressed on the *Iago*. Damned miserable, in fact." He looked around him at the mill he and Merrill's crew had resurrected here on Rice Creek, just above its juncture with the Wateree near Camden. "This is the best time of my life, Jake. This is what I've been working toward since I was eighteen. At last it's ready to spin cotton for me, and even though I'd like to see the British set back on their heels, I don't know that I can leave this just yet. Perhaps the Mistress of the Seas will call off her embargo on our coast, and this will all blow over yet. I think I'll wait with signing my name until we see what's asked of us."

"Well, militia's musterin' on Wednesday. I imagine I'd best be there, since I'm about done workin' here for you, anyhow."

"You must keep me informed of what you hear."

"I will, though word travels slow enough around here. But some of the lads are eager to get their rifles at the ready."

It had been a long time since Fox fired a gun. A rifle, anyway. Aboard the *Iago* he had spent time behind a long tom and an eighteen-pounder, and there had been muskets on board for close combat, but there had been little of that. Since he had returned to solid ground, he had not had enough time to hunt, or to practice at targets. No, that one day with Hugh Vardry had been his last small-arms fire. And it had been enough to last him a good, long time. A lifetime.

"I'll try to keep at the ready as best I can here, Jake. And you let me know if I'm needed in Camden. Once we get everything running here, we'll have lots of time to drill."

"Might. Then again, might not. Got a man wants me to build a cotton mill for him over in the Sumter district. Name of Mayrant. Might be gone a good long time myself doin' that. He's got nothin' but a piece of ground, not an old place to rebuild like you took. It'll be a big piece of work."

"Then we'd both better hope Mr. Madison gets this war to come to an end a whole lot faster than he got us into it. When I think of how much disagreement there's been since back when Jefferson put the embargo on in oh-seven, I'm surprised it hasn't come to war before this. And perhaps it would have been better if it had."

"Yeah. Lot of folks lost money these past few years. But there's always some gettin' rich. Rich enough to build mills," he said with a wink.

"Like the South Carolina Homespun Company men, you mean?"

"Well, they were rich, *once.* Most of 'em probably still are. They don't put all their eggs in one basket. A few thousand here or there won't be the end of 'em."

"But it would be for me. That's why I've got to make this work."

"You will, Gairden. If anyone can, you will."

Three months later, no draft had yet been called, and Fox still drove himself night and day to get the new mill into operation, ignoring the impulses he felt to join the militia. News of the surrender of Detroit to the British by General William Hull, a Revolutionary War veteran, swept the country, but another Hull—Captain Issac Hull of the USS *Constitution*—had made a daring escape against a squadron of British frigates. Fox followed the war news with a guilty interest. The war showed no signs of being quickly concluded, and he *was* needed. But he hadn't been called, and so he did not go. Leaving meant risking what his father and two other men had invested in heavily, and he owed it to them to see the mill into profitable production.

Contrary to what Fox had expected, finding another investor after his disagreement with Richard Celestine had not been difficult. Timothy James, a gentleman from Richmond who had interests in a Rhode Island mill and was eager to do business in the heart of the cotton country as well, had contacted Whit Gairden's law office when he visited Charleston later that autumn, and the connection was quickly made. James fancied himself a new breed of investor, not content with avenues of a provincial nature, and Fox found him both somewhat of a bore and somewhat of a seer. Fortunately, he was rich enough that people indulged his boring side, and by the end of his visit, he and Fox had forged an amiable relationship.

The mill had begun to take shape by the end of 1811 and now, in September of 1812, it was taking in its first wagonloads of cotton and running them through the process from picking to spinning. Most of the cotton would be sold as yarn, but there would be a small amount of weaving done, too—just as Grandfather would have wanted, Fox thought with pride. Fox had managed to obtain one of the new fly-shuttle looms Colonel Taylor had been so taken with when Fox had worked at his mill. It offered a kind of speed that Grandfather had found worrisome. Like other weavers, he had valued speed, but had questioned the worth of a machine that would put weavers out of work. So far the fly-shuttle loom did not work well on water power, but Jake Merrill had some ideas for modifications he was hoping to work on before he left to build Mayrant's mill. In the meantime, Fox had hired three local weavers to work for him, two of them using their own looms. Gradually they would become part of the mill itself. Gradually, it would be as big as anything Colonel Humphreys could ever want, Fox told himself.

Going through the building of his own mill, Fox couldn't help but think back to Anne Vardry's mill. Starting from the ground up hadn't taken much longer than the renovation of Anne's mill had, perhaps because Vardry's ghost did not seem to lurk just beyond every turn the way it had at Beaver Creek. But the ghost was not gone completely, and every time Fox thought of Anne, it was Hugh Vardry's face he saw most vividly. He had avoided race week in Charleston last February, not just because he was too busy with the mill but because he had no desire to go back to the

scene of the duel. And he avoided thinking of Anne
Vardry, too, when he could. Letting himself want her,
even a little, had been wrong. He thought of writing to
her and trying to explain it all better than he had that
day a year ago when they had held each other close in
the late-summer sun. But he didn't do it. He wrote to
no one, saw no one. He only worked.

He did receive letters, though, and grew to look forward to the ones he received rather frequently from
Timothy James, who liked to forward advice and news
alike:

Dear Mr. Gairden:
    I have shipped this day, July 1, 1812, three of the
Edgwell jennies like those we are now using. They
are an improvement over the mules you were accustomed to at Lapham's, and the price is not extreme.
The shipping, of course, is an entirely different matter. Our newly declared war makes sea travel peril-
ous, and overland travel is exorbitant in price as well.
The cargo, however, is to be shipped aboard the *Alfred* out of Providence, and if she be making a lucky
run this, it should reach Charleston by August. I
have purchased insurance, as you requested, so that
in the event of loss . . . but we will not speak of
that. Our American navy with its seventeen ships can
most certainly keep our ports clear of British scows
that would blockade us, right Mr. Gairden? . . .

The letter had been in his possession for over two
months, but the cargo had still not arrived. So far the
mill was running with two old jennies Fox had bought
from Taylor's mill in Columbia, which had closed that
summer of 1808 when Fox returned to Charleston for
the Fourth of July that was to change his life, and then
never reopened. They were a beginning, but in no way

could the mill operate at full capacity with them alone, and Colonel Taylor had sold off the rest of the machinery. Fox's father was keeping lookout for the *Alfred*, but so far there was no sign of it in Charleston Harbor. It could have been taken as a prize, or sunken by a British ship of the line. Privateers were doing a lively business along the coast, and the fledgling American navy was winning some battles, but losing many more. It was difficult to say where his jennies might be, but again and again he imagined the *Alfred* sunken somewhere in the Atlantic and wondered why James had chanced sending them by water.

James had gone on in his letter to say that a hastily recruited and minimally trained armed force was being turned back by Indians led by the brave called Tecumseh in the lands near Lake Erie. In the western lands, too, fighting with the Indians was going on, but here in South Carolina, there was little sign that any war was even taking place. People talked about it, but there was no frenzy to compare to what had been experienced during the Revolution, at least according to the old-timers.

All the while, Fox sat waiting for the arrival of his spinning jennies, knowing that he should be fighting, too. He should be with a militia unit, or on board a ship. He should be doing something to help the nation win the war—not sitting by watching, working for personal gain. It was not what Grandfather Gairden had done thirty-five years ago. But then, this was not thirty-five years ago. And this war didn't feel much like a war as Fox saw it from the banks of Rice Creek. Along the coast where there was the threat of British invasion, no doubt it felt like war. Along the frontier, too, there would be no mistaking the war for what it was. But here, war seemed very far away.

"Many here are violently against this war," Mr. James had written.

The state refuses to call up militias or provide funds for them. There was even talk in Massachusetts of withdrawing from the Union if this business was not settled without war and disruption of the shipping business that is so vital there, but that has died down somewhat now. Still the hot breath of the Federalists blows upon those of us who favor what Mr. Madison does, and life is not altogether peaceful here. *Sedition* is a kind word for some of what passes here as free speech.

Fox folded the letter and put it back in the pigeonhole in his desk where he had been keeping it since it arrived. Political opinion had been divided enough when he had been in the North. It sounded as though it was even more so now. A few men, like Buffin, understood the threat of becoming once again European chattel, but for every one like him there were hundreds who understood only money, only their own well-being. The ideals of the Revolution had been lost in the nation that rose from its ashes. Thank God Grandfather did not have to live to see that.

Of course, Grandfather would have tried to change it. Grandfather would have talked, would have written, would have organized and would have acted. Grandfather had left his own manufactory to go off to war more than once—and it had cost him dearly. Fox looked around at the three-story structure he had built, at the machinery, at the people working there. Other people depended on him to keep it going. Other people's lives were directly intertwined with his own. Despite Richard Celestine's grim predictions, Fox had had no difficulty in finding workers. The docks were idle places now, with the British blockading the port, leaving many without work. Small cotton growers, too, could not keep growing a crop for which there was no sure market, and looked to his mill as a means of riding out the storm of war. The men depended on him as much as he depended on them.

My God, how many times must we fight this same fight? he wondered, knocking his fist against one of the rough oak beams that framed off a corner of the second floor into a small office for him. He looked around the space, which contained only a desk and two chairs. The millwright's drawings for the building were tacked across one wall, and on another hung the hank of yarn that had been the first one off the jenny when the mill opened, along with some samples of long-staple cotton and the newer green-seed cotton, both of which were being tried here. Next to them, though, hung the strip of coverlet Grandfather had been weaving the day before he died. "American Beauty," he had called it, his names for his creations always seeming to have a patriotic turn to them. He saw the country as a beauty, loved it as one might a woman, fought for it as one might for a woman. Its future filled his waking thoughts and certainly his dreams.

Fox walked over and touched the unfinished coverlet. It was made of handspun, indigo wool weft on cotton warp. Grandfather had still had his own spinners, women who had spun for him for decades and who still brought him their finely spun yarns to be woven into works of art like this one. Fox had cut it from the loom himself, the day before he left Charleston on his long journey north, folded it and put it in a drawer in his bureau, still too full of Grandfather's death and the whole Hugh Vardry situation to be able to do more than clutch at the fabric and mourn. But he had made a silent pledge that day to carry on what Grandfather had started. At the time he had thought only of carrying on the weaving tradition, but more and more he had come to understand that Grandfather represented a great deal more to him than just a weaver. Grandfather represented love. He represented ideals. He represented action.

Grandfather had made difficult choices, had left behind his own small weaving shop to go off to fight in both the Cherokee War and the Revolution. But he had had to. Life and personal safety had depended on it. In this war, people depended on these jobs he had given them. Perhaps his way of helping the country was meant to be different from Grandfather's or Francis Marion's. Not as noteworthy, not as bold as the way the Swamp Fox had served, but a service nonetheless.

Already Fox had faced some difficult choices. He had bought up the site of a mill that had failed and built on its foundation. He had turned away the opportunity for a large investment from Richard Celestine in favor of free labor. He had settled for old machines when he had hoped for newer ones. Making this mill a success could prove to be a war in itself. He needed to be here, because he needed to win it.

13

September 1, 1813

"I want to see you, Fox. Tomorrow. Our house." Sally Hudson Harnstron whispered as she caressed Fox in the delicate way that decorum mandated a woman friend comfort a man mourning the loss of his father. Whitcomb Gairden was dead at age forty-three, the victim of a heart attack as he struggled against the winds of a hurricane that had devastated Charleston just three days ago. Sally wore black, a mantilla of fine tulle and a dress trimmed with more tulle that fell in soft ruffles from throat to bosom. She was in her own mourning. Her marriage to Elliot Harnstron of Savannah last year had ended one month after it began when he died of smallpox. Her only brother, Jurian, had been lost at sea nearly four months back when his sloop had gone down in a squall. A friend and two women from the French Alley had been rescued later, clinging to the small, single-sailed craft. Talk of it was still whispered in Charleston, but no one spoke openly.

Fox looked at Sally as she stepped back, not certain he had heard her correctly. "Tomorrow?"

She nodded discreetly, and it was obvious she did not wish for others to hear what she had to say. "I'll be leaving within the week," he said, as if she had asked how long he would be staying.

"You must stay longer. Your mother will need you." Now the conversation was spoken for the benefit of other ears. It was the polite conversation of Charleston that could be interchanged from mouth to mouth among any one of a hundred people and not deemed anything other than correct. Fox had almost forgotten how practiced it all was.

"I intend to do all I can to assist her," he said. "And I'll come home as frequently as I can, too."

"We'll all be glad for that," Sally said, smiling in that way of hers that made him feel that she would be the one most especially glad. Fox felt the old flirtatious flutter. Then remembered Ceely's ears.

"And Ceely? What's become of her?" He asked this with all the pleasantness of an inquiry about an old friend.

Sally lowered her eyes slightly as she answered. "She's still with us. A very fine asset to our household now that she's trained and knows her place." There was no flirtation in these words. Instead their tone implied that Fox, too, should learn his place. He smiled.

"We all need to learn our places in life, I suppose," he said, shifting his eyes to the line of people waiting behind Sally to give their condolences. "I think I have." He kissed her hand, but gave no response to her request to appear at her house. He sensed her beauty as he stooped close to her, the way he would be moved to touch a fine painting, but wouldn't. He could not will himself to dislike such a painting. The sight of it would simply set off a flood of emotion that would overtake him like a fast-running current. Sally Hudson, as he still thought of her, was like that. Sally seemed never to be in his thoughts unless he was near her, and then she was all he could think of. Fox found himself holding her hand longer than he should, even as he began to speak to the next person in line.

They will charge it to my grief, he thought, and gave the slender hand a pat before letting it go. Her eyes gave him one last query, which he pretended not to see, and then she was gone.

Fox had left Charleston almost two years ago on a cool, winter day when the city glistened in all of its iron-gated, shuttered-windowed beauty under a crystalline frost. Now, four days after the hurricane, the city seemed weary of itself, the sea was not calmed and life was far from back to normal. Debris was everywhere, and Fox's horse shied away from upturned tree roots that lay in his path as Fox set about the task of putting his father's affairs in order. Glass shards littered lawns and streets; pedestrians picked their way around glass on the sidewalks where storefronts had been destroyed. Gardens were stripped of flowers and shrubs lay bent and leafless. This day, even though the sun shone and the heat of early September was its normal suffocating self, the city stood shrouded and silent.

It occurred to Fox that perhaps he was just giving the city the attributes that he, himself, felt at the loss of his father in so unexpected a fashion. Struggling to board up the windows of the family home on Maiden Lane near the bay, Whitcomb Gairden had overdone himself. His heart had given out, the doctor said. He had fallen, or been blown, from the ladder outside the front window in the torrential rain. Mother had found him, had gotten the servant, Tully, to help her bring him in, and he had still been breathing. Tully had gone for the doctor, but gotten no farther than the end of the block before he had been driven into Pratt's carriage house for what little protection it offered. There he had sat among splintering glass and frightened horses until a lull had come, consumed the whole while by a sense of failure, a concern for Mr. Gairden's pain and Mrs. Gairden's fear. When he completed his mission to the doctor's office and returned with him to Maiden Lane, he had found Mrs. Gairden stonelike in her grief, Mr. Gairden dead since no more than a few moments after he had left. In the deluge that had followed the winds, it was Tully who had ridden to carry the word to Fox at the mill, and the two of them had made the trip back home together.

Black bunting still hung at the door of his father's house as Fox left it this morning. Inside the house, blackness was artificial, induced by the still-boarded windows, except for the one that had been left unfinished by Fox's father. The storm had not broken its glass or damaged it in any way.

"He wouldn't have needed to do that one," Susan Gairden said over and over, every time her eyes shifted to the beam of light coming through the half-boarded window where her husband had fallen. "If only he'd stopped. If only he'd left that alone, he might still be here."

She wouldn't hear of Fox's taking the boards off. "There might be another . . . don't take them off . . . I feel safe this way," she would say, never looking at anyone as she spoke. The meaning communicated by her voice and eyes were entirely at odds.

"You've always been safe without them boarded up, Mama. You will now, too. I'll wait until tomorrow, though. We'll watch the weather for a few hours. That'll make you feel better, won't it?" he asked.

"The world is such a dark place—hurricanes, war. I don't want to let too much of it in."

And so, with the funeral over, Mama had sat staring at the shaft of light and wishing there was shattered glass all over her parlor floor instead, ruminating on her regrets and chiding herself for her shortcomings, of which Fox knew there surely were very few. But that was her grief. And he had his own. He might have been present more. He might have listened to his father more. He might have been less headstrong and more judicious in his actions. And yet he knew his father had been proud of him—about the mill, at least, and, he thought, even about the duel, although he had never said it. His father had been the only son of doting parents, well schooled and protected as Fox himself had been. But Fox, somehow, had been drawn to the active side of Grandfather Gairden, while his father had been drawn to the contemplative side. Fox and his father had been as different as father and son could be, and yet the loss struck him the way the hurricane had the coast. The storm had slowly built from the moment he had first learned the news from Tully, and now it hit him full force, missing no part of him, sparing nothing. Watching his mother mourn only made it worse. He had to leave, and yet, as the only son, he also had responsibilities to bear. He started at the State Bank of Charleston with the stern, well-dressed man who had always handled his father's affairs, John Frost.

"I've come in to see to my father's accounts. I want to be certain that my mother will not have to face any difficulties in her delicate state," he told Frost. He noticed the somber look on the banker's long face and held his breath a moment.

"I'm afraid only you can see to that, Fox. Perhaps he didn't tell you, but all he had he invested in your mill."

"That was it? There is nothing more?"

"The house is paid for, but he really had nothing else. Business has not been good here for several years, as I'm certain you know. With trade limited or nonexistent, your father's practice was also affected. There was always work, but there were many who did not pay. He has managed—and managed without borrowing, which is more than many have done—but he could not have managed for much longer unless your mill started showing a profit. Since it has only just opened, we can still hope that it will, for your mother's sake, but you must know that I cautioned him against such an investment, even if it was for his own son. Such enterprises are not the way to wealth in South Carolina that cotton is. I told your father so. But he wouldn't listen."

"But something must be made from the cotton. Why let the northern mills control the price of our cotton and then increase the profit on their yarns later? Doesn't it make sense to build the factories where the supply is?"

"Obviously you and your father thought so. But unfortunately so did the investors of the South Carolina Homespun Company, and soon they were coming to me for loans, going to the legislature for operating capital and asking for a lottery to raise funds for their operation. Even with all of that help, they still could not make a profit. Their experience should teach all of us a lesson."

"Still, we need to encourage industry. The northern states are doing it, rewarding people who invent new machines and financing mills and factories as much as they can—"

"But that is because they cannot grow cotton. We will always have an agricultural advantage over them that they must compensate for."

"And what if cotton fails, the way indigo did once the bounty went off? Then what?" Hugh Vardry's words, Fox thought, understanding them now in a way he hadn't that Independence Day five years back.

"Then your mill will be worth even less than it is now, Fox." Frost was so confident of his opinion that Fox wanted to reach across his desk and shake him. He was glad, suddenly, that his father had no money in this bank—and no debts.

"That's where you're wrong, Mr. Frost. People will always need clothing, and bags for their grain and sails for their ships and blankets for their homes, and someone has to make them. It doesn't always have to come over on a ship. We can make it *here* and we can make it as inexpensively as England can once we're mechanized for it."

"Still, you can't expect the government to subsidize you. You—"

"And why not? What has England been doing for two hundred years but subsidizing her textile industry by imposing the very navigation orders that have gotten us into this war? Parliament is going to protect its wool weavers and cotton workers any way it can—by controlling the shipping of foreign nations if it chooses. Our government might at least show some interest in its own industries."

"I'm afraid our federal government doesn't know what it should support, judging from Mr. Madison's indecision on this war business. It's no wonder Charleston cannot even raise enough militiamen to guard the local powder magazines—why should they? They're not certain the threat is real."

"British ships off the coast, and they're not certain the threat is real? All it will take to make the threat real is for Napoleon to surrender in Europe. If he does, and England turns her guns on us, it's going to seem very real, very quickly." Fox heard himself almost shouting this last, appalled by the self-satisfaction in the words that had come from the mouth of someone he had always been told to regard as a wise man. Perhaps Papa had misjudged John Frost as much as Frost had misjudged the cotton manufacturing business. Fox stood, and Frost did the same. "Forgive my outburst, sir. I am overly agitated by the loss of my father, but I do hope you will think about what I've said. Chasing cotton profits is too narrow a path for me, and for South Carolina."

"I wish you luck, Fox," Frost said, indulgent as if he were speaking to a child, which, to him, Fox knew he still was.

Two slaves were still cleaning up the garden that afternoon when Fox approached the Hudsons' black-draped door. Sally had returned to live with her parents the day after her husband died. Now the wrought-iron fence that had stood so proudly around their garden was knocked on its side, and a large orange tree lay uprooted over the top of it. Their windows had already been uncovered, but the boards were still piled beside the house to be put away after the men had completed their other tasks. The sight of the severe damage around the city only added to the feelings of grief and helplessness that had weighed Fox down ever since he'd received news of his father's death. Even the thought of seeing Sally did not seem to cheer him. Of course, he would feel differently once he had actually seen her. He always did.

It was Sally herself who opened the door when he arrived. "They're all gone for the afternoon, and I even sent Ceely to the Griswolds to help clean up from the storm," Sally said. Excitement had replaced all sign of mourning in her eyes, and for a moment Fox shucked off the cloud that had been hanging on him. "And I know it's just awful to say it, but I am so happy I could scream. You don't know what it's been like, Fox. Mourning is such an awful thing, especially when everyone is whispering about Jurian like he was some kind of pariah. What gentleman in Charleston doesn't have secret lady friends? Jurian was no worse than anyone else—except you, perhaps."

"No, of course he wasn't," Fox said, taking the seat she offered him in the upstairs parlor and ignoring her inference. "And Jurian wouldn't have minded a bit of whispering, you know. In fact, he might have enjoyed leaving a daring myth behind him. Think of it that way, Sally."

"You always say just the right thing, Fox. You always have." She moved closer to him and lowered her eyes, as if there might be a tear coming. Fox took her hand.

"There, there, Sally. I know how you must feel."

"You're the only one who does, Fox." She brushed the back of his hand, clasped to her own, against her cheek and looked directly into his eyes. There was no tear there. But there was something else. "I need someone—now that Jurian's gone, I mean. Please say you'll come often, to be with me."

"As often as I can, Sally. But there are so many in Charleston who will be right here to comfort you, many of them men more prosperous than I. I'm needed at the mill, and I can't be here as much as I'd like to—as much as you'd want me to."

"Everyone wants to be of comfort, but I just want . . . you." At this, she looked him straight in the eye. He could see that for a second she chewed at the inside of her lip, but after a moment's indecision—or was it decision?—she leaned forward and kissed him, igniting him the way her nearness could. His arms surrounded her then, in an instant of desire and thoughtlessness, the way they had wanted to sometime ago, a lifetime ago, when she had stood under a lacy parasol on Harleston's Green and watched him play at golf.

Two years had gone by since he had held Anne Vardry in his arms, but this was different. At the first touch of Sally it was different. It wasn't the way he remembered it with Anne. Sally was soft, her body against his was pliant and sweet scented, eager. And he could lean her back against her mother's settee and love her right now. He knew it. She gave every indication of it in the way she moved against him, arousing him and then moving so that her breast was at his hand, ready for his caress. She moaned slightly, the way he remembered from one of the women Grish had led him to, and her breath came heavy and deep. Move the hand an inch, just an inch, let it squeeze that lump of flesh, and then let it begin to undo the buttons at her throat. She's willing and you want it. Admit it, he thought to himself. You want it.

But you don't want her, he thought just as quickly, moving away and breaking out of the kiss. "Oh, Sally," he said. "You are moved by grief, not by affection, and I am, also. We must not. Not now."

"I know," she said, eyes downcast as she straightened her gown and pretended that the intimacy she had offered had not been rebuked. "I don't know what I—"

"Grief takes us out of ourselves, Sally," he said, excusing himself as well. "But this isn't the time. And I'm not the one, Sally. You know that. I'm not ready to marry, to give you the kind of life you want."

"I see. I'm a widow and you're not interested anymore."

"Not at all. You're as lovely as ever. But I think you're seeing me as an old friend of Jurian's you want to hang on to, as if you're hanging on to part of him. I shall always be your friend, Sally, as I was his. Beyond that, I just don't know right now." He touched her cheek in apology, half expecting her to turn away, but she didn't. She cuddled into the curve of his hand and kissed his palm.

14

November 1813

"Let me introduce my cousin, Adelle Durant, from Philadelphia. Adelle, Sally Hudson Harnstron. Sally, my cousin."

As he spoke that November afternoon at tea in his mother's house, he could tell that Sally was taking stock of Adelle, and that Adelle was coming up as rather more than Sally expected any cousin from north of the Carolinas should be. Adelle stood poised in a mourning gown of black wool crepe, styled with a high neck and buttoned almost to the waist with tiny silver buttons. Grandmother Gairden's silver earrings dangled elegantly above her straight shoulders, and Fox was struck by the loving way the years had treated his cousin.

"Adelle! How pleased we are to have you here in Charleston. I understand you traveled here all alone." Sally was in lighter mourning now and wore a dove gray gown of her favored, low-cut variety with a short, tight-fitting jacket trimmed in black braid that gave her a lively, if well-tailored, appearance. She spoke in a hushed tone. Word of Adelle's arrival in Charleston unescorted had flown throughout their social circle with alarming speed.

"Her family wished her to be safely away from the threat to Philadelphia, Sally," Fox explained. "They thought Charleston as far away from the fighting as she was likely to get. And, of course, they knew she would be a comfort to Mother."

"Of course," Sally said, smiling sweetly. "We *do* need family in times like these. But weren't you frightened, traveling alone?"

"We saw British ships on the eastern horizon each day, and in the Chesapeake we saw them even closer, but our little packet was of no interest to them. I think I might have had more fright had I been traveling overland through Frenchtown, Maryland, or the place they call Havre de Grace. The depredations there were awful. A fellow traveler told me that the British Admiral Cockburn's actions were—"

"Ah, well, we are most fortunate here in Charleston, aren't we, Fox?" Sally interrupted, as though any vivid details would send her into a swoon. "We've lacked for nothing, blockade or no blockade."

"Is that right, Sally? I seem to remember being all but unable to get the machines for my mill, until finally they creaked down here from Massachusetts by overland route, nearly six months after I was ready for them. And I think the prices of coffee, sugar, salt—almost everything of that nature that must come by ship—have made buying them a hardship for many."

"I suppose," Sally admitted. "I don't trouble myself about such things."

"You sound like a Federalist, Sally," Fox teased. "To hear the New Englanders tell it, we aren't even having a war down here. It is only they whose businesses suffer from the ways of war. Still it is they who are not blockaded by the British. Suspicious, isn't it?"

Sally dropped any pretense of understanding what Fox was talking about at the same time Adelle was nodding eagerly. As if she sensed that Fox was about to take up the conversation with Adelle rather than with her, Sally returned once again to a subject she knew something about. "Your mother didn't come . . . she married a Loyalist, didn't she?" The sweet smile never left Sally's face.

"The old stories never die in Charleston, Cousin," Fox said, hoping to save Adelle from having to defend what was not hers to defend. "I think your mother's activities are more myth than fact here, now."

"She wouldn't mind," Adelle said, smoothly. Fox saw Sally's shock and chuckled inwardly. "She did what she felt she had to do, and she learned that war is bad business from either side. It was the very reason she insisted on shielding me from it now."

"My, Fox, what an interesting family you have," Sally said, linking her arm in his. He felt her draw him gently away from Adelle and tried to accommodate her and yet not to turn away from his cousin, who seemed to be taking in Sally's performance with a little inward humor of her own. Fox caught her eye and winked. He and Adelle stood apart from the rigid social rules of Charleston, Fox realized just then, feeling good in a way that he hadn't since he'd been back. At last there was someone else like him in the city—and who else but his own cousin?

Sally would never understand him the way Adelle just had in a single meeting of their eyes. Sally's expectations were not his own. He had seen that on each of his two visits with her since his father's death. He sensed that, since Jurian's accident at sea, she hoped Fox would step in to fill his place, only not as a brother, but as a husband. Fox, in his own mourning, had been able to sidestep her intentions.

"Fox, did you know Joseph purchased the mill from Papa? The mill is busy with war contracts. We have an order for three thousand yards of sail duck and ten thousand bags just this month."

"My," Sally said, still smiling. "That sounds . . .

wonderful. Your mill must be making you rich, too, Fox."

"I'm afraid I haven't been quite so lucky, but we are able to keep busy."

"And how long will it be until you are *not* so busy up there?" Sally asked, twining her gloved fingers through his. "You are spending far too much time there and not enough here."

"My work is there, Sally, not here. That is where I must be."

"Why?" Sally crooned. "A mill is just like a plantation, isn't it? You hire someone to run it, and you live in Charleston like Papa does. We go out to The Hollows for a few months, but that's all. We don't *live* there."

"A mill is not very much like a plantation, Sally. At least mine isn't. And I *want* to be there."

"You certainly came home from Connecticut with some odd ideas, Fox. I thought you might be going back to the university."

"I should have finished there, I give you that, Sally. I still try to read Cicero and Aristotle when I can, but the college life was not for me. No, once I left, there was no going back."

Adelle nodded. "We all need to keep educating ourselves, Cousin. You do the right thing. You may end up knowing more than some of those who gain a degree."

"Perhaps, although there were some fine scholars in Columbia with me. Hugh LeGare, for instance. Studied all the time. Memorized whole books of philosophy and reams of poetry. I was too busy wanting to know why gears locked and card cloth ripped. I knew I could never be the equal of lads like Hugh. Even if the duel had not come along to change my life, something else, I think, would have drawn me away from college."

"Perhaps a young lady," Sally said, dropping her eyelids and then looking out from the corner of her eye as she teased.

"Perhaps," Fox conceded. "I shall never know." He gave a finality to the words that Sally couldn't help but hear. He slipped his arm free of Sally's, took her hand and brushed it lightly with his lips. "Thank you so much for coming today, Sally. We do want Adelle to meet all of our dear friends while she's here."

"Yes, thank you, Sally," Adelle put in, polite but not effusive.

"It was my pleasure." Barely any smile accompanied Sally's words. "*Do* come see me while you're home, Fox," she said in an aside to him as she walked away.

"Thank you, Sally," he said. Neither yes nor no. And he liked it that way.

As Fox spoke to a few other guests, Adelle took up minding his sister Miriam's daughter, Philalura. She held the infant, cuddling her inside her tiny blanket, talking to her in soft, low tones to quiet her while Miriam took a short rest. Thinner than he remembered, stately in the black gown, Adelle struck a pleasing contrast to Miriam's postnatal heaviness. The baby had taken to Adelle from the first day she had come, his mother said, and she to her. She would be a great help to Miriam while she was here, Mama was certain. She had brought with her a certain spirit that was not foreign to their state of mourning, and yet helped them all to be carried beyond it.

It was true. Adelle had lost none of the spirit he remembered, and she had not married, as he had supposed she would. Sally Hudson had married and lost a husband already—she had her own kind of spirit, Fox supposed. Sally probably hadn't married for love, and so her loss had been only one of time. Oh well, what he had told her was true: There were plenty of other men in Charleston—she didn't need him.

* * *

"You didn't come back." As she placed another card on the table that evening, Adelle looked at Fox instead of at the game. It was their first opportunity to speak to each other alone in the two days she had been there. The lamplight cast a soft glow on both of their faces while the rest of the room was dark, the rest of the house quiet.

"I couldn't," Fox began. Adelle's full lips parted slightly, as if to interrupt, but she waited for an explanation she appeared determined to collect. "Something happened that was . . . difficult for me. I had been working hard at the Vardry mill, and then when I received a letter from Papa I decided to come directly back to Charleston instead of stopping off in Philadelphia."

"Were you angry that Joseph took over the place you had offered to fill? Mama said yes, Papa said no. I didn't know, but I knew there was something that made you stay away." She slipped out of her shoes and rubbed one foot against the other, her feet no doubt tired from their walk along the Battery after tea.

I didn't come because I was running again, this time from wanting Anne Vardry. Should I tell her that? he wondered. The answer came quickly and he held his tongue.

"It wasn't that, Adelle. Not at all."

"We all felt most regretful, but when Joseph came home we had to make a place for him. He came back . . . very much changed."

"I knew it was Joseph's rightful place to take over your father's mill, so I want no regrets from you, Cousin. I think it was more that I was a different person after my impressment, Adelle, and when I thought of seeing you again I . . . well, I was certain you must have married while I was away, anyway. And then, when I found Mrs. Vardry still not recovered from her grief, I knew I had to finish what I set out to do that summer when I left your house. I had to try to make up for the hardship I had caused even if it was unintentional. By the time I was done in Connecticut, Papa was urging me to hurry back here, and I must be honest . . ." He paused a moment, wondering if she could read not only what was in his eyes but also in his heart. Unsure of the answer, he went on, ". . . there were things I wanted to get away from. Memories . . ."

"Of your friend Grisham. You mentioned he was lost at sea."

"Yes, of Grish. He was ordered to a mast in a storm because a lieutenant hated him. When lightning struck, he was thrown off into the heaving waters in the dark. We threw out lines for hours but never saw him again." Fox swallowed hard. "It was a great loss. He had a brilliant mind."

"I see. No doubt you were still grieving once you got back to Connecticut. And then seeing Mrs. Vardry, too . . . I'd been thinking it was something I said, something I did, perhaps, that kept you from coming back to Philadelphia. We didn't hear from you for so long. We all wondered."

Looking at her as she sat across from him at the table by the window in the drawing room, he noticed the way the black crepe of her mourning dress contrasted with the pure whiteness of her skin. Her heart-shaped face was set off by a strong jawline, her eyes brightly punctuating the upper regions to give her the look of a person who knew what she was about. So unlike Anne Vardry, he thought, who had never known the security of her own decisions, until now, perhaps. I hope I gave her that much.

"I've wondered about you, too, you know, even though I haven't written. I suppose I've been so busy thinking about myself I've taken too little time to think of others—even my own mother. I had to go back to Camden only two days after Papa's funeral—"

"And now you mean to go to sea, again." Adelle's voice was very soft as she said this, and Fox sensed her own disappointment.

"It is the last thing I wish to do, Adelle. Trust in that. At first, when our navy was taking British ships at every turn, I tried to tell myself that I wasn't needed, but this year the tide, so to speak, has turned, and I can no longer deny I am needed. Serving in the Charleston militia would be a worthless pursuit. Four units refused even to report when called to guard the city's powder magazines by Governor Alston last May. And then all charges were dropped against them last month. What good will such people be to the defense of our shores, or such government? Having each state pay for and direct its own military does not work. Look at Massachusetts, for instance. The Federalists there do not favor the war, and so they refuse to raise any forces. Let those who benefit from the war pay for it and fight it, they say. Are we a nation or just a group of states? Ahh! It angers me!"

"Feelings run strong against them at home, too. But the New England states coddle the British. You notice they were not blockaded as the rest of us were. The British believe in the axiom of divide and conquer, it seems. But aside from all that, could you not fight them just as well with the army? Must you go to sea? I thought your mother had written that you would never go to sea again."

"I said that once, I suppose. But now I wonder if part of the reason I was impressed was to train me for a higher service? Anyway, Fort Johnson and Fort Moultrie are both already garrisoned, so my enlistment with the army would still mean leaving Charleston for

some faraway place. Serving at sea seems the best way
to help the country, especially now that Napoleon is
facing defeat. Once England wins in Europe, all of her
guns will be aimed at us. We need to be ready."

"What about signing aboard a privateer? There are
some in the harbor here. I saw them when I came."

"Little more than legalized pirates, they are—I
learned that firsthand. Not that they're not doing a job
by bringing in British prizes. But their main job is private gain—disrupting His Majesty's commerce is just a
side benefit. Nay, the next naval vessel that sails into
Charleston harbor, I'm for it. They tell me at Fort
Moultrie that the navy is crying for men. No one wants
to go in for seaman's wages when they could just as
well go off on a privateer and make themselves a fortune."

"But you do."

"I have to. I let Grandfather down by making a challenge when perhaps I shouldn't have. It would be letting him down again to turn away from a challenge
when faced with one. The future of our whole country
may rest on the outcome of these naval battles, even
though now the land war seems in our favor."

"It isn't just that I'm here, is it? You learned I would
be coming and decided you should go to sea?" She
smiled as she spoke, but Fox could tell that beneath the
banter there was a real question.

"No. I signed the papers the week after Papa died,
actually. His dying so suddenly made me think about
some things I had avoided since Grish died—about
duty, responsibility. About how short life can be. I
might not get another chance to right some of these
wrongs, Adelle, though I would have chosen not to go
now had I known you were coming. I've already put
this off far too long. Now I have to go."

"Will your mill keep running without you?"

"I'd be lying if I said I wasn't worried about it. But I have a man, Ezra Merrifield, to manage it for me. It's a small operation. I'll have to hope for the best."

"Let me help."

"What about going back to Philadelphia—your teaching? I know you could manage the mill, but I couldn't let you. And I couldn't pay you. I'm not even taking wages from it myself yet. And you know no one there."

"But I know mills. I could keep an eye on things for you. And I could teach, too, if you wanted. I won't be thinking of going back to Philadelphia until news of the war sounds more promising. I'd be happy for something useful to do while I'm here—besides seeing to your mother, of course."

"You're not like most other women, are you, Cousin?"

"Would that be a compliment or not?"

"It is most certainly a compliment. Few women have your confidence, or your vitality."

"Are you speaking of Mrs. Vardry?"

At the sound of her name, Fox took a deep breath. "Mrs. Vardry was . . ." He searched for a word to describe what she was, how he remembered her that sunny, golden day and other darker days. "Had been . . ." Fox shook his head. Of course it was Anne he had been thinking of. It must be written all over his face. But then, could anyone ever understand all that had passed between him and the wife of the man he had killed? "No. I don't know . . . I don't really know," he said. "She was . . . I tried to . . . she lacked your confidence. I don't know how to explain her."

"You don't have to. I think I know." Her eyes were shadowed by the dim lamplight, but Fox couldn't have looked into them anyway. He hung his head, remembering. "But that doesn't change my offer to help out at the mill while you go off to war. It would be my way of doing something to help the Union—and I don't think I'll ever fit in here in Charleston with Sally, or any of these other young ladies who've come to call."

Fox chuckled, and this time he did look at her. "You know, I don't think I'll ever quite fit in here again, either. I don't know if I ever did. I just thought I did. I just thought I was part of the code of honor of the grand old city. But now I'm not so sure. Maybe that's part of what's sending me back to sea. . . . Still, I don't want people to talk about you. Anyone who earns money is seen as less than those born to it."

"And being born to it makes them so good they can own other people to earn their money for them. I'm sorry, Fox. I find that attitude appalling."

"I agree, with some reservations."

"I know, or I would never have offered to help you. I think what you are doing by hiring white workers at your mill is the right thing. I want to help you succeed."

Fox thought for a moment, still overwhelmed at her suggestion. His mother would question the whole idea, although if he could find her a suitable chaperone in Camden . . . Little by little the idea began to take root. Merrifield could see to the mechanical needs of the jennies. And if Adelle could see to the orders and sales, even for a few months, perhaps the business could actually grow while he was away, instead of just trying to hold its own. "You would have to see the mill first," he said, thinking aloud. "I wouldn't want you to agree to something without even seeing it. It's not like Philadelphia."

"I would love to see it, Fox. But I will give you my word before we go that I will help you, no matter what. Were your father still living, I know he would have

come to your aid. As it is, you have no one. Your sisters
are already married with babies to care for, and their
husbands have no knowledge of mills. They think of
mills only in terms of the failed South Carolina Homespun Company, from what I could gather in talking to
them the night I arrived."

"That has been a blot on the industry I can't seem to
erase. It will make getting future investors even more
difficult than it has already been. Few people want to
take a chance on industry when they can make a sure
profit in cotton."

"Your brothers-in-law said as much, even though I
tried to dissuade them. I think they thought a woman
out of place speaking on such matters. They quickly
changed the subject. My family is used to such talk
from a woman. After all, you know Mama." She
paused a moment, and Fox could almost see her
thoughts switch back to Philadelphia. "How pleased
she will be to think that I shall spend my time here
helping the family."

"You think that?"

"Had Joe not come back—or you—I would have
asked Papa to allow me to take over his mill. I want to
do it, Fox. I can do it. I will do it. I can pretend to be
only a teacher, but I will actually do much more."

Once again Fox was struck by her confidence, by the
difference between her and the woman who had a mill
and was afraid to run it. Of course, the difference was
that Anne Vardry had a millful of bad memories to
keep her from meeting her challenges head-on. Adelle
had nothing like that. "We'll go to Camden as soon as
Mama will allow it, but no obligations. You know it's
not as large as your father's mill, not nearly so large.
And it's not in a great city like you're used to."

"Stop finding reasons for me not to do it, Fox. There
aren't any that are good enough. And don't worry. I

won't embarrass you. I'll be very quiet and ladylike about my work."

"I don't know that I could ever repay you, Adelle."

"I don't know that I would expect it, Fox. I just want you to come home again, safe and free."

"Anyone who survived two years with the Royal Navy can surely come home from one with the American navy in one piece."

"Will the war be over that soon?"

"It could be. Already there are negotiations for peace. But if we are to win our sea rights, we must negotiate from a position of strength, not weakness."

"One year, then. I'll help you for one year, or until the war ends."

"Or until you marry. If you should meet someone while I'm gone I wouldn't want to—"

"Good heavens, Fox. I'm twenty-five years old, just like you. If I haven't married by now, I'm not likely to in the next year. Not any more than you are. Or are you?"

"Hardly," he said, shaking his head. "I seem to run away from anyone who gets close."

"Even Sally?"

"She likes to be close, I have to admit," Fox said, less delicate than he should have been when speaking of a lady, but it was true. And it seemed all right to say it to Adelle, for some reason. "Sally sees in me a replacement for her dead brother, I think, more than anything else. But she has many suitors. She does not need me."

"Mama has always told me not to marry before I know what it is that I want, not to marry as a means of running away from something, as she did the first time. Still, people ask questions, raise eyebrows. They wonder if I'll ever marry."

Fox felt his face color. "Dear Adelle. Of course

you'll marry. You're just unwilling to settle for what other girls take for granted. You are wise where they are foolish."

"I was betrothed, Fox. Last year. I accepted a young man I met at an antislavery meeting."

"I didn't know." Fox felt a chill on his cheek. The fire was burning low.

"Before I had even written to you of it, it was over. He wanted to carry his ideals west. He had a band of followers, and they wanted to build a new town somewhere in Illinois Territory where escaped slaves could settle and be free."

"And?"

"I suppose I didn't love him enough to go out there with him. The way Joseph looked when he came back from the Ohio was still with me. I was not strong enough to face the hardships, though I shed many tears before I actually admitted that to myself. But I am strong enough to help you. I promise."

"Of course you are, Cousin. I could never doubt your strength. And now I have you to escort me on Christmas visits before I leave. Since neither of us seems to have the heart for marriage, we can keep each other company and not have to worry about asking or not asking anyone else to accompany us. We're both in mourning, and we can decline some invitations if we want to stay home and tell our old ghost stories—or would you miss seeing the whole of Charleston's famous social season?"

"All I want to see in Charleston is right here, Fox." She was beautiful just then, smiling back at him, content with his suggestion. There was an aura she had, almost like the glow from the peg lamp between them.

"We should have a ghost story now, just as we did that last time you visited Charleston." Fox reached out and turned down the lamp wick, partly afraid to pursue her last statement, partly wanting to recapture the childlike camaraderie that had never really left them. Their faces barely illuminated, the setting was perfect.

"Last time you made me cry," she said, pretending a frown.

"Then this time I should make you howl with laughter." He took her hands in his while he closed his eyes, evoking the mood and seeking out the proper story for telling. Opening his eyes again, he found her with head tipped back, eyes closed and face in complete repose. "You don't look frightened," he said.

"I could not feel frightened with you holding my hands, Fox. And besides, you promised to make me laugh." Still she did not open her eyes, as though she were already transported beyond the confines of Charleston, and Fox felt himself not wanting to spoil the moment by beginning a tale of stupid mistaken identity or imagined ghouls.

"Ah. Well then. Let me see. Here's one, not exactly a ghost story. A true story, actually, or so they say. There was a woman, a Mrs. Shubrick, who woke her husband in the midst of a dark night saying she had had a dream of her brother, whom they knew to be on a homeward voyage from your own city. In the dream, he was out on the ocean, all alone, holding a stick with a rag tied to it like a flag. She was frightened by this dream, but her husband bade her go back to sleep, and she did. A second time that night, the woman had the same dream, and a third. Each time, her husband assured her that it was just her imagination taking over in her sleep, and each time he bade her go back to sleep, until the last time she would be quieted no more.

"The next morning, Mrs. Shubrick insisted her husband go into town, hire a pilot boat and have it cruise the sea-lanes north of the city in search of her brother, and her husband did as he was asked, at no small ex-

pense. At the end of the first day, the boat came back
having seen nothing. Mrs. Shubrick sent it out again a
second day. Again nothing. Then on the third day, just
before dusk, a small white speck could be seen on the
water, and the pilot boat found a man, floating aboard
a hen coop, which was all that was left of the ship on
which he had sailed. Not Mrs. Shubrick's brother, who
later came home safely, but another man was saved by
Mrs. Shubrick's dream."

When the tale was done, Adelle opened her eyes.
"You didn't make me laugh," she said.

"I didn't frighten you, either. Give me that, at least."

"You made me think of you at sea, of what you
might face."

"I might turn that around and tell you the story of
Theodosia Burr Alston, the daughter of Aaron Burr,
who was lost at sea sailing north to see her father after
he returned from abroad. You might face dangers at
sea the same as I. We all face dangers. Some quite
unexpected."

"I simply think you have faced enough of them. I
wonder if Grandfather were still here, if he would
think you should go off to war. I thought he wanted all
wars to cease."

"He did, but—"

"And I don't know that you should always try to live
up to what Grandfather was, or wanted. You have your
own life to live, Fox, as I do. Grandfather's time has
passed."

"You can say that, Adelle, because you did not see
him that last day, as I did. The image of his death,
coupled with Hugh Vardry's, is one that never leaves
me. You asked if it was anything you had done that
kept me from coming back to Philadelphia . . . and it
wasn't. It was my past, chasing me like a dog's tail. I
cannot get away from it entirely, Adelle, no matter how

hard I try. Grandfather is the only touchstone I have, sometimes."

"Perhaps you'll find another. Sometime," Adelle said, eyes on the cards still spread before them. "One that will be less demanding."

"Perhaps. But I think we only give of ourselves what is demanded. And if we are to give our best, the demands must be high."

"They should not be so high that they keep us ever running, though, Fox. They should give us time to savor a day's sweetness and a night's good rest as well."

"For a time, Adelle, after I got away from the *Iago*, I never knew a good night's rest unless I was soaked through with whiskey. Thank God I weaned myself away from it. And I do rest well now, after a hard day's work in the mill. The only thing that keeps me from my sleep is my dreams of what it all can be. Those dreams I would put in your hands if you take over for me."

"You must have been related to the Shubricks somewhere along the line, Fox, the way all of these other Charlestonians are related. I hope your dreams are as fruitful as Mrs. Shubrick's were. I'll do what I can to help them be."

"I apologize, Adelle," Fox said without preamble.

"For what?"

"For not coming back to Philadelphia. I had written you that I would, and then I didn't. It was inexcusable. But at the time, it was impossible for me to do otherwise. Thank you for being forgiving enough to come now. I'm different from the cousin you knew that week in Philadelphia, but I'm still a Gairden and I won't lie to you. I just can't quite explain everything to you the way I'd like, the way I should. Not yet."

"Remember, Fox, I'm a Gairden, too. We're known not only for our long arms and deep pockets, but also for our patience."

Fox laughed. "More stories tomorrow night, Cousin?" he asked. "Some scary ones, perhaps?"

"Tomorrow night. And, by the way, I've learned some stories of my own since the last time we met."

"I don't doubt you have, Adelle. I don't doubt it for a minute."

The card game forgotten, Fox looked across the table again to where the cousin with whom he had a lifelong bond looked back at him with new, mature eyes, eyes unafraid of ghosts—in story or in life. He rose and took her by the hand to the stairs, where he kissed her lightly on each cheek before she went up to bed.

Returning to the drawing room, Fox poured himself a glass of what had been his father's whiskey. This time, the toast he made to himself was very different from the toasts he and Grish had made over cups of grog parceled out aboard the *Iago*. The toast was to his late father and grandfather. To Adelle, who was so much like them. Fox smiled as the familiar warmth came to him when the first swallow hit his stomach. He closed his eyes. And for once, Hugh Vardry did not appear in front of them.

15

Fox walked past the *Saucy Jack*, one of three ships tied up at the Charleston docks. The other two were its British merchantmen prizes. Today's issue of the *Gazette* carried the news that the *Jack*'s total now stood at thirteen prizes captured since the war began. Fox shook his head. He was daft to be thinking of going to sea again, although this time, he had to admit, he had a better reason. Still he remembered the close-up combat of the seas, the shots fired amidships, the grapeshot and the chain shot piercing and maiming and killing, the rigging of sail in heavy weather.

"I'd like to sign on with your crew," he told Captain Thomas Drummond of the *Jack*.

"You and over a hundred and twenty others since last night," the captain replied with a confident laugh.

"My offer is to serve with you, without pay, until such time as I can get onto a naval vessel. With the blockade as it is, I don't know when one might ever dock at Charleston." Fox saw the skeptical way the captain looked at him.

"Without pay? But you'll be wantin' a share of the prizes we might take?"

"No, sir. Those I would forego as well."

"An honorable intention, lad," Drummond said. "But you'll be cryin' for your share if we take a rich prize. I don't think—"

"Please, sir. I have experience. I was impressed to the *Iago*—most illegally, I might add."

"Ah, so you've a reason to want to strike back at the Royal tarry-breeks. But why not just take up with us, then? We're doin' more than the navy at takin' prizes."

"So you are, but I've made up my mind. I owe it to my country."

"And you're lookin' for a commission you can use along with your name forever the way these Charleston gents like to, maybe? Never seen such a place for military titles!" The heavily bearded man shook his head with obvious distaste.

"I care nothing for titles, military or otherwise. I simply feel it necessary—my duty. My grandfather died still worrying that the Union would not hold together unless people were willing to carry on the sacrifices he and others had made during the Revolution. The longer this war goes on, the more I see why he was so concerned. We need to gain against England while she is still occupied with Napoleon, because should she turn her full strength on us, we have little chance for success."

The captain eyed him seriously for a few moments, then scanned the long list of names, some marked with only an X next to a name written in his own hand. "We really shouldn't take even one more. But I suppose we've left Charleston manned heavier—always need to have extras to sail back the prizes we get."

"Thank you, sir. When do we sail?"

"One week from today. And you'll get a share of any prize taken just like any other man long as you're aboard. It'll go easier on you that way."

"I can take care of myself."

"Very well, then, Gairden. Enjoy your last week of freedom."

"Let us hope the navy can ensure a lifetime of freedom for us all, Captain." Fox saluted reflexively, the way he had been taught aboard the *Iago*, then turned smartly on his heel and left the ship, knowing Captain Drummond was no doubt still shaking his head. Privateersmen didn't think much of the navy, and didn't have to. Men were flocking to ships like the *Saucy Jack* to stake a chance at a share of the big prizes, while they avoided the navy. For a long time, he had avoided it, too. Even now, the idea of sailing left him with an angry feeling inside he couldn't completely overcome. It was the feeling that had never left him on the *Iago*. This time will be different, he told himself. You are right to go, even if it means leaving the mill. And leaving Adelle? That was a question he hadn't expected to have to answer when he had made up his mind to enlist. But he had signed his name on that long list for Captain Drummond, and in a week he would be gone. The captain had ordered him to enjoy his last week of freedom, and so he would.

"Stop off and visit us at The Oaks." Jonathan Simms made his invitation with the amiability that was expected in such situations. He owned a large plantation and enjoyed guests. No matter that he hadn't been to the plantation for six or eight months, a friend visiting in the general vicinity was welcome at any time. Dustcovers could be quickly removed from the furniture, and Cook could find something for them. A country house should be ready at all times for guests, or pretend to be.

"Thank you, Simms," Fox replied, shaking his hand before each of them returned to his own carriage. "We haven't time, though, I'm afraid. I'm showing my cousin around Columbia and then taking her out to see the mill. After that, I need to return to Charleston with all haste. I leave on the *Saucy Jack* next week."

"Very good. Bring back some prizes—some with coffee and sugar on them. Things are getting a bit scarce."

"I know. Maybe we'll get lucky, although sometimes they just take off the specie and sink the ship, cargo and all. It's faster and easier to make away with the money and destroy the ship. I think that's how the *Jack* can claim so many prizes."

"That may be. And besides, the smugglers have to have some reason to stay in business, I suppose. I hear there's a regular run between St. Amelia Island off Florida and the south coast coves." Simms raised one eyebrow, waiting for confirmation of what so far was only gossip in Charleston.

"I've heard it, too," Fox replied carefully. He didn't add that he had reason to believe Richard Celestine was the primary beneficiary of the thousands to be made from the risky business. At his noncommittal answer, Simms dropped the topic and stepped back up into his coach.

"Good seeing you, Fox. You, too, Eliza. Dobbs," he said with a nod to Fox's sister and her husband, John Dobbs, who were serving as chaperones. "Pleasure to meet you, Miss Durant."

The Simms carriage rolled away, and Fox took Adelle's arm in his to stroll a short distance so that the dust might settle before they resumed their journey. A crisp frost had touched the upcountry this early November day, leaving the roadside weeds dull green and limp.

"It must be odd to live in two places," she observed, watching the Simms carriage go.

"They only stay through New Year's. Most of the planters will be back in Charleston before race week in February."

"So this is almost like a vacation for them, this trip to the country house."

"It is, I suppose. Much of life is very like a vacation for them, I think. That is why they think it odd for anyone to want to get into a business like milling that constantly interrupts that vacation."

"I should think sometime their vacation must end," Adelle said.

"I think for some it already has, but they won't admit it. No one wants to admit that with cotton prices so low they are actually losing money, lots of money."

"But that is only because of the war, isn't it? Once the war is over, they will once again be rich?"

"Probably. I don't know. I know nothing of the land. Like Grandfather, I was never cut out for the life of a farmer or planter."

"I wouldn't like it either."

"Not even after Sally and Eliza and everyone else telling you about all the balls and hunts and social life? Surely they've made it all sound glamorous."

"It's not all that different from social life in Philadelphia, actually, for the very rich. It's just that in Philadelphia there is more social life for people of an in-between sort of class. You know, merchants, artisans, shopkeepers. Here it is different. Rich and slaves. Nothing between."

"At the mill you'll see a difference," he told her. "There are small farmers—people who are a kind of 'in-between.' More than there used to be. The place where we built the mill was a mill seat just after the Revolution, but it failed because rental slave labor didn't work out. It did duty as a gristmill for a while, then burned. We rescued what was left and built it into what you'll see later. The countryside is changing. Other people are realizing they can't make it on the land against the planters, who can afford their own gins, their own transport to market and all the rest."

"That makes me more anxious than ever to see your mill, Fox. It sounds almost like home."

"Perhaps it will be, at least for a while." We marry

our cousins in the South, he had told her that day in Philadelphia. He had been teasing, in part, but perhaps he had been looking for her reaction as well. He knew he was now, but he didn't know quite how to draw it out. He didn't want to in any way damage what was growing between them, and yet his time was short. In a few days he would be aboard the *Saucy Jack.* Despite what he had told the Captain, he *did* want to enjoy his last days of freedom. He wanted to spend them with Adelle. Just like this.

In Charleston, everyone could trace family lines back through marriages and intermarriages for at least three generations. "Harriet Baines married her cousin, Thaddeus Burke, whose mother was one of the Goose Creek Pringles, and, of course, his father was Simon Burke, descended from the Smythes of Long Pines. Colonel Smythe fought with the Penscott Rifles in India, you know," the stories went. Fox's own family had no such easily defined lineage, except that the Gairden name had been carried from generation to generation by men who were proud of it. He was one of them.

Fox and Adelle walked slowly back in the direction from which they had just come, the late-morning sun turning the frost to sparkling dew on the leaves of toadflax and plantain. For a long time, neither spoke. Warblers perched on young beech trees near the road flew away as the couple approached with long, slow steps. I'm going to leave all this behind again, Fox thought. He patted Adelle's arm linked through his, but said nothing.

"Fox! Adelle! Come along! We should be going if we're to get to Camden by nightfall!" Eliza Gairden Dobbs's call from the carriage carried clearly on the morning air, and Fox gave a wave in answer.

"It seems our chaperones are eager to be off," he said. "I suppose they are right, but I hate to end our beautiful walk. Soon my only walking will be on the slippery deck of the *Jack*, and my only companions tars who in no way compare to you, Cousin."

"Then you shouldn't go," she said, favoring him with a smile. "In fact, the more I think about it, the more I think I should not let you go again so soon. The last time I bid you farewell, it was five years until I saw you again. And you know, you aren't the most faithful correspondent I've ever had. Remember, I agreed to one year here, then I want you to come back."

"I remember, and I stand properly chastised for my poor habits in writing letters. They just never seem to say what I wish they would."

"But at least they say something. I love to get a letter. To read it again and again. Don't you?"

"I do. I admit it. Although I write so few that I get very few. And, of course, on board ship there is no post. It will be a very long wait until I hear from you, unless the peace negotiations speed along."

"I pray they will, then," Adelle said, her face close to his as they covered the last few yards to the carriage.

"I will as well." The chaperones were well inside the carriage, and there was no one to see, but somehow stealing a kiss just now didn't seem quite right, no matter how much he wanted it. He couldn't be certain she did, and until she did . . . well, he would wait.

"A man named Hugh Templeton tried to start a mill here right after the war," Fox told his guests when they arrived at the Valley Mill near dark that evening. "Slave owners would withdraw their slaves about the time he got them trained for the job, and finally he just gave it up altogether. Mr. Madison's war and its embargoes and blockades made it once again profitable. Of course, to keep it profitable, we must win the war."

"The Wateree River is the very place Papa intended

to build his own mill, before he and Mama decided to stay in Philadelphia. I've heard him talk of it."

"It was your father who gave me the idea for this site, Adelle. We talked of it when I was in Philadelphia. But he had far too many unhappy memories of the war to want to come back here, he told me."

"And I think he and Mama both felt it best to keep a distance from Grandfather, even though they loved him."

"He was the sort who had a way of wanting people to bend to his will," Fox said with a fond chuckle. "Only because he thought he knew best—about everything."

"They call that stubbornness, don't they?"

"They call it being Scots-Irish, I think. There are lots of his countrymen hereabouts, and they share his temperament."

"But you don't, I suppose?"

"I . . . Sometimes. All right, I admit it. More than I'd like."

Eliza and John had wandered back down to the first floor of the mill, not much interested in it, but Fox and Adelle lingered in the office, going over the order and receipt books and other records.

"Was this his?" Adelle asked, her fingertips brushing the rich texture of the American Beauty coverlet hanging on the wall.

"You can tell, can't you? It fairly shouts: Thomas Gairden, hand weaver. Aye, it was his. I cut it from his loom the day he died and tucked it away in my drawer. Selfish, I know, but at the time I just had to have a little of him to come back to, something his hands had touched."

"You know you should quit blaming yourself, don't you? Grandfather lived a good, long life. Nothing you could have done would have kept him alive once his body was ready to stop."

"I know, Adelle. It's just that on the day he died—the day of the duel—my whole life changed and has never been the same since."

"Each of us has a turning point, Fox. Not all as tragic as yours, I'll grant you, but a turning point nonetheless. Mine came when Joseph left. Suddenly I became the oldest child. I became the one Papa and Mama relied on. And I liked it. When Joseph came back, everything changed for me, too. And I can never go back to the way I was before, any more than you can."

Fox walked from his desk to join her next to the American Beauty coverlet. He let his fingers roam over it for a moment, as if making that connection with Grandfather that he had so often tried to make. "I like you this way," he whispered, close to her ear.

"And I would not change one part of you, either, Francis Marion Gairden. Neither would Grandfather, if he were here. I know it."

Fox brought his lips to hers, gently at first, but then feeling the passion that seemed to streak between them, he took her in his arms and held her close to him the way he had been wanting to since that evening in the parlor. She whispered his name again and again, and he kissed the fingertips that wandered feverishly across his cheeks and down his jawline and neck.

"What would Grandfather say about this?" he said, his arms still enfolding her, her head nestled comfortably against his shoulder.

"Well, let me see . . . I am a Catholic, but I am not too old for you—or too young—and so . . . I think he would say very little. What is important, though, Fox, is what *you* say."

"I say . . . I have never found an evening's work in

the mill office so pleasurable as this one. And I've never before seen an agent so beautiful."

Her laughter was soft against his neck, and he smiled with a contentment he had not known since the day a younger, more ingenuous Sally Hudson had flirted with him on Harleston's Green. "We'd better go, though, Cousin. Eliza and John will wonder what's taking us so long."

"I know," she said, her voice an almost sleepy sigh. "But I don't want to leave."

"We'll have more time together, Adelle. We'll make more time. And the time I'm gone will go quickly."

"Not quickly enough," she said, giving him a last kiss before they made their way by lamplight down the narrow wooden stairs and outside for the short walk to the mill's boarding house. He held her hand the whole distance, the way a gentleman should, except that where flesh met flesh the sensation was more intimate than could ever be considered gentlemanly.

"She *is*, after all, from a family of weavers—our family, Mama," Fox explained the next day when the group returned to Charleston.

"But ladies do not *do* such work, Francis. Your Aunt Lily and Uncle Paul would be most disappointed in me should I let her undertake such a task."

"Quite the contrary, Mama. In fact, Adelle says she thinks her mother would be most *pleased* to hear that she is doing something useful with her time down here."

The widow Susan Gairden shook her head. Her chestnut hair was curled tightly around her face, then pulled into a roll just above her neck. Her square face had been a pretty face in happier days. She had lost a great deal of weight in the weeks since her husband's death, however, giving her features a sharpness they had not had before.

"I never knew Lily well," she mused. "She was grown up and gone before I knew your father, but people still talked about the way she ran off with that Loyalist, and then with her father's partner. I don't think we need them all talking about how her daughter is a willful young lady, as well."

"She is a willful young lady I am very fond of, Mama," Fox said, trying the idea out for the first time. He saw that it was not completely a surprise to his mother. "We have grown very close these past few days."

"All the more reason we do not wish the whole of Charleston to whisper about her actions. She came here to escape the war. Her parents expect us to care for her, not to have her labor for us."

"Her parents were concerned for her safety, and rightly so from the sound of it. But from what I know of them, they would not object to her assisting us."

"But what would we tell people? How would we ever explain?"

"Women work at the mill, Mama. And children. Only a handful of men—"

"But they are not our sort of women."

"And Adelle would not be in *their* sort of situation. She would be serving as my agent, nothing more. Once I come back, she would step aside. But I am going to war, Mama. And I should have gone a long time ago— so should many others. We've become lax, wishing to grow rich and prosperous at the expense of other people's sacrifice. Now I have to serve. She wishes to serve as well, in the only way she can, by helping us."

"Us?"

"You, too, Mama." Fox paused, thinking of the best way to tell her what he wanted her to know before he set sail. "Papa invested all of his money in the mill. If there is loss, you will feel the pain of it as well as I until I can make it up to you. I trust Adelle, Mama. And I know she knows spinning. Weaving, too. She's worked with it all of her life. And certainly no one of 'our sort' will ever go up to visit the mill."

"Perhaps we could say that she was teaching the mill children, rather than taking your place. People would not think that unusual for a northern cousin."

"And she will teach, Mama. She has already spoken to me about it, and I think it's a fine idea. Evenings, and perhaps some Bible study on Sundays. Tell your friends that and no more."

"And what should I tell them about you and Adelle?"

At this Fox crossed the room and glanced out the window, his back to his mother. It was a question he was still wrestling with himself. "I think it unfair to bind her to me in any way before I leave on the *Jack*," he said, which was part of what he really meant.

"Of course you know that by entering into this business arrangement with her, you are binding her to you in one way."

"Aye. But even if she were to go back to Philadelphia today, there would be a bond between us. We have . . . grown close, as I said."

"You make a handsome couple, Francis. And she is a very lovely cousin, indeed. But what about Sally? I thought—"

"Sally and I . . . I don't know, Mama. Anyway, there are plenty of men in line for her hand, I'm sure."

"Her mother is one of my closest friends. And Jurian was one of yours. You *do* owe her something. She has had such a tragic loss in her young husband."

"But Adelle is my cousin, which makes her closer than either of them. Besides, I doubt Sally is suffering

Harnstron's loss all that much, since she has his money. I had never thought I would marry a cousin—I've always thought that one quaint Charleston custom I would not take part in. But perhaps I'm more of a true Charlestonian than I give myself credit for, no matter how much of the world I've seen."

"You should be proud to be a Charlestonian, Francis. Your father was."

"I am, Mama. But there is a whole world out there. And I'm going out into it, I know not where. I may not come back."

"Do you want to come back?"

"Yes, Mama. Very much. More than the last time I left. And when I come back, if things have not changed between us, I may marry Adelle."

"I see." Susan Gairden shook her head. "No one has ever been able to change your mind on anything, and you are the head of the family now that your father is gone."

"What makes you so guarded in your remarks? I know you think well of Adelle. You have always said what a darling she was, even when she came here as a child. And she has made me see myself in a new way. I see my life beginning to change: My decision to enlist with the navy has rid me of the guilt that has plagued me ever since the war began. I will be through with it once and forever. Finally my past begins to seem less important than my future. Adelle has done that—all of it."

"You deserve great happiness, Francis, and I hope you will find it. There is another matter, though. A letter that came while you were away. I'll leave you alone with it."

"Please say nothing of what I've told you," Fox said, not even looking at the envelope his mother handed him. "If her feelings should change while I'm away, I want no constraints upon her."

Susan Gairden nodded as she silently opened her chamber door and let herself out. It was only then that Fox took a good look at what she had handed him, and when he did, he understood her cautiousness. He took a seat as he began to open it. Some things were not ever through with forever. He had been fooling himself to think they were.

My dearest Fox,

How long it seems since I saw you, and how much has happened since you left. I have begun many letters to you, then stopped, not knowing what you would think of hearing from me. Now, I have not only the desire to write, but the need. The Beaver Creek Woolen Mill is no more, burned last week for reasons that are yet unknown, although I suspect the stove on the first floor of burning too hot. Your hard work, and my own, are gone.

My first thought was to leave and go to Hartford, or another city, but my workers entreat me to stay and to rebuild. It is because of their requests that I write you now after so long a silence. I know you are busy with your own work, perhaps even your own mill, but it would be my fondest wish that you would come back and oversee the rebuilding here. We will not be able to do much until spring. Already the autumn winds begin to blow and soon snow will come. I have hired Samuel Buffin to come and cap off the lower floor, and he may begin the upper frame if the weather holds, but the rest of it will have to come later. My workers will stay on here until spring if I can promise them work by summer. Some of the machines were saved, and Mr. McNitt will repair them over the winter. I will give lodging and what food I can to keep their families over the cold months.

I know this must seem odd to you that I, who did not even want to touch the mill in the first place, would now want to rebuild it, but our business has been very good, and I can see more profits ahead. The workers like it here and want to stay. We have our own little community and I cannot bear to destroy it.

Then, too, I would be lying if I said there was not more to the request than just your skill and advice. I have missed you more than I should ever say, and have many times regretted that you left without my speaking to you again. My disappointment in your insistence on leaving grew beyond my control, and once again I reacted by avoiding you, the way I once had done with Hugh. It's taken me all of this time to admit to myself you were right in thinking that perhaps too much had happened for us to ever be able to forget it, although I think the passage of time may have changed that. It has for me. I can almost forgive Hugh. I hope you can, too.

You once came to my aid when I sorely needed it. I need it again, dear Fox. I need you. Please send me an answer by return post. The past is behind us. Forever.

With affection,
Anne

Fox reread the letter, then folded it and tapped it against his knee as he tried to think. He pictured the mill flaming above the waters of Beaver Creek, and at the thought, the sensation of struggling in the cold water to free the bevel gear came rushing back to him. Then it was the image of Anne against the late-summer sun two years ago.

The act of simply rereading the letter brought with it a feeling of betraying Adelle. He had told her nothing of his feelings for Anne Vardry, though he knew she might have guessed. He had thought his feelings for-ever buried, but now, all those feelings were loosed in-side him again. Anne Vardry. He had let himself want her at the same time he had known the world would say he had killed her husband to get her. And then he had walked away from her when she wanted him at last. It had been the right thing to do, even if it had been a hard thing to do.

Now the opportunity was there again. And she promised no ghost of Vardry to stand in the way. She promised. And Fox knew that for her, at least, the promise was genuine. She had hated her husband. She would not let him stand between them. For Fox, though, the absolution would not be so easy. For Fox, the face of Hugh Vardry still remained a sometime companion. For Fox, forever was a more elusive quan-tity than for most others.

Why not last week, Anne? Why did this letter not come before Adelle brought me the joy of a new start? Or before I made up my mind about the navy? Why do you do this, Anne?

Fox hung his head, his hands clasped tightly as his arms rested on his knees. You were right, Grandfather, he thought for the hundredth time. You knew. You warned me. Once I fought Hugh Vardry, nothing would ever again be the same for me. You did not tell me, though, Grandfather, that it would be a curse. That it would keep me from knowing happiness with either of the women I would come to love. The first I could not love because I had killed her husband. And the second . . . the second I may not be able to love because she will not understand what it is that I feel toward Anne Vardry, why it is that she would ask me to come to her aid. Why did this letter have to come now? Why not while I was gone to sea? Why was it not lost on some packet sunk by the British? Why has this found its way to me, and how should I respond?

For a long time, Fox sat pondering these questions, his happiness dimmed, nearly extinguished, by the choices before him. Now, for yet another time, he faced the haunting image of Hugh Vardry, who always seemed to be laughing. The ghost stories I told Adelle were nothing compared to this, he thought. She wouldn't have believed this tale had I told it to her.

And then, as quickly as he thought it, he knew what he must do. He would tell it all to Adelle, every haunting morsel of it, not as ghost story but as truth.

On his last evening at home, Fox and Adelle once again lingered in the parlor long after the rest of the household had gone to bed. Susan Gairden had somewhat self-consciously excused herself earlier than usual, and Tully and Jemma had gone to their room downstairs once dinner was over. With his father gone, there was no one else in the house, and Fox realized anew how alone his mother would be once he and Adelle left.

"Perhaps I was selfish in accepting your offer to serve in my absence at the mill. Mama will be so alone." Fox tried to settle into a high-backed wooden chair next to the table but seemed to find himself all arms and legs. He leaned forward and folded his arms on the table, finally. Adelle sat across from him, just as she had that first night, her feet resting on a small needlepoint footstool and her hands folded in her lap.

"And perhaps I was selfish in offering."

"You don't want to stay with Mama?"

"I would not object to it. But I would rather be where I could *do* something."

"I know. The quiet of a house of mourning is a confining thing. I mourn my father. And I respect his memory. But—"

"So, in other words, you are thankful for an excuse to be off to war." Adelle could tease him like this and make him enjoy it. She was like Grish in that. She knew the right things to say. Except that tonight, nothing seemed quite right.

"I hope Mama does not sense my motives as accurately as you do, Cousin," he said with a wink. He let his eyes linger on her as he spoke, hoping Adelle was accurately aware of his motives, and of the important way she had influenced them in this new and right-feeling direction.

"She thinks you quite brave, I suppose," Adelle said. "And I agree, of course. Neither of us needs more than that to keep us until your return."

"But there *is* more than that." Again Fox shifted uncomfortably. The chair seemed hard, narrow, cold. He stood and walked across to the fireplace, where a small fire fought against a cool November downdraft in the great chimney. "And bravery's the last thing you should hold in your hearts of me." He saw her troubled look and longed to go to her, but instead he stayed where he was, steadying his long arms against the mantel and holding his eyes on the fire. If he turned around again, he might never say what he needed so much to say.

"There was a letter two days ago, Adelle."

"From Mrs. Vardry. I know. Jemma told me." At this he did turn to her. Her concern was now mingled with a kind of simple questioning.

"And you thought it not odd?"

"Not so terribly odd. You did work for her for several months. It does not seem odd that you might correspond occasionally."

"Her wish was for more than correspondence. She

expressed a need for me to come—her mill has burned. She wishes me to help her again."

"And will you?" Adelle shifted in her chair now, as if she, too, was less than comfortable, but she made no move to come to him.

"I don't know. It's so sudden. I'm to leave on the morrow. I would have to break my word to Captain Drummond. To you."

"We've exchanged no pledge that cannot be broken, Fox. If your duty lies elsewhere, I shall—"

Fox crossed the room in the space of one breath and knelt beside her, taking her hands in his. "We've made no pledge because I did not want you bound to a man who might not come back again from the sea. I did not want to see you waiting for something that might not come. And now . . . I must be honest with you, Adelle, because I care for you. There was between Mrs. Vardry and myself more than just a debt to be repaid. There was an emotion so strong I literally ran away from it. That was the real reason I did not stop in Philadelphia before I came home here to Charleston. That was the reason I could not see you. I was ashamed."

"Ashamed to have fallen in love?" She asked the question quietly, yet there was a stiff quality to the words. Pain.

"Aye. Ashamed to have fallen in love with the wife of the man I had killed. Can you imagine how deceitful that made me feel? How nether human?"

"And she?"

"She felt it, too, at first—the deceit, I mean. Then she convinced herself she didn't feel it, that there was nothing wrong in it, that I had saved her from a life with a man she despised. But I kept seeing his face. It is my own ghost story, Adelle. More vivid, more real than any I've ever told you. I am haunted by Hugh

Vardry just as surely as the sea is haunted by the ghost of Theodosia Alston."

"And so you will not go back to Connecticut, then?"

"I will not . . . and yet, I feel wrong to simply walk away when she calls for help. Oh, Adelle, I feel I will never be free of the Vardry curse. Now—"

Adelle stopped the lament, kissing his palms, drawing his head close and stroking his hair as she let her own head drop back and breathed deeply, closing her eyes.

"We have had only a week's time together, Fox. And it has been the most wonderful week of my life. I shall carry it with me while you are away and pray there are many more such weeks when you return—wherever it is from: the sea or the Connecticut mill country. I know I have never known anyone quite like you before, never cherished anyone the way I do you, never felt as I do at this moment. That is all I need to know." She brought her eyes back to meet his as she spoke the last words, then received the kiss he offered with the same passion he remembered from the night at the mill and the few moments alone together they had stolen in between. Taking her hand again, Fox rose to his feet and drew her to him, embracing her and feeling her return the embrace in a closeness he did not think he could live without for a year at sea.

"You are so certain, Adelle? How can you be so certain of things? Do you never question what you should do? What is right?"

"I have questions. But I know you, Fox. The same blood runs in our veins. We are more than friends, more than lovers. Right now, I am as certain of you as I have ever been of anyone in my life. I came a thousand miles to have you find me, Fox, but I found you a long time ago in Philadelphia. Maybe even as a child here in Charleston. I've made up my mind. Now you will have to make up yours."

"Adelle. Adelle. Please. I have. And it is you I want, only you." He held her close. "I love you. There, I've said what I promised myself I would not say before I went to sea. But I had to. I can't lose you, Adelle."

"I love you, Fox. I loved you even when I was a little girl and you told those stories. I always wished you would be the one to comfort me, not Aunt Susan."

"Had I only known how it would feel, Cousin, I surely would have." When their lips met this time, nothing was held back. The bond was made. The history revealed. The future certain.

"Tell me again how quickly the time will pass while I'm away," he whispered, brushing her ear with soft, urgent kisses. "Tell me how right it is for me to go. Tell me . . . tell me . . ."

"The time will pass quickly while you are gone, Fox. And it is right for you to go. And the sun rises in the west. These things we know are true, if we make ourselves believe them."

"And you would think less of me if I didn't go?"

"I would, no matter how selfishly I might wish to keep you here. It would not be right, any more than it was right for the militiamen to refuse to serve when called. They will have to live with their consciences, even though the charges against them were dropped. You should not have to do the same."

"I'll write Mrs. Vardry. She'll understand that I cannot help her, and that even if I were not going to sea, I've made another choice. That is the best thing for both of us, for all of us." His eyes focused on the lamplight as he held her and looked over her shoulder in the ebb of the embrace. "The hurricane, Papa's death, the mourning, the war, Anne's letter—it all seems almost unreal, like I might wake up again some morning and it will never have happened. Only I thank God that the result of all these darker happenings was your coming. I need you, Adelle."

The hours ticked by on the mantel clock, and the gray dawn of his departure found Fox and Adelle still locked in each other's arms, settled comfortably on the tufted settee by the window when Tully tiptoed in the next morning to light the fire. Fox raised his eyebrows when he caught Tully's look of surprise and shook a finger good-naturedly, but neither spoke nor woke Adelle. Fox sat with her in his arms, knowing that by noon of this day his life would take yet another unpredictable turn, no matter how much he might wish he could hold this moment in time. But when you come back you can marry her, he told himself. Remember that. You can marry her. That thought will carry me, he told himself. And perhaps I should ask her today, no matter what I told Mama. Then I could tell Anne when I write. . . .

16

He should have asked the favor of his mother, he realized later. He should have asked her to write Anne Vardry saying that her letter had arrived after he had left for the war. Then Anne would have understood why he had not answered her letter and could have gone ahead with her plans for the mill. Instead he chose to do nothing. He didn't answer the letter before he left Charleston, and once he was at sea there was no opportunity. Nearly half a year passed, in fact, before he could post a letter at all, and that one was owed to Adelle.

May 7, 1814

Dear Adelle,

I might have stayed longer in Charleston with you had I known what an odd shape this voyage would have to it. The *Saucy Jack* carried me northward, on its way toward Halifax in search of prizes, then put me aboard the *Mona*, a prize being sent into New York, where I was put aboard a new naval sloop called the *Peacock*, carrying twenty thirty-two-pound carronades and two long twelves. Fast enough to sneak through the blockade, it is one of three new sloops designed by a Mr. William Doughty of Georgetown, D.C. Two others, the *Wasp* and the *Frolic*, are also on the water, but none of the new frigates are—too slow to clear the blockade, I'm told.

In early March, sailing past my home harbor, and

you, and on to Georgia, I found myself longing more
than ever for your company. Much of the time we
were under chase, but we made it safely to Savannah, where we unloaded stores, and thence to the
Bahama Islands. We have encountered the hostility
of HMS *Epervier* and come away handsomely. Of its
men, I saw what I'd never thought to see: a British
crew not drilled in gunnery and mutinous in spirit. I
think there is hope for our own little navy after all.
We took our prize back to Savannah, arriving on
May 4, and once again I was struck with my nearness
to you, yet my infernal distance. The nearness was
short-lived, and we now embark on what may be a
long cruise, once again to the north in ·search of
whatever British we may find.

I can write you all of this, knowing my letter will
not leave the ship until long past the time the news is
history and no strategy is endangered by my ram-
bling. I know not when I may see you again. My duty
is one year, or until the end of the cruise nearest that
date, but Captain Warrington speaks daily of peace
coming before that time. The English, he says, are
tired of war. Who is not, when it tears them away
from those they love?

Know that you are one of those . . .

                                        Fox

When he posted the letter in Savannah, Fox knew he
should be sending one on to Connecticut as well, but
he didn't. He didn't know what he would say after all
this time, anyway. Buffin had no doubt proceeded on
the mill just as well without him. It was probably running again by now. Anne had some good people working for her. She didn't need him. Not as a millwright, at
least. And as for the other, he was going to marry
Adelle when he got back. He had as much as told her

so. No, everything with Anne was behind him now. Everything.

Five months later, he was finally able to post another letter to Adelle:

September 30, 1814

My darling Adelle,

One hundred days we've been at sea this cruise. One hundred more days away from you, and farther from my own shores than I ever again hope to be. Newfoundland, the Azores, Ireland, the Portugese coast. All names I formerly knew only from books. The summer found us seizing prizes here, there and everywhere, but the last month has brought a change. Of the last twelve sail seen, only two were British. It seems they've taken notice of us, after all. Captain Warrington tells us the last captain with whom he spoke told him British insurance rates are soaring, and British merchants are clamoring for peace and the resumption of their normal trade now that peace in Europe has been achieved. In the meantime, they are cautious on the water—if they sail at all.

We hit a squall last eve I thought would end our search for these now-elusive prizes. One man lost overboard, then retrieved. I thought of Grish, afloat in a storm and never heard from again, and I clung to my post with a resolve I was chided for this morning. I thought only of my return to you, however long it might take. Calm seas today near Barbuda in the West Indies. The beauty of this place makes me long for your beauty and companionship. One day, perhaps, we may sail these blue waters in a world at peace.

All my love to you,
Fox

As the *Peacock* approached New York in October, the shore appeared a mix of reds and golds, and the city itself was spotted with eruptions of color that reminded Fox of Connecticut. He had spent autumns in the North twice before, and the odd feeling these colors had evoked in him returned at the first sight of crimson maples, rusty red oaks and the yellows of aspen and sugar maples. The colors signaled finality to him, the end of warm days and the portent of cool nights and frigid days to come. Still there was a glorious warmth to these colored leaves, a warmth he remembered from an autumn day at the riverside with Anne Vardry. He closed his eyes for a moment, remembering, then opened them again to face reality. The waterfront was treeless, colorless and dirty. Fox longed for a liberty that would give him time to go out into the countryside, even if only for a day.

That liberty didn't come until three weeks later, and all the leaves were gone by then, but fair weather held and the sky kept its October blue well into November. His leave of four days was enough to get him into the countryside, or onto the water again. He took the water—a packet boat to New Haven, and from there the stage to Derby. Avoiding the questioning he knew would come if he set foot in the tavern, he headed straight for the livery, rented a horse and rode to Beaver Creek.

The rebuilt mill was there, just as he had guessed it would be, and the absence of anyone outside told him the day's work was not yet done, though daylight was nearly gone. Stepping inside, he was greeted with friendly waves from Tillie Gooding and two of her children. McNitt, the mill foreman, happened in at about the same time, though Fox hardly recognized him with the bushy brown chin whiskers he had grown. Gray was creeping in here and there, too, Fox noticed, but Mc-Nitt knew him at once and was eager to talk.

"Get that uniform off and find yourself somethin' else to wear, man. We've work to do here!" McNitt clapped Fox on the back, smiling broadly, and then pumped his hand again and again as he questioned Fox about the navy and the mill in South Carolina. Before Fox could answer, McNitt was filling him in on how Beaver Creek had been rebuilt after the fire. All the while Fox looked around at the new arrangement and the new workers McNitt was pointing out, he waited patiently for word of Anne Vardry.

"Is Mrs. Vardry here?" he finally had to ask.

"Not here, no. You can find her at home, though. Got her house finished soon after you left. She stays in it a lot, too. More than she should, I think. But then, she doesn't pay me to worry about such as that. So—"

"Thanks, McNitt. I'll look for her there. Tell the others I'll join them at supper if they don't mind."

"Glad for the company, Gairden. We'll be back to the boarding house within the hour."

Fox walked the short distance to Anne's house, nothing more than the other, standard mill houses. Outside, he hesitated for a moment, wondering just why he had come. Finding no good answer, he knocked.

When she opened the door wearing the same blue-and-cream-striped dress she had worn back when he had been the mill foreman, he had to catch his breath. She hadn't changed, except that she had lost the gaunt look he remembered. A soft pink highlighted her cheeks, bringing warmth to her whole face. She was clearly not expecting guests. Her table was covered with some pieces for a dress she was working on, and several pins were fastened to the puff of her left sleeve. A fluffy gray cat ran from beneath the table to hide itself somewhere in the back of the house, and a pair of shoes stood in the middle of the room.

"Fox! You're safe! Come in and get warm. It's going to be a freezing night, I just know." She opened her arms to him and he held her lightly, kissing both cheeks.

"So you knew I was at sea?"

"Your mother wrote. When I didn't hear from you after the fire, I wrote to her. She said you had sailed on a privateer but hoped to get on a naval vessel. She was very distressed for you, and so I have been, too. I can't tell you—"

"It hasn't been so bad as all that, Anne. We've seen a few battles, but much of it is pure sailing."

"Better than the British navy, though, is it?"

"Infinitely. Our captain is a fair man. Firm, but fair. I have a great deal of respect for him."

"And for me? Can you have any respect for a woman who so brazenly invites a man to come to her? Please forgive me, Fox. I shouldn't have written you like that, but I was so discouraged and it seemed as though if you could just come you could make everything better."

"But when I didn't come, you managed on your own, just as I knew you could. The new mill is a wonder, Anne—better than the old one ever was."

"Samuel Buffin stayed with it all the way through. James and Stewart Karr and the other men worked along with him. And, as it turned out, there was very little damage to the machines. All in all, we were lucky. We saved a great deal."

"And you had a bevel gear this time. I think you'd have gone ahead without me before if it hadn't been for that." Fox heard the clanging of the bell outside the mill announce day's end. He looked out the window and saw a half-dozen young boys running toward the boarding house, saw lamps extinguished in the mill windows. "I promised McNitt I'd join the clan for supper. I suppose I should get over there before it's all gone." His hand rested on the latch as he stood by the door, searching for the right words to say before he left.

"How long do you have?" she asked before he could find them.

"Tomorrow. I have only a four-day leave."

"Then eat with McNitt and the rest. But come back as soon as you're done."

"Don't you ever eat with them anymore, the way you used to?"

"No. Sometimes they bring me something. But—"

"You're not getting to be that hermit Anne Vardry again, are you now? I wouldn't want that."

She shrugged. "I don't seem to relish company the way I did at first. Tillie visits every evening for a while."

"You don't go to the mill at all anymore? You just stay here?"

"There's no need for me to go over there. McNitt takes care of everything."

Fox looked at her, really looked at her for the first time since he had come through the door. Though healthier than before, she still had the look of the frightened doe Buffin had once described her as. "I'm going to talk to him, Anne, about putting you to work, owner or not. You can't stay here alone so much. I'll be back within the hour. You be thinking about what you're going to do to get yourself out of this house more while I'm gone. All right?" He tried to keep the comments light and hoped his concern would not have the reverse of the effect he wanted. "All right?" he asked again, tapping his foot on the floor while he waited for her answer. When he saw her smile, he knew it had worked. "Be back soon," he said, letting himself out and nodding to himself as he crossed the dark roadway between Anne's house and the boarding house.

"She was glad to see you, wasn't she, Mr. Gairden?" Tillie Gooding wasted no time in checking into what had passed between him and Anne.

"She was, though I can't imagine why. When she could have used my help, I wasn't here to give it. In fact, I was halfway around the world."

"She forgave you that once she had the letter from your mother. Took to worryin' about whether you'd come back safe or not, so it's good you've come to let her know her prayers were answered. We've room for you here at the boarding house if you don't mind a few others in the room with you until—"

"Thanks, Tillie, but I won't be staying. I'm just on a short leave. Need to head back tomorrow," he said between mouthfuls of biscuits and ham gravy.

"Oh."

Fox could tell from the children's giggles and the looks that passed surreptitiously around the table that this was not what everyone had been expecting. "I signed on for one year. Three months of that are left. I took a room in Derby for the night," he lied, "but thanks for the offer."

"When you're done sailing, then?" Tillie pressed on, and Fox remembered the Derby nosiness he'd almost forgotten once he left here last time.

"Well, I doubt it. I have my own mill now—or at least I did when I left. Hard telling what I'll go back to."

"You know you're always welcome here if things don't work out for you down there," McNitt put in before Tillie could, and the conversation turned to news of the Beaver Creek Mill for a while before Fox excused himself, walked toward the river while he smoked a cigar and pondered the course of the evening, then ambled back to Anne's.

She had changed into a clean dress of soft, rosy pink cotton by the time he returned, and had put away her sewing and combed her hair, pinning it back with a large, pearl-studded comb.

"Now I feel I should have changed, too. This uniform was clean when I left New York, but now . . ."

"You couldn't look any better wearing an admiral's uniform, Fox. I wish you'd exchange it for some work clothes, though. Stay here, Fox," she said before she even asked him to sit down. "Don't go back."

"But I can't do that, Anne. I've enlisted, and if I don't go back the navy will consider me a criminal. Besides, I've a stake in this war. You know that. I don't know that we're winning—or losing—but we're close to an end. I mean to be there for it."

"You and your sense of honor! Do you never think of yourself?"

"I . . . Sometimes it seems I think only of myself, like in coming here without letting you know first. But I had to come. I couldn't stand being so close and not knowing how you were doing. Then to find that the mill had burned and you had rebuilt . . . It wasn't just the mill, though, Anne. I had to see if there was anything . . . I left in such a rush that day. But if I had seen you again I might not have had the strength to say no again, and we could never have been together with the ghost of your husband between us."

"And yet you've come back now. Why? Don't you believe in ghosts anymore?"

"I do. And the ghost of your husband is still with me sometimes. But . . . I have feelings for you, too, and I realize it isn't right to run away from them because of what might be, either. Perhaps it's time I face Hugh Vardry."

"There is only one way for you to do that," Anne told him, crossing the room to close one last drape before she returned to stand before him. "Stay with me. Let me face him with you. I knew him. I know how to chase away his ghost."

"Anne . . ." Fox sighed, looking away from her. "It's not that simple. I am in love, Anne. With my cousin, Adelle Durant from Philadelphia. I—"

"She's far away, Fox. By the time you get back to her, much may have changed. And you may not get back to her. War is very uncertain business. Two boys from Derby were killed at the border with Canada near Montreal, and two more at Fort George."

Fox looked into her eyes, remembering anew the passion that could fill them when she let it, when she did not make herself afraid of people or situations.

"You said yourself you had feelings for me," she went on while he tried to think of an answer for her arguments. "Don't you owe it to yourself, at least this once, to put honor aside, to put everyone else's wishes aside and just do what you want to do? Would God strike you down for that? Or would your captain? Or your mother? Of course they wouldn't. Everyone deserves such freedom. Is it not the very thing wars are fought for?"

"And Adelle? What would she say?"

"If she loves you even half as much as I do, she will want you to do what you feel you need to do. She won't want you coming back to her still wondering if you love someone else. No woman does."

Fox brought his hands to rest on her hips, then drew her slowly toward him in just the way he had imagined doing many times since that sunny afternoon on the rocks up Beaver Creek. And he said no more, just letting his body respond to hers the way it had that lazy Sunday three years ago. Their lips met in a rush of stored emotion that humbled him. It hadn't just been that she was afraid to have him leave that day, it had been that she had loved him. He could feel it in the caress of her hands at the back of his neck and the feel of her tongue against his, yet in a moment he felt her pull away.

"Come," she said. "When I call you, come to me." She hurried up the narrow stairway, and Fox watched her go just as he had that day in the mill before he had known her and wanted her as he had come to later. He glanced to the door, knowing he should open it and go on his way, then he thought again. Maybe she was right. Maybe there was only one way to chase away the ghost of Hugh Vardry for both of them and that was to face him in the one way they had not. He heard her call his name, took one last look at the door, slipped out of his boots and stood them next to it, then padded slowly up the steps.

No lamp was lit, but she met him at the top of the stairs and took him by the hand. The moment he touched her he knew she wore nothing at all, that her hair fell loose across her back and had been brushed through enough times to make it flyaway. There was nothing to say, nothing he could say. What he had dreamed of many times was now before him, waiting to see if he would run away again. She began to unbutton his shirt, then his breeches, and with every touch of her body against his, he lost some of the apprehension he had carried up there with him. She had said she loved him, and even though he had said he loved Adelle, he knew there were feelings for Anne he had kept carefully buried until he had let himself make this journey. Perhaps she was right. He might as well find out what they were before he married Adelle and ruined her life.

"Fox, Fox," Anne whispered again and again as they made love. He had been with women before, but never with one he had feelings for—perhaps even loved—and the experience left him weak with an ecstasy he had heard other men boast of. He had always thought them lying, but now he knew why they chose to tell and retell the stories of their amours. Drunkenness had no charms as powerful as this, he thought, drifting off into a heavy sleep.

A misty dawn was already beginning to break when he woke with a start to see a fully clothed Anne Vardry kneeling beside him on the bed.

"You were having one of your dreams, weren't you, Fox? About Hugh, I mean."

"I was." Fox took a deep breath and swallowed back the gasps that tried to force their way out as he remembered the image of Hugh Vardry shooting him in the head with a pistol, the same pistol he had used the day of the duel, as Fox made love to Anne. Calming himself after a moment or two, he reached for the comfort of her body. "We didn't quite chase him away. We may have to try again."

As soon as the words came out, Fox knew they hadn't been the right ones. "We shouldn't have tried last night. I was . . . I let my fancies run away with me. I had no business asking you to stay. I should have known Hugh wouldn't let us be together. He will never—"

"But I don't understand, Anne. I thought you didn't believe in his ghost."

"I didn't. Until I watched you sleep. I did, you know. All night. I saw you in torment. Haunted. Restless. And I knew it was Hugh. It was really him, not just your imagination. And I want none of him back, Fox. Not in any way, not even in your dreams. I hadn't realized how far I had been able to get away from thinking of him until he came back in here last night, and as much as I have wanted you, you're not worth the price.

Having you is not worth having to have him back again, too."

"But he wouldn't—"

"Oh yes he would. If the power of our love last night was not enough to keep him away, nothing ever will be, don't you see? No, Fox, I was wrong to ask you to stay last night. To tempt you as I did, but I was hungry for you, like a bear is hungry for honey." She pushed back away from him and off of the bed. "Put your clothes on and go, Fox. Before anyone sees you. They'll be going to the mill soon. And don't ever come back, no matter how much duty you feel here, no matter how far away the ghost of Hugh Vardry seems. He's won, and I finally admit it. I'm going to go away from here myself as soon as I can sell the mill."

Fox wanted to tell her she was wrong, to say that time would erase the bad memories, but the vision of Hugh Vardry was too real to him. And the vision of Adelle was there, too. He had done her a terrible injustice in his effort to settle what was between him and Anne. "I hope the flames of hell are licking at your heels, Vardry. If ever anyone deserved them, you do." Fox spoke under his breath after Anne had left him to dress alone, muttering as though Vardry were real instead of a dead man, and from the far corner of the room, he almost thought he heard him laugh.

January 5, 1815

My Dearest Adelle,

In sending you wishes for the happiest of New Years, I cannot help but lament that I was unable to see this one in with you. How I wished you in Philadelphia this autumn that I might have seen you whilst we refitted here in New York harbor. We landed October 20, and have been here weeks now, waiting for nothing more than the right conditions to once again escape the choking blockade. We are not idle, of course, for there seems an endless amount of work to be done—most of it below decks where the constant dampness has given me a cough I fear I shall never lose.

My naval duty should be done January 23, but the officers have their ways of getting men to stay on. Still a shortage of new recruits, and in case of need I would find it hard to walk away. We hear news of victories along the border with Canada, and further depredations along the Chesapeake seem unlikely, but we must be ever watchful. The news of the burning of the capital sickened us all when we heard of it, weeks after the deed was done. I pray Charleston's defenses remain in place, and that you are in no danger of any kind. I await the day when I can be there to hold you in my arms again. May this war be over soon.

> With all of my love,
> Fox

The letter was short, but it was all he could manage. The trip to Derby stood between him and Adelle like a mountain, and while he knew it wasn't impossible to climb over it and get things back to the way they had once been, it couldn't be done in a letter.

17

In Fox's last weeks aboard the *Peacock* there had been few actual battles but much time to regret the trip to Derby. On his return to Charleston, though, the Vardry episode was quickly overtaken by all that awaited him: Adelle's pleasure at having him home and his at being there, news of the family and of the city.

"I'm afraid I've carried them with me everywhere these past few months," Adelle said, taking the three letters she had received from him from her reticule. "I had a great fear something might happen to you since your last voyage began after the war was actually over. It seemed bad luck."

Soft with folding and refolding, the letters were all he had been able to post. The rest of his days had been recorded here and there in a journal, most of it little more than soundings and wind direction, but some of it about Anne. He had tried to figure it all out during his lonely days at sea, but he hadn't been able to. Now that he was home, Adelle seemed able to make everything fit together just as it should. The moment she came back into his life the Vardry troubles seemed to fade in importance. "If only you could have been in New York when I was there," he said, kissing her lightly on the cheeks as the rest of the family looked on, but holding her close long after the kiss had ended, afraid to let go of her strength now that he had it back again.

He kissed her once more, this time on the lips, before he had to let her go so that he could greet his mother and his sisters, in turn. His homecoming had been awaited from the time the *Younger Sister* had been sighted at the bar, and he was overwhelmed with thankfulness to be back home again. Among the crowd in his mother's parlor, however, his eyes sought out only one and he returned to her side determined never to leave it again.

"Our last cruise was of very little consequence," he said, mechanically stating what the weather had meant for him and the rest of the men aboard the *Peacock*, while his eyes lingered on Adelle. No longer in mourning, she wore a walking gown of sage green cambric with a three-quarter-length jacket that draped pleasingly on her slim frame. You are going to have to tell her about Anne, he thought, if you are the man you claim to be. And you risk losing her when you do.

"We sailed south to rendezvous with the *Hornet* at Tristan da Cunha in the South Atlantic," Fox went on, speaking of his naval adventures instead of what was really on his mind. "Encountered almost no sail along the way, and when we got there the *Hornet* had already seized the British sloop of war *Penguin*. That was in March, but still no word of the peace had reached any of us. We saw His Majesty's vessel sunk, then sailed for the East Indies in search of British sail. Found it, too. Four East Indiamen loaded to the rail, picked off like quail on a hunt. Then we met the *Nautilus*, one of the East India Company's armed ships. She hove to when Warrington ordered, then hailed that peace had been declared. Warrington, unfortunately, suspected a ruse and fired off two broadsides. He was later convinced of his mistake and released the *Nautilus*—and us—to sail for home. My God, what a feeling! It made up for all the nights of eerie silence and days of boredom between encounters. We had done it! Fought for an end to British rule of the seas and won."

"The *Courier* reports that in England people feel that *they* have won. Has anyone won, really?" Susan Gairden's face had lost the frightened, distant look it had had upon her husband's unexpected death at the time Fox went to sea, but her tone seemed still mournful, not quite in keeping with the occasion.

"Indian matters are unsettled as ever, from what I hear. The British wished to establish territories for the Indians; we did not. Boundaries will go back to what they were before the war, prisoners are to be returned, so no one really won there," Fox said. "And the Treaty of Ghent said nothing of impressment, illegal search or blockades—the very things we fought the war for. But I tell you, we won their notice! We stood up to them and did not back down. And our little navy, with speed and with courage, outfought the bigger men-of-war. Oh we lost some, I'll grant you. But we won many."

"You sound profoundly pleased for such a reluctant sailor," Adelle observed. There was pride in her smile, coupled with a certain wistfulness.

Nearly two years of separation stood between them. He had changed, he supposed. No doubt she had, too, although if looks meant anything at all, she was even more beautiful than he remembered. And she'd picked up a soft, Charleston accent, probably without even knowing it. He liked the result.

"Profoundly pleased to be home here with you." He didn't even try to hide whom he meant as he looked into her eyes. "The getting here took so long, I didn't know what I might find. No letters ever reached me."

"And you didn't write of this beard you've grown, either, my son." Susan Gairden cast a disapproving look his way that brought laughter and an end to the private moment between Fox and Adelle.

"It was the style among the seamen, Mama, and I

see it's come on land as well. New York was filled with bearded faces. I find I like it."

Sisters and spouses and nieces and nephews all offered their opinions, but Adelle just smiled. We still share a special bond, she seemed to say, and Fox was able to let the other comments go with nothing more than a smile. Nothing mattered except Adelle. He had finally learned that. "You must tell me all the news of Charleston—and the mill," he said, changing the topic. "I'm eager to know—"

"The Charleston Theatre is open once again," his sister Miriam said quickly. "You won't recognize it now that it's remodeled. We went there just last week to see one of Mr. Shakespeare's plays."

"And cotton prices are climbing every day," put in her husband, planter Robert Stockbook, "just as I told you they would."

Robert had aged, Fox noticed, but he hadn't lost the tone of superiority he had always been known for. Miriam had been taken with his wealth and ignored his character, disappointing their father beyond words. Fox had forgotten that while he was away with more urgent things on his mind. Now it all came back. "Congratulations," he managed to say, not mentioning his divided loyalties. High cotton prices were good for the planters and the factors, not good for the mill owners. "How's the—"

"Sally Harnstron married Richard Celestine." Fox's sister, Eliza, interrupted him before he could ask about his own business. "Finally," she added with a sigh, giving the news some undertones everyone but Fox seemed to understand.

"Finally?" he asked.

"She was unpleasant," his mother said. "She made it known about the city that she was waiting for you, Fox."

"Me? Whatever for? We had no agreement of any kind." He shot a quick glance toward Adelle. "Adelle, I'm sorry for this confusion, but I did nothing—"

"That was part of the problem, Francis," his mother said. "Sally assumed that your friendship with her, and with Jurian, insured a future union since she was left a grieving widow and a grieving sister all at the same time. The fact that you did not speak to her before you left, in either direction, unfortunately gave her reason to go on thinking that. It wasn't until Adelle spoke of your . . . friendship . . . that Sally made public what she thought to be your intentions toward herself."

"I shall speak to her and demand an apology," Fox said, his eyes holding Adelle's in regretful frustration.

"Please, Fox, no. I'd rather you didn't." Adelle's face colored as she spoke, and Fox wondered just how unpleasant Sally had been.

"As you wish, Cousin, but I am saddened to think of your position in all of this. Please forgive me for not speaking to her more plainly before I left. I simply never thought."

"Sally likes attention," Susan Gairden pronounced. "If she doesn't get it one way, she will get it another. Celestine will find that out for himself soon enough. And I thank God you did not bring her home as a daughter to this house, Francis." Mama had a way of closing a discussion with her statements, and before long the conversation drifted to family matters and further talk of the Treaty of Ghent. Adelle was quiet, he noticed, but seemed more one of the family than she had before he left. She was obviously close to his sisters, adored by their children, a companion to Mama. All he could ever hope for in a wife.

She had done it. Without even being there, Sally Hudson Harnstron Celestine had managed to cast a pall over his homecoming, and part of him wanted to knock down the Celestines' door and slap Sally's pretty face. The rest of him wanted to admit that the news of Sally's "unpleasantness" wasn't the only reason he felt as he did just now as he waited for Adelle in the parlor that evening. She had seemed especially reserved earlier, almost as if she could read his own apprehension about this private homecoming that would surely take place between them. Was he imagining it? Or was it his own guilt that was making him *think* she must see his indiscretions in Derby for the despicable act they had been?

"I helped your mother with her buttons. She's resting now," Adelle said softly when she came up the stairs from Susan Gairden's first-floor chamber.

"Her rheumatism has advanced greatly while I've been gone. I couldn't believe the change," Fox said, taking Adelle's arm and showing her to the settee by the window instead of taking her in his arms as he wanted to. A gentle breeze filtered in through the filmy lace of the tieback draperies, and she fanned herself slowly as he pulled a chair close to her. Fox unbuttoned his multicolored Marseilles waistcoat and loosened his cravat. It was warm for September, and the old brick house showed no signs of cooling off.

"This humid weather makes it worse, I think. She has had better days, though few. Uncle Whit's death affects her still, Fox."

"She seemed good, though, today. Cheerful. Happy."

"For you, Fox. All for you. In your absence she was quite melancholy. I suspect the feeling will return."

Fox held Adelle's hand in his, and she looked at him as she spoke, but he sensed once again her reserve. He felt once again his own guilt. "But I do not wish to speak of Mama, Adelle. It is you I have longed to see. It is you I have come home to. I—"

"I have something to tell you," she said before he could finish his sentence. Fox blinked once. Again, quickly. The sound of her voice set off a tremor inside him. She knew. Anne must have written.

"It's about the mill," she went on. "And we decided not to tell you right away. Your mother didn't want to spoil your homecoming. No one did. But I can't let you go on thinking everything's the same as when you left, Fox, because it isn't. You left thinking I would take care of it all for you, and I failed."

"You didn't fail, Adelle. You couldn't fail, at anything. Don't say that." He moved to the settee and took her in his arms, hearing the sobs that had been held in behind that face of calm reserve and the quiet statements of the afternoon. "How bad is it?"

"Very bad." She drew away from him, sitting back and folding her arms tightly beneath her breasts, almost as if she were cold. "Cotton prices shot up, but we were forced to purchase ten bales to fill an order Mr. Merrifield had already quoted too low. With prices still high, we purchased more cotton, only to have nearly half of the spinners quit and go home to their own crops. Two went west to better land at the call of their family from Virginia. Then the war ended, and within a month's time the shops and stores were flooded with British goods again, cheaper than our own. Orders were canceled. . . . For a time, it looked as though we might be saved. Richard Celestine was about to cover the shortfall when Sally found out that you and I . . . were more than friends. She turned immediately to Celestine, and on your mill, and he withdrew. We—" Adelle turned away, and Fox heard another sob catch in her throat. "We had to close it, Fox. There was nothing else to do."

Now it was Fox's turn to sit back, to look away. He had known the mill might be having difficulties. He had seen a newspaper in New York. Another in Savannah. There was a feeling of good times in the tone of the news now that the war was over, but the reality was that, just as they had said this afternoon, in many ways the war had changed nothing. England planned to monopolize textiles in the United States and had wasted no time getting back to matters of trade now that the issues of impressment and search and seizure were issues no longer: Once the war was over, England had no need for extra seamen. She had no need to impress them, or to search ships for them. Fox had read of the demise of three spinning mills in Rhode Island. Now he heard of the demise of his own. He could not, in any way, blame Adelle. Or even his agent, Ezra Merrifield. Or even himself. No, perhaps he could blame himself.

"Could it be that Grandfather was wrong? He always said that mills were the future of the textile business. He could see the day when not just spinning, but everything from the wool on the hoof or cotton on the stem to the coat on a man's back would be manufactured under one roof by machines, not hands. Not by people laboring with aching backs but by people guiding machines to do that labor for them. And to do that, we needed our independence from England. He fought a war for it. I fought a war for it. And now? Has it all been for naught?"

"Not unless you give up on it, Fox." Adelle's voice made a soft blend with the heavy, warm air. Darkness had descended completely, but the light of a full, harvest moon cast the two of them in a silver-white contrast to their surroundings, and neither made a move to light a lamp, to move closer together or farther apart. Like marble statues, they sat erect in their own spaces.

"I think perhaps it is myself I should give up on,

Adelle. It is my own doing, this loss of my mill and my father's money."

"Not at all. Why, you weren't even here." Adelle reached out her hand to comfort him, but he rose and walked away from her and into the shadows at the edge of the pool of moonlight.

"No, I wasn't here. But I should have known. I should have been able to see what was happening. The South Carolina Homespun Company, with many more investors and better equipment than we had, could not stay in business. Why did I think I could? Because I always think I'm right. Just like when I fought the duel." He laughed a bitter little laugh as he thought of it all. "Forgive me, Lord, for I am hard to turn."

Adelle stood and looked out the window, her profile delicate but well defined in the silvery light. She smiled. "You and Grandfather—and my mother. You are all hard to turn. It's one Gairden trait I don't seem to have. I can bend, when I have to. You can, too, Fox. We will bend together, do what we must to get the mill going again. There has to be a way, if we do it together. I just didn't know which way to turn on my own. I didn't know what you would want me to do—"

"I wouldn't have wanted you to borrow money from Richard Celestine, though you couldn't have known that. He's a very hard man, Adelle. And once he had some leverage he would have pushed for slave labor in the factory, and we might have had to give in."

"Why would he do such a thing? He seemed most cordial to me."

"We had words once, back when I was getting the mill started, about slaves. I objected to using them, and he thought me less than a true South Carolinian for it. He's a man who likes retribution. Not a good man to do business with."

"But Sally—"

"I think Sally did us a favor there, without ever intending it." Fox laughed at the irony of it. "But I'm sorry she was unkind to you in the process." Tell her now, he thought. Tell her Sally was not the only one who was unkind to her.

"I survived. And won some friends, I think. There are those who feel Sally is a bit . . . forward in her actions. You have many friends here, Fox. People will help you get the mill going again."

You are far too good for me, Adelle Lambert Durant, Fox thought. Your energy, your talent, your steadfastness. He took her in his arms, in the moonlight and shadows of the parlor, and he knew he could tell her nothing. This hurried union of lips and heart and hands and breath spoke not of betrayal but of promise, not of distance but of longing. Words spent, no more than murmurs and whispers broke the long silences of love that bound them as the harvest moon inched across the sky.

Fox half expected his mother to peek into the parlor during the late hours when he and Adelle still lingered there, she on his lap the way a child might cling to a long-lost parent, but he less content. Loving the feel of her body against his, he wanted more of it, wanted to carry her up the stairs and into his bed. And perhaps soon he would be doing just that, but there was the other matter. The other bed he had not yet told her of, and perhaps shouldn't. Perhaps there was nothing to be gained by confessing to her that he had gone to see Anne Vardry after all. But then, was his love for her nothing more than a matter of gain? In a heartbeat, he knew it was not.

"Adelle," he whispered. The moon had risen high and its light no longer filled the room, but their eyes, catlike in the darkness, saw enough. And Fox wanted to see enough, but perhaps not all, nor did he want to be entirely seen. "There is something I must tell you, too."

She was sleepy now, and her body, relaxed against him, tensed not at all. Yet she lifted her face to him. Their noses touched. Then lips. "Yes," was all she said.

"I've seen Anne Vardry."

"I don't care, Fox."

"How can you *not* care, dearest Adelle? I promised you I would not see her and then broke that promise. You say you do not care? Do you think so little of yourself, then, that you would align yourself with a man of such spineless character? The guilt of it almost kept me from coming back to you."

"I care so much for you that whatever made you go to her, I know it must have been important. I know there must have been a reason. And, after all, you did come back to me." Adelle stopped then, as if perhaps she weren't as certain as she would like herself to be. "I think I knew you would go, actually. I saw your indecision when her letter arrived."

"I felt torn, Adelle. I felt a duty, and, to be honest, I felt I . . ." He shook his head as if to shake away the memory of it. "I was only a short packet-boat ride away and . . . I had some feelings for her. I thought I might be able to settle things inside myself by seeing her again."

"And did you?"

Hugh Vardry's face, now a sadly distorted memory, came to him and Anne's with it, both of them part of him now. "I think you need to know, Adelle, that a part of the Vardrys, both of them, will be with me always. In shooting Hugh Vardry, I destroyed another human being who, from his widow's accounts of him, was a mean-spirited, hollow man. Yet he did not deserve to die, and I did not mean to kill him. His death freed Anne from his abusive ways, but, like me, she will never be completely free of him, either. There can never be anything between us, because he will always be there. Like one of the Charleston ghosts, he will walk with me all my days."

"The stories of Charleston ghosts are just stories, Fox. I've known that since your mother convinced me of it way back when. Hugh Vardry can be a ghost to you only if you believe in ghosts. And you don't, I know you don't. That's why you could delight in the telling of the stories that scared a cousin nearly out of her wits." She tweaked his nose with her finger and brought back, in her touch, the happiness of innocent times. For a moment, Fox was back there with her, but the memory was fleeting.

"Then why is he ever with me, Adelle? Why is his face the first thing I see in the morning, even before I open my eyes? And why does he come along to spoil every chance for happiness I find?"

"Because you let him. Because honor demands that you not forget him. And it is good that you not forget him, or what happened that day at Washington Course. But something my mother told me about her struggles with Grandfather might help you, too. She said that she could never forget that Grandfather tried to deny her Papa's hand, but that she did forgive him. You should never forget Hugh Vardry. But you should forgive yourself, Fox." Adelle lay her head back against the settee, her eyes closing with smooth perfection. "And if forgiving yourself allows you to seek out Anne Vardry, then that is as it should be. I want you to be certain, Fox. I want you to *know*."

"And you *do* know, Adelle? You know you would be willing to spend a lifetime with a man who is deeply in debt with no clear way out?"

"Many are in that same situation, Fox. The end of war has brought bad times. Mama wrote that it reminds her of the year after the Revolution. Men are coming home from war to find farms out of production, jobs gone. Money is scarce. Everything is unsettled. But better years will come. Look at Papa and Mama. Look how well they've done. We can, too."

"You, Adelle, are . . . I can't even say all that you are. I can only say that I love you. And I haven't asked you formally, the way a Carolina gentleman should, if you'll be my wife." Fox rose, but never let go his gentle hold on her right hand. Dropping on one knee, he brought her hand to his lips, caught the elusive lavender scent of her, felt the softness of her skin against his lips. "Adelle. Will you do me the honor of becoming my wife?"

"It is you who do me the honor, Fox. And I will. Oh, I will!" She leaned toward him and met him in a kiss of no sleepy nature but one filled with the urgency of tomorrow.

"As soon as I've been to the mill and talked to Merrifield and to the bankers, I'll know what we're going to do. After that, if they're not going to put me in debtor's prison or the stocks or something equally distasteful, we'll make our plans, if that's all right with you, Adelle."

"I was going to suggest the same thing. We've waited long enough. Not even Charleston's social rules should find fault with a war hero being married with all haste. I shall write Papa and Mama in the morning—oh, but my, my, it is morning already. Anyway, they may not come, but I want them to know. I know they will be so happy for us, Fox. They love you. As I do."

For once, when Fox closed his eyes, it was not Hugh Vardry's face that appeared, but the vision of Adelle with flowers in her hair. He was kissing her. The flowers smelled of lavender.

18

Three days later Fox arrived at the mill. The dust of absence covered every machine, every inch of floor, every windowsill, every belt and pulley in what had been the Valley Cotton Mill. Outside a cool west wind blew, promising rain. The sky was gray as the inside of his soul, Fox thought as he looked around him at the still-born dream. He had talked to some possible investors before leaving Charleston, but none of them had been willing—or perhaps it was able—to sink funds into what they saw as yet another example of why South Carolina should stick to growing cotton and forget about processing it.

He made the trip to Rice Creek by himself, even though Adelle had wanted to come. He thought he should see it by himself, as he had that first time when he had come riding out to the abandoned site and paced off its dimensions, envisioned its future and set his plans. Perhaps some similar inspiration would come to him now. Perhaps he would see a way out of the pit he seemed to have fallen into. Would it have been different had he been there to manage things himself? he asked himself again and again. He wanted the answer to be yes, even though he placed no blame on Merrifield or Adelle. He trusted them. He knew they had done as well as they could. As well as he could have. No, it was the economy that had caused the end of the Valley Mill, just as it had many others across the country. He was not alone in his failure, but it was small comfort.

Damn! His finger traced the word in the dust of an idle belt that connected an overhead shaft to one of the Edgwell jennies. What am I going to do? He sneezed at the dust he had raised with his writing and headed back to the office. Go over the figures, Fox, he told himself. Look for ways. There's got to be a way.

He punched Grandfather's coverlet as he walked by it, sneezing again as dust flew out of it. What am I doing wrong, Grandfather? What can I do? What can I do? He looked back at the coverlet as he sat at his desk, the account book open before him. Owed, to D. Poignand, $31. Owed, to R. McLane, $27. Owed, to A. Lawrence, $78. Note, Whitcomb Gairden, $13,486.38. "I couldn't make it on weavin' alone," he remembered Grandfather saying. "If I hadn't started some tradin' on the side I'd have starved to death. Twas the tradin' that carried me, son. But 'twas the weavin' I loved." He chuckled at the memory of the wink Grandfather had given him as he said it, knowing that his son, Whitcomb, had never liked a single thing about the weaving business, but that his grandson liked it all.

Grandfather had never held it against his son that he hadn't continued on at the Sign of the Shuttle. In fact, he had been proud that Whit had become a lawyer. No man should have to live his life to suit his father, Grandfather liked to say. No woman, either, he had learned to add. But that hadn't stopped his delight when Fox would sit next to him on the loom bench and beg to be taught how to weave. Fox had known from the first time he threw a shuttle that he was going to follow after Grandfather, not his own father, and Grandfather had been careful to teach him that he was going to have to change along with the industry. Weaving was not always going to be a matter of small manufactories like the Sign of the Shuttle. Water-powered mills were going to take their place, and if he was smart he would build one.

Well I am smart, Grandfather, Fox thought. And I have a mill, though I didn't build it all. And I've tried to keep up with the changes. But I can't compete with the British, any more than you ever could. They're back in our markets just the way they've always been. What would you do? What should I do?

Fox searched out every memory of Grandfather he could summon. There is a clue here somewhere, he told himself. Grandfather had another business to keep him going, but I have no capital to start such a business. Grandfather couldn't go back to Philadelphia, so he went to Charleston. . . .

Fox looked again to the coverlet, the solution coming to him in the space of a glance. He had a voucher for 160 acres of land in Illinois, part of his pay from the war, something he'd thought to sell to someone going out that way, another soldier perhaps, who could pair it with his own grant. Try it yourself, he seemed to hear Grandfather say. You'll never know if you don't try. Fortunes to be made in the West, he heard other voices say, voices on board the *Peacock*, voices in New York, the voices in two wagons he had passed on this very trip to Camden. People were heading west to get away from the hard times here. Take the carding equipment, fulling hammers, too. Set up a new mill. Get into the land business or the lending business or some other business to give you enough income to expand. Just as Grandfather had done.

The thought of taking apart this mill that so much of his heart had gone into building was a difficult one for him. A fulling or carding mill was a far cry from what he wanted any mill of his to be. And yet, there was nothing for him here. There was no money to buy more cotton and no one to borrow any from, no one to work the machines and no market for the cloth even if it could be made. There was always the possibility of going back to college. To read law, as his father had done. But there was no joy in either thought. His heart had not been at college that last time he had tried. Now he was even older and less interested. And he wanted to get married. He did not want to wait any longer for Adelle. She had told him once that she was determined to go west sometime. So that was it. West was the answer. They would build a new life. And someday, a new mill.

Fox touched the coverlet again, remembering how as a boy he had wound bobbins for Grandfather's shuttles for other coverlets in other patterns. There were many patterns, he thought as he straightened the coverlet's corner and headed out the door. Grandfather had delighted in drafting new ones. And Fox felt delight in the new pattern that had spread itself before him now.

A wintery drizzle had begun to fall just as he neared the edge of Charleston, but he did not go directly to his mother's house to shed his damp clothes. He rode, instead, to Lamboll's Book Shoppe.

"A book on the Tennessee," he asked of the clerk, a broad-shouldered young man who looked as though he would be more at home driving horses than selling books.

"Our last copy. They're popular now that soldiers have land grants in the West. You going?"

"Aye. Just made up my mind." He thumbed the pages of the little pamphlet. "It's a long way from the sea," he said, almost to himself, as he looked at the map inside the first page.

"A long ways from anything, but I'm going one day,

too. Nothing in Charleston for a clerk like me. I'm going to have my own land out there. Grow cotton."

"They grow cotton out there?"

"Some, I hear. Might get rich there, they say."

"Might, I suppose," Fox replied with a wry laugh. He came to another page with a list of things needed for the journey: tarpaulin, ax, trade goods, medicines . . . It wouldn't be an easy trip, from the looks of the list of supplies.

"Going with a group?" the young clerk asked.

"A small one. My wife."

"That's big enough, I'd say," the clerk replied with a wink. And Fox could picture Grandfather winking, too, somewhere overhead.

Fox let himself in the front door of his mother's house, hurried through the hall and was on his way up the stairs when he heard voices in the parlor. Adelle and Mama were waiting for him. Possibly one of his sisters was as well. There seemed more than two people talking. Slipping the book into his breast pocket, he stepped into the doorway, almost bursting with his news. Anne Vardry's face was all he saw.

"Welcome, my son. We have a visitor." Susan Gairden gestured for him to take a seat, but first he greeted Anne with a bow and kissed her hand, all the while feeling his face burn, a feeling not completely caused by the wind and the rain of his journey.

"Anne. I'm surprised to see you."

"Perhaps the two of you would prefer to speak alone," Adelle said, and Fox sensed that the level of her discomfort approached his own, and Anne's. Only his mother looked secure in her Charleston face.

"Not at all, Adelle. I'm certain Anne is eager to become acquainted with the whole family. After all, she's heard a great deal about all of you. Tell me what brings you to Charleston, Anne. I . . . never expected to see you here."

Across the room, she smiled politely, but with a shyness she had not been completely able to shed. She was well dressed, in a broad-brimmed bonnet that sat low on her forehead, short kid gloves that met the tight-fitting sleeves of the pale blue pelisse she wore over a gown heavy with Mechlin lace. She was a far cry from the waif in black homespun he had first known, so different, in fact, that she appeared quite at home in the Gairdens' well-appointed parlor, except that Fox could tell by the way she twisted and untwisted her gloves, once she removed them, that she was anything but calm.

"We docked in Charleston on a voyage to New Orleans. You see, I sold the mill. Mr. Humphreys offered me enough to make leaving it behind seem the wisest choice. I've developed a cough." At this she coughed lightly. "And the surgeon recommended a warmer climate. He suggested I winter elsewhere, at the very least. I may have to live there the year 'round." She coughed again, very lightly. "I wish to congratulate you on your forthcoming marriage, Fox. Your mother has just told me."

"Thank you, Anne." Fox looked to Adelle and saw relief in her eyes. He had said the right thing. "I must say, I'm concerned about the condition of your health, though, and about who will care for you in Louisiana. Have you someone?"

"I have a friend traveling with me, Miss Dolan. She has a similar complaint."

Fox recognized the name at once. A child from the mill. He remembered her from his brief visit to Derby last year. He knew what had brought Anne here, and when he looked at her as she spoke, he could see she knew that he knew. But no one else need know. How incredibly fickle was life's course from hour to changing hour. The little Tennessee book felt heavy in his pocket.

"Perhaps once you are away from the dust of your mill you will find your cough disappearing," he heard Adelle saying. "You may find it is not the climate at all, and be able to return home after a short time. I have found mill dust, either cotton or wool, to be quite aggravating since I was a child, and often wear a cloth covering my nose when working there." She turned to Fox then, concerned and anxious, he could tell. "What did you decide about your mill, Fox?"

"We're done, I'm afraid," he said, hoping to sound less defeated than he felt just now. "I talked to Merrifield. We've just not enough capital to keep it going—or enough workers. People can't afford to work on promise of payment."

"I've some money, Fox. Perhaps I could help." Anne's cough seemed gone now. Her voice, though tentative sounding, was anything but weak.

"I don't think so, Anne. Thank you, but I couldn't. You'll need that money where you are going—or when you come back. I've already taken too many people's money and failed them. I couldn't do the same to you."

"Were it not for you, I would have *no* money. It would give me great pleasure to—"

"No, Anne. Thank you, but no." He tried to give a polite but firm smile, to let her see through his eyes that it could not be. He thought perhaps she understood, but his mother was quite another matter.

"I doubt you can afford to turn down such a generous offer, Francis. You should at least—"

"Mama, I agree, the offer is most generous. We simply cannot accept."

"But then, what *will* you do? How am I ever to regain your father's investment unless the mill reopens?" An oppressive silence fell in the room with each of the three younger people understanding some of the intricacies of the subject, while Susan Gairden did not.

"I wanted to speak to you privately first, Adelle," Fox said, "but it seems I must reveal my plans earlier than expected."

"I don't want to interfere, Francis, but—"

"No, Mama, you have every right. I realize your future is at stake as much as my own and Adelle's—and yours, Anne," he added. He drew the little pamphlet about the Tennessee from his breast pocket and held it up. "I've made a decision I know you will find as exciting as I do, Adelle. Since there is no hope for the mill, I've decided we should break it down, take the carding and fulling equipment and head west." He saw his mother's extreme agitation and spoke quickly to quell it. "I know, Mama, this seems preposterous to you, but I think there are fortunes to be made there, and it seems the only way I will ever be able to pay you back. The carding and fulling will give us a start we can build on and the market there will be less affected by British imports. We can—"

He stopped in midsentence as he tried to quiet his mother's fears. Adelle's face had gone completely white. Only Anne Vardry seemed to see the rationality of the plan. He looked to her gratefully as he gathered his thoughts to go on.

"We have one hundred sixty acres of land in Illinois we can settle on if we want—part of my naval salary— or we can buy land in the Tennessee. They say there are mill seats aplenty there, lots of little streams perfect for a mill, and lots of settlers needing the service." He waited a moment for a response, but when it didn't come he went on. "I know it comes as a surprise to both of you, but the idea occurred to me as I sat looking at Grandfather's old coverlet hanging on the wall in my office at the mill. I thought about what he would do, and this just seemed right. I hope you'll agree, Adelle."

"I don't know, Fox. I'd never even considered such a thing. I mean . . . I don't know." Adelle's head drooped and her eyes did not meet his as she spoke.

Fox swore to himself. You fool. You should have waited. You should have spoken to her first. At once he was angry with Anne Vardry for coming back into his life, and at his mother for insisting that he reveal both the status of the mill and his future plans as well. And at Adelle for her hesitation. It had gone badly. All of it. Three women faced him, each with her own disappointment in his actions. No matter what happened, someone was going to be upset, and he was going to be angry with himself.

"Forgive me, Adelle. We should have discussed this alone. I didn't think."

"Perhaps I should go," Anne Vardry said, rising and walking toward him. "I—"

"Not at all, Mrs. Vardry," Susan Gairden broke in, getting up and moving to Anne's side. "You'll stay for dinner with us. I insist. It's the least we can do." For the wife of the man Francis killed, Fox knew his mother was thinking, though she did not say it. At least she had not seemed to realize that there was any kind of feeling between him and Anne Vardry. Allowing his mother to deal with Anne, Fox walked across the Turkish carpet to take Adelle's hand.

"I'm sorry, dearest. Forgive me." Even as he tried to apologize to and comfort Adelle, he felt Anne's eyes on him from across the room where she talked with his mother.

Adelle nodded bravely but didn't speak. She took the arm he offered, and the four of them made their way back down the stairs to the dining room, where Jemma had a meal of shrimp, steamed corn and angel biscuits waiting for them.

"You live close to Hartford, don't you, Mrs. Vardry?" Susan Gairden asked, starting the dinner conversation on a new track. "Where those awful Federalists met in secret and planned to break away from the rest of the Union?"

"Yes, it's only a short distance from Derby, though we knew very little about the convention until it was all over. Most in Connecticut think those men patriots, though—men who tried to save the Union by getting it to change its course."

"Well, however they are seen, they were too late to change the course of the war and improve their own fortunes, which is what they really wanted," Susan Gairden replied sourly.

"Yes, they traded with the enemy, then complained that their own government was weak and that the South was unfairly represented in the majority. The whining of the Federalists shall long ring in my ears." Fox found himself becoming angry just thinking of it. "Massachusetts and Connecticut had refused to raise any troops in support of the federal government and found themselves naked before British troops preparing for an attack on Boston soon after Washington was burned. They supposedly called the convention to discuss means of mutual defense and support, but the twenty-six wise men of the East really met in Hartford to discuss nullification of any federal laws that didn't suit them—secession."

"I suspect they only wanted to hold their party together, Fox. There aren't as many Federalists in Connecticut as you remember," Anne said. "Anyway, it is over. The war is won. Let us speak of happier things."

"Yes," Fox agreed, but a tense silence filled the room

when the talk of politics was done. "You haven't forgotten how to cook shrimp the way I like them, Jemma," he said when the cook came back in with poached pears caramel for dessert. "Mmmmm," came sounds of agreement from around the room, but little was said, and Fox could hear the sound of his own teeth chewing against each other in the quiet.

"Francis, you and Adelle should see Mrs. Vardry back to the hotel after dinner," Susan Gairden suggested at last.

"Of course, Mama," Fox agreed. "We will."

"Would you mind, Fox?" Adelle asked, shaking her head. "I'm feeling unwell. I think I should lie down."

"Are you all right? I could call Doctor Olcutt."

"No, it's nothing. I simply feel fatigued. I think I'll go up now. Good night, Mrs. Vardry," she said, hurrying from the table as other farewells were spoken. Anne Vardry rose soon after, and four plates of dessert sat barely touched as the group made its way toward the door.

In a few minutes, Fox and Anne Vardry were on their way to the Planters' Hotel, where Anne had taken a room. It would have been only a short walk, but owing to the weather, Fox had brought out the carriage. As the Gairdens' old mare, Patsy Girl, clip-clopped down Maiden Lane, the quiet of the dining room continued under the steady rhythm of the rain.

"Cough, eh?" he said, at last. "I must say I didn't notice it much after that first announcement."

She coughed then, a little forced cough like the one she had managed earlier. "It comes and goes," she explained.

"Hardly enough to send you to New Orleans, though, Anne, is it? There is no ship to New Orleans, is there? That's why you're staying at the hotel and not on board, in your cabin. And 'Miss Dolan' isn't with you, either. She's at home with her mother and father playing with her dolly, isn't she? I'm sorry, Anne, but I thought everything over between us when I left Derby. You called me there, and then you sent me away. We agreed things could never work out between us. When I came home, I asked Adelle to marry me. And I am going to see it through. We were never meant to be together, Anne."

"I told myself I was right to send you away, Fox. I'm older than you, a widow. And you were going to sea, and I couldn't face the possibility that you wouldn't come back. That's why I sent you away that last night. Not because of Hugh."

"I should have thought you would have been quite glad not to have me come back. I acted less the gentleman than I should."

"You acted, in every way, as I had hoped you would, Fox. I had longed for you every bit as much as you had for me. Our time together was so perfect that all at once I became afraid of it. Afraid of the happiness you offered me. And so I sent you away. Later I thought better of it, even though I knew about Adelle. I just had to try once more, away from Derby. Away from Hugh."

"I admit I was angry with you Anne, just the way you were with me when I left that September to come back to Charleston, but I knew you were right."

"I shouldn't have written you and asked you to come back. I could have saved us both all of this."

"Perhaps. Then again, perhaps we needed that night together in Derby." He pulled back on the reins, slowing the horse in order to give them a few more moments to talk. "There isn't anything else, is there, Anne? There isn't something else that's brought you here—a health matter?" He watched her face, saw her confusion. "I thought you might be with child," he said quietly.

"No. I am not. Although there was a temptation to tell you otherwise. I am healthy. And, thanks to Mr. Humphreys, I am almost wealthy. And I am never going back to Derby. Like you, I am going to move on."

"But where? What will you do?"

"I understand yours isn't the only mill that's failed here in South Carolina. Perhaps I should buy one of them and bring it back from the ashes the way I did the Beaver Creek Mill. I know how, you know. You taught me."

"You knew most of it without me. You just needed a hand."

"I would need a hand again. I could give you employment. Help you get ahead enough to get your own mill running again. Who knows, we might even think of merging the two sometime."

"You won't make it easy for me, will you, Anne? But you know it can never be. It wouldn't be fair to Adelle. And probably not to you, either. We need to go our own ways, Anne. No matter that we've both changed our minds about each other a dozen times, no matter what has been between us. My course is set for me, clear as if my grandfather had handed me a map."

"And Adelle? Will it be so clear for her?"

Fox sighed as he pulled back on the reins and urged Patsy Girl right, to pull up in front of the Planters' Hotel. "Adelle will be a fine partner, Anne. Just as you would have been," he added, trying to smile. He let himself kiss her cheek but no more, then swung down and offered her his hand. Rain fell in heavy sheets as they stepped beneath the hotel portico, and the street was deserted except for the two of them. He could have taken her in his arms one last time, but instead he allowed himself only a long, deep gaze into her eyes, the kind he hadn't been allowed that last morning when she had sent him away saying only that she had been wrong.

"I must get back," he said. "I wish you well, Anne. I wish you happiness. I wish time had treated us differently."

"So do I, Fox." She loosened the ties of her bonnet, took it off and turned it back and forth in her hands. "I'm going to be in Charleston for a few days. If you change your mind—about the money, I mean—the offer stands."

"I appreciate it, Anne. Truly I do. But I can't. To Charleston, I would always be the man who built his mill on another man's bones. I don't want that, for either of us. Invest your money more wisely, Anne. Good night." He tipped his hat and turned away, climbing into the carriage and driving off without so much as a last look, but he knew her eyes never left him until he turned the first corner.

What made him turn the opposite direction from the way home he couldn't say. It was poor judgment to keep the horse out on such a night, poor judgment to drive about the city after nine o'clock, too, he supposed. There were thieves and vagrants out, even in the rain, but Fox didn't care. He didn't want to go home just yet. He knew Adelle would think him with Anne, and he cared what she thought, but somehow he could not go home to face her just yet. Anne's appearance had opened that old wound, that old Vardry sore he thought had almost healed. And he drove on in the rain, toward the Neck, then circled back again, past the hotel, but she was gone.

His mother's house was quiet when he returned in the early hours of the morning, but his sneezes punctuated the silence, coming closer together than they had even in the dust of the abandoned mill. Never changing out of his damp clothes, he took a whiskey and tiptoed into the parlor with it. Embers gave off some little heat and a glow that allowed him to see his way to a chair, and he slouched down, stretching his feet across the hearth. It seemed the alcohol warmed him more than the fire, and so when he placed another log on, he also filled his glass once again. His sneezes subsided. So did his worries. And morning found him just where night had left him, except colder. And his eyes opened to the sight of the Tennessee book still lying on the table.

Last night's downpour had decreased to this morning's dreary drizzle. The house was cool, and Fox coaxed the parlor fire back to life, then lit the dining room fireplace and the front hall fire before Tully got there. He caught a look at himself in the hall mirror—his red eyes, wrinkled clothes and pale face—and tiptoed up the stairs to change. It was barely daylight, and the third-floor hall, lit only by a window at either end, was a tunnel he hurried through, until he stopped at Adelle's door. Quietly maneuvering the knob, he peeked in for a glimpse of her in sleep, the way he had never seen her before. Her dark hair was strewn wildly across the plump pillow, and her face framed by ruffles of point lace. With the covers pulled tightly to her shoulders she was lovely, and she was cold. Fox brought a coverlet from his own room and placed it over her. What must you think of me? he wondered. Please give me another chance, Adelle. Please.

He saw her eyelids flutter. She was awake. At least a little. But she said nothing, pretended to roll to her other side, back to him. Instinct told him to touch her, kiss her, be with her. Reason told him to leave.

"Won't you have some ham, Mist' Gairden?" Jemma wanted to know when he got downstairs a short time later. "Got a good ham at the market this mornin'.

Like to slice some off for you. Like to give you a good meal—you look like you never ate the whole time you was gone to that navy. Time Jemma changed that."

"A cup of coffee's all I need, Jemma. I feel the ague coming on. Not much appetite. Thanks, though. Maybe at dinner."

"I heard you sneezin' an' coughin' up here. You must' caught your death out there in that rain last night."

"Aye. It was a chilling rain. Patsy shivered in her stall when we came back, too."

"And what time was that, Francis?" Susan Gairden asked, coming into the dining room with a cup of coffee that Jemma had brought her earlier.

"Late, I'm afraid, Mama. I went to the . . . coffee-house after I took Mrs. Vardry to her hotel. I thought since Adelle had retired anyway, I might look up some friends." He was not oblivious to the way his mother pulled up her nose and chin at possible untruths.

"A poor night for it. I see you've caught the sneezes."

"I do feel like the very devil this morning, Mama, I admit."

"And Mrs. Vardry? How do you suppose she feels? To have come here and then to have her offer of assistance brushed away with so little regard."

"Mama. I tried to tell you. I cannot take money from Mrs. Vardry. As I explained to her later, the whole of Charleston would say I built my mill on Hugh Vardry's bones. I can't."

"So now you care what Charleston says, though you do not otherwise. You seem to forget that you owe me a great deal of money—money I doubt you can repay by running off to the Tennessee."

"I have not forgotten, not for a moment, that I am in your debt, Mama, and I plan to do all I can to clear your affairs before I leave. But there is no market for our product now that the embargo and nonimportation laws have been repealed. I can't change that. And borrowing money from Mrs. Vardry would only put me into her debt as well, and another failure would leave not just one widow without funds, but two."

"But perhaps your mother is right, Fox," Adelle said, joining them over the last exchange. She, too, looked as though she hadn't slept, though she was not sneezing. Or coughing. "Perhaps you should have been less hasty to refuse Mrs. Vardry's offer. Capital *is* what you've been needing, after all. Perhaps her offer is a godsend."

Susan Gairden took her cup and left the room, shaking her head.

"How can you say that, Adelle," Fox whispered, reaching across the wide, mahogany table to take her hand, "knowing what you do? What I told Mama about building on Vardry's bones is true, as far as it goes, but you know there is another reason—and it is *you*. I cannot invite Anne Vardry into our lives to have you ever wondering if there is something between us, if she loaned me the money for some reason other than pure friendship or pure profit. Mama does not know that, but you *do*. Don't ask it of me, Adelle."

"She wouldn't need to stay here, Fox. She could go back to Connecticut again. We wouldn't need to see her."

"And if she didn't go? We couldn't force her, you know. And she told me last night she will never go back to Connecticut, nor to her parents in Massachusetts. And she is not going to New Orleans. That was only a bit of dissembling. She is in Charleston, and I suspect that here she means to stay."

"But if we moved to the mill at Camden, we would be far enough away that you need never see her. And if whatever was between you is truly over—if you truly love me—then it should not matter how close she is. It simply shouldn't matter."

"Oh, Adelle. How much you trust in me. And how I love you for it. But it is just because of that love that I want to leave this all behind. I want to be free of Hugh Vardry, don't you see? And whether I yet have any feelings for Anne or not, I could never be free of him while I used his money to fund my business and support my family."

"But it's *not* his money, not really. *You* rebuilt the mill so that there was something to sell. You have as much right to that money as anyone. And if you took it, we could stay here, Fox. And I could help you at the mill, and—"

"It's not so much that you want me to take Anne's offer, is it, Adelle? It's that you don't want to go to the Tennessee? Why?"

Adelle grew quiet, slipped her hand free of Fox's, but she met his eyes. "I won't go to the Tennessee. Not ever. I love you more than I have ever loved anyone, Fox, but I won't go off into that wilderness."

"Why, Adelle? I don't understand. I remember when you told me how you meant to go west one day. It was that day at your father's mill. Now that we have this opportunity, what holds you back?"

"Joseph." She looked away, and Fox saw that her eyes were filled with tears.

"Tell me, Adelle. Tell me what it is. What about Joseph? He went west, then came back, I know that. But his failure does not need to stop us."

"He was not the same when he came back, Fox. He was sick. He was weak. And I heard him telling Papa terrible stories of what happened out there. He said no one should ever go there. He said it was not fit for human beings."

"But we are not going where he was. He was in the Ohio, Adelle, and he was there when Indians threatened—before the war. That has all changed now. People are moving west each day, and they are not coming back. They are making lives there, and we can, too."

"Ask anything of me, Fox, but that. I can't do it. I won't."

"You would rather stay here and live on Anne Vardry's money than go with me where we might have a new life on our own? Don't you know I will care for you? I will not let anything happen to you, Adelle. I promise."

"Joseph told Margaret that same thing. But he couldn't protect her. Not all the time."

"I don't know what happened out there, Adelle, and you don't have to tell me. But bad things happen to people here, too. Think about it. You came all the way to Charleston because soldiers were doing bad things to women all along the coast. It's not just in the West that life is hard. And if we stay here we have no life at all just now."

"We could have a good life here. And we will repay Anne Vardry within the first year that prices go up, and then you will be free of her—"

"And what if prices don't go up? Then what?"

"Then you can't build a mill in Tennessee, either."

"Point taken, Adelle. It may not turn out as I hope. So far in my life, very little has."

"Please, Fox, don't say that. Anne Vardry has offered you a chance to make your mill a success. I don't care what you once felt for each other. I know that now you love *me*, and that together we can build a life here."

Fox stood and walked to the door. "You are far too certain of me, Adelle. More certain than I am of myself. I cannot take the money from Anne Vardry, but I will once again seek out other investors, though I can think of no one I haven't badgered already. If I find no one, though, I mean to go west. I want you to come with me."

"I'm sorry, Fox. But if you say I am too certain of you where Anne Vardry is concerned, then perhaps this whole question of the West is pointless. There can be no togetherness for us if she is between us."

"But don't you see, Adelle, that she will not be between us in the Tennessee? She will be far away, somewhere back here in Charleston."

"Will she, Fox? I don't think you're certain of that. I know I'm not."

"God, but you are a single-minded woman, Adelle Durant!"

"And you, too, are hard to turn, Fox," Adelle said softly. "But I love you. And I don't want to lose you."

"Are *you* sure?" he asked. His eyes flared as he took a last look into hers, then turned out into the hall. The fire he had built an hour ago still crackled brightly as he tore his coat off the hook and slammed the front door behind him. She wanted him to take Anne Vardry's money. Well, by God, he just might.

He got as far as the lobby of the Planters' Hotel. As far as asking the desk clerk for her room number. As far as the bottom of the great, ornate staircase, before he turned around, went back outside into a day of clearing skies and soft sea breezes, and down the street to the sign of J. Weems, wagoner.

He found Adelle in her room when he returned late that afternoon. A large trunk stood at the end of her bed, and he could see that she was filling it with her clothes.

"Not for our journey west, I suppose?" he ventured, letting himself in and quietly closing the door behind him. It really didn't matter how much noise he made.

Mama was gone to a meeting of the Ladies Benevolent Society, and Tully and Jemma were washing the carriage house windows. They were alone.

"No, Fox, I've decided it would be better if I went home. Back to Philadelphia, I mean."

"Without even talking to me about it? Adelle, let's not be this way. I love you."

"Enough to stay here in South Carolina with me? Or better yet, why not come back to Philadelphia with me? Papa could help us get a start there. There are other ways besides this notion of yours to go west."

"It's more than a notion, Adelle. It's a feeling. I don't know quite how to explain it. I know there are other ways, other places to go, but this feels like the *right* way. I can't help that."

"And I can't help it that I feel that it would be the very end of everything for us, Fox. That within a year or two we would come back here, beaten and drained the way Joseph was. I've seen it, Fox, and it's awful. You haven't seen it."

"I've seen war, Adelle. I've seen foreign ports clogged with naked, dirty children and hungry, pox-ridden men. I've seen men killed for the price of a decent meal. And I see the life being choked out of this city with every month that goes by. It's time to move out of here, Adelle, and forgive me, but something in me does not want to take direction to the north. Too many memories. And what I tell you of the West is true: I will keep you safe, I will make you happy. I promise it to you."

Adelle folded a lawn petticoat and placed it in the trunk. "Did you stay with Anne Vardry last night, Fox?"

"By the heavens, woman! If I'd been with Anne, would I be here with you now, begging you to go off with me? I was as shocked as you to find her here last night. I don't know what she expected, but she knows now that it's you I'm going to marry, you who will share my life. She's a good person, Adelle. She'll not interfere."

"But she would go west with you, wouldn't she, Fox? She said as much last night. And isn't that why you are so determined? You want me to say no so that you can go off with her with a free conscience."

"What? That is so preposterous as to be ridiculous! I'll never see her again. I don't *want* to see her again. If I did, I'd borrow the damned money from her and be done with it! Your imagination's run off with your heart, Adelle. Call it back, call it back, get it in control."

"My imagination remembers that you said something like that before. I think Mrs. Vardry a seasoning you can't seem to do without in your soup, Fox. And I think it's time we both admit it. I'm leaving on the first ship to Philadelphia. I'd welcome your company, but the only direction my compass knows is north."

"So this is the end of it? This is the end of our love? A few nights back we lay curled in each other's arms, as close to man and wife as two people can be, and tonight we are strangers. I love you, Adelle. I want you to come with me."

"No you don't Fox. I know you better than you know yourself. What you want is at the Planters' Hotel waiting for you."

"I resent that."

"And I resent your saying that you spent the night at the Carolina Coffeehouse, because I asked, and you weren't there." She stopped her packing long enough to take a step away from him. "I'm sorry, Fox," she said. "I just don't believe you."

Fox leaned back against the door, closed his eyes. So it was all to turn on this? A little lie he told his mother? His mother! Not even Adelle, but his mother? "Have I ever lied to you, Adelle? I admit I told you I would write Anne Vardry that I couldn't go to help her at her mill, and then I went there instead—and I failed to tell you about it until much too late, but it was not because I wished to keep it from you but because I was afraid of losing you. Just like this."

"You want us both, Fox. Isn't that it? You can't choose, and honor does not permit you to stand up to either of us and bid farewell."

"Honor does not permit me to entertain thoughts of another while I am so very much in love with you, Adelle. I want you for my wife. You have to see that."

"I want to, Fox. But all I can see is Anne Vardry's face in the parlor yesterday when your mother introduced me as your fiancée. You hadn't even told her about me, had you, Fox?"

"I had told her I loved you, but I had not told her you were here in Charleston. I'm certain she thought you at home in Philadelphia, or she would never have come here. She's not the sort to go about hurting others, no matter how it may look to you."

"Would you have stayed with her had she not sent you away?"

"I think not. I think in time my own good sense would have caught up with me again, but after the months I had been at sea I had convinced myself she needed me desperately, when, in fact, she was doing quite well without me. Anne and I could build nothing —not a relationship and certainly not a business venture—with Hugh Vardry's death ever present somewhere in our lives. At last she has realized that, too. I'm glad she came, Adelle, because at last that's over. I wish it would have happened sooner."

"I wish I could agree, Fox. But I can't. I know the look of a woman in love. I saw it in Sally Celestine's eyes when she talked of you. I saw it in Anne Vardry yesterday."

"And you do not see it in yourself, Adelle? Is that what's happened? You've found you don't love me, after all?"

"I don't know anymore, Fox. I just don't know."

"I see. I'm sorry I've badgered you this way, then. I didn't understand the change in your feelings. Perhaps it is best that I go on my way and let you go on yours. Farewell, beloved Cousin," he said as he opened the door. "I hope someday you can forgive me."

❦ Part Four ❧

1816–1818

19

Tennessee
1816

Seth Butter was true to his name. The large square corners of his body were gently rounded by the butter he ate on everything from radishes to venison jerky. The result was a powerful build that made him the perfect traveling companion for the long, uncertain trek through the Appalachians, which Fox planned to make following along the French Broad River route west from Asheville, North Carolina. Butter, the young man Fox had first encountered as a clerk in Lamboll's Book Shoppe, now rode, saddleless, astride one of the two horses that pulled the wagon, steering both animals from his lopsided vantage point with considerable skill. The first four days had been different. In those first days, the best that could be said for Seth Butter was said by Fox: "As a driver, you're a great bookseller."

The horses Fox had acquired from a planter near his now-abandoned mill were young and not well broken. They were prone to following any path that suited them and not to following the team of oxen Fox drove. Fox looked back once to see them pulling their load off into a shallow stream, another time off the trail and into a sandy barren spot, where nothing but the strength of the oxen—after they were unhitched from Fox's cart, the horses unhitched from Seth's, and then the oxen rehitched to Seth's, and then the whole process repeated in reverse—saved the wagonload of Fox's precious mill equipment from an eternity in the tractionless barren. By nightfall each day, both men were ready to relax.

"I first smoked one in St. Eustatius," Fox told Butter one mild evening in late February as each lit a cigar. They had set up camp along the French Broad River after an especially long day. "And now I wonder when I shall ever smoke one again. I'd hoped that boxful would last us the whole trip."

"We'll have to take up chewing, I suppose," Butter said. "Chewin' tobacco's plentiful wherever you go. There's bound to be a store somewhere in this Tennessee. If there isn't, maybe I'll start one."

"Your training at Lamboll's should stand you at the ready . . . perhaps we'll start our own town. I, the miller; you, the merchant. We'll call it—"

"Shhh!" Butter bit down on his cigar and motioned for Fox to be quiet, then moved his hand to the rifle at his side. "Who's there?"

Fox, still not hearing anything, looked around him, then stood up and reached for his own rifle next to his bedroll where he'd put it when he took out the cigars. He, too, heard something. It sounded like a sniffle. "Hello?"

"Halloo yerself." The sniffle became a full-blown snort as a giant of a man stepped out of the darkness and into the glow of Fox and Butter's firelight with another, smaller man at his side. The giant was clothed in buckskin and draped in a blanket of crudely stitched fur and hide. A broad-bladed knife was prominently displayed at his waist. Both men carried rifles, one pointed at Fox and one at Butter. "Ye can put yer rifles down, boys. We've got ye in our sights."

"And we have you in ours," Butter said, never flinching. All rifles remained raised, and Fox could feel his heart beating fast. There would be no survivors at such close range if shooting started. "We'll be out of here by morning, and mean you no harm, but we won't be run off like scared deer."

"You're a mouth an' will die a lip," the giant said, taking a step forward. "Now set those rifles down at my feet! Hand me that seegar, too. Both of ye! Now!"

Butter stood firm, bracing himself for the kick of the rifle, when Fox said, "We've nothing you'd want, just tools and milling equipment." Butter was like a statue, the end of his rifle barrel not more than two or three feet from the barrel of the small, toothless man who seemed to squint into the firelight. "Be on your way and there'll be no harm to you."

"Hah! You're quick to blabber of harm. We do the harm on this road. We're the Whittle boys, an' we take what we want. Sell it. An' we mean to take whatever ye got." The giant smiled. "After we cut ye open an' scoop ye out we'll load ye with stones an' dump ye in the river, here, just the way we been doin' it fer ages."

The smaller man chuckled as his partner described what was to come, then began to bend his finger around the trigger of his rifle. Seth Butter's finger was faster. Fox fired in the split of the next second. So did the giant. In an orange flash against the night sky it was over, and only Fox still stood. With one swift motion he tossed the intruders' rifles away from them, then knelt at Butter's side.

The giant's shot had taken Butter in the right shoulder, and either shock or his fall had left him unconscious, but Fox felt a pulse in his neck and grabbed the bedroll to prop beneath his head. Butter's eyes fluttered open as Fox tried to make him comfortable.

"Are they gone?" he asked.

"Far gone, I hope. Let's take care of you first. There now," he said, packing his extra shirt inside Butter's coat to stop the bleeding, "just rest there, Seth. You're going to make it."

Butter fought against the packing, twisting sideways until a sharp stab of pain stopped him. He'd managed a better view of the intruders, though, and saw the two bodies on the other side of the fire. "My God, Fox. I killed them."

Fox saw the panic on Butter's face. "No choice, Seth. Them or us. You took one, I got the other—not quite fast enough, though. Sorry."

"I can feel their ghosts over me, Fox. They're over me! I can see 'em."

"Close your eyes, Seth. Rest. There are no ghosts here. Only the wrongly dead come back to haunt their killers. Surely you know that after all your time in Charleston." Fox tried to joke with Seth, but inside he felt the presence of his own ghosts. Hugh Vardry laughed at him as Seth lay shaking beneath his hands. Don't die now, Seth. Don't die. Don't.

Fox rose and stepped between the giant and the smaller intruder, and checked each one for a pulse, cringing at the touch of the unwashed strangers. They were both dead. Fox looked over his shoulder at Butter, wounded, and an almost otherworldly feeling came over him, as if he were not there, taking the heavy capes from around the dead men's shoulders to use to cover Seth; as if he, too, were actually dead and not, instead, the only one untouched by the power of the rifles and of man's will to stay alive.

The feeling passed. He willed it to pass just as he had willed himself to pull the trigger that had leveled the giant. Nothing will ever be the same, Grandfather had said. Vardry. His father. War. Now this. Was this what Grandfather had meant? That death would follow him because he had taken a life?

Butter stirred under the heavy fur capes as Fox shiv-

ered by the fire, head in hands, suddenly weak. He
picked up his cigar and sucked in a long, smooth draw,
then gagged on it and threw the precious smoke into
the fire. They had come through long miles of rough
country down the French Broad and seen few people.
Taking Seth back to South Carolina again would be a
long, hard trip. And taking him farther west? Well, who
knew what lay ahead, how many days it might be to a
house or a settlement? Butter thrashed, then whim-
pered as he once again moved the wrong way and set
off the pain in his shoulder. You knew this would happen, didn't you, Adelle? You told me, but I wouldn't
listen. Fox pulled a blanket around his own shoulders
and felt a chill shimmy the length of him as he kept
one eye on Butter and one on the dark perimeter of
their camp. What if these two weren't alone?

At the thought, Fox got up and reached inside the
wagon for a shovel. Best to bury them yet tonight, he
thought as he started digging in the rocky riverside. He
little more than pried out a shallow oval, then dragged
the two men to it and pushed them in, head to toe, on
their backs, and covered them with what soil he could,
then rocks. Marking the grave with a small aspen trunk
that lay uprooted by the water's edge, he stood back
and hung his head. "I'm sorry you came by tonight,
men, whoever you were. And I ask you, God, to let
Seth Butter live. He saved my life by shooting when he
did, though I wonder if I'm worth saving. Amen."

With that simple prayer, Fox turned and made his
way in the darkness to the circle of firelight that
marked their camp. Butter was quiet, and Fox checked
his breathing once again, found it ragged but still there.
Kneeling beside the younger man, Fox felt the weight
of fatigue upon him, and rolled in next to Butter beneath the hefty furs that just short hours ago had covered two strangers who had entered this camp . . .

and changed everything? Was that what Grandfather
would have said? He tried to make his mind search for
the answer, but the heaviness that had overtaken him
wouldn't allow it. He couldn't think. He couldn't sleep.
He could only wait.

By morning, with the shadows of the night vivid memories, Fox helped Seth Butter to the top of one of the
wagons, and they drove on toward Knoxville. At the
sign of smoke curling up from a cabin they stopped.

"The Whittle boys? You say you buried ol' Nate
Whittle? Well, I'd say you'll be the heroes of Knoxville
when you get there," Hazo Parsons exclaimed when
Fox told the story of the night before. "Those boys
been terror on the hills here the last months. Strike at
night an' then ride off into the mountains again."

"Seth heard them before they were ready for us,"
Fox explained, "or I'm certain we'd be the ones buried
back there along the river. I expect they intended to
wait until we were asleep, but one of them—the big
one—had a fever of some sort. Seth heard his sniffle.
That was how it started."

"Ol' Nate Whittle, caught by a sniffle. Ha! Damn but
that makes for a good story. Might likely make a good
song, too." The man began to hum and tap his foot as
if Fox had given him word of a wedding or birthday
instead of a killing. But then, nothing had seemed real
since last night when Seth first motioned for him to be
quiet. Maybe they weren't in the Tennessee at all but
back in Charleston, dreaming in their beds.

"Rotten sheep like that, time their day come," Parsons said, ceasing his music. "More an' more folks
comin' out here all the time, especially since the war
ended. We can't have lawlessness. There's a fine courthouse in Knoxville. Tell 'em your story when you get
there. If they have any questions, send 'em here. I

know a man tellin' the truth when I hear it. An' I know I'm glad for the news the Whittles is gone." Once again, the foot tapping and humming began.

Fox nodded, relieved. "I need to go back and get the other wagon. Can my friend—".

"Take my mule," Parsons offered with a wave of his hand. "Your oxen are worse off than your man Butter. Mebbe I should go with ye?"

"There's no need," Fox said, not eager for company just now. After a meal and seeing to Seth's comfort, he rode back to where he did not want to go, no matter how much a hero Parsons or anyone else might think him. He half expected to find the Whittle brothers' grave empty, such a poor job had he done of burying them, but it remained as he had left it. He piled it over with more rocks before he went on to the wagon, thinking of Hazo Parsons's words as he worked: "Ol' Nate Whittle, caught by a sniffle . . ." And Fox found himself smiling as he piled the last stones.

By the time Fox returned, the two days' rest inside a warm cabin with soup and bread instead of trail food had brought Butter's color back a little, and he no longer confined himself to the bed Mrs. Parsons had made for him on the floor. He insisted he could once again resume his driving of the wagonload of mill equipment Fox had retrieved, and so after one more day, they set off. Butter did not use his right arm, favored his right shoulder and grimaced frequently by late afternoon, but he never complained. And he never again spoke of the Whittle brothers or of what happened back along the French Broad.

Farms sat randomly among tall stands of ash and hickory, and as Fox and Seth began to descend into the Tennessee Valley, there was even an occasional settlement of a half-dozen houses or more. It was backcountry, no doubt about that, but it was not uninhabited.

Cotton, corn and oats grew in the rich valley soil, but the plots were small, the houses were mostly log, and life was very different from the big cotton plantations they had left behind them in the South Carolina low country.

Knoxville sat, islandlike, between the Tennessee on the east, First Creek on the north, Second Creek on the south and Fish Pond on the west. Fox and Seth ferried their wagons across at Cunningham's Ferry after waiting in line for four other wagons to go first.

"I thought we were going into the wilderness," Seth said as they waited. "This looks like some kind of convention."

"Market day," Cunningham said as he guided their freight onto the raft that would be pulled across the current. "Thursdays and Saturdays. Just built that new market house over there." He pointed to a log building near the edge of town that was circled with wagons and people, livestock and poultry in crude cages. "Folks bring in what they have. There's still no money out here, so we have to make do with barterin'."

"What about the surplus? Do you send it back east?"

"Some ends up there, no doubt. Most goes down the river, then down the Trace and on to New Orleans." Cunningham eyed Fox, then Butter, then the heavily loaded carts. "Miller, are you?"

Fox nodded. "I've a grant for lands in Illinois from my naval duty. We're not certain yet just how far west we'll be going."

"What kind of mill?"

"I've enough sawing equipment to get a mill built, then I'll do fulling and carding. I'd like to add spinning equipment later on, if there's a market. Butter, here, hopes to open a store."

"I don't think you ought to look any farther west

than right here, lads. There's work aplenty in Knoxville. We've a wool carder on First Creek, but no one to
work the cotton—and there's more of it than ever bein'
grown hereabouts." He looked to Fox, then to Butter.

"It all belongs to him," Butter was quick to point
out. "I'm just the driver—but this looks to be a very
likely spot. You ought to hear the man out, Fox."

"What about you, Seth? You'd best do the same."

"It's a growing village, gentlemen," Cunningham
said. "I been here almost twenty years, and I wouldn't
go anywhere else. First capital of the Volunteer State
and proud of it. Besides, we need folks like you," he
said, sincerity in his lined face and baggy eyes. "Cotton
growers comin' over the mountains every day. Land's
played out back in the Carolinas, I hear. We've got a
gin, we might as well have mills, too. No point in having *everything* in Nashville." There was a hint of bitterness in his words about the loss of the capital, but
Knoxville appeared to be active and alive in spite of it.
It wasn't as big as Charleston, and it certainly wasn't as
beautiful. There were only two brick buildings he could
see. But after all, it was young. And that was what Fox
was after.

"We have some business at the courthouse we'd better take care of before we do anything else," Fox told
Cunningham as he gave him a five-dollar bank note on
the State Bank of Charleston for the trip.

Cunningham looked at it and shook his head. "Better put another one with it, Gairden. I doubt I can get
my dollar out of this."

Fox took another note from his wallet. "If it's that
way at the bank here, I won't have to worry about starting a mill. I won't have enough money."

Cunningham handed the second note back to him.
"This banking business is such a confusion with different banks issuing their own notes, you never know what

anything's worth. Drive a hard bargain, Gairden. Your money'll grow faster here than in any Charleston bank."

"I hope you're right, Mr. Cunningham. And thanks." Fox and Butter were about to drive away when Cunningham called out after them, "Look at the plat while you're at the courthouse. See about getting some land for that mill. I'd say someplace up on Second Creek would be about right—easy to dam up, plenty of drop. You could be in business by summer."

"If I am, I'll be back with your other fiver!" Fox slapped the reins and urged the oxen on before the ferryman could change his mind.

Settlers were streaming in through the Cumberland Road to the north, then on down the Tennessee River to the rich new lands of the southwest. Many stayed in Tennessee, Fox knew, but there were a great number who followed the setting sun all the way to the Mississippi, and some even beyond that. Still, Tennessee was a state. Had been since 1796. It had sent twice the number of volunteers the government in Washington had asked for in the War of 1812. General Andrew Jackson of the Tennessee militia had raised over two thousand militiamen and volunteers to help him fight against the Creeks in the Mississippi Territory.

Different from South Carolina, Fox thought. Better. He still remembered his shock that the Charleston militia had been so intractable during the recent conflict, so self-consumed and unwilling to protect their own city. It had been the spark that sent him into the United States Navy, and it had burned until it also sent him across the mountains. Charleston was changing. No, that was not quite right. The rest of the country was changing, but Charleston pretended everything remained just as it always had been.

If Charleston was slow and social, Knoxville was hurried and social, at least on this market day. It reminded him, in a way, of the bustle he remembered from Philadelphia, and that, of course, reminded him of Adelle. She might have been killed that night along the French Broad had she come along as he'd wanted. No, she had been right. It was no place for her. It was a state of risk takers. As Fox had looked back into Cunningham's toughened face, he had wondered if he was made of the right stuff to hold his own among them. Then he remembered the Whittles. Maybe he and Seth were tougher than he thought.

Fox looked off downriver as he drove along. Somewhere down there had been Fort Loudoun, a place of which Grandfather had often spoken. Grandfather had never actually gotten as far as Fort Loudoun, but he had known men who had been there, under siege, existing only on corn and water for long weeks until they were freed, and then were attacked outside their own walls. The few who had escaped told the tale, and Grandfather never forgot it. The lesson he took from it was not a hatred for the Cherokee, though, but a realization of what people will do when desperate to protect what is their own. We will fight the Cherokee War again, Grandfather had often said. And again and again, until we learn to stay off their land and they off ours.

As Fox looked at Knoxville, he wondered if Grandfather had been right. The army had driven the Creeks and the Cherokees farther west and south, killing many, supposedly to keep them from helping the British in the war. But there had been another reason, too: to open up lands just like this for settlers just like him. In every wagon that headed toward the market there was a rifle or two hung behind the seat, with good reason, if the experience with the Whittles was any measure. He wouldn't have wanted Adelle to be there that

night, but, God, how he wanted her here now. He
could see her in this place—at the market, on the
street. And if what Cunningham said was true, their
dream of a mill could still come true. Another dream.
And why not? This whole trip was built on a dream, set
off by the manifestation of Grandfather that had visited him that night at the mill. She might as well be a
part of it. There was no point to small dreams, because
dreams were all he was ever likely to have.

20

Knoxville, Tennessee
1817

"Never saw such a thing in my life," Butter exclaimed on a cold January evening as he entered the lean-to addition to the mill he and Fox had built on Second Creek during the better part of 1816. Butter's shoulder was healed but pained him on cold nights like these. Possibly a chip of bone lodged near the ball and socket joint, the Knoxville surgeon had told him. No cure. Seth Butter took the diagnosis at face value, and took considerable whiskey for the pain. He was not always sober, but he didn't complain.

Gairden and Butter had been fulling cloth and saw-ing lumber for the mainly Scots-Irish neighborhood since late November, even though the building itself, a small, log affair that made Fox shake his head each time he looked at it, was far from finished. It bore little resemblance to the mill he left behind on Rice Creek, and Fox wondered if it ever would. Tonight the wind whistled in beneath the door, and Fox was glad at least that the Tennessee hills offered a never-ending supply of firewood. He sat with his feet on the hearth and a blanket covering his shoulders, resting his back after another long day. "What's that?" he asked, not getting up.

"I didn't get the cigars you wanted. Couldn't. Storekeep says there's a tariff on British goods.

Would've cost him dearly to stock them, so he didn't. A tariff—the damn British bastards."

"I suspect we're the bastards, Seth," Fox said. "And too late to do me any good, I might add. As usual. They were talking about it in Washington before we left Charleston, but I doubted they'd ever *do* anything about it. A tariff sooner might have helped me keep the Camden mill going. Washington let the Britons dump goods on us for months before they did anything. By the time they did, it was too late—for me, at least."

Fox's thoughts jumped immediately back to Camden, and Adelle. She had said he should try to hang on. And he had been quick to point out that he couldn't. If he had sat idly by in Charleston until Congress acted, things might have been different between them. But no, they wouldn't. Anne Vardry's visit had seen to that.

Nothing seemed to happen in the right order anymore. The war started after England had decided to make peace, and then was still fought after peace had been declared; he had gone to Anne and been sent away by her, made his plans to marry Adelle only to have Anne say she had changed her mind; he had seen his mill destroyed by the glut of English yarns and fabrics on the market at bargain prices, and now learned of an American tariff that would protect industries such as his. He was always too quick to act, too anxious to be first. He needed to learn patience . . . the kind Adelle had once told him she had.

"I brought a copy of the *Register* back for us. Says Monroe was elected president. The Federalists are dead. Jemmy Madison's gone home. No more war, Fox. Monroe says good days are coming. We'll get rich out here yet, Fox."

When Fox didn't respond right away, Butter tried again. "You don't seem happy, Fox. This is good news. Isn't it? We should be gettin' out that jug of corn brew to celebrate, shouldn't we? I mean, even if we can't get a decent cigar, at least we're not going to be stuck buying British goods, either. American, strictly American. We don't need anyone else. We can make what we need. Maybe a cigar factory's what we need."

Fox gave a flat chuckle. "Took my own mill apart, and now I've nothing in either place, do you know that, Seth?"

"But you said you were going to bring the jennies out here as soon as you could. This just means you can do it sooner."

"I could, but the markets are on the other side of the mountains. Folks out here can only buy what yarns they need at home. We would need orders for hundreds of hanks at a time, or we'd need to be able to weave it into cloth, as well, and even back on Rice Creek I didn't have much luck at that."

"You start spinning it, and I bet you'll sell it."

"Perhaps if you get your store started—"

"No need for that yet. Besides, I've taken a liking to this milling business."

"I know, and sometimes I think I should just leave everything to you and go back."

"Go back? What? You're just getting started here. We're not even done building the mill. You can't just go off and leave me here. I don't know anything about this except what you tell me. And I can't exactly turn *this* into a store."

"But what will ever come of it if we *do* finish it, Seth? We can card and full for people, saw boards for them, but that's not what I want."

"I think what you want has gone back to Philadelphia, Fox, and you might as well start looking elsewhere."

"You know me too well, Seth. I was a pigheaded fool

to choose this place over wherever Adelle wanted to be. She was right, but I just couldn't admit it."

"John Wofford wants to marry a daughter off to you —and one to me, of course. Why not do it? These long, cold nights wouldn't seem so lonely with some wives to warm us."

"I'm not ready to jump out of the frying pan into the fire yet, Seth. I don't know what I want."

"Then you're the only man out here who doesn't. If you don't marry Jenny Wofford, someone else will."

"Then someone else should. I don't love her."

"I don't know that you can wait around for love out here, Fox. Wives are for raising sons, for helpmeets. They're something you need, like a good horse and a good gun."

"Well, since I have neither a horse nor a gun anymore, I think I can do without a wife as well. You do as you please."

"Just don't pine so for your Adelle that you up and leave me here."

"I won't," Fox said, more positive than he really felt. "Not now, at least. I can't. I've nothing to go back to, anyway. I've lost Adelle, I'm still in debt to my mother and I sent Anne Vardry off for good. My mill is in pieces on both sides of the Appalachians. All things considered, I think it best I stay." He managed a weak chuckle.

"If we don't like it here, we can move on. We can go to New Orleans if we want, or over into Missouri Territory. No need to stay in one place while there's a whole land out there waiting for us."

"No. Not for me. This is as far as I go. I've been north, and halfway 'round the world, and I think I'd better stay in one place and try to quit this guessing game of what's best in life. I'm ready just to live it and let come what may."

"Then you're not going back?"

"No. That was just disappointment talking. . . . I could almost taste those cigars. This was what I wanted, and I got it. Now I'd better do something with it."

"I'll never go back, Fox. But I may go on west. Still some wanderer left in me. Why not see what the tariff brings? Could be the government will make up your mind for you what to do."

"It has a way of doing that sometimes, I agree. For now, we'll keep our fulling hammers pounding and our wheel turning dawn till dusk. And we'll let the future take care of itself."

"Done," Butter agreed, clapping Fox on the back. "Now let's get some more logs on the fire and read the news."

Fox gave Seth one sheet and kept the other for himself. He pulled the blanket tighter around his shoulders and looked at the row of advertisements wedged between the stories on the front page of the Knoxville paper. Livery. Dry goods. Jeweler/gun maker. Knoxville was growing. And his mill could be growing, too—but not until he started spinning. And to do that, he either had to take what money he had—payment owed to his father's estate—and order new equipment from the North, or he had to go back to Camden and get the old equipment. Or try starting over there again. Admit to Adelle he had been wrong.

Patience, he reminded himself. For once, try to be patient. He tossed his half of the paper back to Seth, leaned back in his chair and closed his eyes.

21

Quakers. A whole string of them, fifteen wagons at least, Fox thought, were lined up across the river at Cunningham's ferry stop, waiting for passage. They weren't the first ones to come through Knoxville out of the Carolinas, but they were one of the biggest groups. Usually it was a couple of families traveling together. Always their reasoning was the same. They wished to remove themselves from a place where slavery was an ever-increasing source of spiritual discomfort and showed no signs of reversing itself. Most of them did not plan to stay in Tennessee, either, where slaves were becoming more numerous as cotton became more cultivated. They were going west and north—many into Indiana and Illinois—but they came through the mountains the same way Fox and Seth had, and they restocked in Knoxville before starting out again.

They were easy enough to pick out by the broad-brimmed beaver hats of the men and the shades of brown and gray they all wore, with nothing more than a white collar or bonnet for trim. Even their wagons were painted a dull gray, and their horses wore no fancy harness. Fox shook his head, remembering a little more than a year ago when he and Seth had landed at that same ferry crossing. He was glad he did not have to go any farther. He had made up his mind to stay. He had sent an order for two spinning mules on the last mail, two weeks ago, and at the same time he had sent a letter to his mother asking her to bear with him. Like the other letters he had sent her this past year, he expected it to go unanswered. He gave her leave to have her creditors sell the rest of the equipment and the land at Camden. His ties with South Carolina were severed for good.

It was late that afternoon when he heard voices outside the door. Seth and a customer, no doubt. He was wet to the waist, fulling a length of homespun that had splashed him once too often, and kept to his work. Seth was good at the business end of milling, dealing easily with customers who responded to his hearty laugh and generous disposition. There was no need for Fox to interrupt his work.

A few minutes later, he lifted the homespun from the suds vat to the water bath, looked up and saw her watching him.

"Adelle? Adelle!" Disbelief left him in the single utterance of her name, and he dropped the cloth back into the vat, wiped his forearms on the towel that hung from his belt and started toward her. With a half-dozen feet still separating him, he stopped.

"How did you get here?"

"I came with a group of Quakers. Sister Emeline, a woman I knew in Philadelphia, was among them. She encouraged me." Adelle wore a charcoal gray traveling outfit with a matching cape. From her right hand hung a fur muff, and a large bonnet framed her face, hiding far too much of it to suit him.

"Then you're . . . with them?"

"A Quaker? No, though I find their thinking very much like my own. They are greatly against the institution of slavery, as I am. We all began to feel quite out of place in Charleston."

"You've come from Charleston—not Philadelphia? I thought—"

"Did you think about me, Fox? Ever?"

Emotions long held inside bubbled up, and Fox felt the corner of his mouth turn down. He stepped behind Adelle to fasten the hook inside the door. "Did you think I could ever *quit* thinking of you, Adelle?" His voice was low, not much more than a whisper as he stood very close to her, but he could barely get the words out. The distance between them reminded him of sailing past Charleston on board the *Peacock* and being so near to Adelle but not being able to reach her. Just now his arms felt leaden at his sides. A draft of cold air shot in beside the door and a chill touched his wet skin.

"You should have. I was foolish. Disloyal. Afraid."

Fox felt every muscle tense as he lifted his hands to her shoulders. "Oh God, Adelle, I should never have made you afraid. I should have stayed in Camden the way you wanted. But I felt the pull of this place so strongly. And then when Anne came—I couldn't blame you for what you thought of me." He closed his eyes, fighting back a tear, and felt her come to him. "I'm soaked," he started to protest. He wanted that nothing would ever hurt her again, not even the discomfort of a wet workingman's shirt.

"I should be here working beside you, Fox. I should have my petticoats soiled with fuller's earth and my hair linty with carding. I should bring you a warm coat to put on when your work is done. I have come very far, Cousin Francis," she said, drawing him to her and laying her head against the damp shoulder of his shirt, "and I am still afraid of many things, but not of a little soap and water."

Looking down into her face he saw that tears streamed from her eyes, too, and he bent to kiss them away, first one eye and then the other. He licked the salty sweetness from his lips and let his head rest against hers for a moment before he sought her lips and felt her response, even more intense than he'd remembered it those sublime days in Charleston when they had been betrothed, sure of their love and naive of the future.

"Oh, Fox . . ." Adelle's words were whispers of release he matched with his own as their lips met. "How I've missed you."

"Missed? Not even you could know about missing as I do. I had given up hope—"

"And I lost heart. I should have come sooner. I wanted to come sooner—as soon as Mrs. Vardry told me that there had been nothing between you, I knew I had been very foolish."

"You talked to Anne Vardry?"

"She came back. About three days after you left. She had been at the Planters' Hotel the whole time, deciding where to go from Charleston, she said. But she had sensed a tension between us over her unexpected visit, and she wished to assure me that she had come only out of regard for all you had done for her, now that she found herself in a position to travel and to see you again. She said that . . ."

Adelle paused, and Fox touched her chin, bringing her face close to his own so that he could see what was behind the words, behind her eyes. "What did she say, Adelle?"

"She said that . . . she had had feelings for you, but that you had been too honorable to pursue them." Adelle's lip quivered. "I thought too lowly of you, Fox. And I am so ashamed."

Fox hugged her to him, wishing with all that was in him that just this moment had not come. "Adelle, no matter what you thought of me, it was not too low. I am the man who killed Hugh Vardry. I have killed another man since then—a man who ambushed Seth Butter and me along the trail coming out here. And I did have the complete lack of backbone to let myself have feelings for Anne Vardry. She was too kind, Adelle, in saying that I was honorable. I tried to be, but I don't know if I was."

He stopped short of saying there had been a point at which he would have thrown all thoughts of honor aside had Anne Vardry not stopped him. There had been a moment in Derby when, far away from Adelle and in the midst of war and uncertainty, he had made love to Anne Vardry. It was she who had been honorable. He had been what he always had been: her husband's murderer.

"I know. I have always known. And that was why I fell in love with you in the first place, Cousin. Being honorable does not mean being perfect, or even always being right. Being honorable means trying to do what is right. I know you could never do anything else. Grandfather knew it, too. That was why he talked so much with you of his life and his dreams. He wanted you to carry on what he had begun."

"I sometimes wonder what he would think if he could see me now." Fox turned his head to the vats and machinery that filled the room. "He was doing all this sixty years ago. I haven't come far, except in miles. I haven't made the progress he wanted for me."

"But you are not at the end of your years, either, Fox. You are just at the beginning. Grandfather had some moments of doubt, too, as I remember hearing my mother tell it. That does not mean there can't be successes ahead."

"Oh, Adelle . . . the people having the successes are the people buying up land, growing cotton. Sometimes I wonder why it is that I stay here, working at this, instead of following them. I still have the land grant for Illinois Territory I got from the navy. All I have to do is go there and claim it. But, I don't know, I can't seem to get this out of my head. I think about it, even at night when Seth and I quit for the day. I dream of a big mill—spinning, weaving, everything—like the ones I saw in the North, only bigger."

"Grandfather's legacy. How could you imagine anything else? He gave that to us when he could not give us anything else."

"I suppose you're right. He thought he'd lost it, with my father I mean. Papa wanted nothing of Grandfather's past. He'd seen too much of the ups and downs of the weaving business. He thought law a more secure way to carry out his life. In the end, his security was destroyed by overinvestment in just what he had vowed to stay away from: a mill. Mine."

"I brought your American Beauty coverlet along," Adelle said. "I got it from the mill before I left. I thought you should have it."

"Ha. You know, I couldn't bear to take it down when I left. I saw it hanging there on the wall at the mill, and I suppose I thought I might be back for it someday. Now that I know that will never be, I thank you. I will give it a place of honor here."

"I brought some other things, too." Adelle looked into his eyes, not quite smiling. Fox waited for the answer he hoped meant that she was staying. "The Friends helped me. We brought Grandfather's pattern book. And two of your jennies. Your dream is going to come true, Fox. Mine, too."

"Adelle, how—?"

"I found Merrifield and got him to break them down as much as he could. And I certainly hope you know how to get them back together, because I don't. But I had nothing else to bring and so—"

"So you just went to Camden and got them? You are a marvel, Adelle Durant, and a credit to Grandfather's line—more than the grandson who abandoned all of it. Was the mill still standing? No fire claimed it, I hope."

"No fire. But your mother claimed most of it, I'm afraid. She sold off what she could. There's a Colonel Green who's building a new mill in the northwest corner of the state somewhere. He offered to buy what equipment was there. She took up his offer."

"Well, she'll have something to go on until I can make enough here to start helping her out again. Thank God."

"I don't think you have to worry about her, Fox." Fox was surprised at the words. She had been one of his main worries since the day he left South Carolina knowing his father had left her almost penniless. "She's remarried, Fox. To Mr. William Tatham."

"The planter?"

"Yes. He lost his wife a short time after you left. They were married two months ago. It was one reason I finally got up the nerve to go—they were selling the house. She moved into his city house."

"Mama? I don't believe it. I can't imagine it."

"She had an independent streak you probably never knew, Fox. She called it up when she had to—like after you left. I think your leaving was the best thing that ever happened to her." Adelle smiled up into his eyes, daring him to believe what he so obviously couldn't.

"But she never answered my letters."

"At first, she couldn't. Later on, she wouldn't. But before I left, she told me that if I ever did find you out here on the 'heathen frontier,' I was to tell you she would write—though she had little hope any letter would ever reach the edge of the world where you must be. And, of course, she's been busy, ordering her new life. She and Mr. Tatham have a busy social schedule."

"And lots of slaves." Fox uttered this last with a pronounced flatness.

"Sometimes we do things for love . . ."

"Like bringing wagonloads of machinery across mountains, you mean?" Fox looked into her eyes, forgetting in that look his mother, Charleston, slaves and everything that was other than Adelle. "How did you manage it? The cost? The wagons? I don't see how you could do it."

Adelle looked down, her chin almost on her chest. Her smile was gone completely, and a long silence hung between them before she spoke again.

"I asked Mama and Papa for the money. As my dowry. And if that makes me too forward, too brazen for you . . . I know I shouldn't have, but—"

There were no words Fox could summon to reassure her the way he felt his own nearness could, and so he simply held her close, swaying her gently back and forth, feeling her body so delicate inside the circle of his arms, but her will so strong. "God bless you, Adelle, and promise me you'll marry me—dowry or no, for I love you in ways I never knew it possible for one person to love another."

"I love you, Fox. And I will marry you, and work with you and bear your children. I will never leave you —or let you leave me—again."

"Can you stay here, then? For I've decided I'm staying, Adelle. I've been here a year, and my life is in these walls."

"I want to go no farther west than this, at least not now. I've had enough of rutted roads and crossing streams to last me a good long while. But even in my few hours in this town, I can see in it a bit of what you do. And I do see some brick houses. I know a city cannot be far behind."

"We will build our own brick house—perhaps not as fine as the ones on Meeting Street or South Bay, and not as soon as I'd like. I must tell you one more thing, Adelle."

He saw her face fall, saw her take a shallow breath. "It's not as bad as all that, Cousin. It's just that—I've taken what money I had and ordered two spinning mules from Philadelphia two weeks ago. I was hoping —I was hoping your father would let you know where I was once he read my letter . . . but in any case, the money's gone for now, and we'll have to get by here as best we can. With Seth Butter as our housemate, too, I'm afraid."

"I've met Mr. Butter."

"Oh yes, outside." Fox had already forgotten what had happened such a short time ago. So much had happened in between.

Adelle smiled a coy smile, so unlike her. "The moment he heard my name, he laughed and said that I had ruined any chance of his ever having a double wedding with you and some girls he called the Wofford sisters, but that he might just marry one of them anyway."

"Well, perhaps we could still make it a double wedding . . ."

"Perhaps we could," Adelle said, "if he doesn't take too long in asking her."

Two days later, Francis Marion Gairden and Adelle Lambert Durant stood before Reverend Henry Roane at the Presbyterian meetinghouse. Gathered with them was most of the population of Knoxville, and two pews filled with Quakers. It was a young group, barely anyone over thirty, but a fair number of crying babes and squirming youngsters. There was a handful of folks in Knoxville in their forties and fifties who had come out there at the end of the eighteenth century when the town began, but those coming through the mountains

tended to be in their early twenties. It was no trip for
the elderly. Many of those who had come out earlier
had already moved on farther west when Knoxville became too civilized for them. They wanted to relive the
feelings of self-sufficiency and strength they had once
known by just getting across the Appalachians, leaving
behind Knoxville to a new group of young fortune
seekers.

The Quakers, too, were a young group, although
there was one family of three generations among them,
the Downdes. Their leader, Mr. Middleton, looked to
be no more than twenty, Fox thought as he saw him
there in the front row, but he had kept his flock together—and he had brought Adelle. Fox brushed the
sleeve of his blue waistcoat, noticing the neatness and
clean styling of the array of Quaker garments before
him as they waited for some guests to be seated near
the back. The Friends did not believe in excess or in
much adornment, but they did believe in quality, and
the crisp broadcloth of the men's suits advertised it.
Once again he gave his own apparel a quick check:
boots, polished; breeches, clean and pressed; shirt, ruffled at the collar; vest, brightly colored stripes that
probably offended the Quakers. Still, he judged his appearance passable and took another look at his bride.

Adelle stood before him in the wedding gown she
had so brazenly, as she put it, brought with her along
with her dowry. Made of white satin with gauze trim, it
was heavily embroidered for several inches above the
hemline. Its high ruffled neck and sleeve puffs at the
shoulders suited her figure to perfection. She had had
plenty of time to do the embroidery, she had told him,
teasing. He would always smile when he thought of
that.

"Do you, Francis Marion Gairden, take this woman
to be your wedded wife?" Reverend Roane's voice

bore the trace of a Scots accent, as did the voices of many of those here in the settlement. Fox answered, hearing his own soft Carolina "I do" sound less like "ah do" than it used to. Adelle's vows, though, had a Carolina softness to them she had picked up in her years there, waiting for him. Fox swallowed hard. Forgive me, Lord, for my many foolishnesses. For ever leaving this woman. Let me honor her and keep her always.

As he looked into her eyes and prayed his silent prayer to her, the ceremony ended and the guests rose in a din of booted feet to usher the new husband and wife out of doors. April 7, 1817. A spring-scented day greeted the party outside the meetinghouse doors, where Fox was roundly thumped across the shoulders and Adelle hugged and kissed.

"For a Catholic, you made the best looking Presbyterian wife I've ever seen," Fox whispered to her, kissing her earlobe as he spoke between rounds of congratulations.

"For a Presbyterian, you seemed very willing to marry a Papist," she countered.

"I'd have married you even if you were a Federalist," he teased, this time kissing her mouth and smiling out upon the cheering, clapping guests.

"Don't believe everything he tells you, Mrs. Gairden," best man Seth Butter put in, overhearing. "That last would be stretching belief, I can tell you."

"You mean I did not leave politics behind when I left Charleston? My!" Adelle feigned shock. "I may as well go back."

"You'll find the politics here a bit different from Charleston, I think, Mrs. Gairden," Butter said, and the small group around them nodded in assent. "Not just a few rich men running everything. Here, men of any and all sorts seek office—or the office seeks them. Isn't that right, Fox?"

"If you say it is, Butter." Fox smiled, rolling his eyes at his friend and hoping he would not pursue the subject. But the hopes came too late.

"And you'll be one of 'em, won't you, Gairden? You could just as well be in Washington as here. We've had enough of them that vote themselves higher salaries without asking the people. We voted out a lot of them that lined their own pockets with gold, but there's more left. You'd be a good one to go there and straighten things out." J. H. Kennedy, the big blacksmith, had a way of making his voice heard in a crowd, and a way of giving his statements a ring of authority not much different from the ring of hammer against anvil. It was not a good idea to get in the way of either of them.

Adelle looked to Fox, not surprised but questioning. He hadn't spoken to her of politics. There hadn't been time. In the two days since she had arrived they had talked of nothing but the past, and the wedding. He hadn't held any of this back from her—just hadn't had time to explain it all to her the way he wanted. For one thing, he wasn't sure he wanted to get into politics, even locally. He had a business to run. Now he would have a family to support, too. Politics was bound to take him away from all that, at least some of the time. Still, what Kennedy said was true. Over two-thirds of the House had been replaced in last fall's election because of the outrage over their salary increases, but there was still a core of self-inflated, self-serving men in Washington that rankled frontier minds. His was one of them. "I don't know about that," he told Kennedy and the others. "Any of you could represent us well." Fox smiled, hugging Adelle close to his side. "Besides, I'm going to be rather busy now."

Adelle blushed, the guests cheered again and the

whole party moved off toward the school building next door where a feast had been prepared by the parish ladies.

"You have a way of getting yourself in the middle of things, don't you, Husband?" Adelle whispered as they walked arm in arm at the head of the crowd.

"Well, Wife—oh God, Adelle, that has a good sound to it—if I do, I came honestly by it. A lawyer for a father and a general old-time saucy jack for a grandfather. How could I be anything but what I am?"

"And I, the child of parents who wished to leave politics behind them forever, am to be thrust into the swirl of this? I must have been cast under a Quaker spell to have ever left Charleston for this."

"It was no Quaker spell, darling. It was our spell, one we cast between us sometime long ago. When I came to Philadelphia—"

"No, when you first told me ghost tales in Charleston—"

"Or when Grandfather ordained it. Something like that. We were born to be together, Adelle. And we've waited a long time for it. But the waiting is over. We are together. All life is new for us. The past is far behind us in Charleston and Philadelphia and on ships and in others' lives. We will not be without our hard times and our sorrows here, either, but I pledge to you my honor, and my love."

As they took their places at a small table set for them, Seth Butter and Emeline Minns brought them each a plate heaped with venison, fowl and pork, nut bread and a tiny piece of maple cake made with precious white flour. Fox looked to Adelle as the plates were set before them. He was not hungry. Not for food. Her face told him she wasn't either. Beneath the table he clasped her hand. "I love you," he whispered.

"And I, you," she whispered in return as she looked

into his eyes, and they both forgot there were any wedding guests in the room. The small school table was low, and they perched like king and queen on the tiny bench that went with it. And felt like king and queen, Fox thought. Because they were. To each other.

22

1818

"I don't even know where Missouri is," Seth Butter said. "I don't even think I care."

"I don't think we have a choice. We have to care. Mr. Jefferson bought the land for us from Napoleon, and now we have to take care of it. People are moving there, more all the time. You know that, Seth. You see them coming through here, overland, on the river."

The two men dripped with sweat as they unpacked cotton bales in their picking room. Still a two-man operation, the Gairden mill was on the verge of needing to hire more help, but so far Fox's choice was for longer hours and no other employees. He could do it for as long as he had to: He did not intend to let this mill fail. Seth and Fox were hard-pressed to carry out all the many phases of cotton spinning alone—or with the help of their wives, now that Seth, too, had married. Maddie Wofford Butter was a quiet, hardworking girl of sixteen and made for a fourth person now housed in the small quarters Fox and Seth had once found crowded.

"Why not let them do as they please out there? If they want slaves, let them have slaves. If they don't, like us here, nobody's making 'em. What's wrong with that? People have to do what they think is right for themselves and leave others alone."

"But we're all one country, and there are those who

don't think slavery is right for anybody—especially not for the slaves. And we have to give them an ear, too."

"Well, I say slaves are already in Missouri and it'd be a damned hard time to get them out of there. We sure as hell don't want another war over it."

"There I agree with you, Seth. And that's why I'm hoping they'll settle this Missouri business."

"This so-called Era of Good Feeling has more than a few bad feelings in it, too, doesn't it, Fox? People can always find something to argue about."

"So it seems, though we're so busy trying to make a living here we manage to stay out of most of it."

"What about the elections this fall? Are you going to run?"

"Kennedy still wants me to. Roane as well. Even Adelle says I should. But I don't know. I'm pretty happy right here, toting armloads of cotton and getting lint in my hair. I'd like to stay in one place for more than two years, get settled in. I've been running from place to place for a long time, Seth."

"But if you're the only man with education, you're the man who should go."

"Some think that. Others think just the opposite. They don't trust anyone who is rich or educated. They think them one and the same."

"Ha. They should have a look at our ledger, then, eh, Fox?"

"How true. We're doing all right, but far from rich by any standards."

"Ahhh. People want everyone else to do what they don't want to do themselves. They want the government to make all the right decisions, but they don't want to give up any of their time to go and help see that the right decisions are made."

"Are you referring to me?" Fox jibed.

"You know I'm not. I know you'll run if you think

you should. But some of these folks wouldn't give a minute of their time or a penny of their money for anyone else, and yet they're quick to complain if somebody else is getting fat at the statehouse or in Washington."

"I suppose I've been one of them." Fox could recall some of his own words after the House salary increase just two years back, but he hadn't run for office then. Now he had talked a lot of politics and still had not done anything. Perhaps he was no better than the people Seth talked about. "How about you, Butter? How about you go? You've a good head on those big, broad shoulders. Maddie wouldn't mind going to Washington, from the sound of it. I'd support you. That way, the mill would be here waiting for you when you came home. You'd have a job when the Congress was out of session."

He could see that Seth was pleased at the suggestion but clearly not interested. "You could talk a mule into flying if you wanted to, Gairden," he said with a laugh. "That's why you're the one should be in Congress. And I'm going to tell a few folks that, too."

"You do that, Seth. Butter 'em up, Butter. I still don't know that I'd do it. I don't know how I'd vote on this Missouri question. I'm not in favor of slavery, but I don't see how it could be stopped altogether, either."

"I read that a Representative Tallmadge from New York said Missouri should free all slaves in the territory at age twenty-five, and that Washington could force them to do it," Butter said.

"If Washington can force that, then maybe they can force some things on us we don't like, too. I don't like slavery, but I also don't like the idea that any government can come out here and tell us what to do. Why do we have states if we can't make up our own mind about what goes on inside our own borders?"

"You're right on that. That's the kind of thinking makes folks want you to run. You've got to get thinking about it, Fox."

"Oh, I'll be thinking about it, sure enough. But not for a couple of days. I'm going to take Adelle on a belated wedding trip, next week if you think you can handle things here, though I'm not so sure I should leave you and Maddie here alone."

"We *are* married, you remember. Nothin' we can do would bother anyone."

"I don't know, Seth. I just don't know. It's been a while since I've left you on your own—not since I left you wounded back at Hazo Parsons's cabin."

Butter shook his head. "We've come a long way since then, haven't we, Fox?" They were both silent for a moment, remembering that sober time, that moment of kill or be killed.

"And God willing we'll never have to go back to it." Fox met Butter's eyes in a moment of shared awareness. Seth wasn't cut out for the real frontier, and neither was he. Already settlers had moved far beyond their Knoxville security. But there were different kinds of frontiersmen: trailblazers, farmers, town starters and town builders. He and Butter, Fox knew, fit best in the last category. And they knew they fit there. And they would see to their responsibilities to that town in their own ways.

"You've been a man of secrets, Fox Gairden," Adelle said as they walked their horses south along the Tennessee River on a warm, sunny morning a few days later.

"A man shouldn't have to tell all of his intentions to a woman just because she's his wife," Fox teased.

"Not as long as they're honorable." Adelle was quick to return his teasing, just as she always had been. She knew him, understood him the way perhaps only someone in the family could.

"And I am ever honorable, isn't that right? Isn't that what's gotten me into so many scrapes in my life? I think I'll try to be less honorable on this trip."

"Why, Fox Gairden," Adelle said, eyes flaring in luscious flirtation, "I do believe you have some rather worldly ideas in your head."

"I do believe you're right, Mrs. Gairden." He put his arm around her waist and hugged her close to his side, tickling her ribs. "And if we weren't so close to civilization I'd throw a blanket on the ground right here and love you the rest of the day."

She blushed, and he hugged her closer. "You . . . I wouldn't even make love with someone who wouldn't tell me where he was taking me."

"Ah. Well then. The time for secrets must be past. And actually, we're not going far, I don't think. But we're going to try to find the site of old Fort Loudoun."

"I can't quite place the name, but I know I've heard it," Adelle said.

"Grandfather liked to talk about it. When he first came to Charleston, around 1750, the British had built the fort, and it was about as far west as anyone ever hoped to go. During the Cherokee War, it was burned. Grandfather never actually got there, but he heard tell of the deprivations suffered by the men, and I think he had quite a clear picture of it in his mind."

"Is there anything left of it?"

"I don't know. Not much, I suppose, but I've always wanted to see it. It sits at the confluence of the Little Tennessee and the Tellico River, and I imagine it affords quite a view—those fort builders knew how to pick their sites."

"They just didn't always know how to defend them, obviously."

"Well, actually, I think they defended Loudoun for a good long time, but toward the end, when they were getting desperate, they made a deal with the Cherokees. Some of the Indians honored it, and some didn't. The ones who didn't thought the others were giving up too much to the white man, and so they took it upon themselves to ambush the soldiers as they left the fort in surrender. The few who escaped were led back to Charleston by some of the tribe who had made the agreement in the first place, and they told their story to the assembly."

"And then there was more trouble."

"Some, yes. But I think that was more or less the end of it. Eventually the Cherokees released the prisoners they'd taken, and a treaty was signed soon after that. The settlement line was moved out about this far, and the Cherokees pushed a little farther west, but nothing was written down about who owned what or who could be on what land when, according to Grandfather. He often said there would be more trouble with the Indians. Judging from the stories I've been hearing about General Jackson and the Creeks, and the stories we hear from teamsters coming back from Nashville and down from Lexington, he was right."

Adelle looked back over her shoulder. "You're making me nervous."

"Sorry, my love. I didn't mean to. And there are no Cherokees here anymore. We're on a holiday, after all. It's just that I've wanted to go to the old fort ever since I first got the idea of coming west. Now that you're here—well, it just seems the perfect time."

"It does," Adelle said, smiling into his eyes and pressing her lips lightly against his cheek. "Grandfather would want us to."

"He would. And I think he would be most happy that we are going together, as man and wife. He had a romantic bent, that grandfather of ours."

"Did he? That was a side of him I never got to know, living so far away. I only remember some of his stories. And that odd little smile of his."

"If only he hadn't died so suddenly—" In a flash, the memory of the duel, and Grandfather's death, came back to Fox, but Adelle was quick to intercept it.

"If things hadn't happened the way they did, Fox, you would never have come to Philadelphia. And we would never have fallen in love. Put away the bad memories, Fox—I see them trying to get hold of you, but you mustn't let them. Think of the good things that have happened. Hold on to them."

He stopped then, and his horse stopped behind him. Adelle had already made a step or two when she stopped and turned back. "I want to hold on to you," he said softly.

Dropping the reins of her horse, Adelle opened her arms to him and he stepped into her embrace with all the ardor of a first encounter. A sense of the oneness that was his with Adelle flooded him in a way that it hadn't up until this moment. They were alone, with the mighty river at their side and the hazy mountain ridges in the distance, the whole of them tree green and lush with summer's scent. As he held his wife in his arms and felt the softness of her hair and the warmth of her body, Fox knew contentment in a way he had not quite known it that first night in the marriage bed, or even during their many happy months since.

"Fox? Fox? Are you all right? Is something wrong?"

Fox knew Adelle had felt the tear that had rolled from his eye and that she would think a man's tears cause for alarm. Yet he could not stop the well flowing from within him. "Everything is perfect, Adelle. So perfect I am touched. Forgive my lack of—"

"There is nothing to forgive except my thoughtless questions. How I love you, Francis Marion Gairden. How I love you."

Ever since their marriage, except for their wedding night, they had shared quarters with Seth Butter, and not long after that with his wife, too. It was cramped, and not the most congenial arrangement. Maddie Butter, born in Tennessee, had had no schooling until she was in her early teens, when her father sent her to board in Knoxville for three months in the winter when she could be spared at home. She and her sister, Jenny, found school hard work compared to the freedom of their father's farm, and spent more of their time wishing themselves home than wishing themselves learned. Once married, she helped in the mill for long hours, but always, always her eyes strayed out the windows at every chance. Let's get some land, Seth, was her constant refrain. She had large, dark eyes that gave her a kind of mystic beauty, once you got behind her plain dress and straight, lifeless hair, but she was no kindred spirit to Adelle. She had a suspicious nature, borne of too many stories told on dark nights around a small fire far away from any people who might dispute the so-called facts. Fox sometimes wondered if once Seth's lustier notions were satisfied, he wouldn't wish himself married to someone else.

Still, the four of them coexisted in the small quarters while they watched the business grow and Fox planned the kind of house he would build for Adelle. He had already talked to a brick maker and a mason. Adelle was going to have her brick house if he had to use his own spit to bind the clay. For now, though, they would have to be content with a few hours to themselves.

It was late that day when they reached the site of the

old fort, and a west wind ruffled their hair as they stood atop the knoll and looked out across the broad valley below.

"Do you feel their spirits, Fox? The British, I mean. It's almost as if they were still here, walking about."

He wanted to answer yes, he did feel them. But tears and restless ghosts would be too much for one woman for one day. She needed his strength, not his demons. "I don't know. They might be. You know the old saying about those unjustly killed. Some of these men were, no doubt. They have every right to walk, to be on guard."

"I can almost see the Cherokees out there. How awful it must have been."

"For them, you mean? Or the soldiers?"

"For all of them, I suppose."

"I think you're right. Too many people wanting the same things—us, the British, the Cherokees, the French, even the Spanish. My God, what a mess. And still it goes on . . . When I think of it, I think I *should* take up the party banner and run for Congress. You know they still haven't given back the land guaranteed the Indians in the Treaty of Ghent. The British insisted that the boundaries of the Indian lands be restored to the way they were in 1811, before the war started, and Congress agreed to it but now looks the other way."

"I think you *will* run for Congress, Fox. You just haven't had the time to decide it for yourself yet. Perhaps while we're away these two days I'll try to be quiet enough for you to have some time to think and settle these things in your own mind."

She squeezed his hand and then started down the trail from the bluff top back to where they had pitched their tent in the shelter of a grove of ancient white pines just to the side of a broad shallows in the bend of the river.

Fox stayed inside the expanded diamond-shaped site, stooping here and there to pick up the chip of a charred timber, or a button or cup handle. Deep defensive ditches overgrown with thorny locusts once planted to keep out invaders still marked the outline of the once-important fort. Stones from its well now lay tumbled about and the deep hole echoed back "hello" when he called into it. On the whispers of the wind he heard the voices of the men who had served there. British voices, some imperious, some acquiescent. Cherokee voices, too. Some of women, inside the fort. Some of calm heads, some of the bitter, the suspicious, the malicious. Many, inside the walls and out, starving.

Why do we think we can tame the wilderness? Fox wondered as he looked out and saw no civilization other than his own tent pitched at the riverside. Why do I think I can do what other men have not been able to do? How could I succeed when so many others have failed? How can we decide what to do with black men in a single vote when we have not been able to do anything right with the red man in almost two centuries?

Hugh Vardry's voice came to him then, just as it had a thousand times before. "A bit gray at the muzzle to be speaking so fondly of the future, are you not, old man?" If I'm going to do it, I have to do it before I'm too old, Fox told himself. I can't wait until I've made my fortune and then see to my responsibility. By the Eternal, Vardry, if you're going to talk to me, I'm going to talk back.

23

"Are you certain?"

"Absolutely certain. We are going to have a child, Fox. Another Gairden, the first one born in the West."

Fox held her close and kissed her, feeling at once frightened and ecstatic. A child. Him a father. "Are you all right, though, Adelle? What did Dr. Carrick say?"

"He said I seemed fine. Very healthy, in fact."

"We'll have to hire someone for the mill. You can't—"

"There's no lifting for me in the mill. I can help out there for a while yet so that we can save for our house. After the New Year will be soon enough to look for someone—maybe even one of Maddie's younger sisters could be trained."

"No doubt there's someone could use a little extra money. That Mr. Jenstere I talked to last week told me most of the mill workers back east now are girls and young women. They work for two or three years before they get married, then leave and some new girls take their places."

"We aren't so lucky out here. Not enough women to go around as it is, but surely there will be someone. We have time."

"But we have to get our house built, Adelle. We can't have our new babe living in the lean-to with another whole family, too. There's a land speculator who wants to buy my Illinois land. I was going to hang onto it, but now I think I'll let him have it. The money will help a little toward our house, and . . . I don't think we're ever going any farther west than this anyway. No matter how rich the land, I'm not meant to be a farmer. And I never want to start another mill."

"Never is quite a long time," she teased. "Let me see, this is number three—and the best of all of them." She kissed his nose. "You are doing what you're meant to do."

"Ahhhh, Adelle, at last life is going the right way for us. The mill is doing well. We're going to have a family. And it's all because of you. Until you came, I was ready to go back to Charleston and forget the West. It was you who gave me the energy to work and make the mill what it is." He kissed her, tasting sweetness in each new touch of their lips. "I can't wait!" he said, picking her up and holding her above him the way he would, someday soon, his own child.

"Nor I, although I almost can't believe it yet. I've never thought much about motherhood, I must confess."

"We'll need to let the new grandparents know right away. The mail goes out next Tuesday. I'll write tonight after I get home from talking with the Republicans."

"You'll have plenty of time to write before the mail goes out. Calm down, Papa. All things in good time."

"Easy for you to say. You've had a few weeks' suspecting this that you haven't told me about. I'm still giddy as a gander. Let me enjoy it."

"I wouldn't have it any other way. You enjoy it. But don't be telling everyone in town. Not yet. It's too soon."

"Can I tell Seth?"

"Of course. And Maddie. But that's it."

"That's it, then, my love—and now I've got to rush off to the meeting. I shouldn't be late."

Fox walked the two blocks to the schoolhouse with a spring in his step and with his eyes on the golden September sunset. Thank you, God, for this life. And for the new life to come. And for Adelle who brings it, he prayed inwardly as he hurried along, waving at people without even seeing who they were, turning out for piles of horse droppings without actually noticing them. When he entered the schoolhouse, he searched for Seth's face, bursting to tell him the news. But Seth was late, probably at Rogan's getting a drink of something to take away the pain in his shoulder that was beginning to act up as the nights grew colder and the weather damper. But he would be here soon, and when he came, Fox would take him aside and tell him the news.

In the meantime, he looked forward to the meeting of the Knoxville Republicans. There really was no other political party in town—or in the country for that matter. In the 1816 election, James Monroe had swept the nation, and the Federalist candidate, Rufus King of New York, received only thirty-four electoral votes. Since that time, the Republicans had adopted some Federalist views, and the Federalist party had died away. It was, after all, the era of good feeling the Boston paper had said it was, thought Fox. Especially for him.

"Caucus of the Knox County Republican Party will come to order. John Steadman presiding. Clerk will read the minutes of the last caucus."

The room quieted at the heavy, deep voice of John Steadman, and men, mostly familiar faces, listened with some interest to what they had talked about at the last caucus. Alabama statehood. Tax reform. Militia payments. The minutes were approved with no discussion. The men were eager to get on to the question they had come to discuss—Missouri statehood. They hurried over the lesser questions they needed to address: road building; tax reform, again; banking.

"Missouri statehood—free or slave? As most of you know, the territory of Missouri has applied to the Union for statehood as a slave state. With Alabama likely to come into the Union next year as a slave state, Missouri would tip the balance: twelve slave states and eleven nonslave. I think I know how all of us here feel about the question, but for the records, let us voice our opinions and then show our vote. Kennedy, you first."

J. H. Kennedy, ever free with his opinions, was quick to rise and speak. "The only reason *not* to admit Missouri as a slave state is to keep the voting even in the Senate. As it is, the North now has more votes in the House than we do—their population is growing with all the cities bulgin' out at the seams. They're mightily afraid we might go 'em one better in the Senate."

"I agree with Kennedy," came the voice of Martin McKay. "If we're goin' to be lettin' in more states, there are goin' to be times when there's one more slave than free. We can't stop Missouri from becomin' a state just because some rich Philadelphia gents are afraid they won't get their way on somethin'. Missouri needs slaves for cotton, just like we do. I say we vote for it."

"Gairden? A word from you?" Steadman stilled the din that had risen in the room at the two men's statements with the timbre of his voice once again and called on Fox.

"The way we deal with the slavery issue should be more than a matter of numbers, it seems. I don't own slaves, and don't intend to, but I don't feel it my right to say no one else should."

"You say that now, but if you're elected to Congress it would be mighty easy for you to slip that around to where no one should own slaves, wouldn't it now,

Gairden?" The accusation came from Jerome Bishop, a cotton planter from west of Knoxville.

"There is nothing about the subject of slavery that is easy, Mr. Bishop. It is not easy to regulate, and it would not be easy to stop. There are those, like the Quakers, who find it difficult to tolerate. A representative must try to represent all the people, not just a few. So far in Tennessee, slaveholders are in the minority. Should their wishes be acceded to any more readily than those of the minority of wealthy industrialists in the East who take the other view? Did not Mr. Jefferson build this party on the belief that government, while directed by the educated and intelligent, should respond to the wishes of the people? And should not the people, in small groups just like this one, take responsibility for their decisions and for the future effects of their actions?"

Bishop shot to his feet. "You, Gairden, have a Yankee wife and a lot of Yankee ideas floatin' around in your head. We send you to Washington, an' before we know it you'll have Tennessee undeclared a slave state."

"Tennessee's status, I'm afraid, is unchangeable, though we might well come to wish it weren't someday. As long as there is a division between free and slave, there is a division in this nation, and no matter how we resolve the question of Missouri, that division is going to remain."

"An' is that Missouri's fault? Those folks can't help it. The slaves are already there."

"And the Indians were there ahead of them. But they've been pushed farther west. Is that Missouri's fault? Or Washington's? I say it is the fault of all of us if we are citizens of one nation."

"I thought you said each state should make up its own laws. Now you're sayin' every person in the country should have the same laws? You don't know what you're sayin', Gairden." Bishop dismissed Fox's arguments with a wave of the hand the way he might send a field hand off to a day's picking.

"What I'm saying is that whoever goes to Washington from Knox County, whether it be me or someone else, had better be prepared to look at questions many ways. It isn't enough for us to come here and just get together and make up our minds without even considering the rest of the questions. If we want to do that, why are we even part of the United States? Why not form our own little country out here west of the Appalachians—get Kentucky and Alabama to go in with us, maybe?"

"Well, maybe we'll have to do that someday. I thought you'd be willin' to see it, too, Gairden. You keep sayin' that the federals shouldn't be able to tell us what to do. Now you're sayin' we're all federals. Do you even know what you think?" Bishop's voice had grown louder now, and Fox thought his own had probably gone up a few notches, too. All across the room, men talked between themselves, pointing up first one side and then the other.

"I think it's not as easy a question as lots of folks would like to have us think it is. And I wonder what we'll think if the next six or seven states admitted to the Union come in as nonslave. What then, friends? Will we be singing a different tune when the score is twenty to twelve?"

"But that won't happen! It couldn't!" At once, the two dozen men in the room all spoke at once, each one louder than the next to make himself heard, each one aghast at such a suggestion.

"Order! Order!" Steadman rapped his gavel on the bench before him and once again tried to quiet the din of voices. "There will be order! Gentlemen. Let's keep this orderly. We're here to draft a resolution, and we're getting farther from the point instead of closer. Take your seats, men, and we'll continue the discussion."

Jerome Bishop's face was still an angry red, but he sat down. Fox, too, felt his cheeks warmer than usual, and caught his breath as he waited for the rest of the men to stop their private discussions before he spoke again.

"I recommend that Missouri be entered as a slave state if her entry can be balanced with a free state in the North," he said. "That way the balance is kept—for now. Others have suggested it, and it seems fair to me." J. H. Kennedy looked Fox's way as he spoke. He had come, like all the others, expecting the recommendation to pass after nothing more than a little discussion. Now it was clear he wanted the debate to end. A rustle of agreement went around the room.

"I move the recommendation," said McKay.

"Second," said Bishop, stomping his foot on the floor as he spoke.

"All in favor?"

Everyone in the room voted in the affirmative. The recommendation was what they had all expected, but still Fox asked Steadman for the floor again.

"You've talked of sending me to Washington. And even though I've just voted with you on this recommendation, I suspect most of you are asking yourselves whether you'd want me there or not, because, as Mr. Bishop pointed out, I don't seem to know what I think. Perhaps it looks that way because for a long time I've said only part of what I think. I've said I don't believe the federal government should be able to tell the states what to do or how to run their business. And I do heartily believe that. It was the belief of Jefferson, who founded this Republican party of ours. And a good example of it is this national bank business that's got everyone in a panic after loaning money to anyone and everyone with no collateral for land out west. There's a lot of folks ruined by it, and a lot more to come. And our Republicans are to blame for it, we can't deny that —but we should learn from it. Leave the banking—and most other things—to the states.

"What I haven't said is that I don't want a dedication to slavery to run our state either. Jefferson didn't want it. He spoke often of freeing the slaves. He knew it should be done, but he didn't know how. I don't either. Maybe this Mr. Tallmadge from New York has a solution with the amendment he's suggesting to the Missouri bill: prohibit the spread of slavery into the new territories and gradually free the slaves already there. You can bet the northern states are not going to let a majority of slave states rule Congress. Tallmadge's plan may be a solution we'll need to consider.

"In time, I hope, the peculiar institution will wear itself out. Planters will find machines to do their work. Slavery will become a holdover from the ancient world we will one day find as a footnote in history instead of an issue to be as hotly debated as it is just now all around this country. I will support this state's right to govern its citizens as they see fit, but I can never be a strong advocate for slavery as such. And if that's what you're looking for, you'll have to look to someone else. Right now, the quarrel is over votes—who has 'em and who wants 'em. It's not over the inhumanity of a system most of us have lived with all of our lives. But it's going to be. The Presbyterian General Assembly last summer took a stand against slavery, and so all of us here who call ourselves Presbyterians are called to consider that. In the North, abolitionist societies are springing up in every little town and all the big ones. There are going to have to be compromises, and changes, not just in Missouri, but here in Tennessee, too. We're men who invite change, if moving out here over the mountains is any indication." Fox paused and stopped short of saying that the change he had in mind was the abolition of slavery, but the hint was there, and he could see that many of the men had heard it.

"If all of this makes you think I should be kept as far away from Washington as possible," Fox went on, "I don't blame you. But I think you should know."

He sat down and was overwhelmed by the silence in the room. Though only a handful of the men there owned slaves, Fox's remarks affected them all, he could tell, forcing them to face their own beliefs about a subject they had for a long time tried to live parallel with but never intersect, until now.

He felt a moment of great relief, which was odd, because at the same time he could sense the force of feelings against him from around the room. Jerome Bishop broke the moment.

"Come outside and say that again," Bishop challenged. "A pistol at twenty yards says you haven't got the guts to back up your thinkin'!"

The quiet in the room became a hush as the twenty-four men drew in a breath of surprise at once. Fox was one of them.

"Do you want to die, Bishop? Is that it? Because I'm certain I can oblige you if that's your wish." The image of Hugh Vardry loomed inside Fox's head just the way it had so many other times throughout the ten years that had passed since that Independence Day in Charleston.

"I want to teach you somethin', Gairden. That's all. I've lived here a lot longer than you have, and I know a thing or two about slaves you oughta learn."

"I killed a man in a duel once," Fox said, "for saying something not half as bad as what you imply. I told myself I did it for honor—to save my grandfather's

honor. But you know what? It wasn't actually for honor
at all. He made me angry, and I challenged him, just
the way you're challenging me now. And I found out
that the old saying about no honor among thieves is
true, because a duel steals your very life away from
you, even if you win. I'm still trying to get mine back,
Bishop, and I don't want to take yours."

"Don't make no difference, Mr. South Carolina I'm-
Against-Slavery Hypocrite. You're interested in nothin'
but yourself. You're one of them welcomed the tariff so
you could get rich sellin' your wares, but that tariff
liked to kill off farmers like me. You didn't see us gettin' any more for our crop, but we sure as Betsey's ear
had to pay more for everything we bought. An' you
don't need any slaves to run your mill 'cause you can
hire women and kids for nothin', but I can't *find* a man
to work for me. There aren't any. If you don't buy 'em,
you don't have 'em."

"I know that, Bishop. Did you hear me begrudging
you a chance to make a living? Never. But if farmers in
the North can do it, something tells me we can. They're
no different from us."

"Different crop, man! And that means everything!"

"I'll talk about this with you till we both grow old
and gray, Bishop, but I'll not duel with you tonight, or
in the morning, or any other morning."

"Why . . . you're a low-lyin', nigger-lovin' son of a
bitch, Gairden."

Fox bristled. His hand itched for the grip of a pistol,
or even a stick of wood to beat in Bishop's head.
"You—" Fox started to speak, then checked himself.
What was it he had said to Hugh Vardry? I challenge
you to defend that remark? Something like that. And
what was he going to say this time? You can't say that
about me? Well, of course Jerome Bishop could say it
if he wanted to. He could say it all over Knoxville and

all over Tennessee if he wanted to. And he didn't have to prove it. And Fox didn't have to like it. But he also didn't have to kill him for it.

"I don't believe I owe you the courtesy of a response to that, Bishop," he said.

"An' I don't believe you ever killed anyone. You haven't got the spine for it."

"Believe what you like. It's a free country."

"Hah! You're a fine one to talk like that. You who's lookin' down his nose at the slaveholders."

"It's one thing to disagree and another to try to dictate what they should do. As I recall, I only expressed my opinion. One I knew wouldn't be popular. I didn't want anyone thinking of electing me under false pretenses."

"An' I don't want anyone electin' you under any pretenses. That's why I want to meet you in the morning. I'm going to take your skulkin', Yankee-lovin' ass out of this state for good. You're a yellow—"

"I'm a yellow coward not worth shooting. Go ahead. Think that if you want." Fox paused, and in that second, it was not Vardry's face that he saw but Adelle's. "But I'm going home. I've got a good wife waiting for me. With child, she is. And I'm not going to make that child's father a killer—or a dead man."

All eyes in the room shifted to Bishop. The next statement was his. Instead, he stomped out the door, the noise of its rattling hinges singing out behind him.

"Don't be so quick to think we'll be lookin' for someone else for the election, Gairden," McKay said. "Anyone can step around Bishop like that can surely hold his own with Tallmadge and everybody else up there."

Kennedy slapped his back and shook his hand. "You maneuvered that one good, Gairden. Ol' Hickory could've used that golden tongue of yours to get himself out of a couple of his scrapes, I'd wager."

"Just don't go thinkin' you can vote out slavery," Irod Havens cautioned. "Talk is one thing, votin's somethin' else. We aren't hurtin' anyone with the few slaves we've got."

The comments came and went, some applauding and others cautioning, and there were a half-dozen men who went out the door to join Bishop, too. Passing a resolution was a very small part of what had actually taken place here tonight.

The walk home was a slower, more pensive journey than the golden-toned early evening stroll to the meeting had been. It was a troubling walk, in many ways, as Fox looked around him at what the town of Knoxville really was and who the people were who lived there. Rugged individualists, yes. Had to be, or they wouldn't have gotten there. Brawling at Rogan's each night was just one manifestation of it. Quickness to settle a score was another sign. Sharp words another. Still, these people could work together when they wanted to. Hadn't some of them helped him build his mill? And didn't they cooperate to keep their streets in some kind of repair? And to keep law and order as best they could? But could they ever see themselves as part of the greater whole, tethered to at least some of its rules and expectations? Could he? If I give up the notion of my own rights, he wondered, am I less of a man? Or more?

Makes no difference, he told himself. You have someone new to think about now. Another generation of Gairdens. And you have to make the best world for him or her that you can. You have to be willing to stand up for what you believe. You have to be willing to sit down and be quiet sometimes, too. Fox chuckled. Not too good at that part, much of the time. Adelle

was helping him to be better. She would be the one
person who would be glad for what he had said tonight.
She would have been in one of those Philadelphia abolitionist societies if she were still there, he imagined.
Or if she hadn't found him in Knoxville, she might
have gone on west with that group of Quakers she'd
found.

But there was no right in that, either, he told himself. Trying to get away from slavery was almost worse
than trying to live parallel to it. Only the people who
were willing to talk about slavery and face up to its
peculiar problems were ever going to do anything
about it. And the more he thought about it, the more
he wanted to be one of them. So why had he just
thrown away any chance he had of doing that from this
district? Because for a while there he had let himself
be goaded by Bishop, he admitted. But then he had
overcome it.

He was about a half block past Rogan's when he
heard a step behind him and glanced back over his
shoulder to see who it was.

"Ho. Fox? Lend me an arm, could you, man?" Seth
Butter staggered up the street from Rogan's, his bulky
form sidling clumsily between buildings and street dust
with a regularly irregular gait.

"Glad to, Seth."

Butter shifted his weight, almost toppling Fox as he
threw his arm around his shoulder, then righted himself and clapped Fox heartily on the back.

"Miss anything at the meeting? I got . . . detained."

Fox chuckled. "You did, friend, and I'm sorry for it.
You missed seeing me called out by Jerome Bishop as a
yellow son of a whatever you want to call me, and seeing me walk away. Quite a show for the Republicans."

"My hat to you, Fox," Butter said, trying to lift a hat

he wasn't wearing. He patted his tousled hair absently for several seconds before he gave up the search and instead honored his friend with a song:

Pass, pass the sparkling bumper round
And join the drum and clarion's sound
While social hearts and cheerful glee,
Warm the rapt bosoms of the free.

Fox joined in on the chorus:

Let the cannon's thund'ring roar,
Loud resound from shore to shore
Sing, and dance, and laugh and play,
This is freedom's holiday.

"You're drunk as a lunk, Fox Gairden, are you?" Butter asked as the chorus ended. "You never sing unless you're rightly drunk."

"I'm drunk on the telling of truth, friend. And oh. One more thing. Drunk on the news that I'm to be a father."

"Then we should be goin' back to Rogan's! I'll buy you one and get you rightly soused. This is great news."

"No drinking for me tonight, Seth. I don't need it. But I'll sing with you." He started the next verse, one with special reference to the war just past:

At Orleans and at Baltimore
We met their legions on the shore.
Our gallant troops led on the fight
And put the myrmidons to flight.

No grave, no cov'ring but the sky,
The bleaching bones of thousands lie;

England, behold your useless toil!
No slave pollutes Columbia's soil.

Another chorus and they were back to the mill, Fox trying to lift the latchstring quietly and keep Butter upright all at the same time. Before he could manage it, the door opened and Adelle's face, lit by a small lamp, appeared before him like an angelic vision.

"I heard you coming," she said, holding back a smile.

"I told him," Fox said, not holding back one of his own. "And a few dozen others. I couldn't help it."

Butter slid to the floor beside them as Fox took Adelle in his arms and held her close. "I didn't know I'd married a singer," she said, lifting the lamp close to his face.

"How I sang tonight, my love. How I sang." Holding Adelle while Butter sang another thick-tongued verse of the familiar battle song, Fox's thoughts went back once again to the caucus, to Bishop's challenge. And this time it was Fox who smiled at Hugh Vardry.

The historical romances of
JEANNE WILLIAMS
from St. Martin's Paperbacks

Award-winning author of *Creole Fires*

"Kat Martin has a winner. *Gypsy Lord* is a page-turner from beginning to end!"

—Johanna Lindsey

GYPSY LORD
Kat Martin
He was Dominic Edgemont, Lord Nightwyck, heir to the Marquis of Gravenwold. But he was also a dark-eyed, half-gypsy bastard...
_____ 92878-5 $4.99 U.S./$5.99 Can.

SWEET VENGEANCE
Kat Martin
A woman driven by the fires of vengeance...
A man consumed by the flames of desire...
A passion as dangerous as it is irresistible...
_____ 95095-0 $4.99 U.S./$5.99 Can.